"YOU'RE A BEAUTIFUL WOMAN AND A SPLENDID lover," Jack whispered huskily. He lifted her hand and gently kissed each delicate finger.

Giddy with pleasure and a sudden wave of fatigue, Katie nearly giggled. "Thank you," she replied, smiling radiantly, then closed her eyes.

Jack smoothed the silky black curls from her brow and drank in the sight of Katie's face in repose. Her long lashes brushed her cheeks and her lips were full and tender looking. When Jack felt his heart clench, he was almost afraid to wonder why.

Oh, God, he thought, what have I done?

BRIGHTER THAN GOLD

Cynthia Wright

BALLANTINE BOOKS • NEW YORK

Library of Congress Catalog Card Number: 89-91552

ISBN 0-345-33486-8

Manufactured in the United States of America

First Edition: April 1990

For my beloved husband, Jim,
who has shown me that passionate commitment
and unconditional love can coexist joyously,
not only in romance novels, but in real life.

and

Special thanks to the friends of Bill W.
God bless you all.

PART
ONE

CHAPTER
1

Columbia, California
June 21, 1864

Riding slowly down Main Street, the tawny-haired man on horseback reflected that Columbia had certainly known better days. A dozen years ago, it had been heralded as the "Gem of the Southern Mines," the largest and most prosperous of all the towns that had sprung up during the rush for gold in the Sierra foothills. More than fifteen thousand boisterous people had lived here, making and spending fortunes in Columbia's thriving gambling palaces, saloons, fandango halls, theaters, restaurants, and bawdy houses. Stores were stocked with merchandise delivered by a constant stream of freight wagons from Stockton. Stagecoaches rumbled down Main Street morning and afternoon, dislodging a colorful variety of eager newcomers, including a French chef who charged outrageous sums of money for gourmet meals and imported champagne. The town's four theaters had hosted Edwin Booth, Lola Montez, and circuses with elephants and lions. Columbia even had a Chinese theater that offered an impressive array of talented Oriental performers for the particular benefit of its immigrant citizenry.

In the town's first decade, more than $87 million worth of gold had been discovered in its diggings. The grand scales at the Wells Fargo office weighed an average of $100,000 of gold a week, and the lucky miners often spent their newfound wealth in one explosive celebration, then repeated the process the following day. It was said that the rich earth around Columbia was laced with gold, and in the heady decade of the 1850s, it seemed that the supply would never run out.

Unfortunately, the days of unrivaled prosperity had passed. On this particular dusty afternoon, the man on horseback rode into a town of fewer than five hundred people. Tucked behind hills that staggered down to the dramatically beautiful Stanislaus River, Columbia was surrounded by pine trees. The wide, heat-shimmering streets were sleepy now. Many of the houses were uninhabited, but the town had acquired a haunting serenity lacking in its heyday. Delicate, locustlike trees of heaven lined Main Street, and many of the homes were embowered with climbing roses in full bloom. The clamor was over, yet the traveler felt a surge of respect and fondness for this tenacious community. Built initially in a haphazard, hurried fashion, it had been ravaged by two fires in its early years, but the citizens had staunchly rebuilt Columbia with sturdy brick and sent to San Francisco for several ornate fire engines. When water, essential for mining placer gold, had proved to be in short supply, a sixty-mile aqueduct was constructed. And finally, when the placer gold began to play out, Columbia reacted with grim determination and refused to accept its flagging economy: it introduced hydraulic mining, a controversial yet undeniably effective new excavating technique. Using nozzles to shoot the water at high pressure, the miners blasted loose the gold-bearing gravels and sifted out the gold, leaving behind deep pits, exposed boulders, and peculiar-looking pinnacles and ragged rocks.

The sandy-haired man on horseback, like so many others in the foothills, disapproved of the desecration wreaked upon the land by hydraulic mining. But he had to admire Columbia's fighting spirit. Unlike so many other gold towns, it simply refused to die. True, it had changed, but he found he preferred its more peaceful atmosphere. Farther ahead down Main Street, he spied the familiar sign for MacKenzie's Saloon. Hot, tired, and in need of friendly conversation, the traveler decided to stop there for refreshment.

At the far end of the polished mahogany bar, Katie MacKenzie was perched on a high stool, drying glasses and reading *Wuthering Heights* at the same time. It was a quiet afternoon. The shafts of sunlight that streamed into MacKenzie's Saloon were mellow and golden, scented with roses. The corner tavern was large, with burnished pine floors, a magnificent carved mirror behind the bar, and numerous tables ringed with chairs. Once upon a time, Mac-

Kenzie's had echoed with the laughter and raucous conversation of men from all walks of life. Now, however, the place was an ornate mockery of a bygone era, a golden age long since passed. Katie looked up to see two lone, grimy miners, clad in red shirts and dungarees, who slouched at a distant table, dozing before their empty bottle. Farther down the bar, Brian MacKenzie poured a whiskey for his third patron, then approached his preoccupied daughter.

"I'm thinking this is a fine way for a lass to celebrate her eighteenth birthday," he murmured, his ruddy face and curly white hair reflected in the twenty-foot mirror behind them.

A sweet smile brightened Katie's delicate features. "Nonsense, Papa! You sent all the way to Boston for this book you knew I wanted, and you gave me these beautiful flowers." Lovingly she fingered the vivid bouquet of blue larkspur and orange Humboldt lilies that filled a vase at her elbow. "It's a perfect birthday!"

Brian wrapped her in his bearlike embrace and smiled. "You're a blessing, Kathleen Elizabeth. Why don't you put away the towel and glasses and go outside? It's not a day for chores."

"I'm fine, Papa." Already her attention was wandering back to the first chapter of *Wuthering Heights*.

Sighing, Brian studied his daughter's flawless profile. It was almost a shock to realize, daily, how beautiful she had become . . . and that she was now a woman. More and more Katie resembled her mother, who had died eight years before. She had inherited Mary's lustrous ebony curls, her breathtaking azure eyes with long, thick black lashes, her cream-and-pink complexion, tip-tilted nose, beautiful white teeth, and radiant smile. Even Katie's body reminded Brian of his late wife, for she was small and trim, yet endowed with feminine curves.

Katie's temperament mirrored his own, however, and that worried Brian increasingly as she grew older. If only Mary had lived to teach their daughter ladylike ways! he mused, watching her with a mixture of pride and fatherly dismay. Growing up in the rugged atmosphere of a mining town, Katie was used to working hard, but otherwise she dressed and behaved to please herself. Today she wore a faded rose calico dress with one petticoat, but she was just as likely to be clad in trousers and a shirt if the mood struck her. Worst of all, Katie had declared that she had no interest in marriage or, as she put it, "becoming a slave to a *man*." And she did indeed seem to prefer helping him run the saloon, Brian admitted ruefully, or writing articles for the *Columbia Gazette*. Women were at a premium in the foothills, especially beauties like Katie, and he prayed nightly that his headstrong daughter would come to her senses one day soon and begin acting like a woman. Hadn't he a right to grandchildren?

"Quite a romantic hero in that book, eh?" Brian inquired slyly. "What's his name?"

"Heathcliff." Katie gave him a fond smile, familiar with his ways.

"Heathcliff! Why, seems to me that that name alone would be enough to turn a maiden's thoughts to love!"

The swinging door creaked to announce the arrival of a customer, and Brian trundled back to work. He squinted as the man approached the bar, then smiled broadly as recognition dawned.

"Why, it's Jack, isn't it! Where've you been these past weeks?" He set a shot glass on the bar and reached for a bottle of whiskey.

Jack, settling onto a stool, spread a tanned hand over the glass. "Save your whiskey for someone who'll appreciate it, Mac-Kenzie," he said in a husky voice underlaid with ironic amusement. Surveying the dazzling array of decanters, squat vases of cigars, and jars of brandied fruit reflected in the mirror, he ventured to ask, "Do you serve *water*?"

"Ah, that's right!" Brian laughed, remembering, as he poured spring water from a pitcher into a larger glass. "You don't drink liquor. Tell me, do you belong to that there Dashaway Society that's been promoting temperance in these parts?"

Jack's answering laughter was sufficiently roguish to make Katie, who had been eavesdropping from the first instant she'd heard his voice, look up at last. "Lord, no," Jack replied. "I'm neither a Dashaway nor a Son of Temperance. I've just never seen the point in drowning what few wits I have in liquor. Can't tell when I might need them."

His expression and manner made it clear to Katie that Jack's wits were far more considerable than he so modestly implied. His looks were not insignificant, either. Katie's first thought was that he reminded her of a tawny tomcat. Jack's hair, wind-ruffled and dusty, was nearly the same color as his sun-darkened skin, and a two-day growth of beard glinted like flecks of gold against his lean cheeks. There was something appealing about the shape of his nose, the smile that lingered on his mouth, and the grooves on either side that hinted at dimples. She was most intrigued by his eyes, though, and wandered down the bar for a closer look.

Cat's eyes, she decided after a few moments. A clear, sage green dusted with gold, slightly hooded, as if a bit weary of surveying the world, and framed by laugh wrinkles and sandy brows. Katie was disarmed by the sight of his mischievous smile and the sound of his frank, husky laughter, but she sensed that, like the tomcat he resembled, this man could be dangerous.

"Ah, here's my Katie girl," Brian announced, wrapping an arm around her slim form. "Katie, have you met Jack Adams? He's new to these parts. Came in here the first time just a couple months back. Jack, this is my pride and joy, my daughter Kathleen."

Seeing the appraisal in his green eyes, Katie put out her hand and smiled. "I'm pleased to meet you, Mr. Adams."

He smiled back, noting the rosy color that stained her cheeks. "The pleasure's mine, Miss MacKenzie," he said in his appealing, rough-edged voice. "Call me Jack."

"I'm Katie." She shook the hand he held out, glancing at the well-tended nails. It was a strong hand, tanned against the faded blue shirt he wore but only slightly callused. Katie wondered what he had done before coming to the gold country. "Where are you from, Jack?"

He shrugged. "Nevada, lately. Placerville last week. I have my eye on a couple different claims, but can't decide whether they're worth working. One's near here."

"Just because the boom's past and so many miners have moved on to Nevada or Canada, that doesn't mean our gold's gone!" Brian declared, seizing on one of his favorite topics. "A man with a bit of patience can still get rich here, and live a more civilized life in the bargain!"

"Columbia does look permanent these days," Jack agreed, finishing his water. "Until I decided to take up mining last fall, I hadn't been in the foothills for years. The towns were all wood and canvas when I was here in my youth; a real mixture of imported luxury and make-do. A lot of them are gone completely now that so much of the gold's been mined, but what's left *does* look more like civilization." His eyes crinkled at the corners. "Maybe that's what drove the miners away! They may have missed the wild life."

"There's still enough wildness up here for any man," Brian snorted. "And enough challenges. They're destroying the land with that new hydraulic mining now!" He frowned. "As for the town looking more civilized, you know it was the fires that forced us to build brick buildings. The others kept burning down."

"You must admit that Jack's right, though, Papa," Katie remarked, pouring more water into Adams's glass. "Times *have* changed. The people who came here looking for wealth and adventure a dozen years ago have either moved on or settled in to more permanent lives. Columbia's a different town."

"Quieter, that much is true." Brian sighed, gazing around the nearly deserted saloon. By evening it would fill up, and the gaming table, where miners gathered to play faro at the far end of the room, would turn a tidy profit. But Brian no longer expected his saloon to make him a rich man.

Deftly, Jack changed the subject. "Missouri Dan rode down from Placerville with me, and we spent last night a little ways north of here. I didn't get much sleep, though, because Dan made me dig most of the night. . . ."

Katie responded to the gleam in his eyes. "Dig?"

He chuckled, the sound agreeably scratchy. "Yeah. Seems that last fall Dan discovered some gold over near Fraser River and brought it here to be weighed. There was more than five thousand dollars' worth, but he decided to put it away for safekeeping rather than take it along to Placerville—"

"Or have it stolen by the Griffin!" Katie exclaimed.

"I think the Griffin specializes in stagecoaches, lass," her father murmured.

"Anyway," Jack continued, "Dan chose a clump of five pine trees near a stream, and buried the gold there. The winter in Placerville didn't prove to be very financially rewarding for him, so Dan was pretty anxious to get to his pine trees last night and dig up that treasure." The corners of Jack's mouth slowly turned up as he paused to sip his water. "The stars were out as we came over the crest of the hill, but instead of lighting up Dan's clump of pine trees, they shone down on a vast, cleared field and a newly built cabin."

Katie gasped. "Someone had settled there!"

"That's right." He nodded, more than a little amused, his green eyes twinkling as they met hers. "They'd not only cut down Missouri Dan's pine trees, but they'd also planted grain. Of course, he wouldn't give up without a fight. Made me dig alongside him all night long until that field of grain was covered with holes. I just prayed that the farmer wouldn't wake up! As it is, I shudder to imagine the look on his face when he saw his field this morning."

"Don't suppose you found the gold?" Brian asked hopefully.

Jack laughed. "Of course not! Dan's in the blackest of moods. I left him digging one last hole, before dawn, but I heard that he was at Big Annie's this morning—" He cut himself off, realizing that he shouldn't have mentioned Big Annie's bawdy house in front of Katie. "Well, no doubt Dan'll be appearing here any minute to drown his sorrows. He was ranting all night about the good old days when people didn't go around cutting down trees in these parts. According to Dan, a man can't count on anything around here now.''

''I'll ask the dealer to see to it that he has a winning hand or two in faro,'' Brian murmured sympathetically.

''He should have put the money in the bank,'' Katie said.

''Now *there's* a civilized suggestion! Not Dan's style, I'm afraid.'' Jack laughed lightly, then his eyes wandered over her face and settled on the thick braid that hung down Katie's back. ''You're an uncommonly pretty girl, Miss MacKenzie. You'd have men lining up outside just to look at you if you'd change *your* style. Why not free your hair?''

Katie took a step backward, bumping her elbow against a decanter of brandy. ''I prefer to wear it this way. It's cooler.'' Her cheeks felt hot. ''And neater.''

''She's a stubborn girl,'' Brian told Adams.

''I don't give you men advice about what clothes to wear or how to comb your hair, so I suggest that you show me the same courtesy,'' Katie said, recovering her composure. ''Besides, why would I want to be examined by a lot of strange men?''

''I can't imagine.'' Jack's eyes were twinkling. ''I humbly apologize.''

''Apology accepted. If you are starved for the sight of female beauty, Mr. Adams, you ought to visit Darling's Dango Hall. Rumor has it that some German dancing girls have been imported,'' Katie replied defiantly, chin tilted upward to avoid his amused gaze. Picking up *Wuthering Heights*, she turned to her father and said, ''Papa, since you have urged me to do as I please today, I believe I'll go over to the *Gazette* and write an article about Missouri Dan's adventure. I think our readers might find the story very entertaining.''

''Wouldn't you rather spend your birthday seeking some entertainment for *yourself*, darlin'?'' Brian asked hopefully.

''I love to write, you know that! And thank you again for the beautiful book and the flowers.'' Katie kissed his cheek, then smiled politely at Jack. ''Meeting you has been very interesting, Mr. Adams. Have a safe journey.''

''That's kind of you, but I'm not leaving Columbia just yet, Miss MacKenzie. I feel certain we'll meet again.'' He gave her a lazy smile. ''Happy birthday.''

Jack watched Katie cross the saloon and stride out into the sunshine, idly noting her slim back, narrow waist, and gently curving hips. When he turned back, he discovered that Brian was contemplating him thoughtfully.

"I don't know what to do with that lass," MacKenzie said, sighing. "Eighteen years old today she is, and acting like there's no hurry to marry. I don't think it even crosses her mind! Not that any of the men around here are worthy to claim her hand. Many of the best are off fighting in the war between the North and South." Brian's blue eyes turned speculative again. "It's a difficult bride who's not only beautiful, but also smarter than most men. It will take a man as rare as she is to appreciate Katie and win her love. She's hardworking and has a mind of her own, but she's quick to laugh, too, and—"

"MacKenzie," Jack put in softly, his expression knowing yet amused, "why are you telling me this?"

Brian looked down the bar at the bouquet of lilies and larkspur. "Well, I—I've no idea!" he stammered, and heaved another sigh of mournful confusion.

"Neither do I. . . ." Jack leaned over to pat the older man's shoulder, then stood up and brushed the dust from his smooth buckskin pants. "So, I'm off to have a bath and a shave, get my clothes laundered, and take a room above the U.S. Bakery and Coffee Saloon." He put some coins on the bar and grinned. "Thanks for the water and conversation, MacKenzie. Buy Missouri Dan a drink for me when he comes in, will you?"

"Be glad to." Brian picked up the coins and looked at them for a moment. "Jack—if you want a clean bed and home cooking, you're welcome to stay with us. I like you."

Jack stopped at the door and glanced back, his wide shoulders and lean hips outlined against the sunlight. "That's a kind offer. I'll consider it."

Katie made her way down Columbia's dusty Main Street, which was shaded by rows of trees of heaven, their spreading boughs abuzz with bees. She waved to the blacksmith across the street and greeted an elderly couple coming out of the Cheap Cash Store with a basket of groceries, but otherwise the town's main thoroughfare appeared deserted. Constructed since the fires of 1854 and 1857, the handsome brick buildings lining the street had sturdy doors and windows with tall, green shutters made of fire-resistant iron; many of the two-storied facades boasted fancy ironwork balconies cast in Troy, New York, and brought by ship around Cape Horn. Such evidence of Columbia's prosperity would have been heartening if Katie weren't so aware that the source was quickly drying up.

"Hello, Katie!"

She looked over to see her friend Lim Sung emerging from his father's Chinese laundry. Lim was a thin, wiry boy of sixteen whose cheery smile never failed to brighten her spirits. "Hello, Lim! Can you come to the *Gazette* with me? I have to write a story."

He fell in beside her, his smile fading. "You know they don't like me there."

"That's ridiculous," Katie said, airily dismissing her friend's comment with a wave of her hand. "Besides, I doubt anyone will be there now. You just have to stop acting uneasy when you're around other people. It makes them all the more suspicious!"

Lim Sung and his parents were among the handful of Chinese who had been allowed, grudgingly, to remain in Columbia after all Orientals had been ruled out of town following the fire of 1857. Prejudice against the race was rampant throughout the gold country. People insisted that the Chinese were sneaky and untrustworthy, blaming them for thefts, fires, and various other crimes. The customs and beliefs they had brought with them from China made the miners all the more mistrustful, but Katie knew that their prejudice was rooted in ignorance and jealousy. The Chinese people she had come to know were hardworking, industrious, and patient. Indeed, it was their infinite patience that maddened the other settlers. Many a miner had given up on a claim only to have it taken over and worked painstakingly by a Chinese family with successful results. Now that the gold was playing out, a great deal of general frustration was increasingly being taken out on the Chinese population.

As they passed the D. O. Mills Bank Building, which also housed the post office and the Tuolumne County Water Company, Katie glanced over at Lim Sung and sighed softly. In a fresh white shirt and loose black silk trousers, he looked alien and out of place. His hair was drawn back into a long queue, which accentuated his high cheekbones; his eyes were dark and fathomless, uptilted and veiled with heavy lids. To others he was a foreigner, an outcast to be feared and rejected. But to Katie he was just Lim—her childhood companion, her trusted friend.

Lim met her gaze and smiled. He couldn't imagine life without Katie. She was his bridge to the white world, his friend, teacher, and counselor. When they were little children, they had sat under the trellis of morning glory next to the MacKenzie house while she shared her lessons with him, teaching him not only to read and write in English, but to speak the white man's language without a trace of his parents' accent. He would never forget the debt he owed her; he would honor her, and her friendship, all the days of his life.

"Look what my father gave me for my birthday," Katie said

now, holding up her book. "*Wuthering Heights*. It's a wonderful, tragic romance set in Yorkshire, England."

Lim grinned as they turned up Washington Street toward the *Gazette* office. "How can a romance be wonderful and tragic?"

"This one is!" Katie laughed, her long black braid swinging in the breeze. "Emily Brontë is a very talented author."

"A lady wrote this book?" he exclaimed in surprise.

Opening the door to the *Gazette*'s cramped offices, she was about to reply when Gideon Henderson called to her from his desk. "Kathleen! I'm glad you're here. I need you to take over Owly Shaw's duties. He's ridden over to Murphys to talk to the stage driver."

"The stage driver?" Katie echoed.

"Haven't you heard?" Gideon's glasses slid down his nose as he sorted through the papers littering his desk, perpetually in search of the one that wasn't there. "The Griffin robbed the Sonora stage this morning! Took a thousand dollars in gold off one of the passengers, but left the others in peace. He's the confoundedest stagecoach robber I've ever heard of!" As an afterthought, Henderson picked up a piece of white linen from among the papers and tossed it to Katie. "Care for a souvenir?"

Her blue eyes were huge as she stared down at the snowy handkerchief, its corner embroidered with the figure of an animal that appeared to be half eagle, half lion. Katie swallowed hard and whispered, "It's a *griffin*. . . ."

CHAPTER
2

June 21, 1864

CARRYING A CHICKEN, FRESHLY KILLED AND PLUCKED, AND A bag of potatoes, Katie approached the white frame house she shared with her father. Located on a quiet corner of Jackson Street, it was not as grand as some that had been built with gold fortunes, yet she loved it for its cozy charm.

Beneath the profusion of blue morning glory blossoms that spilled over the porch roof, Katie saw that the front door was ajar. Juggling the chicken and vegetables, she gently pushed open the door with her hip, took a step into the kitchen, and stopped, staring.

A man stood gazing out the back window, his physique framed by lace curtains and sunlight. Katie took in the clean sweep of tawny hair across the back of his head and the curls that grazed his tanned neck. A freshly washed white shirt set off straight, square shoulders and a tapering back. The man stood with his hands on lean hips encased in faded dungarees. His feet were bare.

An unfamiliar sensation rushed through Katie's body, settling in her midsection as she regarded this vital figure. The image of the curls against the male neck and the line of his shoulders and back burned into her brain. The sack of potatoes slipped from her grasp, rumbling upon impact with the scrubbed floorboards.

The man turned, and a thoroughly disconcerted Katie met the

clear green eyes of Jack Adams. Before she could speak, he was crouching to retrieve the potatoes.

"I must have startled you," he said in his husky voice, glancing up to smile apologetically into her eyes. "Your father invited me to stay here, but perhaps he should have consulted with you? . . ."

"Oh, no. . . ." Katie glanced away, saw the taut muscles in his thighs as he rose slowly, then murmured, "Here? You're staying here?"

"If this poses a problem . . ." Jack set the potatoes on the table, which was covered with a cheerful yellow-sprigged cloth. He tried to capture her gaze once more.

"Of course not!" She laughed brightly. "Why would it be a problem? My father and I frequently entertain house guests."

"I just thought that perhaps *I* might be the problem." Arching a sandy brow, Jack smiled slightly. "You don't like me, do you?"

Katie was relieved to feel her wits returning. "You flatter yourself, Mr. Adams. I haven't had time to form an opinion about you one way or the other." She put the chicken on the table, then crossed to get a pot from a cupboard under the pine dresser. Glancing back, she saw that his eyes were twinkling. "As it happens, I have more important matters on my mind."

"Indeed?"

"Yes. The Griffin has struck again!" Katie exclaimed.

"Your tone of voice seems to indicate that this is dramatic news. Isn't the Griffin just another stage robber?"

Katie's blue eyes widened with disbelief as she opened the back door. "Don't you read the newspapers, Mr. Adams? But then, I shouldn't suppose you can read at all. Most of the miners of my acquaintance are not intellectually inclined."

"Oh, I can read," he replied laconically. "A little."

"Well, perhaps you should consider practicing with the *Columbia Gazette*."

Smiling, Jack followed her into the neat backyard. Bordered by a white picket fence, it boasted a row of fruit trees and tidy flower and vegetable gardens. Katie paused to cut yellow roses, then bent beside the small plot of fresh herbs.

"Are you hoping that I'll enlighten you about the Griffin?" she asked, not looking up as she broke off new basil leaves.

Jack laughed, and the sound unaccountably made the tiny hairs on the back of Katie's neck stand up. "Miss MacKenzie, don't make me beg for this favor!"

She stood, her cheeks pink, and found him gazing at her with amusement . . . and something else that made her uneasily aware that he was a man and she was a woman. For the past year, her father had constantly reminded her that she was a woman now, but Katie had never understood what he meant until today. Nervously, she turned and walked back into the house.

"The Griffin is very different from the other stage robbers, Mr. Adams. There has been an air of mystery which has surrounded his every move, ever since he first stepped in front of the Sonoma stagecoach last autumn." Katie put the basil in the pot with the chicken, lit the stove with practiced ease then sat down and handed Jack a paring knife. They both peeled potatoes as she continued. "It's said that the Griffin is a gentleman. He's clean, well-spoken, and has never resorted to violence."

"The mystery, I gather, must be that the drivers continue to turn over their gold to such a peaceful soul," Jack remarked in ironic tones.

"Well, he *does* carry a rifle, but it has never been fired. He wears a long linen duster and a hood with holes for his eyes. When the stage comes into view, he steps out of the trees holding his rifle and says, 'Would you mind stopping for a moment, boys?' "

"Do you suppose the Griffin cares if they do mind?" Jack's green eyes danced with humor.

"Well, no, obviously not, but people are absolutely intrigued by the idea of a hold-up man with breeding. It's said that he often appears to be rather amused by it all, and he's displayed rare consideration for his victims. In *fact*"—Katie leaned closer lowering her voice in conspiratorial tones—"the real mystery is what the Griffin is after. So far, he has only robbed stages containing either Aaron Rush or Harold Van Hosten as passengers, and he only takes *their* money and valuables."

Jack's brows elevated slightly. "Rush and Van Hosten. Aren't they the owners of the big mine near here?"

She nodded, cutting the potatoes into quarters. "That's right. And they aren't very well liked. They bought out a lot of claims for prices well below their value, then used hydraulic equipment to get the fortunes still hidden in the limestone and marble. Miners who have settled here with families are now forced to work in the Rush Mine for miserably low wages. They hate Rush and Van Hosten. Some speculate that the Griffin actually might be one of those miners . . . except that he doesn't behave like any miner I've ever seen in these parts."

"Hmm . . ." Jack leaned back in his chair and stretched out his legs. "Perhaps the Griffin just doesn't like their looks."

Katie gave him a dubious look as she rose to add the potatoes to the pot. "Don't you think, Mr. Adams, that there must be a bit more involved in it than that?"

"What? Revenge? You said he only takes their valuables. What about the box?"

"Well," she allowed, "he has taken that once or twice, but always later some of the poorest families in town have found envelopes of money under their doors. Needless to say, the Griffin's legend has grown, and he's become something of a folk hero in Columbia and the surrounding towns. . . ."

"Ah!" Jack laughed huskily. "The Robin Hood of the Sierras. He keeps none of his ill-gotten gains for himself?"

"Well, yes, I suppose so—" She broke off in midsentence. "This is ridiculous! I don't need to defend the Griffin to you. I am not saying that *I* think he's a hero, but you see, I'm a newspaperwoman for the *Columbia Gazette*," Katie said proudly. "So I have been privy to all the details of these hold-ups. I wouldn't be human if I weren't a bit intrigued."

The corners of his mouth still twitched in amusement. "Confess now, Miss MacKenzie. I promise not to tell. Aren't you the least bit caught up in a romantic dream about this outlaw? Perhaps you're hoping that the Griffin will rob the stage you're riding and carry you off instead of the box!"

Katie's cheeks burned as she whirled on him. "You are insufferable, Mr. Adams! How dare you say such things, even in jest? *And*, for the record, I do not have romantic dreams!"

Jack feigned astonishment. "You don't?" He found himself fascinated by her show of temper and dazzled by the fire in her blue eyes.

"Just how long do you intend to remain in Columbia, Mr. Adams?" Katie asked frostily.

He laughed again, and the sound was almost seductive. "I hate to disappoint you, Miss MacKenzie, but my business shouldn't take more than a week."

She walked over to the table and set down a white earthenware pitcher filled with roses. "That long? I *am* disappointed." Then, her long ebony braid flying off to one side, Katie swept from the room, the sound of Jack's low laughter ringing in her ears.

Nightfall did not bring peace to the town of Columbia. Instead, men of all shapes and sizes clad in flannel shirts of red or blue filled the saloons, fandango halls, and bawdy houses lining Main Street. A mixture of tinkling piano tunes and raucous voices filled the night air, invading even the parlor of the relatively secluded MacKenzie house.

Katie sat curled on the faded calico sofa, an oil lamp glowing near her elbow and *Wuthering Heights* open on her lap. Usually she feasted on solitude and the chance to read, but tonight her mind wandered restlessly. Supper was ready, but neither her father nor Jack Adams had come home. Jack had gone out soon after she retreated to the parlor with her book, his only farewell a maddening, amused glance in her direction as he went out the door. Although Katie told herself that she found him annoying, she also found herself brooding about their conversations. Her mind went round and round as she tried to make sense of Jack and of the intensity of her own reaction to him. Finally she told herself, "It's because he's invaded your territory so abruptly! After only the briefest acquaintance, he was sitting at your table and goading you about your views of the Griffin! It's his eyes! To maintain an attitude of detached friendliness and to stop him from getting a rise out of you . . . you must avoid his eyes!"

Katie smiled to herself. It all seemed simpler now that she'd sorted things out and arrived at a workable solution.

Her thoughts drifted back to the Griffin. What sort of man was *he*? Jack Adams would laugh if he knew of her secret feeling that the Griffin was a true gentleman at heart, reckless yet fair and compassionate. Katie imagined that he held up stages because he was righting a wrong of some sort, and that he was cultured and well read. He had probably traveled widely . . . and was very handsome . . .

"Pardon me if I'm intruding again—"

She looked up in surprise to find Jack Adams leaning against the kitchen door, his hooded green eyes watchful in the half-light. "I didn't hear you come in!"

"I used the back door. You shouldn't leave it unlatched, Miss MacKenzie. Someone less friendly might drop by uninvited." A lazy current of amusement drifted into his husky voice. "The Griffin is at large, you know . . . but then, perhaps you would enjoy a nocturnal visit from *him*."

Irritation boiled up in her again. For some inexplicable reason, his perverse determination to address her formally as "Miss MacKenzie" rankled her to no end. Katie had the feeling that she was being mocked, gently, but she certainly had no intention of repeating her suggestion that he use her Christian name. Moreover, the resolutions she had made moments before now seemed impossible even to implement—let alone maintain! Detached friendliness? How could she, with the maddening Jack Adams? Still, Katie pressed her lips together and tried to smile. "Your concern for my safety is touching, Mr. Adams. However, it is not only unsolicited but unnecessary. I am perfectly capable of looking after myself."

Jack grinned suddenly and sauntered toward her. Bending, he touched her tight smile with the tip of his forefinger. "Careful!" he chuckled. "You might hurt yourself."

Feeling vaguely insulted, Katie flushed. "Are you here to annoy me, Mr. Adams, or is there a *logical* reason for this midevening visit? If it's supper you want . . ."

He backed away, smiling boyishly. "*Am* I annoying you? It's hard to be certain—"

Katie cut him off with an icy stare, then stood up and smoothed her skirts.

"All right," Jack said with an expression of mock contrition. "I'll behave myself. I've come over from the saloon to deliver a message from your father. He's too busy to come home for supper and asks that you bring a plate over to him."

Katie went past him into the kitchen and assembled a fragrant dish of chicken and vegetables, then covered it with a napkin. Turning, she discovered Jack standing behind her. "Must you *lurk* so often?" she burst out.

His tawny brows shot up. "You're the first woman who's ever asked that of me," he said in tones that suggested he was flattered. "I'll try to comply . . . if you'll make a plate for me, too."

Exasperated, Katie shook her head. "I think you're capable of doing that yourself, Mr. Adams. And I won't mind a bit if you stay right here to eat your supper." With that, she picked up the covered dish and swept out the front door.

The night air was cool. Katie, having forgotten her shawl in the drama of her exit, hurried down Jackson Street and had turned onto Main Street when she sensed that someone was following her. She quickened her pace, but the feeling persisted. Finally she looked over her shoulder and recognized Jack's shoulders silhouetted in the moonlight as he walked toward her carrying his own covered plate.

"I should have known it was you!" she cried in relief.

His teeth flashed in a smile. "Was I lurking again? I didn't mean to, but for some reason I thought that you preferred to walk alone." He nodded toward his plate. "Your father suggested that I join him for supper."

Katie sighed and nodded, and they walked the rest of the way to the saloon together. Jack seemed interested in the activity that

spilled into the street from Darling's Dango Hall and the saloons
lining Main Street, while Katie tried to pretend she didn't notice.
Her own father's saloon was one thing; she had grown up with it,
and the patrons always treated her with deference under the stern
gaze of Brian MacKenzie. However, Katie looked with mild disgust
upon the boisterous, drunken goings-on that took place elsewhere
in Columbia.

As they approached MacKenzie's Saloon, she noted with satis-
faction that, although a crowd of heads was visible over the tops of
the swinging doors, there was neither raucous laughter nor shouting
going on inside. Jack held the door for her, and Katie entered to
sudden pandemonium.

"Happy Birthday!" everyone shouted. Stunned, Katie surveyed
the sea of grinning faces. There was her father, pink-cheeked and
beaming behind the bar, and Lim Sung, his dark eyes sparkling
with pleasure. Lim Sung's father stood amidst a group of bearded
miners, and many of her neighbors were present as well, including
Victoria Barnstaple, a talkative sparrow of a woman who had been
Mary MacKenzie's best friend.

Victoria hurried forward to embrace the speechless girl. "Why,
I do think we surprised you, dear! Are you pleased?" She took the
dish from Katie's hands and passed it to Jack without looking at
him. He set Brian's plate on the bar, got a fork for himself, and
retreated to a corner table to eat his own supper and watch the
celebration.

Katie had intrigued him from the moment he'd first seen her that
afternoon at the bar, her scrubbed, pretty face bent over *Wuthering
Heights*. She piqued his curiosity not only because she was an in-
congruity in the gold country—especially in this saloon—but also
because he soon realized that Katie possessed a unique mixture of
personality traits, many of which were rare in the women of his
acquaintance. She was independent, intelligent, capable, adult beyond her years in many respects—all due, Jack supposed, to the
responsibilities she had assumed after her mother's death. In addi-
tion, Katie was blessed with a lovely face and form. With those
qualities, she could have become the toast of the Sierras by this
time, attracting men of quality from miles around. It was entirely
possible that she could have married a rich man from Sacramento
or even San Francisco. Yet Kathleen MacKenzie claimed that she
did not yearn for romance, love, or marriage. Passion, it seemed,
stirred not within her breast.

Jack smiled slightly as he stared across the saloon and pondered
the enigma that was Katie. She seemed slightly ill at ease as she

stood among the group of well-wishers, as if she were embarrassed by this display of affection and uncertain how to respond. Mrs. Barnstaple and the few other women who had deigned to come into the saloon tonight for Katie's sake were clad in fine dresses with wide-hooped petticoats, and they wore their hair in carefully arranged ringlets or smooth chignons. By contrast, the guest of honor's frock of faded calico and her long, lone braid seemed strikingly inappropriate. Jack took a last bite of chicken, pushed his plate away, and wondered whether Katie's apparent lack of interest in her appearance and in men was evidence of bravery—or cowardice.

Having opened and admired an array of modest gifts, Katie was now gazing at the cake that Mrs. Barnstaple had baked for the occasion. "It's really too pretty to eat," she remarked, touching one of the candied violets that decorated the smooth white icing.

"Don't be silly, Katie girl!" Brian exclaimed, handing her a knife.

"It's even prettier inside," Victoria encouraged her.

Katie winced as she cut into the elaborate confection, discovering that bright candied fruit studded the interior. "Oh, my, it's much too beautiful! I'm embarrassed that all of you have gone to so much work on my account."

Lim Sung couldn't hug her in public, but he did lean in close to whisper, "We love you!"

Overcome, Katie blushed as she served the cake. She felt so very warm . . . and out of place, somehow. This party, and the emotions that appeared to be behind it, were more than she deserved. She didn't know how to behave. What did all these people expect of her? Should she have wept with joy?

"Darlin', why don't you take a piece of cake to Jack?" Brian murmured, leaning across the bar. His breath smelled of celebratory whiskey. "Ask him to join the party. After all, he had a hand in the success of your surprise!"

Puzzled, she met her father's eyes. "What do you mean?"

"Jack had to lure you over here without arousing your suspicions." Brian chuckled at the memory. "When we asked him, he assured us that you were already irritated by his presence, and that he was quite sure he could keep you too annoyed to suspect that he might be delivering you to a party in your honor."

Katie lifted her chin, staring across the saloon to where Jack Adams reclined on a chair, apparently dozing. "That man really is insufferable."

"Because he speaks his mind?" Brian teased. "You're used to that; the men around here don't waste time with manners. I think that Jack's found your sore spot because he doesn't back off from you. You can't outtalk him and put him in his place.''

She smiled grudgingly. ''I shudder to think where his 'place' really ought to be. The possibilities are horrifying.''

''*Kathleen*, don't be unkind. Take the man a piece of cake and try to remember that he's our guest.''

Katie bit off another tart rejoinder and accepted the plate, secretly glad for the respite from her party. Across the crowded, noisy room, Jack appeared oblivious, slouched on his chair, bronzed hands folded against his white shirtfront. His strong body was graceful in repose, legs stretched out and head tipped to one side. As Katie drew nearer, studying his face, she began to suspect that his green cat's eyes were open just a fraction. . . .

''Missing me so soon?'' he asked softly, moving only his lips.

Now Katie could see that Jack was watching her from beneath his tawny lashes. ''Papa insisted that I bring you a piece of cake.'' Her tone was cool as she set the plate before him. ''Has he overestimated the extent of your domestication, Mr. Adams? Perhaps you're not yet able to sit up straight and use a fork.''

He arched one eyebrow and grinned slowly in appreciation. ''I never could resist a challenge,'' he replied, stretching and shifting upward on the chair.

She watched him take a bite of cake, then purred, ''Well, I wouldn't want you to overtax yourself on my account, sir. . . .''

''Miss MacKenzie,'' Jack began, then paused to chew, making a boyish face at the sugary taste. Swallowing, he continued, ''I should remind you that I spent last night digging for gold in a field of grain. I'm too tired right now to match wits with you.''

''Oh, dear, that's right!'' Katie exclaimed, remembering. ''Where's Missouri Dan?''

''He's gone to bed, which is what I would have done if—'' He broke off and stifled a yawn.

''If you hadn't been persuaded to lure me here for my birthday party,'' she finished for him, watching as he stood up beside her. She found herself trailing after him toward the doorway, while all around them groups of miners loudly discussed the Griffin's latest stage robbery. Katie scarcely heard, though, more intent on catching Jack's sleeve before he exited the saloon. ''Why, after you went to so much trouble, didn't you join in the party? You deserved to be among the guests—''

He turned to look down at her, one hand on the door, and smiled lazily. Unaccountably, Katie felt a disconcerting shiver race from her scalp to the base of her spine. ''No,'' Jack said in his soft, husky voice, "I couldn't join in the party because I didn't have a present. At least . . . not one I could give you in front of your friends and neighbors." His gaze dropped to her parted lips. "I suppose I could give it to you now—but you'd have to come outside with me."

Heart racing, Katie stepped backward and swallowed hard. Instinctively, she pressed her hands against her burning cheeks, then quickly removed them when she saw Jack's knowing smile. "No. No, I'd rather not."

"Well, then, I'll just keep it for you, Miss MacKenzie, and you can tell me when you want it." Halfway out the door, he glanced back over one straight shoulder, his sleepy green eyes agleam with amusement. "Good night, Kathleen. I'm glad you were surprised on your birthday."

She was too confused to be angry—yet—or to be sure what Jack had meant by his parting remark. Dazedly, she could only whisper, "Good night," but Jack Adams had already gone.

CHAPTER
3

June 24, 1864

"**D**O YOU SUPPOSE JACK *REALLY* WENT TO LOOK AT A claim?" Katie wondered aloud. She was cleaning the surface of the saloon's mahogany bar with a vengeance, rubbing so hard with her soft white cloth that Brian worried she'd strip the varnish.

He looked up now from refilling the liquor bottles. "What else would the man be doing?"

"Well, he said it was just a few miles east, and he's been away a day and a half!"

"Good Lord, child, are you complainin'? I thought you couldn't stand Jack Adams!"

"I can't." Katie rubbed harder, staring at a barely visible stain. Although it was only nine in the morning, the saloon was already stiflingly warm, and damp tendrils had escaped her braid and were curling about her face. "I just wonder what he's up to. I don't trust the man."

Brian laughed. "Oh, it wouldn't surprise me a bit if Jack's indulgin' in something more pleasurable than just investigatin' a claim. Women fancy men like him, and men like him fancy women! Betsy Cartwright over in Shaw's Flat was widowed last autumn, remember? She's a handsome young woman, and it seems to me that—"

23

"Shaw's Flat is south of here, Papa," Katie interrupted, her voice rising.

"Oh, I don't imagine that Jack would mind ridin' a few miles out of his way for a beautiful woman. . . ."

"Truer words were never spoken, MacKenzie!" A husky voice laughed softly from the doorway.

Katie froze in the act of pushing wisps of hair off her moist forehead. Slowly she lifted her head and beheld Jack Adams casually entering the saloon. Unlike normal mortals on a crushingly humid day, he appeared freshly bathed and unaffected by the heat, his caramel-colored hair ruffling back from a tanned, engagingly attractive face. His boots were shined, and his faded red shirt and blue dungarees looked as if they had just come from Sung's Laundry. Katie, on the other hand, was certain that she was the picture of dishevelment.

"Darlin', don't just stand there gaping!" Brian boomed happily. "Get the man some coffee!"

Blood rushed to her cheeks. "I—I was just wondering if Mr. Adams always returns from his trips at such an odd hour, and how he manages to look so immaculate."

Jack smiled at her as if he could read her mind, took a stool at the bar, and accepted the mug of coffee Katie placed before him. "I was up early and didn't have far to ride. And, as a matter of fact, I stopped at home for a bath before walking over here."

"Home?" she echoed.

His green eyes twinkled. "Well, it feels like home, thanks to the warm hospitality bestowed upon me by you and your father."

Only Katie seemed to be aware of the irony in his voice. Brian, on the other hand, appeared on the verge of offering to adopt Jack. Reaching across the bar, he patted the younger man's shoulder with hearty affection. "We couldn't ask for a better houseguest, could we, Katie love? You're a pleasure, Jack, and we've missed you since yesterday mornin'. Why, just before you came in, Katie was sayin'—"

"I was saying that you had been rather mysterious about your errand away from Columbia!" she interjected hastily. "If we hear that the Griffin has been active again, I might begin to suspect *you*, Mr. Adams!"

"Indeed? Why, Miss MacKenzie, I'm flattered! Knowing the exalted opinion you have of the Griffin, I consider it an honor that you could imagine I could be so fine and brave a gentleman. . . ."

Brian looked at his smoldering daughter in confusion. "What's all this? Have you romanced the notion of that outlaw, Katie? You'd do well to remember that men like that—that—*Heathcliff* are only in books. And if you do harbor any sympathy for the Griffin, keep quiet about it. Harold Van Hosten is in here almost daily, and it wouldn't be good for my health if he thought my own daughter was out singin' the praises of the highwayman who's been humiliating him and Aaron Rush for nearly a year!''

Katie glared at Jack. "I think this is just Mr. Adams's misguided attempt at humor, Papa."

"Hmph. Take my advice, both of you, and choose another subject for your taunts. The Griffin's dangerous sport."

Jack drained his coffee and set down the mug with a dull thud. "Believe me, MacKenzie, there's nothing I'd rather discuss less! As a matter of fact, I have an ideal distraction in mind." He leaned closer. "I've thought of a plan to improve business here at the saloon."

"This should be fascinating," Katie muttered, returning to her polishing but staying within earshot.

"Darlin', where are your manners?" Brian exclaimed. "Hear the man out."

A charming smile brightened Jack's countenance. "This notion is so obvious that I'm sure you've thought of it yourself, but were unable to find the right person for the job. You see, MacKenzie, what this saloon *needs* is a female to serve the patrons. A pretty, friendly girl whom the miners could look upon as a friend, yet who would also provide a welcome respite from the other men they toil beside all day long in the mines. I was thinking—"

"Mr. Adams," Katie interrupted, "this saloon is not a hurdy-gurdy house or a dance hall. Those are the only places that use women to lure unsuspecting men for the purpose of getting them to pay outrageous prices for their drinks. I am shocked that you would propose something so . . . so *base* to my father!"

Jack replied evenly, "I wouldn't consider proposing anything even remotely *base* to a respectable man like your father, nor am I suggesting that this saloon become a hurdy-gurdy house or a dance hall." He looked at Brian. "The men are already used to seeing Miss MacKenzie working here, so it's not as if women are forbidden in your saloon. It simply makes sense to me that it might improve business in these less-than-prosperous times if one of your employees was a pretty girl who enjoyed dressing accordingly and being friendly to the lonely, unmarried men of this town."

Katie seethed, more conscious than ever of her plain braid and modest, faded dress. She was further outraged to hear Brian reply, "Well, what you say makes sense to me, too, Jack. But I wouldn't want someone of questionable character, if you take my meaning, and I couldn't pay as much as the girls make at some of the less respectable places here in Columbia. Who'd want the job?''

Jack was on his feet in an instant, grinning broadly. "I was hoping you'd ask me that! Wait just a moment.''

As he hurried outside, Katie whirled on her father. "Have you taken leave of your senses?'' she hissed. "How could you encourage such an immoral scheme?''

"Settle down, darlin'. Let's hear the lad out.''

"*Lad?!* Papa, you mustn't be swayed by that devil's charm! He's up to no good, I just know it!''

"Nonsense.'' Brian waved her off with a chuckle. "I'm a pretty fair judge of character after all these years. Jack just enjoys life— and, in turn, people enjoy him.'' He paused. "I'm thinking that you just might be jealous.''

"Jealous?'' She paled. "That's a ridiculous thing to say. Why should I be jealous?''

He shrugged. "You're used to bein' the only female in the saloon, and the men adore you. It'd be natural for you to worry that another girl might take your place in their hearts.''

Katie laughed, relieved, but broke off at the sound of footsteps across the room. Turning, she saw Jack walking toward them, one arm wrapped protectively around a petite, buxom young woman with curls the color of burnished gold. They stopped a few feet away.

"Abigail Armitage, I'd like you to meet Brian MacKenzie and his daughter, Kathleen,'' Jack said almost gently.

"It's a great pleasure to make your acquaintance,'' the girl said in a high voice. "Jack has told me so many nice things about you both.'' She smiled at them nervously, then looked back up at Jack with huge brown eyes.

Katie decided that Abigail appeared to be infatuated with Jack, but she managed to hide her unreasoning fury behind a smile and say, "Welcome to Columbia, Miss Armitage.''

"Hear, hear!'' cried Brian. "Sit right up here and have something to drink. What would you like, uh . . . ''

"Abby,'' she supplied. Holding up her wide pink hoop skirt, Abby perched on one of the stools with Jack's assistance. "Call me Abby. And I'd truly enjoy a small glass of sherry. It's very kind of you to offer, Mr. MacKenzie.''

Katie blinked, glancing at the clock, but said nothing as her father poured the sherry and heartily insisted that Abby call him Brian. "So,'' he inquired after she had taken a few sips, "what brings you to our humble town?''

"Well, to tell you the truth, Jack said that I should come."

"Did he?" Katie said sweetly, avoiding Jack's narrowed eyes.

"I met Mrs. Armitage last autumn," Jack explained, "just after her husband was killed in a rather questionable accident in the Rush Mine. They had a little cabin between here and Springfield, and I decided to stop by yesterday and see how she was doing." He ignored the delicate arch of Katie's eyebrow. "To make a long story short, Abby's had a hard time making a go of it. I thought that if you could give her work, Brian, the both of you might benefit. She not only needs the income, but it would do her good to be among people again."

"Consider yourself employed, Miss Abby!" Brian declared, refilling her glass.

Her large round eyes pooled with tears, and she leaned against Jack's arm in relief. "You're all so kind. Jack's visit yesterday was like a miracle. He's saving my life. . . ."

"Yes, Mr. Adams ought to be a candidate for sainthood," Katie murmured, looking away. She didn't like the way she was feeling or acting, but kindness and charity seemed beyond her at the moment, and she was convinced that somehow Jack Adams was responsible. Certainly she'd never behaved like this before! He seemed to have the ability to needle her in ways that weren't apparent to anyone else, which infuriated her all the more. Katie glanced back at him now and found him watching her. He gave her a barely perceptible wink, then returned his attention to Abigail Armitage, who beamed up at him with frank adoration.

"Now then, Miss Abby," Brian said, "when would you like to start work?"

"I'd be glad to begin today if someone can teach me what to do." Shyly, she looked toward Katie, who averted her eyes and began polishing the bar again.

"Unfortunately, I have an article about the Griffin to finish for the *Gazette* today, but I'm sure my father would be happy to instruct you," Katie said stiffly.

"Did I hear you mention the Griffin?" demanded an angry voice from across the saloon.

All four turned their attention to the tall, thin, well-dressed blond man who walked up to the bar. His mouth was set in a hard line that was accentuated by a jutting nose and cheekbones. Small, deep-set pale blue eyes stared at each of them in turn.

Brian splashed whiskey into a shot glass and set it on the bar. "Good morning, Mr. Van Hosten. Beautiful day, isn't it?" He cleared his throat. "Uh, my daughter was just sayin' that she's composing a piece about the Griffin for the newspaper. She works there, you know.''

Harold Van Hosten smiled thinly, downed the whiskey, then inquired, "It will come as no surprise to you, Miss MacKenzie, to learn that I am rather interested to hear if any progress has been made toward discovering the Griffin's true identity or his whereabouts."

"None as far as I know," Katie admitted. "My story merely explores various possibilities of identity and motive—who he might be and why he turned to this way of life."

"If you hear anything, even a rumor, I would appreciate it if you would come to me. I'll be glad to reimburse you for your trouble. As long as that outlaw is at large, my very life is in danger."

Katie wanted to say, "Not to mention your money!" but instead replied politely, "I appreciate your concern, Mr. Van Hosten, and I'll remember what you've said."

"Good." He drained his second whiskey, looking at Jack and Abby over the rim of the glass. "You're Adams, aren't you? I think we were introduced a few months back."

"That's right." Jack's voice was low, his gaze even. "It was at the Wells Fargo office in Sonora, I believe. I trust you had a pleasant journey that day?"

"On the contrary, I was robbed by that cursed Griffin!"

Jack's tawny brows lifted. "I'm sorry to hear that. It was fortunate for me that I took the stage to Sacramento instead."

"The criminal only took *my* valuables. It's a vendetta of some sort, but I assure you that I mean to even the score! Rush and I are posting a reward that should bring out a Judas among the miners who revere, and doubtless protect, that outlaw." His blue eyes glittered coldly, then he blinked, regaining his composure. "I seem to recall that you were in search of a profitable claim to work, Adams. Any luck?"

"Not the sort I'd hoped for. I'm here to investigate a claim I heard is up for sale a few miles east."

"Well, such pursuits are risky business at best these days. If you're disappointed again, come and see me at the mine office. I might be able to provide more reliable employment."

The smile that curved Jack's mouth didn't quite reach his eyes. "That's very generous of you."

"Pragmatic, my good fellow," Van Hosten replied coolly. "You're strong and able-bodied, but those qualities are easy to come by here in the foothills. What is harder to find is a man with a quick mind. You're intelligent, Adams, I can see it in your eyes."

"You'll understand if I don't demur." Jack's voice was dry.

Brian was growing increasingly uneasy as he listened to this conversation. It worried him to think that Jack might go to work for Rush and Van Hosten. Glancing over at his daughter, he saw that she was watching the two men with an expression of open contempt. Brian decided that a distraction was in order.

"Mr. Van Hosten," he interrupted, "I've neglected to introduce you to Columbia's newest resident and *my* newest employee! This is Mrs. Abigail Armitage. Miss Abby, say hello to Mr. Harold Van Hosten, one of our most prominent citizens!"

Abby smiled at him warily and extended her hand, which Van Hosten lifted lightly to his lips. After amenities were exchanged, he murmured, "Armitage . . . that name sounds familiar. . . ."

"I believe that you were acquainted with my husband, Ben, Mr. Van Hosten. He worked in your mine. You may recall that Ben staked a claim of his own near Springfield, and it looked very promising. I believe that you were quite interested in purchasing it from him, but he refused, and shortly after that he was . . . killed in an accident in the mine." Abby's rouged lips trembled as she spoke, but her words were fueled by courage.

Van Hosten put some coins on the bar and stood up. "Of course, I do remember your husband, Mrs. Armitage," he said absently. "He was a fine man, a good worker. Mr. Rush and I were saddened by his death. Unfortunately, mining is hazardous, and I know that Ben was aware of the risks. You have my sincere sympathy, madam, and my best wishes for the future."

Abby could only nod, after which Van Hosten made his farewells and strode out of the saloon. Longing to soothe the obviously distraught young widow, Brian poured more sherry.

"Thank you," she whispered. Her tiny hand shook as she lifted the glass to her lips.

Katie felt the stirrings of genuine compassion. Ignoring Jack and her father, she reached over to touch Abby's arm. "I have to go to the *Gazette* for a few hours, but I'll return here later this afternoon and help you learn what will be necessary to perform your job. All right, Abby?"

"You're very kind."

"I thought Miss Abby might stay in that spare room upstairs," Brian remarked. "The bed's good, and there's a balcony overlooking Main Street. With a few female touches, it ought to do quite nicely. Why don't you let me show it to you, m'dear, and you can freshen up if you'd like, and lie down for a bit."

Jack stood up. "Abby's things are still at the Wells Fargo office. I'll go get them."

To her dismay, Katie found that he was walking behind her out of the saloon, and she could feel him watching the gentle sway of her hips. Out on the dusty street, she whirled to face him.

"Stay away from me!"

Jack feigned surprise. "I thought I *was* doing that! You can't accuse me of lurking, either, since I announced my intention to leave."

His tawny hair gleamed in the sunshine, and Katie was unnerved by the way his lazy cat's eyes danced as they stared into her own. "I am disgusted by your proximity," she hissed, then turned and walked away.

Jack kept pace. "That's unfortunate, since we're heading in the same direction. And I had the impression that you had something on your mind that you might wish to say to me. . . ."

Goaded to the breaking point, Katie stopped. "All right," she replied in poisonously sweet tones, "I'll tell you."

"Good!" He broke into a grin, and she narrowed her eyes in return. "I'm sure you'll feel better afterward. Why don't we just step over here under a tree so that we don't attract a crowd."

When Jack's fingers closed around her arm, as if to guide her, Katie wrenched free and walked ahead of him to the shelter of the spreading branches of a tree of heaven.

"Here I am," Jack invited, standing before her, "a willing target. Please begin."

"I don't mind if I do! First of all, you needn't look as if my anger is cause for amusement."

"I'm sorry. I'll try to do better." He strove to settle his features into a mask of sobriety.

"*And*, I am well aware that you are presently being nice only to entertain yourself!" When he blinked in mild surprise, Katie was unaccountably pleased. "Everything you have done today, Mr. Adams, has made me furious! I feel a great deal of sympathy for Mrs. Armitage, and she seems to be a good person, but you had no right to manipulate my father into providing employment for her!"

"Was that what I did?"

"It certainly was! Oh, you were very canny, like a cat with a mouse, explaining the situation to my father in such a way that he was bound to agree! He is kind, warm-hearted, and impulsive, as well you know, for you have been the recipient of his generosity yourself. But, if you were a person with any scruples, you would not have played upon his good nature to achieve your own ends!"

Jack's brows arched slightly. "And what might those be?"

She wished he would be quiet and just listen to her. Casting about for a response, she exclaimed, "I'd rather not sully my mind with the sordid possibilities."

Unable to contain himself, he gave in to husky laughter, eventually wiping his eyes and murmuring, "I'm sorry; I couldn't help it. You should be flattered, Miss MacKenzie. Sometimes the things that come out of your mouth are simply delightful!" He smiled down at her angry countenance. "Is it so difficult for you to believe that my motive was simply to help Abby?"

"Perhaps it was in part, but I also know that there is more to it," Katie said stubbornly.

"Do you imagine that I did it to aggravate you?"

That was precisely what she thought, but when he said it aloud it sounded ludicrous. "Of course not! But you had no right to interfere in the business of the saloon. We have worked hard to establish a certain reputation for quality—unlike the establishments in Columbia which cater to a more . . . lascivious clientele. Now that reputation will be at risk!"

Jack leaned against the tree trunk and folded his arms. "Your father is only at risk to make more money than he's seen lately. Abby likes men, and they'll like her—therefore, they'll come to the saloon to see her."

"You can try to whitewash this, but the fact remains—"

"That you're jealous. You've been the only female in that saloon, and even though you claim to be above feminine vanity, the fact remains that you've gotten all the admiring looks from the men without having to curl your hair or wear a pretty gown or lower yourself to wearing powder and rouge."

Katie longed to slap him, but the curious glances of passersby held her in check. "I do not wish to discuss this matter any further, Mr. Adams. Obviously you are far too rude to listen to reason or admit that you have erred."

"Apparently I am quite hopeless," he replied agreeably. "Are we finished?"

"Not quite!" Her sapphire eyes were flashing, her delicately sculpted cheeks were rosy, and she was breathing hard. The conviction that Jack appreciated even the physical effects of her fury only made Katie angrier. "I also would like to inform you that, if I did not already have enough reasons to despise you, your conversation with Harold Van Hosten gave me another."

The laughter went out of Jack's eyes. "Indeed?"

"It was unpleasant enough to see you being obsequiously polite to a man I have told you is corrupt, and who you know may well have been responsible for the death of Mrs. Armitage's husband. But when you began discussing the possibility of going to *work* for him, I was filled with revulsion!''

Jack opened his mouth to speak, then seemed to think better of it and sighed instead. A muscle in his jaw tensed before he finally replied softly, ''Unlike the Griffin, whose courage you so admire, I cannot wear a mask in the presence of Van Hosten. I must introduce myself by name and show my face, which I happen to be quite fond of. I haven't forgotten Ben Armitage's death; it holds a lesson, reminding me what is necessary to stay alive. If that makes me a coward, then so be it.''

Katie steeled herself against the spell of his eyes and his soft, serious voice. ''We have nothing left to say to each other, Mr. Adams.''

Slowly, he lifted tanned fingers and smoothed a stray curl from her brow. A gentle irony infected his voice as he murmured, ''Somehow, Miss MacKenzie, I doubt that. . . .''

Her heart thudded and she tried to swallow. Pressing her lips together, Katie turned away. She had gone only a few steps when the pull of his eyes caused her to pause for an instant, but then she continued walking, not looking back until she was safely inside the white frame office of the *Columbia Gazette*. Leaning against the door, she pressed shaking fingers to her burning cheeks.

''Odious, odious man!'' she whispered. She had no idea why Jack Adams stirred up such vehement, conflicting emotions within her, but she wished fervently that he had never come into her life.

CHAPTER
4

June 26, 1864

"T HAT WAS DELICIOUS!" BRIAN DECLARED, SWALLOWING the last bite of his toast and poached egg. "Your strawberry jam is as fine as any your dear mother ever made."

"Thank you, Papa." Absently, Katie picked up his plate and walked over to wash it with the other breakfast dishes.

Brian followed, wrapping an arm around her slender waist. "You look real pretty today, darlin'! Is that a new frock?"

She glanced down at the dress of white percale dotted in violet. The full skirt was set off by a violet sash at the waist, and the high, violet-bordered collar was edged in starched white lace. "It's the one Victoria made for my birthday. Do you really like it?"

"You're a picture. Have you thought about puttin' your hair up?" Immediately Brian regretted his words. "I see—that'd be a mistake, wouldn't it? Jack might think you were changin' your hair because *he* suggested it."

"Mr. Adams's opinion is of no consequence as far as I'm concerned, Papa."

"That's my girl! You know, the sight of you so beautiful and grown-up makes me remember something I've been meanin' to give you." He took her by the hand and led her into his bedroom. Opening the top drawer of a worn cherrywood bureau, Brian reached to the back and withdrew a small wooden box. "This was

your mother's, and she wanted you to have it. I should've given it
to you on your birthday, but you know how absentminded I can be.
I forget that you're not my little girl anymore."

Katie held the box for a moment before opening it. She tried not
to think of her mother, avoiding the pain that inevitably accompanied memories, and now she could already feel the familiar sting
mingling with a sense of anticipation. Slowly she lifted the lid to
reveal Mary MacKenzie's three cherished pieces of jewelry. Nestled in a bed of velvet were a lustrous pearl necklace, a cameo
brooch edged with gold filigree, and a beautiful ring that featured
a sapphire encircled by tiny diamonds.

"Oh . . ." she breathed. She picked up the cameo, stroking the
sculpted pink-and-white surface with the side of her thumb. "Mama
wore this nearly every day! I assumed that . . ."

"She wore it still?" Brian whispered. The sight of Katie's blue
eyes shining with tears made his throat close and his voice grow
thick. "No, darlin'. Mary has her wedding rings, but she asked me
to keep these for you. You've never shown an interest in jewelry
before, but seein' you so lovely in that dress made me think that
it's time you had these."

Katie looked into his shaving mirror and pinned the brooch to
the base of her lacy collar. "I love it, Papa. Thank you."

Brian gathered her into his bearlike embrace. He held her for a
long time, awkwardly patting the back of her head until he felt the
warmth of her tears penetrate his shirt. "What's wrong, lass?"

"I miss Mama."

"I know you do. I do, too, but I'm thinkin' that's not all that's
bothering you. Won't you tell your old da what it is?"

She shook her head but wouldn't meet his eyes. "It's nothing,
really."

"Wouldn't have anything to do with Jack Adams, would it?"
Brian pressed gently.

Katie disengaged from her father's embrace and walked over to
lean against the door frame, arms folded across her breasts. "No.
Well, yes, but not in the way you think. I mean, I have no feelings
at all about the man himself—it's the things he does and says that
vex me intolerably!"

Brian's gaze was as tender as he took in the stubborn set of Katie's
chin. "Tell me what you mean, darlin'."

"I feel that this is my home. I'm a part of our family, of this
town, and I've grown to depend on certain things being constant.
You, and the saloon, and my friends and neighbors are my whole
world . . . yet since Jack Adams came to Columbia, everything

seems turned upside-down!'' She took a deep breath, hoping to calm herself. "He's *changed* things that I had come to rely upon. Even you aren't the same, Papa! I always could predict what you would say and do, but that man has convinced you to change things that were just fine until he interfered. He's invaded our home, and everything is different at the saloon. You know that I like Abigail just fine, but I don't think we needed her to work at the saloon. It used to be a place of business, a friendly place with a sort of dignity, where the men could come for a quiet drink, some conversation, wholesome food, and a game if they were so inclined. Now there's this blushing, pretty girl waiting on the customers, who wears gowns that show too much of her bosom when she bends over and who causes the men to act like adolescent boys! And meanwhile, there is Jack Adams, leaning against the bar and admiring his own handiwork. Well, it wasn't his place to interfere! He has you charmed into believing that he's a good man—so charmed that you don't even blink when he discusses taking a job with Harold Van Hosten! Well, I can see him for what he is. I just wish he would go away and leave us alone!''

Brian rubbed his jaw, bemused. "Sounds like you've been holdin' in a whole lot of frustration, Katie love.''

Suddenly she felt like crying, but she pushed down the tide of emotion, merely nodding in response.

"Probably upsets you that I haven't seemed to pay any mind to your objections to Jack so far.''

"Well . . . yes! Yes, it's bothered me that a virtual stranger has had more sway with you than I, that you seem to have more respect for his judgment than for mine. *And*, it bothers me that *he* brushes off my protestations and opinions as if they aren't worth considering!''

MacKenzie wanted to put an arm around his daughter, but he sensed that she wouldn't welcome it right now. "Darlin', I apologize if I've been inconsiderate. I've not meant to hurt you, and I think you know that I have a bounty of respect for your judgment and your opinions. Haven't I listened to you always?'' He paused, then added gently, "You've had a great deal of power in your own little world, ever since your ma died. You've been used to behaving as you pleased and looking as you pleased . . . and having things the way you wanted them. I'm not saying that's bad. You have a strong will, Kathleen, and you're pretty and as smart as any man. It's only natural that you'd stand out in this town.''

"Are you suggesting that I'm spoiled?'' she asked in a quiet, shocked voice.

"I wouldn't put it that way. You've worked too hard to be spoiled. You're just a natural leader, and you're used to that. I'm afraid that Jack Adams is the same way. I happen to believe that other people's opinions can be worthwhile, which is why I've listened to Jack. It sure doesn't mean I put any less stock in what you think! I love you more than my own life. It just seems to me that you're accustomed to people doing what you want, and rightly so. It's natural that you'd be annoyed by Jack busting into your world. Not only are people listening to him instead of you, but you can't get *him* to do what you want, either."

"You make me sound horrid, Papa!"

"Nonsense!" Brian laughed. "And what you're feeling is just part of growing up. Look on it as a lesson. Even in a town like Columbia, you can't always make life turn out the way you'd like. Other people have their ways to do what they want, which may not be the same as what *you* want."

Slowly, she came over to him and rested her head against his sturdy shoulder. "I'll try to remember that, Papa."

"You'll be a lot happier if you can, darlin'." Smiling, he patted her cheek. "Would you listen to a bit more advice from your old da about Jack Adams?"

Katie sighed. "I suppose so."

"You're lettin' him bother you too much, lass. Just let him be. And, don't think that everything he does is to get your goat! Relax . . . accept him as he is, because there's not a blessed chance that you can change him. If he ever does start actin' the way you'd like him to, it'll be because he chooses to and not because you willed it." Brian kissed the tip of her nose. "I have a suspicion that, deep down inside, you like him just a little bit. You know, you're too young and pretty to get so riled up over one human being. Why not look on Jack's visit here as an opportunity for adventure? Try to have a bit of fun!"

Katie made a face. "Why don't I start with something that would be easier to enjoy? Perhaps I could persuade our good dentist Dr. Blake to extract one of my teeth!"

"Have you ever tried this concoction?" Gideon Henderson asked as he set the type for an advertisement of "Dr. Webber's Invigorating Cordial."

Smiling, Katie read aloud from the copy: " 'Do you feel prostration of the nerves, the body, or the mind? Are your nerves unstrung, your spirits low? Is a general feeling of exhaustion, inanimation, and weakness pervading your mental and bodily functions?' " She skipped ahead to " 'Weakness in Females, and Aged Persons, are singularly benefitted.' " Katie laughed. "How interesting to learn that we women are classified with the aged in terms of our health! No, Gideon, I've never tried this miraculous cure. Have you?"

He pushed up his glasses with ink-smeared fingers. "No, but a few years back, my mother was drinking a bottle a day. She smelled like she'd just left a saloon, and she acted that way, too! Finally, Mother set the kitchen on fire one night while trying to light the stove, and my father refused to let her have any more of Dr. Webber's Invigorating Cordial!"

"A wise decision. Did she miss it?"

"Oh, yes. She took to her bed and sulked for a week before announcing that her headaches were completely gone and she felt fine for the first time in months."

They had almost finished with the back page of the *Gazette*. Tomorrow this latest weekly issue, along with her story about the Griffin, would go on sale. Anticipating increased interest, Gideon planned to print an extra fifty copies.

Katie stretched and felt the stiffness in her back from hours of bending over the type bed. "I'm ravenous! You must be, too. Shall I get us something to eat?"

He nodded, watching as she removed the white smock that protected her dress. For a moment, he was uneasily aware of his ink-smudged shirt with its frayed cuffs and the drabness of his black trousers and brown silk waistcoat. The twinge passed, though, as Gideon reminded himself that it would take more than fine clothing to transform him into a man worthy of Katie MacKenzie. "I've meant to tell you that you look pretty today, Katie. Not that you don't always look pretty, but that frock is a beauty. And where did you get such an exquisite cameo?"

She blushed in surprise. Was it her imagination, or was Gideon blushing a little, too? They'd known each other all their lives, though he was two years older, and Katie had never seen him show a romantic interest in any female. Gideon's first love had always been the Adams bed and platen printing press. "Why, thank you, Gideon! I—that's very . . ." She glanced down in confusion. "The cameo was my mother's. Papa gave it to me today." She touched it with slim fingers. "I adore it. I can remember so clearly when she wore it herself, pinned at this same spot on her gowns."

"Your mother was a very beautiful woman," he said quietly. "You look more like her all the time. Have you thought of pinning up your hair?"

She reacted instantly. "No!"

"All right, all right, I'm sorry I mentioned it!" Gideon held up his hands in surrender. "I just thought that it would show off that graceful neck of yours . . . and the cameo."

Katie pursed her lips thoughtfully and wandered over to the tiny mirror that hung in a the corner of the back room. Staring at herself, she slowly unbraided her hair, which cascaded down her back in rich, ebony waves. Almost reluctantly, Katie reached back and wound it around, then carefully arranged it atop her head, holding it in place with one hand. The effect was stunning. She frowned but shyly emerged to show Gideon.

Her friend applauded. "If you don't mind my saying so, I think you've been hiding your light under a bushel, Katie! Or, more precisely, under a braid and a plain, unflattering dress. You've grown into a woman, but kept the transformation a secret. Although I was aware that you were pretty, I can see now that you're a true *beauty*!"

Before Katie could reply, another voice spoke from the doorway. "It's a distinct honor to witness this historic occasion. I hope it isn't too late for you to change the *Gazette*'s headline to KATIE UNBRAIDS!"

She whirled around, freeing her hair to tumble over her shoulders. "You! Have you nothing better to do than lurk in doorways, waiting to mock me?"

Jack's husky laughter seemed to infuse the office's stale atmosphere with fresh energy. He walked toward her slowly, his expression appealingly boyish and innocent. "I'd be obliged if you could accuse me of something else besides 'lurking,' " he entreated.

"Oh, I'd be happy to, Mr. Adams. Shall we begin with appalling insolence? Or would you prefer that I compose a *list*?"

Gideon stared as Jack responded to her angry insults with a grin. Clearing his throat, Henderson murmured, "Katie, will you introduce me to your . . . friend?"

She'd forgotten he was there and now turned to him in embarrassment. "I'm sorry, Gideon. You must be quite shocked by my behavior. Mr. Adams has a singular talent for bringing out the worst in me."

As Katie performed stiff introductions, Gideon looked at Jack Adams and felt puny, pale, and awkward. The other man certainly had presence. Clad in clean, soft buckskins and a shirt the color of ripe wheat, he exuded strength and self-assurance as he came forward, his bronzed hand outstretched. His shoulders were broad, his hips lean and narrow, and his face was not only attractive, but intelligent. Gideon felt Adams's catlike green eyes sizing him up before white teeth flashed in a sudden, engaging smile.

"It's a pleasure to meet you, Mr. Henderson," Jack said, shaking the smaller man's ink-stained hand. "You publish a very worthwhile newspaper here. I admire your work. Are you still turning a profit now that Columbia has . . . slowed down?"

"Uh—thank you for the compliment. I wish I could assure you that the *Gazette* is thriving, but unfortunately, that's not the case," Gideon replied, struck by the inane sound of his own voice in contrast with the male huskiness of Jack's. "I've heard of you, Mr. Adams. You've earned quite a reputation for installing Abigail Armitage at MacKenzie's Saloon. The miners are very grateful!"

"Are they?" His eyes danced. "Well, I try to help in my own small way." He ignored the snort of derision from behind him, instead reaching back to take Katie's arm and draw her forward. "Mr. Henderson—"

"Please, call me Gideon."

"If you'll call me Jack. Gideon, may I borrow Miss MacKenzie for a short while? It's a matter of grave importance."

Henderson nodded soberly, charmed and envious at the same time. "Well, certainly, Jack. Katie's put in a long day, and she's looking far too pretty to waste any more time cooped up here. . . ."

"Excuse *me*, gentlemen, but I am not a piece of goods that you can trade at will!" She tried to wrench free of Jack's grip, but he held her with ease. "Only I can say whether I will stay or go—"

A sudden, quelling look from Jack silenced her. "Would you do me the colossal favor of allowing me to explain? Privately?"

Katie stared back, her eyes flashing sapphires. "I might, if you will *release* me!" She jerked her arm away only to find that he had released it, then was further humiliated by losing her balance and stumbling against Gideon. Marshaling what little dignity she had left, Katie straightened up, elevated her chin, and walked toward the door. "You may follow me, Mr. Adams."

Jack gave Gideon a look of long-suffering amusement, then nodded good-bye and exited the *Gazette* office behind Katie. Out in the afternoon sunlight, he gestured toward the passageway next to the Fallon House Hotel and Theatre. "After you, my dear."

When they were standing close together, hidden from the street, Jack murmured, "Would you like me to avert my eyes?"

"Why would I want you to do that?" Katie asked, irritated.

"So that you can remove the stone from your shoe . . . or whatever it is that's causing your querulous mood."

Her eyes blazed. "It's a thorn in my side, and the only way to remove it is for you to go away!'' She paused, breathing hard, then added, ''And if I am querulous, it is because *you* are captious!''

Jack's tawny brows elevated appreciatively. ''The challenge, as I see it, would be to use both 'lurk' and 'captious' in a sentence. Let's see . . . 'Lurking captiously, he plotted ways to drive the formerly serene young maiden to the brink of madness.' How's that?''

''Apt . . . most apt.'' A smile flickered over Katie's mouth but was instantly suppressed. ''*Mr. Adams*, this is a shocking waste of my time!'' she said sternly. ''What is it you wish to say to me?''

''I wish to ask a small favor.''

''Of me? This should be entertaining!'' She grinned as if already contemplating the pleasure of refusing him.

''Now, Kathleen, don't look like that. I realize that you aren't *fond* of me, but aren't we friends?''

His eyes were gazing into hers in a way that made her feel breathless and confused. Katie realized that she had never understood the true meaning of the word *charm* until Jack Adams came into her life. Merely by using her Christian name and choosing a different form of address, he'd created a sense of intimacy between them. Somehow, too, he could charge his eyes and voice with heady magic, and she was not immune to their spell. Instinctively Katie struggled, but then she remembered her father's advice. Don't let it bother you, she told herself. Relax and try to enjoy him for what he is.

''Friends?'' Katie met his eyes boldly and felt a sudden surge of power as she stopped fighting and let go. Suddenly she saw that not allowing him to upset her was a more subtle form of victory. ''I wasn't aware that there was any basis for that happy relationship between us, but I suppose that anything is possible. And I like to think that I'm a charitable person, Mr. Adams. What kind of favor did you have in mind?''

Jack blinked in momentary surprise but refrained from questioning her sudden shift in mood. ''Just a bit of light-hearted fun.'' He gave her his most appealing smile. ''All I ask is that you pretend to be my wife.''

CHAPTER
5

June 26, 1864

"**H**AVE YOU TAKEN LEAVE OF YOUR SENSES?" KATIE GASPED. His eyes crinkled at the corners. "I don't think so, although you're certainly entitled to your opinion. Just let me explain—"

"Please do!"

As if to calm her, Jack reached for her hand. The instant his warm, strong fingers touched her soft skin, Katie flinched as if he'd burned her. Jack smiled a little, stroking his thumb against the sensitive surface of her palm and watching Katie's reaction. Now she was still, but he saw that she was holding her breath. "Don't worry; I'm harmless," he murmured, his voice a caress.

Katie felt as if her face were on fire. "Are you?" She drew her hand from his.

"For a woman who dreams of being carried off by the Griffin, you certainly seem to be afraid of men!" Jack chuckled softly, then held up his hands in surrender. "Now don't get all hot and bothered again. I apologize. I don't mean to offend you—but you're the damnedest woman I've ever known."

"And probably the only *lady*," Katie retorted coldly.

Jack hastened to make amends. "That's true. Absolutely. I'm just a poor barbarian who can't help saying the wrong thing. But I mean well."

She allowed her anger to melt under his smile. "Mr. Adams, are you civilized enough to come to the point?"

"I think so." The sight of Katie returning his smile disconcerted him. God, but she was beautiful! There was a radiance in her face that he'd never seen before, and deep sapphire eyes twinkled gently. The urge to kiss her was almost overwhelming. Jack bit his lower lip and cleared his throat. "I . . . uh, well, the fact is, I need your help. It isn't so much for me, but to spare the feelings of a certain young lady. . . ." Katie's delicate eyebrows rose, but he plunged onward. "You see, I met Miss Chelstrom in Placerville, and apparently she formed an attachment to me. I won't bore you with the details, but the current situation is that she seems to have followed me here. I was, as you can imagine, quite surprised when she appeared in your father's saloon. As we talked, it became obvious that she was determined in this matter. Finally, seeing no other way out, I told Miss Chelstrom that I could not be a part of her life any longer because I had gotten married." He grinned recklessly as Katie widened her eyes. "To *you*."

She opened her mouth, but no words would come.

"I realize that I may have spoken rashly, but your father joined in, and before I knew it, we had spun quite a tale of impetuous romance. Brian declared that you and I had fallen in love the moment we met. Destiny, he said."

Katie finally made a sound of outrage. "My *father* said that?"

"Oh, that was just the beginning. Once he got started, I thought he'd never stop!" Jack started to laugh, remembering, then sobered at the sight of her stormy expression. "It was all nonsense, of course. We just wanted to convince her to leave on the next stage."

"It would serve you right if she lingered and made you suffer!"

"Perhaps, but would you want your father to suffer, too? I'm not the only one who's been dishonest today. If I'm exposed as a liar, then he will be as well."

"But you are the one who created this situation!" Katie's voice rose heatedly. "You've probably left a string of broken hearts all across the Sierras!"

"Shh!" Jack glanced over his shoulder. "Please, I don't mean to hurry you, but the stage is due soon, and I intend that Miss Chelstrom will be on it. Kathleen, won't you do me this one favor? If not for me, then for your father."

"This is outrageous! What on earth do you want me to do?"

"Well, for some reason, the young lady is suspicious. She won't go until she meets you. She's waiting for us now at the Wells Fargo office." His brows rose hopefully.

Katie sighed. "I don't seem to have a choice, do I?"

Laughing, Jack caught her up in his arms and lifted her off the ground. Katie wriggled free, but he saw the telltale flush that suffused her cheeks. "It'll be fun," he assured her. "All you have to do is pretend to be madly in love with me. That won't be difficult, will it?"

With those provoking words, he tucked her hand through the crook of his arm and started toward the Wells Fargo office. Katie told herself that she despised him and was angry with him, but her feelings were quite the opposite. Never before had she known such a euphoric surge of excitement and adventure, and her heart raced with something akin to joy as Jack smiled down at her and winked roguishly. Even worse, she found that the sensation of his hard-muscled arm against her fingers and the warmth of his body so close to hers were distinctly pleasurable. So pleasurable, in fact, that Katie allowed herself to bask in the moment and not think about the dangerous implications of what she was feeling.

As they turned right on Main Street and approached the handsome, brick, three-story Wells Fargo office, it was all she could do not to beam up at him. Then she saw Miss Chelstrom. The young woman was sitting on a bench outside the ticket office, surrounded by luggage and hatboxes.

Katie felt a stab of raw emotion that she recognized as jealousy. Miss Chelstrom was ravishing. Clad in an elegant summer suit of fawn-colored Glacina stamped with a lace design, the young woman was blessed with a petite, perfectly curved body, gleaming coppery ringlets, huge green eyes, and flawless white skin. Suddenly Katie's new gown seemed gauche and obviously homemade, and her face burned as she realized that she had forgotten to rebraid her hair.

Miss Chelstrom was staring at Jack. "I see that you have found your *wife*," she murmured in tones of disbelief.

He seemed perfectly at ease. "Kathleen helps to publish the *Columbia Gazette*, and she was working this afternoon, but she graciously agreed to come and meet you." His hooded eyes narrowed slightly. "I wish it hadn't been necessary."

Jack wrapped his arm protectively around Katie's waist, and the sides of their bodies fit naturally together. For a moment she rested her cheek against his shoulder, inhaling his clean, masculine scent; then she seemed to recall her duty. Straightening, she smiled at Miss Chelstrom and held out her hand as Jack introduced them.

"How do you do?" she said politely. "I do hope you'll excuse my rather informal appearance. I—well, Jack often likes to unpin my hair, even in public.'' Katie blushed prettily and glanced up at him.

"How interesting to meet you, Mrs. Adams!" Miss Chelstrom declared. "And, you have a *job*! How sweet. I do hope my arrival in Columbia hasn't upset you too much."

Katie relaxed against Jack so that her breast pressed against the side of his chest. He tightened his fingers at her waist in response. "Upset me? Don't be silly. Nothing could upset me these days, Miss Chelstrom, I'm far too happy. I never understood the meaning of that word until Jack and I met. . . .'' She dragged her eyes from his mouth and bestowed a smile upon the intruder. "Surely you don't imagine I'm surprised to learn that Jack knew other women before he met me? On the contrary, I'm certain that there are many, many young ladies who have fancied themselves in love with him. How could they resist? But that's past now. I'm Jack's wife."

Jack himself could hardly believe his ears, not to mention his senses, as Katie leaned against him. He could even feel the outline of her thigh against his hip. Their eyes met, and he swore he read passion in Katie's blue gaze. "You certainly are," Jack murmured, then looked at Cecelia Chelstrom. "I'm truly sorry you had to come all this way, Cecelia, but we did say good-bye in Placerville. Have a safe journey home."

"Oh, I shall. And Jack, shouldn't you buy your dear wife a wedding ring? That is, if you mean to stay married. . . ."

"I plan to, just as soon as we get to Sacramento this Thursday."

Miss Chelstrom's beautiful face was stiff with anger and suspicion as Jack and Katie strolled away arm in arm. Turning his head a fraction, Jack saw that the young woman was sitting forward, observing them. He looked down at Katie, who was leaning contentedly against his shoulder.

"That was quite a performance, Miss MacKenzie. Have you considered a career on the stage?" Before she could gather her wits and resurrect the familiar barriers between them, Jack continued, "I'm not entirely certain that Miss Chelstrom is convinced, however. Would you mind helping me to dispel any lingering doubts she might entertain?"

Katie gazed up into his green eyes, wondering if this entire episode might be a dream. "No," she whispered, "I wouldn't mind."

Aware that he was taking advantage, yet blithely unrepentant, Jack turned to face Katie and slid both hands around her waist. Slim and supple, she melted against him, and with an instinct born of practice, he knew that she wasn't pretending: Katie was as hungry for him as he was for her. His heart leaped with arousal when she artlessly reached up and twined her arms about his shoulders. Her fingers sank into the curls at the nape of his neck, feeling their texture and caressing the warm, bare skin under his open collar.

"Kathleen," he breathed, gathering her completely into his arms. Her firm breasts seemed to brand the expanse of his chest; their bodies were flush, hips pressed together in spite of the voluminous crinoline that belled out behind Katie.

She didn't close her eyes but stared in wonder, savoring the exquisite anticipation as Jack slowly lowered his face to hers. Already Katie's senses were feasting on the sight, touch, and smell of him; her heart seemed to burst with the first, tentative taste of his mouth. Gently, Jack grazed her parted lips, tracing each soft, lush curve before covering them with his own finely chiseled mouth. Through a dizzying wave of arousal, the realization came to him that Katie had never been kissed before. Her lips trembled with yearning as he tasted them for long moments before slowly venturing beyond with his tongue. Katie's came eagerly to meet him, sweet and ardent, and then she was kissing him back, exploring the inside of his mouth as he had explored hers. At length they broke apart, gasping for breath and laughing; then Katie's mouth hungrily sought Jack's again. His hands explored the graceful curves of her waist and back while her fingers caressed his tawny, ruffled hair. It wasn't until Jack felt for the tiny buttons that skimmed her spine that he remembered where they were, and why. Opening his eyes, he saw that Victoria Barnstaple and two of her friends were staring at them from the other side of Main Street.

Katie moaned softly in protest when Jack's mouth left hers. He buried his face in her hair, kissed her neck, then remarked with gentle irony, "We seem to have forgotten ourselves, Miss MacKenzie. . . ."

Startled, she opened her eyes as the flush of passion drained from her cheeks. "I—but—"

"Please don't slap me," Jack begged, smiling, "or our performance will have been for naught." His alert eyes watched the conflicting play of emotions cross her face. "Now, Kathleen, don't look at me like that. Think of it as my birthday gift, the one I couldn't give you at the saloon that night. You're eighteen now, and it was time you had a proper kiss." Jack lifted her trembling hand and pressed it to his mouth before glancing up at her with a hint of mischief. "You can speak honestly to me. Didn't you enjoy it just a little?"

Katie swallowed and took a deep breath, but the storm inside her body would not be calmed. "I don't wish to discuss this . . . incident. Ever. I'm going home."

"We're still being watched, so you'll have to let me escort you." When she nodded dazedly, Jack tucked her hand around his arm and they walked together up Main Street in silence. He sensed that she needed to be left alone, and he discovered that, for once in his dealings with women, he himself was confused.

When they reached the white picket fence that enclosed the MacKenzie house, they stopped, and Jack caught Katie's arm before she could turn away. "Don't look so stricken," he said lightly. "It was only a kiss, Kathleen, engaged in for the benefit of Miss Chelstrom. It doesn't bind you to me in any permanent way."

She nodded, looking away, then Jack let go of her arm and she went into the house alone. Inside, it occurred to Katie that he might be returning to see Cecelia Chelstrom. Hating herself for caring, she peeked out the window and saw that he was walking east, toward Yankee Hill Road. Sighing, she leaned back against the door. The neat little parlor was just as she'd left it that morning, yet everything looked different. Jack's voice echoed in her mind, repeating over and over, "Just a kiss . . . it doesn't bind you to me . . ."

Kissing was something that Jack Adams did all the time, Katie imagined. He'd probably kissed hundreds of women. It might mean nothing to him, but she felt transformed, frighteningly so. Somehow, with his intoxicating maleness and his skilled embrace, Jack had opened a door inside of her that she had been only dimly aware of before. It was as if an entirely new person had escaped from a previously locked room, a woman Katie didn't know, and she wasn't certain if she could force her back into captivity.

She walked into her sun-filled bedroom with its narrow, austere bed against the far wall and stared at herself in the bureau mirror. The beautiful blue eyes that looked back at her glowed with a new light.

"It was just a kiss," Katie whispered. She touched her mouth. It felt slightly bruised, and the memory of Jack's kiss and their mutual abandon sent a traitorously pleasurable shiver through her body. "How could I have done that?" she wondered, and was answered by the puckering of her nipples and a tingling sensation between her legs.

Suddenly Katie was angry—angry at her own body's betrayal, at Jack's cavalier attitude, at herself for loving the taste of him that lingered in her mouth and the male-musk scent that still clung faintly to her skin. She glared at her own reflection. "I refuse to feel this way!'' she hissed. ''It was just a kiss, a meaningless kiss, he said so himself. A frivolous pleasure of adulthood. And Jack Adams is a man. He's certainly no one special, and certainly not deserving of my thoughts! It was a loathsome accident that Jack Adams kissed me for the first time. I would have reacted to such a pleasurable physical sensation the same way with any man.''

The woman in the mirror smiled back at her reassuringly. Katie remembered then that she had promised to bring some food to Gideon. She no longer had any appetite but decided to take him some of the ham, bread, and fruit that were left from last night's supper.

Before she set out on her errand though, she brushed her tangled mane of hair, then braided it so tightly that it hurt.

The headquarters for the Rush Mine had recently been rebuilt of brick after another of the many fires that had plagued Columbia during its fourteen-year history. It was situated on a hillside east of town, overlooking one of the sites of hydraulic mining that had rejuvenated the gold industry in the area.

Harold Van Hosten's office was smaller than that of his partner, Aaron Rush, but it reflected the prosperous image the mining company wished to project. Jack, sitting on a straight chair, was separated from Van Hosten by an ornately carved, mammoth cherrywood desk. There were large, gilt-framed oil paintings on the walls, and as they talked Van Hosten drank his whiskey and smoked a long cigar. Jack thought, with decided irony, that any dusty miner who came here to confront his employer would feel like a serf who had been granted an audience with his king. It was not an atmosphere conducive to honest communication or democratic fair play.

''I like you, Adams,'' Van Hosten was saying in velvety tones. ''It's not often that I meet a miner with obvious intelligence as well as ambition and physical strength. I think that you could have a bright future if you come to work for us. If you're patient, you just might have a position in management one day. On the other hand, you could go on working claims independently, but surely a perceptive man like yourself is aware that the day of the lone prospector is over in the Sierras. The surface gold is played out.''

''That's the rumor, anyway,'' Jack replied laconically.

Van Hosten arched his pale eyebrows. ''I'd say that it's a proven fact. It's very rare for a man to discover an appreciable amount of gold with a pan or a pick these days.''

Jack's eyes looked even more catlike than usual as he gazed

calmly across the desk. When he spoke, however, it was only to say, "I'll have to take your word for it, Mr. Van Hosten. You're certainly in a position to know."

The older man smiled thinly. "I realize that it must be difficult for an ambitious young man like yourself to trade dreams of glory for something more realistic, but you wouldn't regret it. I can guarantee you a fine, successful future."

"What exactly do you have in mind?"

"Well, initially you would be an assistant of sorts. The business has reached the point where there is more supervising than either I or Mr. Rush can handle. You'd be a fast learner, I'm sure, and your responsibilities would increase accordingly." He exhaled a strong-smelling cloud of smoke. "Of course, we're willing to pay handsomely for a man of your caliber."

"Of course," Jack echoed with a barely perceptible note of disdain. He paused then, leaning back in his chair and running a hand through his hair. "Well, Mr. Van Hosten, I would say that you have made me a very attractive offer. I'd like to accept, but I'm afraid that I can't make any commitments. If I find that I'm dissatisfied, or if something serious develops in one of my other business interests, I would be forced to resign."

Van Hosten nodded, considering. "I'm willing to take that chance—and the only commitment I would require from you is one of absolute loyalty."

Jack grinned. "I'm as loyal as an old dog. When do you want me to start, and what do you want me to do?"

"You can come in tomorrow, Adams, and I'll begin to show you the way we do things around here. Then I'm planning a trip by stage to our bank in Sacramento next week, and I'd like you to accompany me. As you might suppose, I'm rather concerned that the Griffin might once again attempt to separate me from the money I am taking . . . or even from this earthly body. Your sharp wits and strength should be of great service."

"I'll be there, sir."

Van Hosten poured himself another glass of whiskey. "Are you certain you won't join me? I'd say that our agreement calls for a toast!"

Standing up, Jack put out his hand. "Have an extra shot for me, Mr. Van Hosten," he said, smiling, as they shook hands. "If I don't leave now, I'll miss dinner with the MacKenzies, and my hostess will be out of temper with me. Actually, she has seemed quite out of temper with me ever since we met, but I haven't given up hope of winning her over. . . ."

"Go along, then, but don't expect Katie MacKenzie to thaw out just because you're on time for dinner. Many a man in this town has tried to discover the way to her heart, and all have failed. If you solve the mystery, you could sell the secret formula and retire a wealthy man!" Van Hosten laughed loudly and drained the whiskey. "Good evening, Adams. I'll see you tomorrow morning. At six."

Jack longed to utter an exclamation of protest but forced a smile instead as he backed toward the door. "Yes, sir. Good night, sir—and thank you."

The scene at the dinner table was comfortable and homey, unnervingly so, as far as Katie was concerned. As she ladled fricassee of rabbit with baby carrots and potatoes onto a platter, she cast a sidelong glance at Jack and her father, who were cozily discussing Columbia's current petition for incorporation. Brian launched into an explanation of his position on the issue, and Jack leaned back in his chair, listening with an affectionate smile. He looked completely at ease and content. Freshly washed, he'd rolled up his sleeves to display handsome brown forearms, and droplets of water still clung to the hair that curled at the back of his neck. Unbidden, the memory of her fingers in Jack's hair rose up to torment Katie. She wished she could scour the feel of it from her hands, erase the pleasure of it from her mind, and was reminded of Lady Macbeth.

When she set the platter on the table, Brian asked, "Are there any more of those biscuits from breakfast, darlin'?"

"I'll get them," Jack said, rising. "You sit down, Miss MacKenzie. You've done enough work for one day."

Unable to meet his smiling eyes, Katie nodded and obeyed. When Jack passed next to her, she breathed in his clean scent and felt her cheeks grow warm.

"Are you feelin' all right, Katie?" Brian inquired, peering at her in the soft lamplight. "You look a bit out of sorts."

"No, no, I'm fine. A little tired, perhaps. It's been a busy day."

MacKenzie sniffed the fricassee appreciatively, then served himself. Jack offered Katie a biscuit, which she took without looking at him. She ardently wished that he weren't sitting across from her and briefly contemplated excusing herself.

"I see your braid has been restored," he observed.

"Yes." Katie spread jam on her biscuit with painstaking care.

"That reminds me!" Brian boomed suddenly, startling them both. "How could I have forgotten? I saw Victoria Barnstaple on my way home and she told me the wildest tale! Sometimes I swear that woman's a secret tippler. She said that the two of you were *kissing* in the middle of Main Street today, with, as she put it, 'shocking enthusiasm,' and that Katie's hair was all unbound, flowing down her back!''

Katie choked on her bite of biscuit while Jack grinned at his host. "What did you reply, MacKenzie?"

"Why, I just laughed and told her that I'd outgrown fairy stories forty-odd years ago!"

"Well . . . Mrs. Barnstaple wasn't completely inaccurate," Jack said carefully. "We weren't in the *middle* of Main Street, but I suppose that, to the casual observer, it might have appeared that we *were* kissing." Katie's eyes flew up to meet his, and he offered her a reassuring smile. "Your daughter very selflessly agreed to *pretend* to kiss me so that Miss Chelstrom, whom you will recall meeting earlier today, would believe that I was no longer romantically available. Miss MacKenzie did me a great favor, and I am now deeply in her debt."

"Oh." Brian swallowed some gravy-drenched rabbit and tried to make sense of what he had just heard. "So it was all an act . . . not a real kiss, then, hmm? I suppose you were just kissin' Katie's chin or thereabouts, and it looked like the real thing, right?"

"Something like that," Jack confirmed with a sober nod. "And, as I said, it was a great sacrifice for your daughter to suffer my touch at all, considering the way she feels about me. You should be proud that she possesses such generosity of spirit."

"Now, Jack, I'm sure my Katie bears you no ill will, and after all, she's aware of my fondness for you, lad. No doubt she did it in part because she knew it would please me, isn't that so, darlin'?"

Both men were looking at her, forks poised over their plates. Katie wanted to scream. "If you don't mind, Papa, I'd rather forget the entire incident. It really was meaningless. Can we talk about something else?"

"Certainly, love, certainly." Brian, his brow knit in confusion, cast about for a new topic of conversation. "Jack, why don't you tell us what else you did with your day?"

He took a long drink of water, then smiled bravely over the rim. "Well . . . I accepted a job from Harold Van Hosten. I start work tomorrow morning as his new assistant."

With a gasp of outrage, Katie leaped to her feet and threw her napkin at him. When Jack caught it deftly, his brows flying up in half-amused surprise, her fury doubled. "That does it! I can't bear another moment in this man's company! And to think that I felt sorry for you, the way I might feel sorry for a starving dog! If I had had any idea what you planned to do, that you intended to work for that corrupt *murderer*, I would never have taken pity on you or suffered your touch for even those few hideous moments!'' Although Katie's sapphire eyes flashed with rage, her voice trembled when she spoke, sounding high and strained, as if she were dangerously close to tears. ''If I never see you again, it will be too soon!''

With a strangled cry, she fled to her bedroom, slamming the fragile door behind her. Jack winced, looked over at the puzzled MacKenzie, and murmured with his usual trace of irony, ''It's no use trying to deny it. She *does* bear me ill will!''

CHAPTER
6

June 30–July 2, 1864

KATIE CLEANED THE JARS OF BRANDIED FRUIT THAT WERE lined up beneath the saloon's huge mirror. It was late, and Brian was hanging a "Closed" sign in the window while Abby swept the floor. At the bar, Jack Adams folded his copy of the *Columbia Gazette* and drained his cup of tea. Abby watched him, brown eyes filled with longing as she dragged the broom over the same spot for the third time.

"That's quite a piece you wrote about the Griffin, Miss Mac-Kenzie," Jack said, handing her his empty cup. "Your store of knowledge about the man is impressive."

Katie ignored the teasing note in his voice. "I take pride in my work, Mr. Adams."

For a moment he was tempted by the challenge of making her smile, or at least look at him, but fatigue won out. All too soon five o'clock would arrive again, and he would be forced to awaken and begin another day of work in the offices of the Rush Mine. Besides, Katie's usual barriers to communication between them had been impenetrable since the day she had learned of his employment by Van Hosten. Most of the time Jack was too busy or exhausted to make more than a halfhearted attempt to pierce her armor. Today it seemed easier to wait for her to grow tired of the game herself.

Now he merely said amiably, "Well, I'm sure that the Griffin, wherever he may be tonight, is flattered by your interest." Before Katie could reply, Jack crossed the bare floor to exchange a few affectionate words with Abby. Then, with a yawn and a half wave at Brian, he left the saloon.

Abby's eyes lingered on the swinging door. Moments later, her sweeping done, she disappeared into the back room. Katie was ready to go home to bed herself, but something in the older woman's demeanor troubled her. After a moment's consideration, she walked down the back hallway and met Abby coming out of the dark storage room.

"Good heavens!" Abby gasped. "Miss MacKenzie, you startled me!"

Katie was certain she smelled liquor on Abby's breath. "Haven't I asked you to call me Katie?" she said, then paused, torn between disapproval and concern. "Abby, perhaps I've been too busy or preoccupied to extend a proper hand of friendship to you since you came to Columbia. In any case I want to correct that oversight now. I know that you have been going through a difficult time lately, and I hope that you haven't felt all alone in your new home. . . ."

In the shadows, Abby self-consciously raised a hand to her mouth. "You're very kind . . . Katie. Thank you." She tried to escape, but Katie touched her arm.

"Is there something in particular that's bothering you? It might help to talk about it."

"I—no . . . well, I can't say that I'm exactly *happy* these days, but that's to be expected, isn't it? Life seldom turns out as we hope, and I'm learning not to hope anymore." Abby's doe eyes glistened with tears.

"What had you hoped for here?" Katie asked gently.

"I know it's not fair to draw conclusions about my future in Columbia after only a few days . . . but I suppose I expected to see a bit more of Jack. Before he came to visit me, I kept pretty much to myself, partly because I just didn't feel like seeing anyone after Ben died and partly because we lived miles away from anyone else. When Jack rode up, he brought hope and laughter back into my world. He's so *alive*, isn't he?" She gazed at Katie with searching eyes, waiting for her nod before continuing, "I see now that it was foolish of me, but I suppose I hoped that I could continue to lean on him here in Columbia. I'm sure Jack cares for me, and would rush to my aid if I were truly in need, but it's clear that he has his own life to lead and expects me to stand on my own two feet."

"That's hard, isn't it?" Katie couldn't forget that worrisome whiff of liquor.

"Well, I have to accept that Jack is one of those lone wolves. He has a good heart, but he'll never be committed to anyone. He needs his freedom."

Katie nodded, mulling this over, then put an arm around Abby. There were many things she longed to say, but she compromised with, "You must reach out to the rest of us. Jack Adams isn't your only friend in Columbia, Abby. If you need to talk to someone, I hope you'll come to me."

Abby managed a faltering smile. "I appreciate that."

The night was warm, and the barest breeze caressed the white curtains at Katie's windows. In spite of the late hour, she found that she couldn't sleep. Sitting on the edge of her bed, clad in a long, filmy nightgown of cotton lawn, she reread her article about the Griffin. The last few paragraphs had taken courage for her to write and courage for Gideon to print.

"The Griffin's legend grows with each new stage robbery. Some feel that his allure stems from the mystery of his identity and the style with which he carries off his crimes. Others contend that he has found favor with the people because they do not perceive him to be a criminal at all, but rather a modern-day Robin Hood balancing the scales of justice.

"Theories abound concerning the Griffin's motive. The most popular casts him as a miner who was cheated by Aaron Rush and/ or Harold Van Hosten, yet he appears to be more sophisticated and refined than any of the miners known to the townspeople of Columbia. In these times, when it is common for revenge to be sought with ruthless violence, the Griffin—with his calm, careful methods and gentlemanly demeanor—is an enigma.

"Many hope privately that this outlaw-hero will never be caught. And perhaps the Griffin will stop preying upon certain stagecoaches traveling the twisting roads of the foothills. Perhaps he'll grant Rush and Van Hosten a reprieve if they begin to deal fairly with the miners of Columbia. . . ."

Sighing, Katie crossed the room and set the newspaper on her bureau. Then, pensively, she opened the top drawer, taking out the fine linen handkerchief with its miniature griffin embroidered in the corner. She'd never known a man who owned anything so uniquely tasteful. The Griffin had style, but more important, he had principles that he upheld above personal gain. Katie felt a surge of anger as she thought of the man who lay slumbering on a cot in her parlor.

She was just about to extinguish the oil lamp on her bedside table when a sound in the kitchen made her straighten up. Peeking out of her room, she saw a shadowy figure fumbling at the dresser shelves.

"What's going on?" she called softly, emerging into the narrow kitchen. "Is that you, Papa?"

"No, it's me."

Outside, a cloud passed, uncovering the moon and sending a silvery ray of light through the window to illumine Jack Adams. He turned to face her, and Katie saw that he wore only drawers that rode low on his lean hips. The moonbeam skimmed the sleek, muscled surface of his chest, the clean, square lines of his shoulders, the long, hard curves of his arms, the ridges of his belly . . .

"Kathleen?"

Her eyes had touched the shadowed indentation of his navel, but now they flew up to meet Jack's gaze, which seemed more penetratingly catlike than ever in the darkness. "I thought you were asleep, Mr. Adams."

"I was looking for a glass. I'm thirsty."

Katie moved around the table to stand beside him, took a glass from the shelf, then felt for the pitcher of water and filled it. When she turned to hand it to him, her left breast, covered only by a thin layer of cotton, brushed Jack's chest. His sudden intake of breath was audible, just as it seemed to Katie that the sound of her heartbeat filled the room.

"Thank you," Jack said hoarsely, taking the glass from her hand.

She wanted to weep with confusion. How could her own body betray her so outrageously? Just when she had convinced herself that she really did despise this man and all he stood for, and that their kiss on Main Street hadn't been authentic, *this* had to happen! Every fiber of her being was tensed and tingling with arousal. Praying for deliverance, she took a step backward. "I'm going to bed now."

To her horror, Jack reached for her hand. The pressure of his warm, strong fingers sent a wave of intense sensation through her body. "I wish you would try not to hate me so, Kathleen," he murmured. "I keep remembering that rare, radiant smile you bestowed upon me the other afternoon. Will you never smile again in my presence?"

Katie took another step backward, freeing her hand. "I don't hate you, Mr. Adams, but I cannot respect you. Now, if you'll excuse me, I'm very tired. You should go to sleep yourself. Your esteemed employer would be displeased if you were tardy."

Jack watched her go. When she had gained the safety of her

bedroom, she paused for an instant in the doorway. The lamplight from within cast its golden glow over the curves of Katie's body beneath her lawn nightgown. Her rich ebony hair swirled as she reached back to shut the door, leaving Jack alone once more in the darkness.

"My father is talking about leaving Columbia," Lim Sung remarked. Perched on a grassy cliff overlooking the magnificent Stanislaus River west of Columbia, he stared pensively at the ribbon of blue-green water far below.

Katie, who had been lying on her back studying the clouds overhead, sat up with a start. "What?!"

"You are surprised? We haven't felt comfortable here since the fire of fifty-seven. Certainly we are pleased that people trusted us enough to believe we were not responsible for the fires or any of the other crimes they were blaming on the Chinese, but it did leave us in an awkward position. After all, being one of the few Chinese families legally allowed to remain in town . . . ." A warm dry breeze mussed Lim's black hair as he plucked the petals from a cluster of fragrant wallflower blossoms.

"But—all your friends are here!"

He gave her a wry look. "Katie, you and your father are our only real friends. And one day you'll get married, and your husband won't want me around."

"That's ridiculous," she said stubbornly. "I'm not getting married, especially not to someone who would try to choose my friends!"

"I must respect my father's wishes. Aaron Rush has offered him a handsome price for the laundry, and Father thinks that we should go to San Francisco and make a new start while he is still able." Lim's fine mouth curved in a half smile. "Unlike you, I *would* like to marry one day. Whom would you suggest among the young ladies of Columbia? Sally Barnstaple?"

"Oh, for heaven's sake, you're only sixteen. Just because you're feeling randy, you needn't get carried away! And how can your father consider selling to that villain Rush?"

"Mr. Rush has made a very tempting offer. You know that Columbia has declined more than ever this year, and the townspeople say that life will return to our town only if buildings are razed so that the lots can be mined. Our laundry sits on an important piece of land."

"If you give in, it will just mean more power for Rush and Van Hosten!" Katie cried.

Lim shrugged philosophically. "Business has been most depressed here, Katie, as you well know. Everything else in Columbia is drying up. If Rush and Van Hosten can revive the mining industry, it will mean renewed prosperity for your family as well."

Katie threw herself back down in the grass and sulked. "This conversation is most annoying! *If* your father decides to sell and go to San Francisco, why can't you stay here for a while? You can work at the saloon, and then, in a couple of years, we can *both* go to San Francisco."

"Well . . . we'll see." Lim knew better than to continue what was obviously a fruitless discussion. "Nothing is definite now, but my first loyalty is to my family. Although I was not born in China, I cannot turn my back on our traditions." He got to his feet and brushed the brick-red flower petals from his trousers. "I must go now, Katie. Will you come?"

"No. I think I'll stay here for a while and . . . rest."

Lim Sung shaded his eyes and gazed down at her. "None of this means I am any less devoted to you. You're my best friend, my favorite flower."

"I know, Lim." Tears stung her eyes. "I don't mean to be a crybaby, but the prospect of life here without you is terrifying."

He smiled. "You will live, Katie. No one will ever quell your spirit."

"I'll see you later, Lim. . . ." She rose on an elbow to watch him wade through the high grass. When he turned onto Parrotts Ferry Road, which curved back around the hill toward Columbia, Katie lay back and closed her eyes, trying not to think about her multiplying problems. When next she opened them, it was to discover that the grassy bluff had grown hazy with pink-tinted dusk. A voice said, "Thank God! You're alive."

Katie blinked and turned her head. Next to her crouched Jack Adams, his hands resting lightly on buckskin-sheathed thighs. His face, which wore an expression of mild amusement, was bronzed in the mellow light.

"Of course I'm alive," Katie said, gathering her wits. "I must have fallen asleep."

He chuckled. "Well, you'll have to pardon my concern. I'm most unused to the sight of you lying prone and silent."

"But what are you doing out here?" She struggled to sit up, hoping Jack wouldn't help her. He didn't.

"Mr. Van Hosten sent me to inspect the water flumes that connect with the river. I was just on my way back. What about you?"

Katie's upper body was nearly touching his knees, and his face was so close that she could see the gold flecks in his green eyes. "I walked out here with Lim Sung. This was a favorite spot of ours when we were children. After he left, I must have dozed off." She forced her eyes away from Jack's compelling gaze. "I should be getting back now, though, and I'm sure you're anxious to report to your employer."

"Not particularly." He was slightly surprised by Katie's instinctive reaction to his words. She glanced up immediately, as if searching his face for a sign that he had not joined the enemy camp after all. "I'd like to talk to you, if you can spare me a moment."

After a slight pause, Katie nodded. "Well, all right."

Jack smiled and reclined beside her in the grass. "My wish is that we might cry truce. You see, I'm leaving Columbia tomorrow morning, and I had hoped that you and I might part friends."

"Leaving!" Katie exclaimed. "Why? You just took that very promising position with Van Hosten."

Idly, he twisted a long blade of grass next to her hand, his fingers brushing hers. "Can you keep a secret?"

"Yes," she answered cautiously.

"I was never very serious about working for the Rush Mine. That's not the sort of employment I find challenging." He looked into her eyes. "I took the job because I wanted to see for myself what was going on there."

"And what did you decide?"

"Let's just say that you are right about Rush and Van Hosten. Their code of ethics has a decidedly foul smell."

"Then why are you leaving? You should stay and help us fight them!"

"That's not possible at the moment." His rough fingertip trailed fire over the back of Katie's hand. "There are other matters that require my attention. That's the reason I have to leave tomorrow, but I didn't want to go with you hating me."

Her heart pounded with a surge of conflicting emotions. "So you're going? You've learned the truth about Rush and Van Hosten, and you're going to turn your back and walk away?"

"There's little I could do anyway, Katie. And perhaps I'll be able to return before too long."

A storm raged within her. It didn't seem that she had any grounds to be angry with Jack any longer, but the thought of him simply disappearing from her life made her feel very confused, and she wasn't sure exactly why. Finally she murmured, "Well, I do appreciate your explanation . . ."

"Will you hold a good thought for me?"

Their faces were inches apart, and suddenly she was overwhelmingly conscious of the fact that they were reclining side by side in the grass. Twilight was deepening, and they were completely alone. Katie took a deep, shaky breath and inhaled Jack's masculine scent. "Yes." The word was barely audible.

He traced the line of her cheek with his thumb. "You'd nearly convinced yourself, hadn't you?"

"Of what?"

"That it wasn't real when we kissed the other day. That it actually was pretend, as we told your father."

"Oh," Katie sighed, "why are you bringing this up?"

"Maybe it's my male pride." One side of his mouth quirked ironically. "And I think you ought to be honest with yourself, for your own good. You felt some things for the first time, and if I let you pretend the kiss didn't count, you can also bury those feelings. That wouldn't be right."

"It . . . wouldn't?" She could scarcely breathe as his hand lightly caressed her throat, then slipped down her arm to her waist. Gently, he turned her body so that they lay facing one another.

"No, it wouldn't," Jack repeated, his voice low and husky. "That kiss was your awakening to womanhood, Kathleen. You're a beautiful, passionate woman, and you should be proud of that." He gazed into her wide blue eyes, which shone with panic and helpless yearning. Slowly Jack moved his hand to her back, drawing her slim, soft form against the length of his strong body. Katie wore one of her faded calico dresses, with only one thin petticoat, and for once he approved of her disdain for fashion. A hoop would have interfered. He slipped his right hand behind her head, then lowered his face to kiss her.

Recklessly, Katie surrendered to the moment. Tomorrow Jack would be gone, and then she would have forever to sample the rewards of self-denial. Now, however, she opened her mouth to his kiss and drank in the taste, scent, and feel of this irresistible man. Her hands caressed the contours of his shoulders, neck, and face while her hips arched against his hardness in the violet light. She had never guessed that a man's body could be such a magical source of delight. When Jack turned her back into the soft grass, the pressure of his chest against her firm breasts made her moan with pleasure. He was kissing her ear, then the graceful arc of her neck, and the sensations his mouth evoked were shocking. Katie felt moist between her legs. She longed to take his hand and press it there.

Suddenly Jack lifted his body away from hers and dropped back in the grass a couple of feet away. "My God," he muttered after a minute, "that was the hardest thing I've ever done." He stared at the sky. "Stopping, I mean." When Katie didn't answer, Jack turned his head and saw that she, too, was lying back and staring upward. Her breasts rose and fell rapidly, and the urge to bare them was nearly overpowering. He could almost see and feel the pale, satiny curves . . . taste the sweetness of the rosy nipples that would pucker in his mouth . . .

Aching to the point of pain, Jack stood up before unbridled lust could overcome his more civilized inclinations. He bent down, took Katie's hands, and lifted her to her feet. She looked at the grass and tensed against the fingers that tilted her chin upward. "Kathleen," he said softly, "look at me. Please."

Reluctantly she obeyed, grateful for the gathering darkness. Jack's eyes were disarmingly gentle. "I must be mad," she whispered.

"No," he answered firmly. "I was completely responsible for what just happened, and you were completely blameless—and innocent in every sense of the word. I only meant to give you the smallest kiss, just to remind you of the other. I lost my head . . . and it's a sign of my respect for you that I regained it before it was too late. Can you possibly forgive me?"

Katie's cheeks burned with shame as she remembered her own wanton response to Jack's body. "Of course," she whispered, tears crowding her throat.

"Come along, then. My horse is tied to that tree over there. I'll take you home." Jack was surprised by the surge of protectiveness he felt as he reached for Katie's hand and led her through the twilight.

CHAPTER
7

July 3, 1864

Birds were singing merrily in the peach tree outside Katie's window as she dressed in the amber-rose light of dawn. Already late for her five-thirty appointment to scrub the saloon floor with Abby, Katie strode into the kitchen and paused just long enough to get a raspberry muffin. She knew that Jack was still sleeping on his cot in the parlor, and she told herself not to look. But this was the end, whispered a little voice. He would leave Columbia today, taking her confusion and conflicting emotions with him.

Katie didn't want to say good-bye. She was wearing a pair of dungarees, since she would be working on her knees, and a thin cotton shirt. Her hair was drawn back even more tightly than usual. For reasons she didn't care to examine, she didn't want this to be Jack's last memory of her.

But she did want one last look at him. Carefully, avoiding the squeakier floorboards, Katie moved into the parlor as silently as a cat. A few feet from the cot, she stopped and drank in the sight of him. Jack lay bathed in the first burnished glow of morning, only somewhat covered by a rumpled blue-and-white quilt that Mary MacKenzie had sewn shortly before her death.

Katie blushed a little as she stared at his foot and calf hanging over one side of the narrow cot. His limbs were beautifully shaped, she thought, and looked strong even in repose. He was sleeping on

61

his stomach, and nearly all of his bronzed, tapering back was exposed to her view. She could see the outline of his lateral muscles and noted a small mole at the base of his spine. Jack's arms made lean-muscled arcs on either side of his head, which was turned to one side. Clean tawny hair fell forward over his brow and curled at the nape of his neck, adding to the illusion of boyish vulnerability. Katie studied the profile that she seemed helpless to resist. It was handsome, though that was not a word she would have chosen to describe the appeal of his looks. The line of his nose, the hard mouth softened in sleep, the rugged curve of his jaw, all seemed uniquely a part of Jack, different somehow from those same features on any other male face. Katie wondered what dreams were hidden behind his eyes.

When Jack's lashes flickered, her heart leaped into her throat. He sighed slightly, and his lips curved in a suggestion of a smile.

"Good morning." Sleep roughened his voice even more than usual.

Katie wished that she could simply vanish, but she froze instead, hoping that Jack might drift off again. Instead, his eyes opened a fraction, and his brows arched quizzically.

"Kathleen . . . why are you staring at me?"

She coughed, conscious of her burning cheeks. "I . . . uh, was just trying to decide whether or not to wake you. I wasn't certain if you had to go to the mine or not. . . ."

Rolling onto his back, Jack stretched, groaned at the effort, and sat up partway, leaning back against his elbows. Katie felt that his sleepy green eyes could discern her every thought.

"It was kind of you to think of me." He gazed at her for a long moment, smiling. "You have a lovely pair of legs, Miss MacKenzie, even in trousers."

Her face grew hotter. It was the first time she'd seen his bare chest in daylight, and she tried desperately not to look at it or to think about how warm it would be or how it would feel to touch the light mat of golden-brown hair that covered it. Jack was, for Katie, the very essence of maleness.

"Abby and I are going to scrub the saloon floor this morning," she said, explaining the dungarees. "Have you said good-bye to her?"

"Yes. I saw her last night."

Katie felt a twinge of jealousy. "She'll miss you."

"Abby needs to begin a new life. It will be better for her to do that without me around to depend on." He sat up completely and said, "Would you come over here? I'd get up and come to you, but that would probably be inappropriate in my current state of undress."

Charmed by his raffish grin, Katie approached the cot. When Jack reached for her hand, a shiver ran up her arm. "I only have a moment," she whispered.

"I just wanted to thank you for the hospitality you've shown me during my stay in Columbia. I know that it wasn't your choice to have me in this house, but you did refrain from poisoning my food, and I appreciate that. If I've done anything to offend you, I apologize."

Katie was nearly overwhelmed by a sudden, inexplicable wave of emotion. There were so many things she wanted to say . . . but couldn't. "I may have overreacted upon occasion, Mr. Adams. Actually, knowing you has been a most interesting experience."

"Has it?" He beamed at her with a feigned expression of surprised delight. "I'm glad, and I am pleased to be able to return that very warm expression of sentiment, Miss MacKenzie." His eyes twinkled. "In fact, I might go so far as to say that I genuinely like you. You are unique among all the women I have known, and I have found every moment in your presence to be highly . . . stimulating."

Helpless, she smiled, acknowledging the pleasure she had experienced in Jack's embrace. "You are very roguish, you know, but perhaps that's been beneficial to me—for these few days."

"Ah, at last! The smile I've been craving." He pressed his mouth against the back of her hand, then stole a bite of the muffin she held. "I am very grateful."

Katie smiled again, right into his warm, dancing eyes. She gave him the muffin and backed away. "You may as well have the whole thing!"

"I'll miss your muffins, Kathleen. I never cared for them until I tasted yours."

She blushed. "I really must go. Godspeed, Mr. Adams." Turning, she hurried out of the house without looking back. Once out on Jackson Street, however, Katie leaned against an oak tree. Her hand felt scorched where Jack had kissed it, and now she touched her own mouth to that spot with an aching sigh.

Harold Van Hosten stood at his office window, looking down at the lots that had already been mined at the south end of Columbia. Main Street stopped and sloped sharply downward to a dirt pit studded with huge, oddly shaped granite, marble, and limestone boulders. They were the products of hydraulic mining, which many felt was destructive to the countryside and wildlife. Already valley streams had begun backing up, causing runoff mud to ruin farmland, but for now the mine owners had too much power to be stopped. Van Hosten smiled coldly. He believed that power was all, and as long as he held fast to what he had, he could overcome any obstacle—disgruntled miners, the Griffin, or the whining editor of the *Gazette*.

"Mr. Van Hosten? Could you spare me a moment?"

Van Hosten turned around, mildly irritated at having his reverie so abruptly dispelled. Jack Adams was standing in the doorway, looking tanned and fit in faded dungarees and a blue flannel shirt. "Certainly, Adams," said Van Hosten, forcing what he hoped was a congenial smile. "Come right on in. Are you prepared for today's stage journey?"

"That's why I'm here." Jack did not take the chair that Van Hosten indicated, choosing instead to stand in the hope that their conversation would be brief. "You'll recall, sir, that when I accepted this position, I told you that I might not be able to stay. Unfortunately, I've been called away much sooner than I expected. A problem has arisen that requires my attention."

"Indeed?" Van Hosten feigned concern. "Is there anything I can do to help?"

"No, it's a family matter. I'm the eldest son, you see, and certain responsibilities fall to me."

"Well, I won't say I'm not sorry to lose you, Adams. And Mr. Rush is due back from New York in a few days, and will be sorry to have missed meeting you. But then, perhaps you'll be back?"

"Sir, I wouldn't presume to think that you might hold this position open." Jack rolled up his sleeves as he spoke. "And in any case, I don't think I will be able to commit to settling anywhere for a long time. Perhaps I'll pass through again one day, though, and I want to thank you for the opportunity you gave me here. I've learned a great deal."

Van Hosten poured himself a whiskey and tossed it back. "Adams, couldn't you make the trip with me today before you leave my employ? I was counting on you."

"I wish I could, sir, but that's impossible. Time is of the essence, I'm afraid." He smiled. "I wouldn't worry, though, if I were you. No doubt, after the success of his last robbery, the Griffin will lie low until he thinks you've forgotten about him. He'd be greedy and reckless to make another attempt while you are so carefully on guard."

Sighing sharply, Van Hosten splashed more whiskey in his glass. "I hope you're right, Adams . . . for *his* sake!"

"Katie, darlin', I've asked Lim Sung to help at the bar for a few days. I'm taking the stage to Sacramento to visit Mrs. Waldner." Brian spoke in an offhand manner as he filled one last glass. "Could you take over until Lim arrives?"

Katie, who was exhausted after scrubbing the floors and then preparing a huge pot of stew, stared at her father. It always happened this way. His urges to visit Mrs. Waldner came upon him suddenly, and he never communicated his plans until the very last moment. Brian had met the attractive widow three years earlier during a trip to Sacramento for supplies, and though he never discussed their relationship with Katie, he made a point of traveling to see Mrs. Waldner two or three times a year.

It had never made sense to Katie before, but now she felt a dawning comprehension. Her father worked as hard as a horse and was a wonderful parent and friend to her. If a private piece of him captured a bit of joy with Mrs. Waldner, Katie was happy for him. She'd experienced that fleeting, luminous bliss herself now and suddenly felt much older and wiser than before.

"Of course I'll watch the saloon for you, Papa." She rested her head against his shoulder and smiled. "You know you can depend upon me and Lim. Go to Sacramento, have a wonderful time, and give my regards to Mrs. Waldner."

MacKenzie's blue eyes twinkled as he wrapped her in a bear hug. "You're my own gift from God, lass. I love you dearly, you know."

"I know, Papa, and I love you. Now, you'd better go or you'll miss the stage!"

Laughing, he released her and wound his way through the dusty miners and mountain men who half-filled the saloon. On a hot day like this, business was good. Brian turned at the door to wave at his daughter, then exited into the sunlight.

"It's a beautiful day, isn't it? We were fortunate that there were no passengers from Sonora, or I'd be riding on top!" MacKenzie beamed first at Victoria Barnstaple and her sister Emily, who sat across from him in the stagecoach, and then at Harold Van Hosten, who was wedged into the seat beside him. "Fine day for a journey!"

Van Hosten merely grunted and raised his *Harper's Weekly* a little higher. The stage had slowed to climb a grade on the other side of the Stanislaus River, so for the moment he could hold the paper still. "I find nothing beautiful about this oppressive heat, Mr. MacKenzie."

"Is there any news of the war?" Mrs. Barnstaple inquired in a small voice.

"Very little, my good lady," Van Hosten replied impatiently. "General Grant's troops are still being held in their trenches at Petersburg by Lee's army. One can only hope that Sherman will have better luck farther south. There is a long piece about the re-nomination of President Lincoln for a second term. As you are doubtless aware, that was effected on June 8, in Baltimore, so this report is rather after the fact." And with a decisive crackle, the paper barricade was erected once more.

Brian raised his eyebrows at the ladies. Casting about for another topic, he said, "There was a fellow passing through from San Francisco the other day who came over to the saloon for a whiskey. Said that Miss Lotta Crabtree's gone off to New York in search of world fame." Sighing, he shook his head. "Well, I wish her well, but I don't think she'll be any happier than she was dancing and singing for the miners at the Fallon House Theatre."

Victoria and Emily glanced at one another, their cheeks pink under wide-brimmed chip straw bonnets. "I daresay," Victoria murmured politely.

The stagecoach was picking up speed now, rumbling downhill and raising clouds of dust that settled over the already grimy travelers. Whenever they rounded a particularly hazardous curve, Emily let out a little squeal and clung to her sister's arm. Brian peered out the window at the hills, covered with a carpet of dry, summer-gold grass and scrub oak trees. California was brown in summer and green in winter, just the opposite of Pennsylvania, where he had lived from early manhood until the age of forty. MacKenzie was offering a silent prayer that the foothills might be spared a fire this summer, when the stagecoach approached a turn so sharp that it slowed to a near stop. The sound of a man's raised voice caused Brian to crane his neck out the window and Van Hosten to fold his *Harper's Weekly* with a snap.

"Would you mind stopping for a moment, driver?" The voice was deep and unremarkable, but the words left no doubt as to the man's identity.

Calling out to the horses, the driver halted the coach, then pulled up on the brake. By now Brian could see the Griffin standing in front of a tangle of brush that had apparently served as his hiding place. He was tall and broad-shouldered, but all other physical characteristics were hidden beneath a long linen duster and a hood that covered his head save for two eyeholes in the middle. He carried a fine double-barreled shotgun, which was currently aimed at the hapless driver.

"Kindly throw down the box—and your gun, sir," the Griffin requested. When the driver had complied, he turned his attention to the passengers inside the coach. "I apologize for having disrupted your journey. Would you men do me the favor of disembarking for a few minutes?"

Emily was swooning, and as Brian opened the door Victoria threw out her beaded reticule. "All my money is inside!" she cried. "Please don't harm us!"

The Griffin seemed amused. He caught the purse with one hand and returned it to her with a courtly flourish. "I don't want your money, madam. Rest easy, no one will be harmed."

Van Hosten glared at the outlaw as he followed Brian out into the scorching sunlight. "Devil!" he spat.

"I suggest that you judge not, lest ye be judged," the Griffin replied lightly, motioning with the barrel of his shotgun. The two men stepped behind the coach. "Now then, I would appreciate it if you would hand over any valuables that you have concealed on your person, Mr. Van Hosten. Mr. MacKenzie, I would like you to search him."

Brian felt no fear at all. He would not venture an opinion as to the Griffin's character or morality, but of one thing he was certain: the man meant him no harm. Clearly his quarrel was not with Brian or Wells Fargo, or the stage driver, or any of the passengers who happened to be present during a hold-up. The Griffin was calmly and deliberately settling a score with Harold Van Hosten and Aaron Rush. Brian looked squarely at the eyeholes in the outlaw's hood, then stepped toward Van Hosten. As he reached into the taller man's coat pocket, Van Hosten suddenly shouted up at the driver.

"You have another gun—I saw to it! Shoot this criminal, now!"

The stage driver's only reply was a slow smile. Incensed, Van Hosten butted at Brian with his head and shoulder, then reached inside his coat to pull a Colt .36 revolver from the waistband of his trousers.

MacKenzie, who was as solid as an oak, was surprised but unshaken. Standing his ground, he raised bushy white brows at the sight of gun in the mine owner's hand. "There's no need for this," he cautioned.

"Get out of my way, MacKenzie! This is no business of yours!" Van Hosten snarled, and cocked the revolver. "I mean to see this outlaw dead once and for all!"

"Put that away! You'll get yourself killed!" Brian shouted, conscious of the strong smell of whiskey on Van Hosten's breath. Desperate to restore order and avoid bloodshed, Brian grabbed for the revolver, forcing the barrel toward the ground. Something in Van Hosten's eyes ignited his fiery Irish temper, fueling all the feelings of anger and frustration and plain dislike he had suppressed in the past. "You're the worst sort of vermin, Van Hosten!" Brian grunted as they struggled over the gun. "You never think of anyone's wellbeing but your own!"

"Leave it, MacKenzie!" the Griffin ordered, his voice tight. "Get out of the way! This is my score to settle." He had taken a step forward, aiming his own shotgun, but Brian held on like a bulldog. "Go on back with the driver—now! Do you hear me?"

Brian knew only that he could not let go of the revolver, or someone would be shot. The stage driver, alarmed by this time, began to climb down from his perch. MacKenzie felt his strength ebbing; sweat dripped down his brow, stinging his eyes, blurring his vision. He heard the Griffin shouting at him to get out of the way but still clung tenaciously to the revolver, praying that he could somehow prevent a tragedy.

Suddenly a shot rang out and Brian moaned, releasing his grip on the smoking gun at last. Wild-eyed with triumph, Van Hosten shoved the wounded man aside, pulled back the revolver hammer with shaking fingers, and pointed it at the Griffin.

In the split second before he could pull the trigger, a shotgun blast hurled Harold Van Hosten backward against the stagecoach. One arm caught in the spokes of the wheel, twisting behind him at an unnatural angle, while a red stain spread rapidly from the gaping hole in his chest. He was dead even before he slumped to the ground. When at last Mrs. Barnstaple mustered the courage to peek out from the passenger seat, she beheld his glassy, unfocused eyes staring up at her. Too horrified even to scream, she paled and fainted against her already prostrate sister.

The stage driver ran forward to find the Griffin crouching beside Brian MacKenzie, who had been shot through the heart. The driver hardly knew what action to take. If he tried to take the Griffin prisoner, the odds were that he'd end up shot himself. Besides, he had always secretly admired the outlaw, sharing the common opinion that Van Hosten deserved to be preyed upon.

"This man is dead," the Griffin said in a hoarse voice, adding as if to himself, "It never should have happened. . . ." He reached out and gently closed MacKenzie's eyes.

"As God is my judge," the driver said, "this is the worst day of my life! I sure as hell can't deal with *this*"—he waved a hand at the two dead men—"and you, too. Someone else can have the job of capturin' you—but you can't stay around here, for God's sake! What'll those women tell the San Andreas sheriff?" He stared at the outlaw, who continued to kneel beside Brian MacKenzie's still form. "Look, you can't bring him back. Please . . ." he pleaded desperately. "D'you want me to shoot you, too? If you don't get away from here, I'll be forced to!"

"More than enough blood has been shed," the Griffin murmured, getting to his feet. "I am . . . sorry. It shouldn't have happened. Why didn't he listen to me? Why was he here?"

The driver hissed, "It don't matter now! Just get the hell outta here!"

CHAPTER
8

July 3, 1864

Although the afternoon was waning, the heat remained oppressive. Katie wiped a thin rivulet of perspiration from her temple as she surveyed the saloon. Two old miners dozed under the south windows, while at a large, circular table, half a dozen men engaged in a friendly game of poker. From time to time they called to Abby for more beer, patting her backside when she hovered at the table. Abby didn't seem to mind. In fact, she didn't seem to be particularly aware of her surroundings. All day she had been gazing off into space, her limpid brown eyes pitiful to behold.

Refilling an empty whiskey bottle, Katie resolved to cheer her up, though she wasn't feeling particularly chipper herself.

"What's wrong with you?" Lim Sung inquired as he finished wiping down the bar. "You look like you've lost your best friend. But I'm right here, so it must be Mr. MacKenzie you're missing. Is that it, Katie?" He watched her with alert black eyes.

She summoned a smile. "Don't be silly, Lim. Papa's only been away a few hours. I think it's the heat . . . and I'm probably tired. I didn't sleep very well last night, and Abby and I scrubbed this floor at dawn."

"As you say. And Abby is just hot and tired, too?"

"I imagine so." Katie propped her elbows on the bar, rested her chin in her hands, and stared into the distance. She sighed, conscious of an unfamiliar ache in her chest, a feeling of emptiness. Why did her father have to go away today, of all days? Not that she would have felt right about discussing her feelings with him. If her mother were still alive, she would have had someone to share her problems with; they could have talked them over together, woman to woman. With that realization came a sudden wave of longing for her mother, compounding her loneliness and feelings of isolation.

"Well, well," Lim murmured next to her. "Here comes someone who might possibly make you feel better."

Katie glanced listlessly toward the door, then straightened. Jack Adams was standing there. With the afternoon sun glinting off his hair and burnishing a halo round his head, he appeared ghostly somehow, an apparition. Summoned to mock her. That possibility was ruled out, however, when Abby let out a cry of joy, ran to him, and threw her arms around his neck.

"You came back! Oh, Jack, I knew you would!"

"Hello, Abby." Gently, he pried her arms from his neck. "I appreciate the warm greeting, but I don't think it's merited; after all, I've only been gone a few hours. Must be pretty dull around here today if my appearance can cause such excitement!" He held her away from him. "Look, I've gotten you all dusty. I'm really not fit to touch."

"Don't be silly," Abby replied, clinging to his arm.

Jack looked slowly toward the bar, and his eyes met Katie's. He smiled slightly, and she flushed in reaction. "Hello, Miss Mac-Kenzie . . . Lim."

Katie's heart swelled painfully at the sight of him, his cat's eyes appearing greener than ever, his hair sun-bleached in contrast with his bronzed face and blue shirt. "Have you become more attached to Columbia than you realized?" she asked. "Couldn't you bear to leave?"

Jack sauntered over to the bar, Abby close behind, and took a stool. He smiled at Katie. "Might I trouble you for a mug of cold water? It's hot as Hades out there." After drinking deeply, he explained, "I got as far as Angel's Camp before discovering that I didn't have my watch. I remembered then that I left it on the table in your kitchen when I bathed this morning. It's valuable to me; it was a gift from my grandfather."

"I'm sorry you've been inconvenienced," Katie said, praying that he couldn't guess the heady elation she felt just being near him again. "I know that you were in a hurry."

Jack nodded. "Yes, and I can't afford to lose a whole day. I'm afraid that, after I have something to eat, I'll have to be on my way again.'' Watching Lim refill his mug, he added, ''It wouldn't do for Van Hosten to hear I'd been in town today, either. I begged off making that stage trip with him because I couldn't spare the time.''

''Well, if he's gone to Sacramento, he doubtless won't return for two or three days. Besides, why should it matter to you one way or the other? You're no longer in his employ, are you?''

''That's true. I don't care particularly, but on the other hand, he isn't a man I'd choose for an enemy.'' Jack rubbed his eyes with long fingers. ''What are you serving today?''

''Boiled mutton with oyster sauce, and there's bread pudding, too. Abby, would you fetch a plate of food for Mr. Adams?''

Reluctantly, Abby let go of Jack's arm and headed off to the tiny kitchen at the back of the saloon. Jack gazed at Katie.

''You must be at least as hot and tired as I am,'' he remarked. ''Why don't you come around here and sit down for a few minutes? Just because you're in charge doesn't mean you have to stay on your feet the entire time.''

After a moment, Katie succumbed to temptation. She gave him a smile, knowing that he found her smiles beguiling, walked around the bar, and perched on the stool next to his.

''It's almost worth the time and trouble just to see you again,'' he murmured, his voice low and husky.

Katie knew that she was bedraggled, but she felt radiantly pretty in Jack's eyes. She wasn't sure what it was that he saw in her, but it pleased her that he saw it. On the other side of the bar, Abby set down the plate of mutton with a thud, rousing them both. Jack had just lifted his fork when Gideon Henderson entered the saloon.

''Hello, Gideon!'' Katie greeted him brightly. ''What brings you here? I hope you don't need me today because Papa has gone to Sacramento, and I promised to look after the saloon in his absence.''

Gideon's face was pale and covered with a film of sweat. ''That's what I've come to talk to you about, Katie.'' He stood facing her. Swallowing hard, he continued, ''The sheriff asked me to tell you . . . well, it's bad news . . .''

''Yes?'' Dimly, Katie felt a strong male hand clasp her own, and then Gideon's face seemed to blur before her eyes.

''There was an accident today. The Griffin held up the Sacramento stage, and Brian was shot. . . .''

''He's not—''

His face came closer, eyes swimming with tears behind his spectacles. ''Katie, I'm so sorry. Your father is dead.''

Jack was on his feet, gathering her into his arms and holding her fast. Katie's knees buckled, and her mouth opened wide to scream, but no sound came out. Her breath came in shallow gasps as she twisted in Jack's arms, looking for Gideon. He reached out to clasp her shoulder.

With an effort, she whispered, "Are you saying . . . that the Griffin shot Papa?"

Gideon nodded. "It looks that way. Your father and Harold Van Hosten were both killed. But you don't want to hear about this now—"

"Yes. Tell me." She leaned against Jack, letting his arms support her. She hadn't the strength to both stand and speak. Jack was stroking her hair, and the rhythmic motion of his hand seemed to be all that kept her heart beating.

"Well, the details are a bit muddled. Victoria Barnstaple and her sister were the only other passengers, and they are both hysterical and confused. The driver was climbing down from the box when your father was shot, so he's not entirely certain what happened, either, but as I understand it, the Griffin asked Brian and Van Hosten to get out of the coach. He took them behind it—to search Van Hosten, I believe—when a struggle ensued. At the end, both men were dead and the Griffin was unharmed. There is some question as to whether your father was shot by Van Hosten or the Griffin."

"Van Hosten?" Katie's thoughts spun crazily. "But that's impossible. He wouldn't shoot Papa, he'd have tried to shoot the Griffin."

Jack spoke up quietly. "There may be more to the story than we know. Perhaps the stage driver will remember more clearly."

"But it doesn't really matter, does it?" she replied. She felt cold, lifeless, her heart a stone. "Papa is dead, and the Griffin is to blame, even if he didn't fire the shot that killed him. If he hadn't robbed the stage, Papa would be alive right now."

"That's true," Gideon agreed, nodding. "Oh, Katie, I wish with all my heart that I could undo this terrible thing. You know that I loved Brian, too. Everyone did. He was a wonderful, kind-hearted man, and he certainly didn't deserve to die. Not yet, and not like this!"

Katie disengaged from Jack and went to embrace her friend. He had begun to weep, and as she patted Gideon's back, her own tears began to flow at last. Great, gulping sobs racked her body. She felt like crumpling to the floor and screaming with pain, but instead, after a few moments, her composure began to return. Jack held out a handkerchief and she took it, wiping her eyes and blowing her nose.

"Why don't you sit down, Katie?" It was Abby, holding a chair for her, her brown eyes poignant with empathy.

She sank onto the wooden chair and drew a deep breath. "Well, there's nothing I can do, is there? I can't change what's happened."

Lim Sung knelt beside her. "You must grieve, dear friend, and leave the rest to us. No worries."

"No . . . worries?" Katie repeated, and gave a bitter laugh. Suddenly she realized that she was all alone. Both her parents were dead—the two people she loved and needed most were lost to her forever. Now she was completely responsible for herself. She would have to run the saloon on her own, live in the house without her father, and be able to make enough money so that she would never be forced to marry a man she didn't love. The future yawned before her—interminable, uncertain . . . an uncharted wasteland. Was it possible that her father would never again wrap her in his bearlike embrace and warmly tell her how dear she was to him? Through a mist of tears, Katie stretched out a hand toward Lim. "You won't leave me yet, will you?"

"Of course not." He tilted his dark head against hers. "No worries, Katie. Not now."

"Let me get you a drink," Abby offered. "That will make you feel better."

"Oh, no, I don't think so," Katie whispered.

"Believe me, it helps," she insisted, and slipped behind the bar to pour Katie a sherry. Soon after handing it over to her, Abby retired to the storeroom at the back of the saloon.

Jack looked on as Lim and Gideon pulled up chairs next to Katie and murmured reassurances. After a moment, he rose and walked quietly back to the storeroom, pushing open the door just in time to see Abby quickly attempt to conceal an open bottle of sherry. Jack winced.

"Have you lost your mind, Abby?" He crossed the storeroom and wrenched the bottle from her trembling hands. "You're *working*, for God's sake!"

"Mr. MacKenzie's murder is a terrible shock to all of us," she cried, eyes wide with panic. "I just needed a little something to calm my nerves."

"Save your excuses for someone more gullible. You've been drinking in secret, haven't you? You've been through a difficult time, what with Ben's death and moving to Columbia, but this has to stop." His voice softened slightly. "You're using the sherry to keep your pain at bay, but drinking won't make your problems go away. Believe me, they'll wait for you and just get worse the longer you hide from them.''

Abby began to weep, clinging to his sleeves. "Please, Jack, take me with you when you go! Don't you see, I love you! The only moments of happiness I've known since Ben died have been with you, and today, when you went away, it felt as if my heart . . . as if I had a knife in my heart. I wouldn't be any trouble! I'll take care of you and love you and—''

Jack held her away from him. "Abby, dearest, you don't love me. You're just grateful to me because I reached out to help you. You have to build a new life, to make peace inside *yourself*, and that will only happen with time—time, and the courage to deal with your feelings instead of numbing them.''

Out in the corridor, Katie stopped at the sound of Jack's raised voice. Then Abby's sobs reached her ears. She'd come back to tell them that she was going home to be alone for a while, but obviously this was not a moment to interrupt.

"No, no! I'm so lonely!" she heard Abby cry. "No one in this town really cares about me. I'll die if you don't take me with you!''

"That's enough. If you are lonely, it's because you haven't tried to make friends here in Columbia. There are many people here who will care for you if you will let them. If you *try*, and have patience, you'll be amazed at the results." There was a slight pause, and then Jack went on in a firm voice: "Besides, I cannot take you with me. There is already a woman waiting for me in San Francisco. She's planning a spring wedding.''

Katie backed away from the door, forcing down the wave of confusion and pain that threatened to engulf her. It was too much. As she returned to Lim and Gideon, there was a buzzing in her ears and she felt as if she were floating. When the faces of her two friends came into focus, she tried to smile.

"Lim . . . you'll come home with me, won't you?''

"Of course." He took her arm. "Mr. Henderson, do you think you can close the saloon? Ask Mrs. Armitage to help you.''

As Lim led her toward the door, Katie looked back over her shoulder. "Tell the men it will just be for tonight. Tomorrow we'll be open as usual. Papa would want that.''

The MacKenzie house was showered with iridescent white moonlight. Standing on Jackson Street, Jack paused for a moment before opening the neat little gate. Everything looked just the same as it had when he'd left that morning. Red hollyhocks marched merrily along the picket fence, and the morning glory vines tumbled over the porch. A golden light shone at the kitchen window, completing the illusion of a contented, happy home.

But everything had changed. Jack's heart ached whenever he thought of Brian. The image of his ruddy, smiling face, blue eyes twinkling under bushy white brows, was painfully fresh in his mind. He could still feel the warm pressure of Brian's handshake when they had said good-bye less than twenty-four hours ago. How could the life of such a vital man be snuffed out so suddenly and senselessly?

Sighing, Jack opened the gate, walked up to the door, and knocked. After a moment, Lim Sung opened the door.

"How is Miss MacKenzie?" Jack asked softly. "I'd like to speak to her if she's awake."

"Katie's bearing up quite well, but then she's a very strong girl." Lim gestured for him to enter. "Come in. She will want to see you before you leave."

Jack found Katie sitting at the table in the kitchen where they had shared many convivial meals with her father. The evening's air of unreality was heightened now by the cheery embroidered table-cloth and pitcher of orange poppies sitting in front of Katie. Her gaze was fixed on them, unseeing, while a cup of tea grew cold at her elbow. Jack sat down and reached for her hand. It was cold as ice.

"Kathleen?" he murmured gently.

Automatically, she turned her face toward him and smiled. "Hello, Mr. Adams. It was kind of you to walk over and say good-bye again. But then, I suppose you came for your watch? I have it right here in my pocket. It was on the dresser shelf."

He blinked, then remembered. "That's unimportant, Kathleen. I've come to see how you are. This has been a terrible shock for you."

Lim cleared his throat. "Katie, I must go home now and share the sad news with my family."

When the door had closed behind him, Jack leaned toward Katie. "I want you to know how sorry I am. Although I didn't know him very long, your father was a splendid man. It was very easy to care for him."

Her great blue eyes were luminous with pain, their long black lashes glistening with tears. "Thank you for saying so, Mr. Adams. I know that Papa liked you very much, too."

Jack held her small, cold hand in both of his. "I think you are right. And, I know he would expect me to take an interest in your welfare."

"I don't know what you mean." Katie searched his eyes and found them curiously intent. There was a light in his gaze that she'd never seen before.

"I know that I should wait, should give you time to adjust to what's happened and to grieve, but it's time we simply don't have to spare. All I am certain of is that I came to know both you and your father unusually well in the time I spent in your home. I know that Brian would not have wanted you to spend the rest of your life in Columbia, running the saloon, Kathleen."

"Mr. Adams, I appreciate your concern but you really have no right—"

"Perhaps I don't. But, I must speak out, to say what I believe your father would say if he could."

A fiery spark kindled in her eyes. "I find your presumption quite extraordinary, Mr. Adams! Do, please, enlighten me! Since you were acquainted with my father for only a few days, and I have known him my entire life, it certainly does seem proper that *you* should speak on his behalf."

"You may think I am being presumptuous, but I do care," Jack replied in an even voice. "And your father talked to me about you. He was well aware of your many gifts, Kathleen, and anxious that you have the opportunity to fulfill them." He took a breath, and she looked at him, waiting. "You shouldn't stay here now that Brian is gone. I want you to come to San Francisco with me."

Katie gasped. "You can't be serious!"

"Oh, but I am. I am completely in earnest."

"Mr. Adams, what exactly are you proposing?" Her mind reeled as she remembered what he had said to Abby earlier about a fiancée waiting for him. Did he expect Katie to be his mistress?

"Nothing illicit, I assure you. Look, Kathleen, I have a family in San Francisco, a home and a life—"

"What do you mean, a family?"

"I live with my grandfather and my brother. It would all be perfectly circumspect. You could learn to explore and enjoy life for a change, attend parties, make new friends—"

"I think you must be mad!" she interrupted. "Do you think that just because I am a woman, you can take me in hand and tell me what is best for me? If so, you're very much mistaken! *I* know what is best for me. I already have a life here, Mr. Adams. I have friends and I have work that I enjoy. Lim will help me run the saloon, and now that Abby is here, too, I shan't be alone. I don't need your help or your patronage, or whatever it is that you're offering!" Tears stung her eyes as she pulled her hand from his.

Jack bit his lip. How had he erred? "I'm sorry if I've offended you," he said quietly. "Believe me, that was not my intention. I came here tonight as a friend, not only of yours, but of your father's as well. I see that I've only made matters worse."

Katie's features were strained as she turned away from him. "I'll survive. We'll all survive." She drew a shaky breath. "Now, if you don't mind, I would like to be alone. Have a safe journey, Mr. Adams."

Jack stood up, then slowly extended his hand and smoothed back the stray curls from her brow. "I do care, Kathleen."

Katie nodded, still unable to meet his compelling gaze. Then she remembered the watch and took it from her pocket. He accepted it, his fingers brushing hers, then the contact was broken.

She listened as Jack walked out of the kitchen and out of her life. The door clicked shut behind him, and suddenly the warm July night felt painfully cold. Under a ray of snow-white moonlight, Katie buried her face in her hands, sobbing as if her heart would break.

PART
TWO

CHAPTER
9

San Francisco, California
July 7, 1864

"**I**T'S SEVEN O'CLOCK, MR. WYATT."

Jonathan Wyatt opened one eye just a fraction. Across the spacious bedroom, Elijah, his manservant, was opening draperies of cream velvet. The tall second-floor windows afforded an impressive panorama from Rincon Hill that encompassed much of the city to the north and the surrounding bay to the east, but this morning, like most mornings, little of the city was visible through its cloak of fog. Wyatt preferred it this way. It was hard enough to wake up without the shock of sunlight.

"I've drawn your bath, sir," Elijah was saying. "Would you care for breakfast?"

"Just tea and fruit, thank you." They always had exactly the same conversation. Wyatt closed his eyes again, then added on impulse, "Elijah, do we have any . . . muffins?"

The black man stopped short in the doorway and glanced back, surprised. "I—I am quite sure we do not. Shall I ask Mrs. Gosling to bake some?"

"Yes," he murmured, smiling. "But there's no hurry. Tomorrow will be fine."

"Yes, sir. Anything else, sir?"

"No. I'm sure you've thought of everything, Elijah. Thank you."

Wyatt listened for the click of the paneled door, then opened his eyes again and stretched. The fine linen sheets caressed his naked body, tempting him to doze, but his bath was hot and his tea would be waiting downstairs in exactly half an hour. It was a routine that servants and employer had perfected over a number of years. If he deviated from it, they would all think he'd gone mad.

Smiling again to himself, Jonathan Wyatt emerged from his tes-tered walnut bed and padded across the luxurious Turkey carpet. A cool, misty breeze filtered through the window, which Elijah had opened an inch or two. Wyatt paused to breathe deeply of the morn-ing air, then continued on to his tiled bathroom. Efficiently he washed, toweled his hair and lean-muscled body, and shaved. Awake at last, he crossed into his dressing room and surveyed the cedar-paneled closets filled with all manner of expensive, tailored clothing. He chose a dark blue morning coat, white shirt, blue cravat, fawn-colored double-breasted waistcoat, and sleek fawn trousers. When he was dressed, Wyatt briefly surveyed himself in the full-length beveled mirror and adjusted the square shoulders of his coat. The tailoring was impeccable. He brushed his hair, de-ciding to stop at his barber's in the afternoon for an overdue trim, slipped his watch in its waistcoat pocket, attached the chain to the opposite side, then picked up fawn-colored gloves and left the dressing room.

The house was deceptively quiet as he descended the wide stair-case. Dropping his gloves on the table in the entryway, he turned into his book-lined study. A tray awaited him on the large Chip-pendale desk, which many thought out of place with the Gothic flavor of the room. Wyatt professed not to care: the desk was not just a family heirloom; it was practical as well. It had ample space for his papers when he worked at home and deep drawers for stor-age.

Now the desk was clear except for the tray, which contained a steaming cup of tea, a wedge of lemon, a translucent china plate of neatly arranged raspberries and orange segments, silver cutlery, a linen napkin, and a newspaper folded in half. Wyatt sat down and opened the newspaper with one hand while squeezing lemon into his tea with the other. He scanned each column with a critical eye and dipped a gold pen in ink to make notations in the margins from time to time. When he had finished, the tea and fruit were gone. Wyatt checked his pocket watch, and as if on cue, a tall woman with steel-gray hair drawn into a bun appeared in the doorway. She wore a severe gray dress, but her appearance was belied by a fond smile.

"Good morning, Mr. Wyatt. Can I get you anything else?"

He stood, holding the folded newspaper, and returned her smile. "No, thank you, Mrs. Gosling. Is my grandfather in the dining room?"

"Yes, sir. He's expecting you, as usual." She paused, as if uncertain whether to deviate from their usual morning dialogue. "The muffins you requested are baking, sir. Would you like one when they are finished?"

Passing her, Wyatt grinned infectiously. "If I'm still here, why not?"

Mrs. Gosling watched her employer walk through the west parlor and enter the dining room. Perplexed, she shook her head and murmured through pursed lips, "Why not indeed?"

Wyatt found Ambrose Summers at the far end of a long, polished mahogany table, sitting under a portrait of John Adams, who had been first cousin to Ambrose's mother. The family resemblance was noticeable, especially now that the old man was nearing eighty. His thinning white hair was combed neatly back from a face with large, keen gray eyes behind round spectacles, an aquiline nose, a small mouth nearly hidden under a drooping mustache, and round, heavy cheeks that were accentuated by white side whiskers. Like Adams, he was short in stature but generous in girth. Ambrose Summers loved to eat.

"Good morning, Grandfather," Wyatt greeted him, coming around the table. Bending, he kissed the old man's pink brow.

"Say good morning to Harriet," Ambrose reminded him, indicating the exceptionally large gray cat curled on his lap. Harriet looked up expectantly, egg on her whiskers.

"Hello, Harriet." He pulled a chair up near his grandfather's. "The two of you are looking quite satisfied."

Ambrose finished his biscuit, then pushed his plate away and wiped his mouth with a napkin. "Hmm. Well, it was a very good breakfast. Mrs. Gosling never overcooks the yolks." Harriet seemed to nod in agreement as she began to wash her face. "You're looking very fit this morning, Jack. Must've slept well. I knew you'd feel better after a night in your own bed. And I'll wager that you're happy to be back to your regular routine."

His grandson smiled absently. "Yes, I suppose so. It is good to be home, and to be myself again, and yet . . . I feel a bit awkward at the moment. I can't quite say why. . . . After all, I've been happy with my life by and large—particularly with the structure that I've created and so carefully maintained. It's always fit like a glove and I've never wanted to disrupt that, yet these past two days I've felt rather . . . *confined* by the habits and discipline that I have imposed upon myself.''

Summers studied him carefully. ''Well, you know that I've always thought you went a bit too far in that regard, regimenting your days and so forth, but it was your choice, and you've seemed to thrive on the discipline.'' He paused to stroke the purring Harriet. ''Your life was in disarray for some years, and it was a pleasure to watch you rebuild with such indefatigable determination. But perhaps the time has come to inject a bit more spontaneity into your routine.'' With a philosophical shrug, he continued, ''Or it may be a simple case of readjustment. You've been away for several weeks, living a very different life. It may take some time to settle back into your normal, day-to-day routine. You have to get used to being *yourself* again.''

''Yes . . . myself.'' He sighed deeply. ''Perhaps I'm not entirely certain who that is anymore.''

''Jack, did something else happen while you were away this time? I know that you're upset about those deaths, but they were not your fault,'' Ambrose said firmly, reaching over to pat his grandson's arm.

''Weren't they? If I hadn't held up that last stage, Brian Mac-Kenzie would still be alive.'' Jonathan Griffin Adams Wyatt pressed his eyes with taut fingers, then looked around. ''Where's Conrad?''

''Elijah just went up to draw his bath, so you can speak freely. Jack, my dear boy, I must urge you to confide in me. I've sensed that something has been bothering you ever since you arrived home, and it will only gnaw at you if you keep it inside.''

''You're right, of course, Grandfather, but I'm not even certain myself exactly what's troubling me.'' He raked a hand through his tawny hair. ''I'm due at the *Morning Star* offices in ten minutes—''

''The newspaper will wait for you, Jack,'' Ambrose replied calmly. ''You're the owner and editor. And here's a chance to bend your routine a bit.''

Wyatt's smile of surrender failed to reach his hooded green eyes. ''You know, it all was so simple in the beginning. When Conrad ran off to the foothills to make his fortune, and then was tricked out of his claim by Van Hosten, all I sought was some justice. And perhaps a bit of the excitement that had seemed to be lacking in my own life since I had straightened it up so meticulously.'' He sighed again. ''God only knows how Conrad would feel if he knew what I've done, especially since I counseled him to put the experience behind him and not seek revenge.''

"Well, you're twelve years older than he. It's only normal that you'd be protective of your brother."

"Perhaps, but Conrad's twenty-one now. I have to let him fight his own battles sometime, don't I?"

"Jack, you're straying from the heart of the matter," Ambrose said, eyeing him shrewdly.

"Am I?" He smiled without humor. "I suppose I'm just trying to unravel things in my own mind, to understand where and how the line between Jack Adams and Jonathan Wyatt became so blurred. . . ."

"Ah. Is that what's happened, then?"

Jack stared back, then raised his eyebrows. "I believe so. As you know, when I first disappeared to the foothills last autumn and became Jack Adams and the Griffin, I was careful to keep moving so that no one would gain more than a fleeting impression of me. I formed only passing acquaintances. The stage robberies were perfectly executed, and I suppose I should have left my revenge there. Not gone back this summer. I told myself that I had to, though, because of all that I'd learned about Van Hosten and Rush. My mission had grown far beyond avenging Conrad's loss. I believed that someone must continue to fight the heavy hand that Rush and Van Hosten had clamped down over the southern mines. The people of Columbia couldn't afford to take the risk, but the Griffin could."

"You sound as if you've taken a second look at your motives," Ambrose remarked, rubbing behind Harriet's ears.

"I've been forced to take a second look at a lot of things, Grandfather, but it's only left me more confused. Perhaps part of the reason I went back to the foothills was because I liked being Jack Adams, and I missed it. I enjoyed the feeling of being stripped of my possessions, my status, my reputation, and the perfectly structured discipline of being Jonathan Wyatt. I justified my masquerade by reasoning that I was righting wrongs as the Griffin." He unclasped and clasped a pearl cuff link. "Now, however, I see that I was deluding myself. Someone was bound to get hurt one day. One might argue that the world is better off without Harold Van Hosten, but I did not have the right to remove him from this earth."

"Jack, it was an accident—"

"An accident that occurred because I chose to play God. If I had allowed God to balance the scales of justice in His own time, perhaps Brian MacKenzie would still be alive."

Ambrose hazarded a guess. "You knew this MacKenzie fellow well?"

Wyatt nodded slowly, then met his grandfather's compassionate gray eyes. "Yes. Another mistake, I suppose, looking back now. Brian owned a saloon in Columbia, and I came to town at a point when I was beginning to really enjoy my new identity. He extended a hand of friendship to me, and I accepted it. It was a line I shouldn't have crossed. I stayed in Brian's home, I began to feel comfortable in Columbia . . . and the beginning of emotional bonds for Jack Adams created an inevitable conflict."

"He had a family?"

Jack consulted his watch. "A daughter. Kathleen."

"I see." They were silent for a moment. "I suppose that you feel very guilty and responsible for her plight now?"

"Of course I do!" Jack shot back harshly. "She's only eighteen, and although she's self-sufficient, she's now an orphan just the same. She and her father were very close, and of course she blames the Griffin for his death."

"And she doesn't know that you *are* the Griffin."

Jack stood up suddenly and paced across the dining room. "No, she doesn't know! And frankly, I'm not sure just who the hell I am, either!"

"Did you offer to take care of her?"

"Of course I did! I tried to bring her home with me, for God's sake!"

"I see," Ambrose said quietly.

"She'd have no part of me. She intends to run the saloon without her father and go on writing her pieces for the *Columbia Gazette* and insists that she will be just fine *alone*."

"But you don't believe her?"

"Oh, I believe her all right, but how do you think I *feel*, knowing that I'm responsible for the death of the one person she truly loved and trusted?" He stood over his grandfather's chair, hands clenched into fists.

"Well, I'm confused by your intensity, Jack. Is it just guilt that you feel, or something more?"

Jack looked away. "Christ, all I know is that I can't go back. The Griffin died with Brian MacKenzie, and I have to get on with my life here. I've done enough damage in Columbia."

Ambrose patted his grandson's arm again. "Just give yourself some time, boy. You'll sort this out—I'm sure of it. And don't be too hard on yourself. You acted without malice."

Wyatt closed his eyes, felt the burn of tears, then gazed down at his grandfather. "Thank you for the advice, sir. Perhaps now, I'd best be off to the *Star*, owner and publisher or not. Tell Conrad I'll see him tonight. Genevieve is joining us for dinner.''

He was leaving the dining room when Mrs. Gosling appeared with a plate of fragrant raspberry muffins. "Won't you be having any after all, sir?" she asked.

"No. Give them to Harriet." Jack continued on into the entry-way and drew on his fawn gloves. Opening the front door, he called back, "And, Mrs. Gosling—please don't bake any more. You know I never eat muffins."

"Well, gentlemen, it appears that we're finished. It's been a constructive day." Jonathan Wyatt shuffled some papers and stood up behind his desk. The fourth-story windows behind him over-looked California Street, which was noisy with the traffic of horse-drawn carts and pedestrians, not to mention the construction of larger, taller buildings, like the one housing the *Star*'s offices. The 1860s was proving to be a decade of new prosperity for San Francisco as the city profited from the silver boom in Nevada.

Edwin Murray, the city editor, stayed behind as the other editors filed out the door. Round and bald, he had a sweeping red mustache that twitched whenever he was excited. It was jumping now. "Mr. Wyatt, could you spare me a few moments of your time?"

Jack checked his watch, tucked it back into his waistcoat pocket, and smiled. "After all you did to keep the paper running smoothly while I was away? Of course."

"It's never the same without you, sir. This is a ship that needs its captain, but I must say that you have chosen a fine and loyal crew. Everyone worked together for the common good in your absence." Murray smiled broadly. "We're all very happy to have you back, though, sir."

"I'm happy to be back."

"You're looking very well, Mr. Wyatt. You must have gotten plenty of sun in Nevada."

"There is a lot of it at this time of year." Jack came around his desk and perched on the front edge. "What was it you wanted to discuss with me, Edwin?"

"It's about Samuel Clemens." Murray's mustache twitched again. "Goes by the pseudonym Mark Twain. He was staff reporter for the *Morning Call* until recently—"

"I'm familiar with his work, and I've met the man once or twice. He did some fine writing in Nevada, before coming to San Francisco. Impressively droll."

"Well, sir, his talents were never used properly on the *Call*.

There simply wasn't the space, and he was worked too hard. They discharged him while you were away, which turned out to be quite fortuitous for us. Now Clemens has resumed his pen name and is working independently, selling stories about life in San Francisco. I would like your permission to hire him to do a series for us.''

''What theme did you have in mind?'' Wyatt asked, brushing a speck of lint from his fawn-colored trousers.

''My inclination is to give Clemens free rein. I have a very strong feeling about this, sir! I think the man has a very special gift, a way of capturing the essence of a place and its people with great wit, and style. Anything he would write for us would be an asset to this paper.''

Jack rubbed his eyes with one hand, then gave the city editor a weary smile. ''You have my blessing, then, Edwin. Make Mr. Clemens a fair proposition and relay his response to me.'' He stood up. ''If he accepts, arrange a meeting between us.''

''Yes, sir! Thank you, Mr. Wyatt!''

''No need to thank me. You know that I'm not in the business of dispensing favors. I expect results.'' Jack patted the shorter man's plump shoulder and gathered up a pile of galley proofs to scan later that evening. ''Now I have to be going. Miss Braithwaite is meeting me.''

Murray's mustache twitched again as he watched his employer head out the office door. ''You wouldn't want to keep a beautiful woman like Miss Braithwaite waiting, sir!''

Jack glanced back over his shoulder and arched an eyebrow. ''I'm certain that she would agree wholeheartedly with that sentiment. Good night, Edwin.'' He made his way past the desks of other editors and reporters, personalizing each farewell. Then, as he ran lightly down the four flights of stairs, Jack experienced a keen sense of liberation. Unfortunately, it was short-lived: emerging onto the board sidewalk, the first thing he saw was the elegant black carriage belonging to Genevieve Braithwaite. Behind the driver, resplendent in red-and-white livery, a lovely face peered anxiously from beneath the leather carriage top.

''Jonathan!'' the young lady exclaimed the instant she saw him.

Jack felt as if he were walking through a tunnel as he approached the carriage. Leaning in, he forced a smile as her slim arms wound round his neck and her face filled his vision. ''Hello, Genevieve—''

''What sort of a greeting is that after an absence of two full months?'' she asked, pretending to pout. ''For heaven's sake, get in and kiss me!''

Seeing no alternative, Jack complied. Genevieve was a lissome blonde with a flawless porcelain complexion and long-lashed green eyes that slanted upward slightly at the corners. Any man would judge it pleasurable to kiss her. She tasted fresh and sweet, her mouth was soft, and she was certainly responsive. Jack had been able to maintain a detached attitude toward their relationship since its beginning nearly a year ago; now, however, something was amiss. Genevieve was a diversion that no longer amused him. In fact, holding her in his arms in the back of the carriage at this moment felt more like a duty than a diversion, and Jack found himself in no mood to pretend otherwise.

Genevieve thrust her tongue into Jack's mouth while one of her hands found its way under his jacket, caressing and exploring. The carriage had started up California Street, bound for the Wyatt mansion, and when the left rear wheel caught in a crack in the plank-paved thoroughfare, Jack pretended to have been jarred from Genevieve's embrace.

"Sorry, darling," he murmured, disengaging completely and glancing down to straighten his clothing. "In any case, this really isn't quite the proper time or place, is it?"

"Well, I'm sure I don't know," Genevieve replied petulantly. "What is proper when two people have been separated for two months? I must say, I'm surprised at you, Jonathan. I anticipated a far more manly and passionate greeting. . . ."

Wyatt cocked an eyebrow and smiled slightly. "Indeed?" With maddening equanimity, he shifted his position. If Genevieve was hoping for an excuse or an apology, or that he would be spurred to kiss her again with new enthusiasm, she was doomed to disappointment. Instead, he gazed out at the crowds and vehicles that milled around them, and seemed to forget her presence.

"I might almost suspect that you took a lover during your travels," she persisted, nettled into goading him to a response.

But Jack didn't hear her. "Look over there!" he cried suddenly. "Isn't that Samuel Clemens? Driver, stop. I want to have a word with that man—the curly-haired one without a hat."

The carriage wound through the traffic and drew up near a young man walking along the sidewalk. Jack called a greeting and emerged from the carriage to extend a hand to Samuel Clemens.

"Mr. Wyatt?" Clemens cocked a dark-reddish eyebrow, his gaze sharp with interest and surprise. "This is an unexpected pleasure. . . ."

"I wasn't certain you'd remember me—"

"I see that modesty is a facet of your celebrated character, Mr.

Wyatt.'' The younger man smiled wryly, his wide mouth partially hidden behind a full mustache. "Surely you realize that anyone working in newspapers in this city today stares each time they pass you on the street. I'd be a colossal fool if, after scheming for most of the winter to attend a party where we might be introduced, and then winning that introduction, I now had forgotten you!''

Jack was bemused by the writer's honesty. "I fear you exaggerate my importance, Mr. . . . Clemens. Or do you go by Twain these days?''

"Call me Sam. It minimizes the confusion.'' His eyes were twinkling.

Genevieve leaned out of the carriage. "Jonathan, are you finished?''

He ignored her. "Sam, would you care to join a group of us at my house for supper tonight?''

"Socially or professionally?''

"A little of both, I imagine,'' Wyatt replied, chuckling softly.

"I like that mixture, and I'm pleased to accept. You'll find that I'm rather expert in the role of dinner guest. If nothing else, I promise to entertain the table at large. . . .''

Jack laughed. "I'll look forward to it, Sam. See you at seven!'' He climbed back in the carriage and waved as they reentered the flow of traffic.

"Who *was* that man?'' Genevieve demanded, her delicate nose wrinkled in distaste.

"Samuel Clemens, also known as Mark Twain. Why do you look that way, my dear?''

"Why, because he was so very horrid! His hair was *too* outrageously curly, he looked like he needed a bath, and he had the audacity to wink at me!''

Wyatt leaned back against the leather upholstery and laughed with delight. "Well, perhaps he just surmised that you needed cheering up, which may well be the case after you learn that you'll be sharing supper with my good friend Sam in just a few hours. . . .''

CHAPTER
10

July 7, 1864

JONATHAN WYATT NEATLY CARVED THE LOIN OF VEAL À LA béchamel, placed aromatic slices on the plates, and handed them, one at a time, to Genevieve Braithwaite, who sat at his right. The glow of candlelight softened the features of the six people at the table, each of whom gazed longingly at the veal and companion dishes of lobster salad, stewed peas à la française, braised ham garnished with broad beans, crimped perch and Dutch sauce, and scalloped potatoes. Ambrose Summers sat at the other end of the table, opposite his elder grandson, while Conrad Wyatt and his heart's desire, Emma Pierce, faced Genevieve and first-time guest Samuel Clemens.

Genevieve usually liked playing hostess in the Wyatt household, but tonight she looked as if she would prefer to be anywhere else. Passing a plate to Clemens, she glanced at his ink-stained fingers and grimaced slightly. He gave her a broad grin in return.

Ambrose, watching the scene with interest, remarked, "I like your style, Mr. Clemens. It is both frank and arousing! Before we were called for supper, you'd begun telling me about the adventures attending your recent move to new rooms. Can I persuade you to delve back into that tale?"

"Well, sir . . ." Sam glanced over at Wyatt, who smiled encouragingly. "I have a typesetter friend named Steve Gillis who shares lodgings with me. We found new rooms not long ago, but Steve forgot to tell his father that we'd moved. Mr. Gillis hunted up the old landlady, a Frenchwoman, who apparently never liked us much. She didn't know that he was Steve's father and launched into a tirade of epic proportions. Said she: 'They are gone, thank God—and I hope I may never see them again. Do you know, sir' ''—Clemens dropped his voice to a confidential, female tone, his features drawing up in distaste to mimic the Frenchwoman's— '' 'they were a couple of desperate characters from Washoe— gamblers and murderers of the very worst description! I never saw such a countenance as the smallest one had on him. Their room was never vacant long enough to be cleaned up, for one of them was always going to bed at dark and getting up at sunrise, while the other went to bed at sunrise and got up at dark. And if the chamberman disturbed them, they would just sit up in bed and level a pistol at him and tell him to get scarce! Oh, I never saw such *creatures*!' ''

Clemens paused for a sip of wine and a bite of lobster salad before continuing, while the others indulged in amused laughter. Genevieve alone compressed her lips disapprovingly.

"Sir," she inquired icily, "do you really consider this proper conversation for a refined dinner table?"

"Refined?" Samuel repeated, tasting the word experimentally. "Is that what this is?" He gave Wyatt a reproving look. "Why didn't you warn me, sir? I might not have come!"

A tight smile curved the mouth of his host. "Surely you jest, just as I am certain that my dear Genevieve also spoke in jest, didn't you, darling?" He gave her a brief, flashing glance that extinguished her sulky retort before she could form the words. "I insist that you continue, Mr. Clemens! Did the French landlady have any other complaints beyond your countenance and the hours you kept?"

"A few." Sam grinned. "I believe that she went on to say, 'They used to bring loads of beer bottles up at midnight and get drunk and shout and fire off their pistols in the room, and throw their empty bottles out of the window at the Chinamen below. You'd hear the bottles crash on the China roofs and see the poor China-men scatter like flies. Oh, it was dreadful!' '' Seeing that Emma Pierce, a diminutive, ginger-haired girl, was round-eyed with con-sternation, Sam gave her a wink before continuing in his falsetto, '' 'Those villains kept a nasty foreign sword and any number of revolvers and bowie knives in their room, and I know that small one must have murdered *lots* of people! But that's not the worst of it . . .' '' He narrowed his eyes and lowered his voice to a disapproving hiss. " '*Women!* Yes, it's true! There were women running to their room—sometimes in broad daylight—bless you, *they* didn't care. They had no respect for God, man, or the devil.' '' Clemens grinned suddenly. "The good Frenchwoman summed up with thanks to God for taking us away from her boardinghouse.''

Conrad Wyatt stared in honest confusion, his red hair and side-whiskers contrasting with his pale skin. "That's a very colorful story, sir, but was it meant as entertainment or truth?''

Laughing, Sam replied, "You raise an interesting point, Mr. Wyatt! My erstwhile landlady seems to be doing no little damage to my reputation. What is the use of wearing away a lifetime in building up a good name if it is to be blown away at a breath by a woman who is ignorant of the pleasant little customs that adorn and beautify a state of high civilization?''

Jack looked down the table to his grandfather, and the two of them chuckled in amusement. Genevieve, still peeved, glared at Jack.

"Has Mr. Clemens described a way of life that you aspire to, Jonathan? You seem so approving.''

One of his brows flicked upward. "Whatever can you mean, my dear? In truth, I was merely amused by my friend's talent for exaggeration. I was sorely in need of that laughter.'' Jack smiled at Samuel Clemens. "Thank you for joining us tonight. I hope to see a great deal more of you!''

Sam took a bite of raspberry-filled meringue and grinned, eyes atwinkle. "Pleased to have been of service, sir!''

From his end of the table, Ambrose Summers sipped port and quietly observed his elder grandson. He was gratified not only to see Jonathan unbend a bit, but also to witness Genevieve Braithwaite's petulance. These, he felt sure, were her true colors.

Genevieve paced the study nervously, her exquisite gown of pearl-encrusted blue silk shimmering in the light shed by wall sconces. She had waited most of the evening for the other guests to disperse, and now her wish had been granted. Conrad had left to escort Emma home, then Samuel Clemens had bade them farewell, declaring that it was time to return to his new lodgings and begin fueling a whole new set of "murder and mayhem" rumors. After another hour, the old man had at last surrendered to fatigue and trundled off to bed. Now that she and Jonathan were alone, however, Genevieve wasn't quite certain where to begin.

Wyatt was leaning back against the edge of the Chippendale

desk, already coatless, his lean fingers working at the knot of his cravat. The merest flicker of his hooded green eyes betrayed the impatience he felt. The hours spent with Samuel Clemens had reminded him so much of life in Columbia that he no longer had any heart for playing the wealthy San Francisco gentleman.

"Why don't you stand still and say whatever it is that's on your mind, my dear?" he said.

Jack's rather bored tone of voice made her feel foolish. "Well, I . . . I . . ." Seeing his brows rise warningly, Genevieve burst out, "I just don't understand why you had that man in your house tonight! I found him to be shockingly ill-bred, and it surprised me to witness your obvious enjoyment of his—his—*performance!*"

"I wasn't aware that I needed to gain your approval of my friends." His voice was cold. "In any case, you might be reassured to know that Mr. Clemens is far from subhuman. He possesses keen intelligence, rare wit, and a unique and considerable writing talent. I like him for those reasons, and also because he is not pretentious, unlike so many of my so-called friends here in San Francisco."

"Well, he is certainly unlike any man in the better social circles."

Wyatt pretended not to understand. "My point exactly." He offered her a tight-lipped smile—a grim twist of the lips that signaled an end to the conversation. But Genevieve had neither the subtlety nor the inclination to heed that signal.

"I think that you have changed since your latest journey to Nevada," she continued stubbornly. "I suppose it was inevitable, considering that you were cut off from proper civilization for so long. Next you'll grow a beard and start wearing red flannel shirts and those hideous thick blue trousers and—"

"Genevieve, it is getting late and I have a crowded schedule tomorrow. If we have nothing else to discuss, I'll have a carriage brought around to take you home—"

"Wait!" She bridged the distance between them in an instant, reaching for his hands. "I missed you so, darling," she murmured seductively. "Have you not longed to . . . be alone with me?"

Jack's face and body grew taut. He gazed into Genevieve's beautiful, intense green eyes, searching his mind for an appropriate response. Her hands, slim, soft, and white, slid caressingly up his waistcoat to round his shoulders and gently stroke the back of his neck. "I seem to recall a conversation that we had several times before I left in the spring. You told me that it would be improper for us to be alone together, did you not? You were quite adamant about avoiding any situation that might compromise your reputation or your chastity.''

"That was a long time ago," she objected weakly. Seeing the way his mouth quirked in surprised amusement, she almost added that she had said those things when he had desired her, when his passion had been undeniable. Hadn't her mother assured her that Jonathan Wyatt was the sort of man who would value his bride's purity, and that his own carnal desires would drive him to propose marriage? Genevieve knew that she was as beautiful as ever. She had eaten like a bird for weeks and now possessed an eighteen-inch waist to set off her high, creamy breasts. What had happened to that desire?

"A long time ago?" Jack repeated, his tone dry. "It was May, I believe."

Genevieve leaned against Jack's chest, lowering her lashes demurely. "Sometimes womanhood comes over one suddenly. While you were away, I . . . grew up. I had time to think about my feelings for you, and yours for me. I missed you, Jonathan. I longed for your embrace, for your . . . touch, as never before.'' Her right hand trailed over the soft white fabric of Jack's shirt, caressing the lean muscles of his arm.

Jack accepted her words and the touch of her cool white fingers . . . and remained unmoved. For some reason, Genevieve no longer excited him. Her fragrant hair was as soft and pale as cornsilk against his cheek, and the curves of her breasts were lightly grazing his chest, but he felt nothing. Now, as she offered him her parted lips in silent invitation, he kissed her experimentally. Their mouths met, his tongue teasing entrance to the silken depths within, while his arms slipped around her supple back. She was moaning softly, her fingers in his hair, her eager body arching through her petticoats in search of a response.

Jack's own body felt surprisingly detached from Genevieve's allures, while his mind traveled back to the bluff above the Stanislaus River where he had lain in the tall grass with Katie MacKenzie in his arms. Every nerve in his being had sung that day, every vein surging with fire. He had feasted on her delicious mouth and now remembered with a pang how their hearts had pounded in unison as he lay against her.

"Jonathan . . . is something wrong?" Genevieve had leaned back to look at him, staring into his distant, catlike eyes. "Don't you want me anymore?''

He blinked, focusing on the exquisite creature in his arms. Remembering his vow that morning to concentrate on the reality of his life in San Francisco rather than the masquerade in Columbia, Jack mustered a smile. "Of course I want you, Gen, but I must be more tired than I realize. The trip home was arduous, to say the least, and it's been taxing to catch up on everything here at home and at the newspaper. I just need a little time to settle in again, I think."

When he touched a tanned forefinger to her cheek, Genevieve reached up to catch his hand and kiss it. "Your skin is so rough!" Her eyes searched Jack's face, and she added, "And you're so brown . . . and the sun has lightened your hair. It's as if you're not quite the same man who left here in May. Have you really changed?"

"Undoubtedly. But there's no cause for concern." He gave her a wry smile. "As I said, I just need a little time."

"Is there anything I can do to help?"

"Yes." Jack pried her arms from his neck and held her slightly away. "Don't press me, all right, Gen?"

Before she could answer, there was a knock at the study door. Genevieve stepped back just as Conrad Wyatt poked his head into the room.

"Oh, I beg your pardon!" He reddened. "I hope I didn't disturb you. I wasn't aware that you were still here, Miss Braithwaite."

"It's all right, Conrad. Genevieve was just leaving. Let me see her into a carriage, then I'll be back."

Silently, Jack blessed his brother for the timely interruption. He was even spared a lengthy parting conversation from Genevieve because he had to return to the library. After the most circumspect of kisses in the presence of the coachman, Jack promised to see her soon, then waved once as the carriage rolled off down Montgomery Street.

Conrad was waiting for him in the doorway. Taller and leaner than Jack, he still looked and moved much like a boy, and his expression was one of youthful exuberance. "You look relieved, Jack. And here I was worrying that I'd ruined your expectations for the rest of the night!"

Wyatt snorted derisively and threw himself onto a wing chair facing the cold fireplace. "Women!" He smiled and cocked an eyebrow at his younger brother. "They're a complicated business, my boy, so beware!"

Awkwardly Conrad took the matching chair, folding and unfolding his long legs. "You must be joking . . . Yes, I can see that gleam in your eye. Either that or you're mad. There's not a male above eighteen in all of San Francisco who wouldn't give a fortune in gold to be alone with Genevieve Braithwaite. I'll wager that she's the sweetest, most beautiful woman in all of California!''

"Ah, youthful fervor!" Jack laughed huskily. "Just remember that love is blind—and passion can be life-threatening. If you have to give up a fortune in gold or anything else of great value to win a woman, you're in grave danger, my boy."

"I never thought I'd say this about you, Jack, but I think you're becoming stodgy."

Jack laughed again, but his mind was obviously elsewhere. Then he said, "How have you fared in life and love during my absence, Con? Any news? Are you still courting Miss Pierce?"

"Nothing of any real importance has taken place. Work at the bank is progressing well. Mr. Braithwaite has spoken of a promotion."

"Good!" Jack flashed him an approving grin. Conrad had tried working at the *Morning Star* but had no talent for either editing or reporting. It had taken all of Wyatt's considerable tact to persuade his younger brother to seek employment elsewhere.

Conrad shrugged. "I suppose. It's rather boring there. And I'm growing rather bored with Emma as well. I long for excitement! Which reminds me—I stopped by Barry and Patten's Saloon after I saw Emma home and heard some rather provocative news. That's what I came to tell you."

"Well, don't fall silent now. Pray enlighten me."

"There were two miners at the faro table, just arrived from Columbia. They said that Harold Van Hosten was killed by that highwayman who calls himself the Griffin."

"Really?" Glancing down, Jack flicked an imaginary speck of dust from his fawn trousers.

"Really!" Conrad sat forward, his voice rising. "I wish I knew who the Griffin was so I could thank him myself. You can't imagine the ill will I have borne toward Rush and Van Hosten for cheating me out of my claim, or the frustration I have suffered since heeding your advice not to seek vengeance against them."

"Perhaps now you'll be able to put that unhappy chapter behind you," Jack suggested.

"Well, I might if it weren't for Aaron Rush. The miners said that he was away when the shooting occurred, but he returned two days later and the town has literally been quaking with his fury. He's vowed to find the Griffin and bring him to justice, and is offering a huge reward for his capture."

"Indeed?" Wyatt's tawny brows flicked upward. "Well, I wish him luck. From all I've heard, the people of Columbia are grateful to the Griffin for all he's done. It's doubtful that any of those citizens will turn him in.''

Conrad sank back on his chair. ''The miners said that the Griffin disappeared without a trace after Van Hosten's shooting, and he hasn't been heard from since. The thing is, people fear that Rush is going to resort to even more disreputable and punitive dealings with the miners, partly out of anger and partly out of a desire to draw the Griffin out of hiding. The townspeople scarcely know what to think or hope for.''

''I imagine this will all blow over in time,'' Jack said mildly.

''Perhaps.'' The younger man sighed and ran a hand through his curly red hair. ''One can't help hoping that the Griffin will return to finish Rush off and put an end to that evil once and for all.''

''Don't count on that, Con. From all I've heard, the Griffin isn't one to resort to violence. My guess is that Van Hosten's death was probably some sort of accident, and I'd further venture to predict that the Griffin will be lying low for a long time . . . if not forever.'' Jack's tone was grim.

''Oh, God!'' Conrad exclaimed dramatically, slumping on his chair. ''What a depressing thought! What's become of courage and honor?''

Wyatt stared into the dark fireplace. ''Perhaps there's more at stake for the Griffin. He's not some character in a fairy tale, Con. The man's a human being.''

CHAPTER
11

Columbia, California
September 11, 1864

LIM SUNG WALKED SLOWLY UP MAIN STREET TOWARD THE
MacKenzie Saloon. It had rained the night before, and the cool
morning air was fragrant with pine. Even Columbia's usual clouds
of dust were dampened, a welcome change after the summer's unremitting dry heat. A quartet of miners passed en route to the Wells
Fargo office, while the stagecoach rumbled into view at the north
end of town.

Entering the saloon, Lim spotted Katie hunched over a corner
table with a number of papers spread before her. She wore an
expression of worried concentration as she wrote, crossed out, then
wrote again. Lim made his way over to her, his brow furrowed with
concern. Katie looked so tired these days, and she was thinner as
well. In summers past she'd ripened like a peach, her skin a soft
golden hue dusted with freckles. She'd ridden her horse daily, pausing to play or lie on the wildflower-strewn hillsides, and wherever
Katie had gone, a radiant smile and ready laughter had been her
companions. Now that smile showed itself only rarely. Her heart-
break over Brian's death was compounded by the burden of work
and responsibility that came with running the saloon. Lim knew
there were other problems, too, that Katie kept to herself. On its
best days the saloon barely turned a profit, and she had hinted to
Lim that a review of Brian's books had confirmed her suspicions

that this had been the case for more than a year. Although Lim and Abby put forth their best efforts to help the saloon prosper, the future looked truly bleak.

One night, Lim and Katie had closed up together. Seeing her sad, faraway expression, he had gently encouraged her to talk about her feelings. Slowly, Katie opened her heart to her friend and shared her deep, unremitting grief for her father, whom she missed constantly. She spoke of her worries about the saloon, questioning whether this was the way she wanted to spend her life. And then, weeping softly, she had told Lim that she was desperately lonely. He had patted Katie's back consolingly as she whispered, "It's as if there's a hole inside me that no amount of work or prayer or even the love of friends like you can fill. Papa's death is part of it, I know, but . . ." Her voice had trailed off, and she'd refused to say any more about it.

Lim sighed now, remembering. He wished there were a man in Columbia who suited Katie—and deserved her. Someone with intelligence, strength, and wit to match her own. . . .

"Where have you gone, Lim?" Abby inquired playfully, coming over from the bar.

He gave her an absent smile. "Good morning, Abby. You're looking well." It pleased him to say so honestly. Slowly, Abigail Armitage was finding peace. Two months had passed since her last sip of sherry, and she was trying to find strength through daily prayer. She now had friends in town and was a great favorite with the saloon's customers. "I was thinking about Katie," Lim continued. "I wish you could give her some of the roses in your cheeks."

"My heart aches for her," Abby whispered. "I know what she is going through. . . ."

Katie looked up then, shading her eyes against the sunlight that streamed through the east windows. "Hello, Lim. I'm hurrying to finish an article for the *Gazette*. I know I said I didn't have time to do them anymore, but Gideon is desperate." She glanced down again, adding distractedly, "It's about the fire at Widow Turner's last Monday, and how our fancy little Papeete fire engine saved the day." The committee dispatched to San Francisco to buy a fire engine had found the charmingly decorated hand-pumper on a ship in the bay, destined for the king of Tahiti. The ship's crew had left for the gold fields, so the Papeete had come home to Columbia.

Lim set a basket on the table in front of Katie. "I brought a few bird's nests from home. Tsing Tsing Yee just got dozens in for his store, and naturally Mother was the first one there to pick the best of the lot. She thought you might want to make soup and sends these with her regards.''

"How very kind of her." Katie touched the three tiny, rather pungent-smelling nests. "I must thank her."

"Are you feeling well?" Lim asked.

"Of course!" Katie declared forcefully. But there were dark smudges under his friend's blue eyes, Lim noticed, and the weight she had lost in recent weeks was evident in her pronounced cheekbones. Katie, who had never been vain, seemed now to be completely without concern for her own appearance. Her faded blue calico gown was mended at one elbow, and her ebony braid had lost its luster.

Standing up, Katie turned her attention to gathering the papers in an effort to avoid Lim's penetrating gaze. "I must go over to the *Gazette* now to give Gideon this story. He's setting type for this week's edition today."

"I hope he's planning to leave out the editorials attacking Aaron Rush and his mine," Lim said. "That man has had a dangerous face the last few times he has come to the saloon. Many thought that Van Hosten was the evil one in that pair, but lately it seems the real truth is coming clear."

"I know!" Abby chimed in. "Mr. Rush may look like a Milquetoast, but there's something in his eyes that frightens me. Gideon has been very brave to print editorials in defense of the miners, but now that the Griffin isn't around any longer to distract Rush's attention . . ."

"Don't ever speak of the Griffin as a hero again," Katie said coldly. "He killed my father. And obviously he's too afraid of being arrested for murder to continue to take risks on behalf of the miners. It's clear to me that the Griffin was never the champion we once believed him to be."

When Katie started toward the saloon door, Abby ran after her. "Wait, please! I'm sorry, Katie. I spoke without thinking. I didn't mean to remind you of your loss. It's only that I've been worried about Gideon. He's been a good friend to me these past weeks, and I'm concerned for his safety."

Katie gave her a sad smile. "Never mind, Abby, it's all right."

"Would you mind if I walked with you over to the *Gazette*? I'd just like to say hello."

"You'll have to come right back. I realize that business is slow, but there's always a chance . . .''

The two young women emerged onto Main Street in time to see the stagecoach rumble past. As they walked, Katie absently watched it stop in front of the Wells Fargo office. Two passengers disembarked, one of them a man with lean hips and wide, square shoulders. Tawny hair waved across the back of his head and curled over his collar. For an instant, Katie couldn't breathe. A shiver ran down her back, and her face grew warm as she stood staring at the man's back, waiting. Finally he turned to catch the bag the stage driver tossed down to him, revealing a sharp-boned profile. Katie's breath returned in a heaving gasp.

"Are you all right?" Disconcerted, Abby followed her friend's gaze to the stage passenger. "Goodness, that man looks a bit like Jack from the back, doesn't he? Did you think it was Jack?"

"I—yes." She was too stunned by her own reaction to lie.

"You two got to be friends while he was here, didn't you? Have you missed him?" Abby was surprised by the sudden glare Katie shot at her.

"Believe me, I've had more important things to think about than Jack Adams. Just because you find the man irresistible doesn't mean every other female shares your weakness!"

Abby rushed to catch up to her, matching her pace. "I'm sorry, Katie! It's just that . . . well, Jack is a very attractive man and you're a beautiful woman, and I think it occurred to many people that the two of you would make a handsome couple. Please, don't be angry. I'm only saying these things out of affection for you."

Katie didn't look at her. "The last thing I need right now is a man—especially one like Jack Adams! Didn't you say not so long ago that he was a lone wolf, that he could never commit himself to a woman?"

"Maybe he simply hasn't found the right one." Abby smiled in spite of herself. "In any case, a commitment may not be what you need. Perhaps a good dose of love and romance would do you more good."

"Abby, for heaven's sake!" Color flooded Katie's pale face. "I cannot believe you are saying these things! What about your own feelings for Jack?"

Abby shrugged. "I think I was just . . . oh, I don't know—afraid, I suppose, and lonely, too. And then when Jack came into my life, I thought he would take care of everything for me." She smiled, remembering. "Instead he helped me to understand that I had to sort out my own problems and not look to a man to rescue me."

"But you think that I should?"

"It's not rescuing that *you* need, Katie!" Suddenly Abby remembered what Jack had said to her about being betrothed to a woman in San Francisco. "Well, I suppose that you'll find romance when the time is right. Jack isn't here, after all, so it doesn't much matter what I think!" As they approached the white frame office of the *Gazette*, she sought to change the subject. "You know, there's another reason I got over Jack Adams so painlessly. This is something of a secret, so I'll trust you not to say anything to anyone else."

Katie stopped and stared at her. "This is the most curious conversation that you and I have ever had!"

Widening her large brown eyes, Abby replied, "Didn't you ask me to be your friend? Aren't friends supposed to confide in each other?"

"Well, yes, they are." Chastened, Katie added, "And of course I'll not betray your confidence."

A beatific smile spread over Abby's face. "I find that I have some very tender feelings toward Gideon Henderson."

"You do?" Katie blinked, nonplussed. *"Gideon?"*

"What's wrong with that?"

"Nothing, nothing!"

"Are we so ill suited?"

"No, of course not!" Katie hastened to reassure her. "It's just that I'm not used to thinking of Gideon in those terms. He's never been in love, as far as I know."

"Then you aren't very observant. I think that he was half in love with *you* when I first came to Columbia. Then, gradually, we became friends. He loaned me some books." Abby's eyes grew dreamy again. "I've always been attracted to a different kind of man, but Gideon's warmth and tenderness, his constancy, make me very happy."

"Is he . . . aware? I mean, does Gideon feel the same way about you?"

"I think so, though nothing's been spoken of as yet. He's rather shy."

Katie felt a rush of emotion and reached out to hug her friend. "I think it's wonderful. If there is anything I can do, please say so!"

Blushing, Abby murmured awkwardly, "Well, if the opportunity should arise, you might speak to Gideon—just in passing, of course. Do you understand what I mean?"

"Certainly." Katie beamed. "I'll be the soul of tact. Let's go in now and say hello. You'll have to be getting back to start preparing stew for lunch—"

She broke off in the midst of opening the *Gazette*'s door, freezing as she took in the scene of chaos—papers littering the floor, office chairs overturned, and Gideon's desk a shambles with ink splat-tered over everything. Quickly, her eyes sought out the Adams bed and platen printing press at the back of the room. The platen had been broken in two by a sledgehammer, which lay on the floor nearby.

"Help . . ." The call came faintly from behind stacks of old newspapers in the far corner of the office.

"Dear God, it's Gideon!" Katie cried. Scrambling over the wreckage, she reached his side in moments, with Abby only a step behind.

"Gideon!" Abby burst into tears at the sight of him. His body looked broken, his clothing torn to reveal bruises and dried blood. There was a gash in the side of his head that oozed blood, and one eye was swollen shut. His spectacles, smashed, still clung to his nose.

Gideon moaned, "The press . . ."

"Never mind that! What about you?" Katie looked back over her shoulder at Abby. "Run for Doctor Morgan. Hurry!"

Abby obeyed without a word, though she longed to tend to Gid-eon herself and her heart was bursting with fear for him. Mean-while, Katie blinked back tears of her own.

"I'll live," Gideon whispered, managing a crooked smile.

"Of course you will!" Her voice shook with emotion. "Abby and I will nurse you back to health. We'll pamper you, wait on you hand and foot, and cook all your favorite dishes. . . ." Katie paused, swallowing tears. "Gideon, do you know who did this?"

"Don't you?" His tone was acid even as he gritted his teeth against the pain. "Two men came in late last night. Wearing masks. When they smashed the press, one said, 'Since you won't print the truth, it's best you don't print at all.' Then they smashed me, too."

Katie's cheeks were wet. "Oh, Gideon, will this nightmare never end?"

An impressive new hotel was under construction across the street from Jonathan Wyatt's office at the *Morning Star*, and the inescap-able racket was a test for his patience. Sipping tea at his desk, he went over galley sheets with a pen and tried not to hear the incessant pounding and clatter out on California Street.

There was a tap at the door, then Samuel Clemens poked his head in. "Good morning! Could you spare me a moment of your time?" His waistcoat was unbuttoned, his curls tousled, and his mustache nearly covered his mouth until he grinned.

Jack leaned back in his chair and smiled. "Ah, Sam! Come in.

You're just the tonic I need—thus far, the day has been far too boring.''

"Well, you're certainly looking very fit.'' Clemens took a seat, his eyes agleam with speculation. Jonathan Wyatt was the last person he'd expect to complain of boredom. Why, the man's looks alone would be enough to satisfy most men for a lifetime. Sun poured through the windows behind him, burnishing his toffee-colored hair and deepening the green of his eyes. His immaculate white shirt and vest of watered gray silk emphasized the broad shoulders and tapering chest—and when he smiled . . . ! Since Clemens's own looks were less than spectacular, he gave them little thought, but he was forced to concede that there must be definite advantages to possessing the physical attributes of a Jonathan Wyatt. That wasn't what he said now, however. "People would be surprised to hear that you're bored, my friend. You own a newspaper, you have a handsome home and a beautiful woman who is desperately in love with you. You're young, intelligent, and a darling of society. What more could a man ask?''

Jack regarded the younger man with narrowed eyes. "I haven't noticed you pursuing any of the goals you think I've attained.'' Sighing, he reached for his tea. "I don't know, Sam . . . something is missing. I worked hard the past few years to discipline myself and instill a sense of order in my life, but now it seems almost . . .''

"Sterile?'' Clemens widened his eyes innocently.

"Yes. Exactly. I've told you that I spent some time in the foothills off and on since last autumn, and when I was there I felt alive. Yet it became rather, uh, confusing—as if I were beginning to lead two lives. My home and my business and my roots are here, so when I returned in July I decided to accept this reality. Stay here and face *it*.''

"But you're not happy?''

"No. I don't seem to be. Something is lacking. . . .''

"Passion?''

Jack laughed suddenly. "You're a crafty dog, Clemens! And, you're smart, too. Do you know, I feel better.''

"Well, don't give me too much credit. I sympathize with your feelings because nothing drives me madder than an ordered existence! I crave adventure, new experiences, something to make me feel *passionate* about life. People have pointed it out on many occasions as a character flaw.'' His tone was dry. "You'll work it out. I think the trick is to strike a balance between listening to the head and the heart, but I can't claim to have achieved that balance yet myself.''

Wyatt glanced down at the galley sheets he'd been proofing and made a derisive noise. "Perhaps it's just a mood. This work, after all, is dull beyond measure.''

"Galleys?'' Sam chuckled and lit a cigar. "That reminds me of a story my friend Bret Harte told the other night. Do you know Harte?''

Jack nodded. "I wouldn't say I particularly like the man, but I have admired his work.''

"I know what you mean. He is showy, meretricious, and insincere, but he has also been a friend to me and a source of professional advice. And Bret can be amusing. He used to live in Yreka, teaching school and editing the weekly newspaper. Once a galley slip was placed on his desk for his attention. It was a flowery, extravagantly written obituary for a Mrs. Thompson. One line read, 'Even in Yreka, her chastity was conspicuous.' Of course, the word was 'charity,' but Harte didn't think of that. He merely underlined the word and put a question mark in the margin, signaling the printer to refer back to the manuscript.'' Sam paused to chuckle, his eyes twinkling. "Well, as you know, underlining is also meant for words that are to be italicized, and the printer saw this correction in a different light. So, when the obituary appeared in the newspaper, it read, 'Even in Yreka, her _chastity_ was conspicuous?'—which of course turned the thing into a ghastly, ill-timed sarcasm!''

Leaning back in his chair, Jack laughed with easy pleasure. When he was with Sam, he knew a sense of freedom and camaraderie that had been missing in his life since he'd returned to San Francisco and left Jack Adams behind. "That's a priceless story, Sam. Did you come over here for the sole purpose of cheering me up, or did you have business to discuss?''

Clemens withdrew folded papers from his inside coat pocket and opened them. "I brought you another story. Have a look and see what you think.''

Rising, Jack reached for the manuscript and glanced at it. "Ah, diversion! You have rescued me all the way around this morning, my friend, and I am grateful.'' He smiled and came around the desk to shake Sam's hand.

"Speaking of diversions, how is the ravishing Miss Braithwaite?''

"The same.'' Wyatt raked a hand through his ruffled hair. "I'm certain that she'd like to be making wedding plans, but I can think of nothing I'd like less. I suppose I continue to see her out of convenience."

"Or until someone else comes along to lure you away?"

Jack was surprised at the immediate intensity with which Katie MacKenzie's image appeared in his brain. His gaze was far away as he replied, "Hmm . . . perhaps. But I don't envision that happening here in San Francisco."

"I've been thinking about journeying to the foothills myself," Sam said casually. "Steve Gillis, who shares my lodgings, has a brother, Jim, who is pocket mining in a place called Jackass Gulch. Whenever we have a bad day, Steve and I dream of going off to join Jim, and one day we very well might!"

"I know Jackass Gulch," Wyatt said. "It's quite a sylvan spot now; nearly deserted."

Clemens opened the door and smiled. "Who knows? We may both see that paradise ere long. When challenge and adventure beckon, a wise man heeds their call!"

CHAPTER
12

October 12, 1864
Columbia

W ARM, SOAPY WATER SWISHED AGAINST THE SIDES OF THE
tin bathtub as Katie MacKenzie stepped out onto the kitchen rug.
Midnight had passed, and moonbeams streamed through the windows, silvering her wet, classically molded body.

As Katie dried herself slowly in the haze of shadow and starlight,
she felt both refreshed and weary. It had been a busy autumn thus
far . . . almost busy enough to prevent her from dwelling on her
father's death. Yet she still felt that familiar ache in her heart and a
yearning to weep when she thought of him, and any discussion of
the Griffin sent waves of impotent anger rushing over her. For the
first time in her life, she hungered for revenge. Katie's friends, and
the regular customers at the saloon, tactfully refrained from mentioning the highwayman.

Beyond her grief and rage, however, were questions about the
future. In their own way, those were the most troubling thoughts of
all. Katie's prospects for the years ahead were uncertain at best.
She owned a business that generated barely enough income to feed
her, Abby, and Lim, whose parents had left for San Francisco in
August. Moreover, she felt isolated in Columbia. There was little
to challenge her intellectually, especially now that the *Gazette* could
no longer be printed, and an unfamiliar, aching loneliness passed
over her at unpredictable moments.

Upon leaving Columbia, Yong and Choy Sung had sold their house and laundry to Aaron Rush, who had now begun to mine the valuable lots. Lim's parents had agreed to let their son stay in Columbia until Katie's need for him was less acute; he had moved into the spare bedroom above the saloon, and Abby had taken Brian's bedroom at Katie's house.

Abby's companionship had eased Katie's loneliness until Gideon's injury a month ago. Ever since, he had been recuperating at the saloon, where the women could take turns caring for him. Then, "for convenience' sake," Abby had returned to the saloon herself, setting up a cot in the kitchen so that she could be near him. In her heart, she was grateful for their time together. It seemed that each day strengthened the bond between her and Gideon. Watching them together, Katie felt happy, and during the day she enjoyed the sense of family she felt with her friends. Still, the nights seemed endless. . . .

Garbed now in a diaphanous lawn nightgown, she padded barefoot into the bedroom and picked up her mother's silver-backed brush. She didn't bother to light a lamp but sat on the edge of her moonlit bed and ran the brush through the mass of damp ebony curls that cascaded down her back. An unseasonably warm breeze wafted through the open window, caressing her, and Katie was lulled into lying back. She spread her hair out over the snowy pillows, closed her eyes, and let the dreams come.

Lately, it was a rare night that passed without a dream of Jack Adams. Often they were intense enough to awaken her and thus imprint themselves upon her memory. Sometimes he was at the bar, burnished by hazy sunlight, his sage-green eyes gleaming as he reached out to touch her. Every detail of him was letter perfect, from the golden flecks in his eyes to the sprinkling of sandy hair across the backs of his hands. Katie could even smell him. She would yearn to touch his body and drink in his warmth. Sometimes they would kiss, but as she became aroused, her conscious mind would interfere and she would awaken, trembling and frightened.

Tonight, though, Katie felt reckless. With the balmy night air whispering over her clean skin, she welcomed Jack Adams to her dreams.

Jack was aware of a distinct feeling of unreality as he walked down Columbia's deserted Main Street. The warm breeze reminded him of the summer night he'd left this town, intending never to return.

For the hundredth time, he pieced together the series of events

and choices that had led him back to Columbia. Yes, it was true
that he'd missed Kathleen MacKenzie. He could admit it, if only
to himself. And he'd grown more restless and felt more stifled with
each passing day. The life Jonathan Wyatt led was now unsatisfy-
ing; he no longer enjoyed being in total control of his world. He
missed the spicy unexpectedness of being Jack Adams in the foothills . . . with Katie.

Still, the idea of returning to Columbia had seemed out of the
question. He'd fought against the urge for so long that he thought
he'd beaten it into submission. His world in San Francisco—his
mansion, his newspaper, his uneasy relationship with Genevieve—
had been created by no one but himself, and now he would have to
accept it. Besides, Columbia was dangerous for him now that the
Griffin was wanted for murder. And what about Katie? It seemed
that the burden of guilt he carried for her father's death overshad-
owed the tentative feelings he had toward the girl. She would wish
him dead if she knew the truth.

But then one day in early October, as he ate lunch with Samuel
Clemens and Bret Harte at the Palace Hotel, Clemens mentioned
that Steve Gillis had received a letter from his brother in Jackass
Gulch. It detailed the destruction of the *Columbia Gazette*'s printing press and the attack on Gideon Henderson. Jack left the next
morning with a new platen for the Adams press in the back of his
wagon.

He'd arrived earlier today in Angel's Camp, a mining town a
short distance northwest of Columbia that continued to thrive thanks
to the recent discovery of some important veins of gold and the
subsequent formation of the Utica Mining Company. Jack liked
Angel's Camp and was, for some reason, in no hurry to reach
Columbia now that he had come so close. Suddenly seized with a
desire to renew ties with a gambling friend from younger days in
San Francisco, he had searched out Mike Dodd. Dodd, whose current game of chance was mining gold, had been happy to see his
long-lost friend, and the two of them spent the afternoon at the
Angel's Hotel, eating, drinking, and reminiscing.

Jack had welcomed the opportunity to relax—and postpone his
confrontation with Columbia and Kathleen MacKenzie. It had all
seemed simple enough to him when he left San Francisco. Gideon
was in need of a working press, Aaron Rush needed to learn that
he couldn't play God, and Jack was able to fill those needs. The
fact that he'd be seeing Katie again was incidental.

Yet once he was fed, bathed, and clad in clean buckskins and a
white shirt, driving in the autumn twilight up the hills toward the

Stanislaus River, Jack could avoid the reality no longer. He saw Kathleen in his mind, wearing the white percale dress with the violet dots and sash, a cameo brooch at her neck, glossy black curls spilling around her shoulders. The fabric of the gown flowed softly over the tantalizing curves of her breasts and hips while the sash accentuated her tiny waist. Her beautiful face was radiant with intelligence and something more—an incipient passion he longed to tap. Jack smiled now, remembering how she'd reacted to his proposition that she pretend to be his wife for the benefit of Cecelia Chelstrom. She had been so animated in her outrage, sparks flying from her azure eyes, her delicate nostrils flaring in a way that utterly charmed him. And then, in front of the Wells Fargo office, she had gazed up at him expectantly. Jack would never forget Katie's mouth. It was rosy, full, and delicious looking. Moist and slightly parted, her lips exuded a heady mixture of innocence and hunger.

It had been late when Jack had hauled his wagon up Parrot's Ferry Road just a few miles from Columbia. Behind and below, the Stanislaus River shimmered with the reflection of countless stars, and mockingbirds had soothed the weary traveler with stolen song. Jack had forced himself to think of Gideon, of the story he would tell to explain the platen. He'd pondered the problem of Aaron Rush, whose constant absence had lulled them all into forgetting that he was Van Hosten's equal partner in evil.

But try as he might, Kathleen simply would not be excluded from his thoughts. His memory of her was as fresh as if he had seen her that morning. Her face, her voice, the sensations of her kiss, and the warmth of her body intruded in his mind. Jack wasn't sure what it meant, and he didn't want to know. His other self had whispered that he'd been a fool to come back. As the wagon trundled over the brow of the hill that sloped gently into Columbia, Jack had flicked the reins and surged forward in reckless surrender to whatever lay ahead. Obviously he'd needed to return for some reason, and, besides, it was too late to change his mind, wasn't it?

Now, strolling down the eerily quiet Main Street, Jack realized that he'd been foolish to stay so long in Angel's Camp: he'd underestimated the length of time it would take him to travel by wagon to Columbia. At well past one o'clock in the morning, the MacKenzie Saloon would be locked up, along with the miners' boardinghouses and the hotels. This small, remote town was not the sort of place where hotel clerks sat up waiting for potential customers. Jack had no taste for sleeping in the livery stable, in the back of his wagon with the printing-press platen. He still had his key for the

MacKenzie house, and he felt it now in the pocket of his buckskins. Brian MacKenzie might be dead, but Jack had slept many nights in that parlor. True, it strained the bounds of propriety to consider arriving at this hour to spend the night under the same roof with an unmarried woman, but at the moment he was too tired to debate the finer points of conventional morality.

Walking up Jackson Street, he convinced himself that she couldn't be living in that house alone. Surely Abby was staying there, too, and she was a chaperone of sorts. He would tell them that he only wanted to sleep and would leave at first light before anyone even knew he had been there.

Jack let himself in through the white picket gate, noting that the vines that had spilled flowers over the porch roof in June were now beginning to change color. Yet the night was so balmy, it still felt like summer. He wished that he had the power to turn back the clock—back to when Brian MacKenzie's snores had rumbled out of his small bedroom.

The house was dark. Jack's heart thudded as he knocked on the door, and the physical reaction surprised him. He anticipated Kathleen's appearance in the shadows, the first sight of her face. How would she react? Would she touch him? His palms moistened suddenly at the thought.

But moments passed and nothing happened. The house was silent, and as Jack's rush of nervousness ebbed, he was aware only of a powerful sense of fatigue. He was utterly exhausted, eyes burning, and without a place to sleep. Perhaps Katie was in her bedroom with the door closed and simply hadn't heard him knock. Or had she moved to the saloon with Abby to avoid this houseful of memories?

Jack was too tired to consider the possibilities any further. After a few hours' sleep he'd have a clearer head, he told himself. Taking the long, slender key out of his pocket, he paused, then inserted it in the lock and turned it. The door swung open gently, and Jack's first sight of the familiar, darkened parlor heightened the dreamlike atmosphere that had permeated his middle-of-the-night return to Columbia. It seemed that at any moment he might wake up and find himself in his bedroom in San Francisco.

Of course, the cot Jack had slept on in the parlor was gone, and the calico sofa looked smaller than he'd remembered. Pulling off his boots, he padded into the little kitchen. The same bright, embroidered cloth covered the table, and a bouquet of yellow chrysanthemums filled the pitcher at its center. Jack felt an unexpected tightening in his chest.

The door to Brian's room was closed. Tentatively, he tried the doorknob and discovered it was locked. Resigned now, he went on to Katie's bedroom and found the door open. He would have to awaken her, apologize for letting himself in, and ask if he could stay the night in Brian's room. His heart began to pound almost painfully as he stepped into the doorway and saw her lying on top of the sheets. The filmy, lace-edged nightgown she wore molded perfectly to the womanly curves of her body and had edged up just enough to expose slim pale legs. With her ebony curls fanned out over the pillows, Kathleen looked like a sleeping angel.

Jack bent over the bed and gently touched her shoulder. "Kathleen," he murmured.

Immediately she opened her eyes as if she'd been expecting him. "Jack." She smiled sleepily. "You're here." Standing above her in his moonlit white shirt, he seemed a perfect product of her dreams, more real than ever before. Sleep washed over her, ebbing and flowing like a gentle wave on a beach.

"Do you mind if I sleep in your—in the spare bedroom to-night?"

His voice seemed to come from far away. With an effort, she whispered, "No, sleep here. Don't leave me."

Utterly exhausted, Jack looked at her sleeping form and sighed. The snowy linens on the bed looked infinitely inviting. I'll just sleep for a few hours, he promised himself, then leave before she wakes up. Easing down on the bed, he pretended Katie wasn't there. The sensation of the cool pillow against his cheek was bliss, and sleep came instantly.

From the sweet, dream-tinged depths of sleep, Jack became aware that he was hot and uncomfortable in his clothes. He never slept in clothes. Removing them was simple reflex; he didn't even have to wake up to pull them off, drop them on the floor, and lie back again. Then, savoring the breeze that caressed his bare skin, he let the current of sleep pull him under again.

Later the air grew cooler, and Jack and Katie both sought warmth instinctively, gravitating toward each other as they lay on their sides. At first Jack was only dimly aware when a warm back touched his chest. But then, as Katie snuggled closer, her derriere molded itself against his hips. Dreaming, he felt his manhood growing warm, brushing his upper thigh as it hardened, twitching slightly with each beat of his heart. A hot, pulsing need began to build within him. Through the gossamer confection of her nightgown, Jack could feel the warmth of her flesh, and involuntarily he tensed the muscles in his loins. A jolting surge of lust left him fully erect. He was burning.

The veils of sleep were lifting one by one, but this had to be a dream. When she snuggled nearer, Jack pressed himself against the delicate niche that bisected her fanned bottom and clenched his teeth as a chill rushed from the base of his neck down his spine to fan the fires of his arousal. His eyes flew open as reality intruded, but he was powerless now to quell the feelings that held him in their grip.

Katie was dreaming that she and Jack were lying in the meadow overlooking the Stanislaus River. It was growing cold, and she liked being held and protected by his hard male body. The contrast between them felt good. The place between her legs was warm and tingling pleasantly, like her breasts. This time she didn't want to wake up . . . didn't want the feelings to go away.

Jack ached with hunger. He touched his mouth to the baby curls at the back of her neck, nuzzling, breathing in the scent of her soft skin and fresh-washed hair. Driven by instinct, Katie pressed her hips against him and moaned softly. She moved again and again, sighing as she instinctively sought the hard male member that fit so perfectly against her.

At last, Jack lifted his right hand and placed it ever so gently on her hip. He swallowed a moan when he discovered that Katie's gown had slipped up nearly to her waist on that side, so that he was caressing bare, satiny skin. Tentatively he rested his palm on her hip and let his fingers curve into the hollow of her belly. On fire, he held his breath, afraid that she would awaken and stop him, afraid that she would sleep on and condemn him to the madness of his desire. At that moment Katie's thighs parted slightly, her right leg slipped backward between his, and Jack was utterly lost.

He heard her breathing quicken and recklessly slid his hand beneath her nightgown. Katie continued to press rhythmically against him as his agile fingers played upward until they grazed the ripe curve of one breast. She was so warm, so eager, but he held himself back, lightly tracing circles around her breast with his fingertips. Finally he took the soft nipple between his thumb and forefinger, rolling it gently as it puckered.

Katie was swimming in a sea of sensitized pleasure, half-awake but unwilling to release the dream. Tingling darts of arousal were shooting from her nipples to her loins, and she could feel her breasts swelling, becoming fuller and warmer, in Jack's deft hands. In the mists between sleep and consciousness, her carefully tended inhibitions were stripped away, for the first time allowing her body to revel in the passions of womanhood. When Jack's fingers slid downward, then pressed with consummate skill against the hidden source of her arousal, Katie moaned and turned in his arms.

Her hunger, suppressed for so long, would be denied no longer. This time she wouldn't flee from her desires. In the darkness her mouth sought Jack's, opening to receive his tongue, while her arms wound round his neck. After an eternity of ravenous kissing, nibbling, tasting, he reached down to slip the nightgown over her head. Then, drawing back, he studied her in the moonlight. Her face, pale against the ebony spill of her hair, was turned to one side. Her eyes were closed, but her mouth was open, and he recognized the telltale cadence of her breathing.

"Beautiful," he murmured, and bent to trail his fingertips over her throat, shoulders, the lush curves of her breasts, the hollow of her tummy, her hips, and her lithe legs . . . Carefully, he avoided the place he knew ached to be touched. Katie stretched and writhed beneath his hands, then moaned as Jack began to retrace her body with his lips. He found pleasure points that had gone undiscovered until tonight: the back of her neck, her spine, the small of her back, the tender insides of her elbows, her wrists, her palms. With lips like butterfly wings, he kissed along her sides, then gently sought the delicate rosebud nipples of her breasts. She sank her fingers into his hair as he sucked slowly on first one and then the other, excited beyond belief by her gasps of pleasure. At last he moved lower, kissing the arches of her feet, then taking her toes into his mouth one at a time. Katie undulated helplessly above him. His lips trailed fire up her calves, lingering on the backs of her knees, then nipping sensuously on her inner thighs. When he reached the soft dark tangle of curls between her legs, he paused, then blew softly. Katie arched her hips in response, and he saw how moist and swollen she was, could smell the faint, musky scent of her desire. Bending, he pressed his lips to the core of her femininity, and almost instantly she strained upward and began to shudder, panting. Jack poised himself above her, eyes glittering in the pale light of the waning moon. He could wait no longer.

Katie cried aloud as the exquisitely pleasurable contractions swept out from between her legs, sending shimmering waves of delight through her entire body. A warm glow settled over her, overcoming the certain awareness that what had just happened was no dream. Jack's face was now above her own, and their eyes met. He braced himself, one hand on either side of her, and Katie reached out to touch his shoulders and the soft tawny hair that covered his chest. The feeling of his lean-muscled male body, so different from hers,

excited her. She drew herself up to nuzzle his neck. He smelled of
soap and, intoxicatingly, of Jack. When she murmured his name
aloud, he smiled down at her.

They kissed then, commingling wonder and passion between
their lips, and Jack lowered himself between her legs. His state of
arousal was beyond any he could remember, and Katie was warm
and moist against him. Carefully, he entered her. Encountering a
thin barrier, he withdrew a little and began again. He pushed forward gently, paused, then pushed again, savoring the pulsing rush
that came with each movement. As hot as he was, Katie was even
hotter inside. Jack took her virginity as tenderly as he could, feeling
her constrict even more tightly around him at the first shock of
penetration. After this initial reaction, however, she relaxed and
arched her hips to meet his. He was careful at first, but gradually
Katie's own rhythm increased, and together they began to soar.

Katie was astonished by her own passion. The sensation of Jack's
thrusts deep within her, the sight of his taut, wild, masculine sil-
houette above her in the moonlight, sent fire coursing through her
blood. Instincts she hadn't known she possessed were freed by the
merging of their bodies. Jack cupped her buttocks in his hands
and Katie wrapped her legs around his waist and clung to his wide
back as they rode higher and higher together, their bodies agleam
with perspiration. This is beautiful, she thought, tears stinging her
eyes. At last Jack arched his neck, froze for an instant, then let out
a long, low groan.

They lay together, panting, their faces side by side. Katie felt
him pulse slightly inside her and tightened her own muscles in
response, embracing him. Warm currents of absolute contentment
washed over her. Softly she ran her fingers down the tapered sides
of Jack's back.

"Mmm," he murmured.

She smiled against the side of his face. Slowly he withdrew and
turned to look at her, bracing himself on an elbow.

"You're a beautiful woman and an incredibly exciting lover,"
he whispered. He lifted her hand and gently kissed each delicate
finger.

Giddy with pleasure and a sudden wave of fatigue, Katie nearly
giggled. "Thank you," she replied, smiling radiantly, then closed
her eyes.

Jack smoothed the silky black curls from her brow and drank in
the sight of her face in repose. Her long lashes brushed her cheeks

and her lips were full and tender looking. He felt his heart clench and was almost afraid to wonder why.

Oh God, he thought, what have we done?

CHAPTER
13

October 12, 1864

T HE SUN WAS WARM ON KATIE'S BODY, HER NIGHTGOWN WAS
twisted around her thighs, and the insides of her eyelids were on
fire. Still, it was difficult to wake up. She was dreaming that she
had come into the house and found her parents eating breakfast in
the kitchen. Her mother, looking up to smile lovingly, was unchanged. She wore the cameo brooch at her neck, and her rich
black hair was pinned up into a chignon. Brian invited Katie to join
them, and she obeyed, not wanting to question their return to her
life.

Then a mockingbird called from the peach tree outside the bedroom window, and reluctantly Katie opened her eyes. Reality returned in a flood of morning sunshine, and the image of Brian and
Mary MacKenzie faded to a cherished memory. What time was it,
she wondered. How could she have slept so late? When she turned
to get out of bed, she became aware of the tenderness between her
legs, and her eyes widened in horror.

The dream came back in a spine-chilling rush. Jack Adams had
been in her bed; he'd made love to her. Blushing as she remembered
each intimate caress, Katie threw back the sheet and saw the spot
of blood. It had been real! He'd not been a dream at all, but flesh
and blood, and their lovemaking had been more sensuously explicit

118

than anything she'd ever imagined. And worst of all, she had been an enthusiastic participant.

Panicked, Katie got up and paced back and forth across the bedroom. What had happened to him? Where was he now? How dare he come into her house, into her bed? She couldn't believe what her mind insisted was true. How could it have happened? It was impossible!

Heart pounding, Katie stripped off her nightgown, washed, and dressed in her plainest faded pink gown. She buttoned it up to her throat and wore no petticoat or adornments of any kind. Sitting at her dressing table, she stared at her flushed face. Was it her imagination, or did her lips look a little swollen? Oh, God! What had come over her? Was she mad? Possessed? Katie brushed her hair back and braided it so tightly that it hurt, then got up and hurried out of the house.

On Main Street, she suffered through a conversation with Victoria Barnstaple about the unseasonably warm autumn, distractedly returned greetings from various townsfolk, then tried to calm herself as she entered her saloon. Her heart was thudding wildly, but all seemed well. A couple of miners were having morning beers at the bar, while a few of the tables were ringed with men eating breakfast. Lim waved to her from behind the bar, but he seemed preoccupied. Katie began to breathe easier as she greeted her customers and made her way toward the kitchen.

" 'Bout time you got a new cook, Miss MacKenzie!'' a grizzled mountain man exclaimed from his table near the end of the bar. "These're the dandiest flapjacks I ever tasted! Lighter'n my sainted mama's!''

"Oh.'' Katie pasted on a smile. "Thank you.''

Puzzled, she backed toward the door of the kitchen, which was a small, makeshift affair off the rear of the saloon. The mouth-watering aromas of sizzling eggs and sausage, coffee, pancakes, and fresh-baked apple muffins wafted out to her as she approached. She could hear muffled voices—Abby's, and then, for an instant, a man's, followed by loud laughter from Gideon.

"Gideon, are you certain you should be out of bed?'' Katie demanded as she entered.

His reply was lost in the fog of the next few moments. Katie froze at the sight of Jack Adams standing over the cast-iron, wood-burning stove, using a spatula to turn flapjacks with practiced ease. He wore a towel knotted snugly around the hips of his faded dungarees, and the sleeves of his blue shirt were turned up to reveal the strong tanned forearms that she remembered all too well. Jack's tawny hair was shorter than it had been that summer, freshly washed and brushed back from his irresistibly attractive face. His grin flashed white in the sunlight, and a day or two's worth of golden stubble glinted on his cheeks.

"Surprised to see me, Miss MacKenzie?" he inquired huskily, the arch of his eyebrow betraying his amusement.

"In my kitchen?" Katie heard herself reply. "Of course I'm surprised. What are you doing here?"

"Cooking breakfast." He turned back to his work.

Abby exchanged looks with Gideon, who sat on a chair near the back stairway. Abby's big brown eyes widened further as she took in the angry set of Katie's jaw. Rushing forward, she hastened to explain, "I hope I didn't make a mistake, asking Jack to cook! It's just that you didn't come in, and I didn't want to disturb you, and I was having a hard time keeping up, so when he offered—"

"Never mind, Abby. It's all right." She indicated the three laden breakfast plates sitting on the oak sideboard next to the stove. "Shouldn't you serve those?"

Her friend scooped them up and made a quick exit, grateful for the opportunity to escape. Katie approached the worn pine work-table that ran down the center of the cozy room and set about turning muffins out of their tins. She tried to pretend that Jack was not standing just a few feet away, even though every breath she took was an effort.

Suddenly Gideon exclaimed, "Katie, did you hear the good news?"

She glanced up from refilling the muffin tins, her blue eyes flashing. "No, but I'd be grateful to hear some."

"Jack's brought us a platen! That's the reason he came back. We can repair the press and resume production of the *Gazette*!"

Jack ladled pancake batter onto the griddle, not looking up as he said casually, "I heard about Gideon's misfortune in San Francisco. I happened to have access to a platen, so I brought it along."

"How selfless and noble of you," she said with biting sarcasm.

He pretended not to notice. "That's very flattering, but I cannot allow such kind words to be spoken without a disclaimer on my part." Bubbles broke on the surface of the flapjacks, and he flipped them neatly. "My motives were a bit more complex than a simple desire to serve justice and restore Columbia's freedom of the press. Certainly I wanted to help Gideon, but I also wanted to thwart Aaron Rush. His methods lack moral decency; he needs to be taught a lesson."

"And you're just the man to do it. I declare, Mr. Adams, you could teach moral decency lessons in the schoolroom!"

This time Jack glanced over his shoulder in response to her acid tone. "Why, Miss MacKenzie, I had no idea you had such a high opinion of my character!"

Abby reappeared then, carrying a stack of dirty plates. "Everyone's been served, so I think we can relax for a moment. It's late enough now that there may not even be any more breakfast customers. I'll go around with the coffeepot, then start washing dishes."

Katie reached for a mug and hastily filled it with coffee before Abby took the pot away. She leaned against the wall, drinking and watching Jack finish the last of the flapjacks. When they were done, he picked up the tins of muffin batter and looked over his shoulder at Katie.

"Do you want me to put these in the oven?"

"Yes. They're good for lunch, too." Their eyes met for an instant, and she felt the heat in her cheeks.

Jack wiped off the griddle, washed his hands, then untied the towel around his hips. "If you don't mind, I could use some breakfast myself."

Katie took a deep breath and stepped forward. "Could you spare me a few minutes of your time first?"

Green eyes twinkling, he replied, "As always, Miss MacKenzie, I am at your disposal."

Her blush deepened. "I would like to speak to you in private. Shall we go back to the storeroom?"

Gideon stared out the window, pretending not to notice as they walked by. Neither he nor Abby could quite decide how Jack and Katie felt about each other, but whatever their relationship, it clearly was intense. It was a relief to Gideon to realize that his own feelings for Katie had changed over the past several months: he still loved her, but he had come to regard her more as a friend than an unrequited love, and he experienced no jealousy in hoping that she'd soon find someone worthy of her. As for himself, his heart seemed more and more to be inclined toward Abby. . . .

Katie led the way through the saloon, back into the shadowed storeroom. She waited for Jack to pass inside, then closed the door behind them. Crossing the floor, she stopped amid the crates. Faint, dusty rays of sunlight streamed through the single window as she turned to confront him. Jack leaned against the door frame, arms folded, watching her and waiting with keen interest and admiration.

"You are more odious than I ever dreamed!" Katie said, her

voice dangerously quiet. "How dare you take over my saloon on this of all mornings? And how dare you pretend that you . . ." She faltered, then took a deep breath and continued, "That you didn't do what you did?!"

Jack suppressed a smile. "Before I answer those charges, it might be helpful to know exactly what you're referring to."

"I am *referring*," she replied, icily ironic, "to your violation of my body last night." Her heart was pounding madly as she said the words. To keep him from seeing how her hands shook, she balled them into fists.

"That's an interesting choice of words," he remarked, looking calmly into her eyes. "Are you suggesting that I forced you?"

Katie's voice rose. "I will not allow you to stand there, the picture of self-possession, and infer that it was I who initiated our—that—what happened!"

"I said no such thing. For God's sake, Kathleen, what we committed was not a crime. It's not necessary to apportion blame! We are adults who have been attracted to each other for some time, and I happen to believe that giving in to our feelings was healthy, not a sign of weakness."

"I did not ask you here to discuss my physical desires, Mr. Adams! They are no concern of *yours*! You obviously broke into my house and seduced me. I was not even aware of what I was doing. I was dreaming!"

He walked toward her. "Kathleen . . ."

"Don't come any closer!" Her blue eyes shot sparks at him.

Jack stopped, then said gently, "You looked at me. You called me by my name."

"I thought I was dreaming!"

"Of me?" he queried softly.

"I don't remember! Why, I barely remember any of it!" Katie's cheeks flamed in betrayal. "It wasn't until I saw the—the evidence, in the daylight, that I realized it had really happened. Still, I tried to think of another explanation. I believed that you were still in San Francisco. Of course, when I came into the saloon this morning and discovered you shamelessly taking over—"

"Unjust!" Jack protested. "I was only trying to help."

"You are an overbearing cad!" Katie cried. "You forced yourself into my bed, and then you had the nerve to impose yourself upon my business! That is the simple truth, and I will not allow you to attempt to justify your behavior!"

He gazed off into the distance for a moment, then shook his head and sighed. "All right. I'm going to admit that what happened last night between us may have been a result of poor judgment on my part—but our lovemaking was completely mutual. You were as eager as I!'' Jack paused to rake a hand through his hair. ''Don't you see, Katie, that what we shared, and what you felt, was not bad. On the contrary—it was natural and beautiful.''

''You took advantage of me.''

''That wasn't the way it happened. I arrived in town late; everything was closed up. I was exhausted, and I thought that I might sleep on your couch. You didn't answer when I knocked. I wasn't even certain you were staying there, so I used my key.''

''You *did* break in!'' she cried triumphantly.

''I wasn't sneaking around. I went straight to your room to inform you of my presence and give you a chance to throw me out. I asked if I might sleep on the couch, and you insisted that I stay there with *you*! I assumed that you . . . that you were lonely, and all I wanted at that moment was a place to close my eyes. Kathleen, I only meant to lie down next to you for a few hours. I don't even remember taking off my clothes—I think I must've pulled them off in my sleep. When you began to snuggle against me, I was only half-conscious—''

''Oh, I see! It was *my* doing! Next you'll say that I seduced you, and you were powerless to resist my advances!''

''Nothing of the kind.'' He strove to keep his voice even. ''But I do think that we both were more inclined to succumb to passion because we were drugged with sleep.''

''I don't remember succumbing to anything,'' she insisted stubbornly. ''All I know is that you forced yourself upon me.''

''I think you remember a great deal more than you are willing to admit, Kathleen.''

The tenderness in his voice was like a caress, and Katie felt a hot chill run down her spine. That was the problem: she did remember, and it was sheer torture. ''Mr. Adams, I feel that it would be pointless for us to continue this conversation. When are you leaving Columbia?''

She was a little fireball with a veneer of ice. Jack's eyes strayed helplessly to Katie's full, rosy mouth, and he almost sighed aloud. Damn, but she was beautiful. ''I'm not quite certain.''

''I thought you came to deliver the platen. Well, you've accomplished that noble goal, so I see no reason for you to linger here.''

He smiled dryly. ''Be that as it may, I cannot make my plans on the basis of your opinions. I have other things to see to here in Columbia, and I have no way of knowing how long that will take.''

Her curiosity was keen, but she affected an attitude of nonchalance. "My goodness, how very mysterious you are, Mr. Adams. Well, I suppose that I shall just have to tolerate your presence in town, but I see no reason why I should have to tolerate your company."

Jack cocked an eyebrow. "Have I been banished from your circle of friends?"

"I think it would be stretching the point to say that we were ever _friends_. And in light of your behavior last night, I see no reason for any further contact between us." Katie tilted her nose upward, thinking it an inspired touch. "Now, if you'll excuse me . . ."

He suppressed a chuckle as she swept past him toward the door. As she turned the knob, he said, "Kathleen, you're a woman. You cannot simply force your desires back into a box and lock it in the attic."

"Once again, sir, you underestimate me!" Katie shot back, then made her exit.

Jack nearly succumbed to an impulse to applaud.

CHAPTER
14

October 14–15, 1864

"Missy Mac want bamboo shoots? Fresh!" Tsing Tsing Yee grinned broadly at Katie across the glass counter of the Chinese store. With his long white queue, silk tunic, and round steel spectacles, Yee looked ancient and fragile. The old man was not even as tall as Katie.

"No, thank you, Mr. Yee. We're cooking Hangtown fry for lunch today. All I need are oysters and eggs."

"Hangtown *fr-ly*?" He repeated the words warily.

"Haven't you heard of it?" Katie exclaimed, her eyes dancing. "My father told me that he was in Placerville back when it was called Hangtown. A miner who had just made a strike came into the Cary House when Papa was having lunch, and demanded the most expensive dish in the house. He was told that the most expensive *ingredients* were oysters and eggs, which cost a dollar apiece. Well, the cook scrambled the eggs with some onions, then folded in oysters, and the dish was christened 'Hangtown fry'!"

"But—" Tsing Tsing Yee sounded perplexed. "But it not new! It egg foo yung! Chinese!"

Katie succumbed to laughter, and Lim, who stood nearby, joined in. "Of course it is!" he assured the old man. "The cook must have been Chinese, too. But white people don't want to know that, or hear that one of us is cooking their food, or they would have to

125

worry about rat's tails or cat's paws in their food. And they can't admit to liking Chinese food, either. They give our dishes new names and pretend they made them for the first time!''

Yee scratched his head as Lim wandered away to study the shelves of spices. ''I don't understand.''

''To tell you the truth, Mr. Yee, neither do I,'' Katie admitted.

He returned to more familiar ground. ''You want mushrooms?'' he said, holding up a box of dark, dried fungi. ''Two kinds. Imported! And fresh, too!'' The small, wizened old man turned, pointing to a bin filled with grayish mushrooms. Katie noticed that Tsing's queue was so thin now that it made only a tiny line down his back, as if it had been drawn there.

She returned his hopeful smile. ''Yes, some mushrooms would be nice. I'll take a handful or two of the fresh ones.''

As he assembled her purchases, Katie browsed around the dim, cool store. Lim was staring at the glass containers of exotic spices that lined one wall. Indeed, everything seemed exotic in this place, even the smells—incense, coriander, pungent bottled sauces, Chinese vegetables, dried fish, peppers, jasmine tea. Tsing Tsing Yee and his wife also sold Chinese silk, fireworks, and, it was rumored along the Caucasian population, opium. Katie had grown up eating Chinese food at Lim Sung's house, and she loved it. It seemed a shame to her that rampant fear and mistrust of the Chinese had prevented her people from discovering Chinese cooking. Now that so many ''celestials'' had been driven from Columbia, Tsing Tsing Yee's business was beginning to founder.

''Katie, have you seen Mr. Yee's egg?'' Lim called softly from the back of the store.

''Not since I was a little girl,'' she replied, going to join him. ''He showed it to Mama and me.''

Yee was taking a beautifully decorated lacquer box from a cupboard. Smiling serenely, he opened it and withdrew a glass case. In it was an exquisite, intricately carved jade egg.

''From Tang dynasty,'' Yee explained in hushed tones. ''Very, very valuable. Egg has always been in my family.''

Katie stared, awestruck. ''I've never seen anything more beautiful.''

''I'll bet it's worth more than all the gold that's ever been weighed at Wells Fargo,'' Lim declared.

Another voice remarked, ''I wouldn't be surprised if you're right.''

The three of them looked up, startled, and saw Aaron Rush drawing near. Although he was a heavyset man, his tread was light and nearly soundless. Smiles wreathed his plump, pink face, and the top of his bald head glistened with beads of perspiration. As usual, Rush wore a brown suit, waistcoat, and a pearl stickpin in his black silk tie. From his breast pocket he withdrew a wilted brown silk handkerchief and applied it vigorously to his brow. "That's quite a treasure you have there, Mr. Yee. Mind if I have a closer look?"

Hesitantly, Yee opened the fingers that he had folded protectively over the glass case at the sound of Aaron Rush's voice. "I put it back now," he said as soon as the mine owner had glimpsed the egg. Moments later the case and its black box were locked safely in the cupboard.

"I don't suppose you're interested in selling that egg," Rush said genially.

"No!" Tsing Tsing Yee cried instantly, his face drawing up in an expression of fear.

"Just asking, friend, just asking!" Rush laughed and clapped a beefy hand on the old man's shoulder. "No need to panic! Now then, might I speak to you privately? It's rather important."

Tsing asked his wife to come out and finish Katie's transaction. Katie stood at the counter and took her time counting the money, one ear strained to catch bits of the conversation between the elderly Chinese and Aaron Rush. They were in the back room, but the door was ajar just enough to permit their voices to filter out when the pitch rose high enough.

Katie said nothing, but she studied Ah Yee. She was a beautiful old woman, as tiny as her husband, with skin like crinkled parchment. From time to time, Ah glanced toward the back of the store, clearly perturbed. Finally Lim spoke.

"Mrs. Yee, is something wrong?"

"Big man want to buy store. Keeps saying he pay more and more. He smile, but not in his eyes," she said sadly.

Katie covered the old woman's wrinkled hand with her own. "Don't worry, Mrs. Yee. Everything will be all right."

"I hope so. Tsing not strong anymore." She looked down and sighed.

Outside, Katie strode angrily down Main Street, her basket swinging in the sunlight. "Why doesn't that man leave us alone? I hoped so much that this evil would end when Van Hosten was killed. I hoped that some good might come of Papa's death. . . ."

"Well, I think that the truth about Aaron Rush has been slow to come to light," Lim said thoughtfully. "We hoped for the best, and he's deceiving."

"I *know*!" Katie cried. "We hardly ever saw him when Van Hosten was alive, and when he did appear in town, he was always so jovial. I doubted that he even knew what his partner was up too. I really believed that everything would be different with Rush in charge."

"Many people are still misled by him. It was his apparent kindness that convinced my parents to sell their land at last."

Katie looked grim. "Well, now that we have a platen for the printing press . . ."

"Thanks to Jack Adams," Lim put in.

"We can start putting out the *Gazette* again. I intend to write an editorial that will expose, once and for all, what Aaron Rush and his cronies are all about!"

"Katie, I think you ought to be a bit more cautious." Lim stopped, noticing that her attention had been diverted to the bench in front of the City Hotel. On it sat Jack Adams and a stunningly beautiful young lady. She wore a stylish black-and-white-striped silk day gown with a braided hem and let her matching parasol drop back to reveal wavy chestnut hair drawn into a flattering chignon. Her face was lit by a radiant, adoring smile that Katie recognized all too well.

"Who's that with Jack?" she whispered.

"Maggie Barnstaple. She's Mrs. Barnstaple's niece. Abby said that she was sent here from New York after some sort of scandal."

"Hmm. She looks the type." Katie's cheeks were flushed. "Miss Barnstaple had better take heed, or she'll find herself in the midst of a worse scandal, courtesy of Mr. Adams."

"What's wrong, Katie? You sound jealous."

She hurried on ahead of him, her braid flying. "I'm going to pretend you didn't say that, Lim. Otherwise, it might mean the end of our friendship!"

A cloud of dust rose as Katie attempted to straighten the papers littering Gideon's desk at the *Gazette*. As usual, cleaning the office was a task that seemed endless. Sneezing repeatedly, her eyes full of tears, she fumbled for a handkerchief. When one appeared in her hand, she gave it no thought until she had wiped her eyes and blown her nose. Then she looked up, expecting to find Lim at her side.

"Please don't yell at me, Kathleen. You're in my debt now, remember!" Jack Adams's voice was husky with amusement.

For a frightening moment, she couldn't get her breath, over-whelmed by the sight of him. Jack just seemed to get better looking each time they met, which maddened Katie no end. Today she was keenly aware of his sage-green eyes with their flecks of gold. Under slightly hooded lids, they seemed sharp and lazy at the same time. And they were knowing. Katie felt as if they absorbed all her secrets at a glance. "What are you doing here?" she demanded. Thinking meanwhile that she must look frightful, her hair coming down, her face smudged, the tip of her nose red from sneezing.

The corners of Jack's sensual mouth curved slowly upward. "I heard that you were going to start up the *Gazette* again, and I felt it was my responsibility to make certain that the new platen was in working order. After all, it hasn't been tested on this press."

"More likely you stopped by to remind me of your generosity and to corner me into thanking you." For an instant she was abashed at her rudeness, knowing full well that as a representative of the *Gazette*, she *did* owe him a vote of thanks. But then pride overcame her better instincts, and she couldn't resist adding, "In any case, I'm surprised that you were able to find the time in your busy schedule."

Jack had been walking toward the printing press, but Katie's words stopped him dead. "What an interesting thing to say!" He turned to stare at her, wide-eyed. "Knowledge derived from my extensive dealings with women over the years leads me to suspect that there might have been a current of jealousy behind your words. But of course, that's impossible, isn't it?"

She damned the traitorous blood that rushed to her cheeks. "Absolutely!"

"Yes, because you despise me, isn't that right? I am an overbearing cad, if memory serves me, and you desire only to sever all contact between us—forever!" He spread his hands wide in a gesture of anticipation. "Dare I hope that you've changed your mind?"

"Certainly not!" Katie cried.

"Well, it's been three days, which in some matters could be defined as forever, don't you think? Your interest in my 'busy schedule,' as you put it—by which I assume you mean the time I've spent with the charming Miss Barnstaple"—he gave her a devilish grin—"has prompted me to hope that you might have had a change of heart."

Katie was furious. How dare he laugh at her? "*Mr.* Adams," she said, mustering her iciest tone of voice, "let me assure you that I have not experienced a change of heart where you are concerned. I wish I could completely erase you from my life, past and present."

One of Jack's sun-bleached eyebrows flicked upward slightly. "Those are cold words, Kathleen."

"I mean them." Pride threatened to choke her.

"In that case," he replied, turning back to the platen, "you won't need to clutter your mind with thoughts of my social activities. Since there is nothing between us whatsoever, it's only natural that I should seek female companionship elsewhere."

"My only concern is for Miss Barnstaple's welfare," Katie said, bristling. "You have a way of infecting unsuspecting females with the stench of scandal."

Jack kept his eyes on the platen as he worked, but his voice was hard. "You're on the edge, my dear. Watch your step."

Returning her attention to the papers on Gideon's desk, Katie found that her hands shook and she could hear the pounding of her heart. Frantically, without giving thought to what she was doing, she arranged everything into piles. When Jack walked back across the office, approaching the desk, Katie didn't look up. She prayed he would leave without another word.

"Let me know when you're ready to print," he said tonelessly. "I want to be certain that it's working properly."

"You needn't bother. Besides, what do you know about printing presses?" She heard the tremor in her voice. "Just because you found a platen for this press, that hardly makes you an expert! I'm sure that I know more about it than you ever—"

His bronzed hand shot out to grip her forearm. "Why don't you hold your tongue for a change?" he growled. "You haven't the slightest idea what I do and do not know. I went to a lot of trouble to get that platen up here, and I'll be damned if I'll let you order me to stay away from it!"

Katie struggled to free herself, but his fingers were like steel on her flesh. "Let go of me, you savage! I'll have Gideon tell you himself if that's what it takes to keep you away!"

"Fine. You do that." Jack's eyes flashed with rage. "Oh, and one more thing, Miss MacKenzie. Stay clear of Aaron Rush. Write about the church social and your latest recipe for soup, but if you value your life, you won't write any more about Rush and his mine."

"Get out!" she screamed.

Jack released her then and strode out the door, which banged shut behind him. Katie threw a bronze paperweight at the door, fighting an urge to weep. She hated Jack so much, her heart threatened to break.

* * *

"What I need is *proof*!" Katie declared, setting a piece of lemon custard pie in front of Gideon.

When he picked up his fork, the pain in his shoulder made him wince. "If only I hadn't tried to lift those pots the other day. . . ."

"Helping Abby again? Your newfound chivalry will do you in yet!" She was smiling, but there was a note of frustration in her voice. "Oh, Gideon, I wish you were well—well enough to come back to work at the *Gazette*."

"Yes, of course, so do I." This wasn't entirely true, for he was reveling in the days spent with Abby, though still uncertain what these new feelings meant. "Now, tell me, what's all this about 'proof'?"

"I need to find some evidence that Aaron Rush has been threatening and blackmailing people to get their land, just as he and Van Hosten did to get hold of people's claims in the past. If I'm going to write an editorial exposing him, I must have some facts to back up my allegations—"

"Katie, my dear, I don't think that would be a good idea." Gideon strove to sound calm, looking around the saloon to make certain no one could overhear them. "Jack was telling me that it would be wise to lie low for the time being and just keep an eye on Rush. He thinks that—"

"Don't bore me with Mr. Adams's thoughts on this or any other subject!" she cried. "I despise that man! He delights in interfering in my life, even going so far as to poke his nose into the activities at the *Gazette*. That's one of the reasons I miss you so much, Gideon. If you were there, he wouldn't be able to meddle because you would be able to test the new platen yourself."

Gideon stared, nonplussed. He still hadn't decided what to make of the animosity between Katie and Jack, but one thing was clear: although Katie had seemed to be living on the brink of frenzy these past few days, she was more *alive* than at any time since Brian's death. Now, watching her get up to pace between the table and the bar, Gideon took a careful breath.

"Katie, I know you won't enjoy hearing this, but I like Jack and I appreciate the interest he's shown in the *Gazette* during my recuperation. Do you have any idea how much trouble he went to getting that platen all the way up here? Not to mention the fact that it didn't cost me a cent—"

"How could he charge you for something you didn't order?"

Gideon tilted his head in a gesture of mild admonishment. "Now, Katie . . ."

"Well, it's true," she muttered.

"I think you're being unfair to the man."

She whirled around, eyes flashing. "Hasn't it occurred to you that I might have reasons? That perhaps *he's* been unfair to me?"

"Obviously, since you haven't shared the facts behind your quarrel with Jack, I am unaware of anything beyond the unreasonable attitude you have toward him. As for myself, I like him and I trust him. Furthermore, I have asked him to do what he can to help at the *Gazette* in my absence, and he was kind enough to agree." Gideon met Katie's furious gaze, adding, "He agreed in spite of the fact that it must be distinctly unpleasant for him to have to deal with you."

Her mouth fell open in shock. "Unpleasant for *him*? How can you say such a thing? Gideon Henderson, I thought you were my friend!"

"I am, but that doesn't mean I have to condone your behavior. I am also the editor of a newspaper, which I would like to see resume production in my absence. Jack apparently has worked on a paper in the past, and I am grateful for whatever expertise he can contribute."

Katie's cheeks were pink with frustration. "But you certainly can't mean to let him dictate what we'll print!"

"I have respect for the man's judgment. If he feels that it would be dangerous to print negative editorials about Aaron Rush at this time, I think it would be wise to take that advice. At least for the time being."

"Well, I don't! Have you forgotten that my father is dead, partially as a result of Rush and Van Hosten?" she exclaimed. "That's the trouble with people in this town—they've been too cautious for too long. Whatever happened to freedom of the press?"

"I haven't forgotten about Brian, or all the others who have opposed Rush and Van Hosten and been harmed as a result. Aaron Rush is a powerful man, Katie, and it may be that other means besides confrontation will have to be employed to bring him down."

"In the meantime," she insisted, "the townspeople of Columbia need to be informed of his methods before anyone else is bullied into selling valuable property. Don't look so worried, Gideon! I won't print anything without proof." Turning on her heel, she started toward the saloon door, calling to Lim behind the bar, "I have to go out for a while."

When she pushed open the door, she nearly collided with a man on his way in. Katie glanced at him and kept on going, calico skirts flying.

Jack Adams paused for a moment to watch her departing figure, then continued on into the saloon. He nodded to Gideon, then inclined his head toward the saloon door. "I don't think she likes me," he murmured, his tone dry.

The younger man sighed. "Katie isn't especially fond of me either right now. Do you have a moment to sit with me, Jack? I thought we ought to talk. . . ."

CHAPTER
15

October 15, 1864

A SOFT BREEZE RUFFLED THE LEAVES OF THE COTTONWOOD trees surrounding the recently completed St. Andrew's Presbyterian Church. It was a plain but handsome wooden building with turrets and a tall square tower that housed a copper bell that had been shipped around Cape Horn. Hauled the rest of the way to Columbia by mule freighter, the bell had just arrived a few days ago and now pealed joyously in the sunlight, urging the townspeople to come and worship God.

Katie was in need of church this morning. The last three days had been confusing and frustrating, to say the least. It felt good now to be buttoned into a prim white blouse, Mary MacKenzie's cameo pinned at her neck and her bible clasped tight in her hand. With Abby beside her, she walked from Jackson Street up the grassy slope to the church. Both of them were preoccupied, but Abby suddenly broke the silence.

"Oh, Katie, I nearly forgot! It doesn't make any sense to me, but Lim asked me to tell you that your friend Tsing Tsing Yee's egg is missing. Do you know what that means?"

"Missing?" Katie stopped for a moment, stricken. "Does that mean stolen?"

"I don't know. Mr. Yee told Lim that he went to get it out last night and it was gone. Was it an egg that he wanted to eat?"

"No, no, it was a very valuable piece of Chinese art," Katie replied distractedly. As they walked the rest of the way to church, she remained preoccupied, held by the conviction that here at last was a chance to prove the full extent of Aaron Rush's villainy. It seemed obvious to her that Rush had stolen the egg, not merely out of greed, but also as a means of pressuring and frightening Tsing Tsing Yee into selling his store and the land under it. Horrid man! Katie raged silently. If she could find evidence that he had taken it, or better yet, if she could recover the egg, she could use the *Gazette* to demand that he be punished and forced to leave Columbia.

A familiar voice broke into her reverie. "Good morning, Miss MacKenzie, Mrs. Armitage. Have you met Miss Barnstaple? She's new to Columbia and longs for some female friends."

Katie pivoted to behold Jack Adams and Maggie Barnstaple standing under a large blue spruce. Maggie's chestnut hair was coiled at the base of her neck, and she carried a pagoda-style parasol that matched her stylish green-and-pink silk gown. She and Jack made a handsome couple, Katie was forced to admit. Clad in a well-tailored gray suit, immaculate white shirt, and pearly-gray silk waistcoat with a matching tie, he looked every inch the gentleman. With his tanned face, tawny hair, and glittering green eyes, Jack was also the most attractive man Katie had ever seen. That realization made her dislike him more than ever.

"How do you do, Miss Barnstaple?" she inquired politely.

"I'm very well, thank you," Maggie replied. "It's a pleasure to meet you both."

"Welcome to Columbia," Abby said with a warm smile. "Did you have a long journey?"

"Very long. I came from New York."

"Goodness!" Katie feigned surprise. "Why ever would you want to travel all this way?"

Maggie flushed prettily. "I came to visit my aunt, Miss Mac-Kenzie."

Deciding not to press the issue, Katie said, "No doubt you have found a kindred soul in Mr. Adams, since he is also new to Columbia and in need of friends. Well, we should be going in now. So pleased to have met you, Miss Barnstaple."

Maggie Barnstaple watched the two young women enter the church, then turned to Jack. "My goodness! I think that Miss MacKenzie is in love with you!"

"Do you indeed?" Jack chuckled softly. "That's the most improbable statement you've made yet. She would be the first person to set you straight."

"Well, of course—because she doesn't know it yet." Maggie ignored his exclamation of laughter. "I recognize all the signs. I was that way when I first met Peter, when I thought that he was unattainable. Of course, even after his divorce, my parents saw to it that I still couldn't have him."

"But you mean to wait it out," Jack put in. "Women are very stubborn when it comes to matters of the heart. Have you never thought that you might just as easily fall in love with someone else?"

"Certainly not! Of course, my parents are hoping that I will do something just that frivolous and fickle." She closed her parasol with a crisp snap. "It will *not* happen! Peter and I are meant to be together. The knowledge that he loves me and is waiting for me is all that sustains me through these months of enforced exile in California. When I return to New York in the spring, and my parents see that nothing has changed, they'll have no choice but to consent to our marriage." Softening slightly, Maggie smiled and touched Jack's arm. "Your friendship sustains me, too, Jack. It's a pleasant experience to be friends with a man, and your company is most enjoyable."

"It's pleasant for me as well, knowing that there will be no romantic complications between us. I've been snarled in those too often lately." He smiled down at her. "I like you, Maggie. Now, shall we go in to church?"

Thundershowers threatened that afternoon as Jack sat in the City Hotel's tiny lobby, where he had taken a room. Reclining on a chair of tufted maroon velvet, he perused a three-day-old copy of the *Sacramento Union*, given to him by the stagecoach driver.

Half of the front page was filled with advertisements for available jobs, jewelry for sale, dentistry, and assorted improbable medicinal potions. The Eureka Bath House and Barber Shop announced "cupping and leeching," adding that they would dye hair and whiskers any color desired. Jack saw that the Miss M. Atkins's Young Ladies' Seminary in Benicia was resuming operations.

He skipped ahead to a long letter from the *Union*'s "lady correspondent" about life in Paris. She was particularly irate about the lack of respect Frenchmen displayed toward women, citing that the testimony of "women, criminals, and children" was not accepted as positive evidence in court, and that Frenchwomen could not walk more than a few steps in public without being insulted. Jack reflected that females seemed to have no such discrimination problems in Sacramento, since the next long article was also written by a woman and concerned her visit to the West Point Military Academy. And that completed the *Union*'s front page, the bulk of which had been written by women. Jack sighed and shook his head. The days of the male-dominated newspaper seemed to be over.

He folded the tattered pages for a moment and thought about Katie and her dogged determination to singlehandedly resume production of the *Gazette*. She was willful and feisty, but to himself he could admit that he admired her strength. Katie had battled on alone after Brian's death, not merely coping, but also running the saloon in his stead. Jack liked the fact that she stood up to him, never acting coy or mooning over him. And yet he could never forget that Katie was a woman. She might braid her hair and cover her body with prim gowns, but he was acutely aware of her innocent sensuality. The memory of their lovemaking was fresh and exciting each time he called it up. Katie's artless passion had infused every kiss, caress, and arch of her hips . . .

Forcing himself back to reality, Jack thought over his conversation with Gideon Henderson. The younger man had spoken of his concern for Katie's welfare and asked that Jack keep an eye on her, despite her demands that he stay as far away as possible.

Jack stood up and stretched lazily. Just because it was Sunday, that didn't mean that Kathleen MacKenzie was resting. . . .

The white frame boardinghouse that overlooked Washington Street next to the offices of the *Columbia Gazette* was owned and run by Mrs. Pondhollow, a garrulous old woman who was known to collar weary miners and solicit business on the street. Today, apparently, was no exception. Jack, clad in snug miner's dungarees and a slate-blue shirt, awakened her interest as soon as he rounded the corner from Main Street.

"Good day to you, sonny!" Mrs. Pondhollow tottered forward on two canes to the edge of the wooden sidewalk. "You look like a young man in need of a cozy room and a hot meal. I just happen to have an opening!"

Jack paused before her, shielding his eyes against the sun, and grinned. "Mrs. Pondhollow, we've had this conversation twice in the past three days. Don't you remember? I already have a room at the City Hotel."

She pursed her lips into a withered smile. "What do you want with that fancy place? I can promise you a clean bed," she boasted. "No bugs! And my cooking is legendary."

"Let me strike a bargain with you. I'll give you some money to reserve one of your lovely rooms, but I'm not certain I'll be able to stay here. Don't worry about me if I don't turn up, all right?''

Mrs. Pondhollow's gray eyes glinted. ''I suppose that's fair. Shall I save you some of my delicious venison pot roast and baked squash?''

''No, thank you, I have other plans for dinner.''

''Plans? Hmmph! Probably carousing at one of them dance halls!'' She waggled a finger at Jack. ''It's the devil's work, son!''

He handed Mrs. Pondhollow a five-dollar bill, which was several times more than the price of one of her rooms, and then backed away. ''Nice to see you, ma'am. Good afternoon!''

She watched him, eyes narrowed and canes trembling, until he entered the *Gazette* office. Then, muttering, ''It's the devil's work!'' she backed shakily onto her chair and resumed her vigil for the next unwary victim.

Jack found the *Gazette*'s front door ajar and entered so silently that Katie didn't hear him. She was bent over a table covered with trays of type, proofreading the original copy of her latest creation.

Jack paused in the doorway for a few moments to imagine the curves of her hips and bottom under the layers of petticoats and skirt. He couldn't help remembering the feel of Katie snuggling backward against his loins, and he sighed involuntarily. She jumped and whirled around.

''*You!* What are *you* doing here?''

Jack gave her his most disarming smile and ran tanned fingers through his hair. ''Gideon asked me to keep an eye on you. For some reason, he's worried that you might print something . . . dangerous.''

''Ridiculous!'' Katie exploded. ''I will not be treated like a child simply because I am *female*. I don't need any assistance from you to put out the *Gazette*—or from Gideon Henderson, for that matter.''

''Gideon might see things a bit differently. . . .''

''What are you talking about?'' she snapped.

''Well, I think he might argue that he has every right to interfere since he *owns* the *Gazette*.'' Jack spoke with wry irony, then softened his tone. ''Don't you see, though, the issue isn't power. Gideon is less concerned with retaining control over the contents of the newspaper than with keeping you safe, Kathleen. We're both worried that your headstrong tendencies will get you into trouble, particularly when it comes to dealing with Aaron Rush and his cronies.''

''It seems to me that men do not concern themselves with their male friends' 'headstrong tendencies' in this matter. You do not rush around trying to protect each other from doing something risky. It just so happens that I am quick-witted, and I am also smart enough to proceed with caution. I need neither a nursemaid nor a guard.'' Katie lifted her chin. ''And I particularly don't need *you*!''

He tried another tack, replying gently, ''You know, when your father was alive, he knew how to counsel you in ways that kept you out of danger. I think he'd want someone to look out for you now. I was very fond of Brian, and I—''

''Oh, no, you don't!'' she cried. ''Don't you dare tell me that you are behaving as my father would have wished! Would he have condoned what you did to me the other night?''

Her words were like a slap in the face, and Jack winced slightly. Privately he suspected that Brian MacKenzie might have realized that it was time Katie unleashed her passions, but he could never say so to her. ''What happened between us was not a willed choice on my part. . . .''

''Nor on mine! Now, leave me alone.'' She turned back to the typeset article and tried to concentrate, but all her senses were alive and tingling. When Jack walked up behind her, Katie caught a whiff of his scent, a mixture of shaving soap, fresh air, and something indefinably male. A sweet, maddening longing swept over her.

Jack looked over Katie's shoulder and read: YEE EGG STOLEN! The facts were laid out in the story that followed, but the text was also interlaced subtly with hints and speculation. The final paragraph read: ''Who could have committed this heartless crime, and why? Privately, some townsfolk have suggested that certain men in power might have reason to terrorize Tsing Tsing Yee. The longtime storeowner has refused to sell his property at any price, and some suspect that the valuable Tang dynasty egg, estimated to be nearly 1,200 years old, may have been stolen in part to frighten its owner. Will a worse crime be committed if Yee does not succumb to this latest pressure?''

As Jack read, he reached forward to brace himself lightly on the edge of the table. Katie glanced beneath her lashes at his strong, sun-bronzed hand, staring at the fingertips that had caressed her so intimately a few nights before. For an instant, she yearned to touch the golden hair that glinted on the back of his hand.

''You can't print this,'' Jack said suddenly, his voice hard. The spell was broken.

''I beg your pardon?''

''You were smart, Miss MacKenzie, setting up this story on a Sunday afternoon, when you thought no one would bother you. But fortunately I can keep up with your agile mind. There is absolutely no possibility of this article seeing the light of day."

Katie flushed slightly. Jack knew her better than she'd realized, for it was true that she had assumed he'd be otherwise occupied with Maggie Barnstaple after church and therefore wouldn't interfere with her work at the *Gazette*. "Don't you have anything better to do than harass me?"

He leaned forward and spoke softly in her ear. "There probably are other things I do better. I'd be glad to show you—again—after you remove this type."

"You are a despicable scoundrel!" She whirled around to confront him and found his lips a mere breath away from hers. Pulling back as if she'd been burned, Katie cried, "I will not allow you to bully me any more than I will stand by silently while Aaron Rush bullies Tsing Tsing Yee! Something has to be done, and—"

"You haven't any proof. You can't print veiled accusations like this," Jack said flatly.

The overpowering nearness of him was making her dizzy. "I'm going to *get* proof!" she vowed, turning her back on him.

Leaning forward so that Katie's body was imprisoned against his, Jack reached forward with his free hand and began to pull out the type letter by letter. "No, you're not. You are going to forget about this and concentrate instead on living a long and healthy life."

Katie thrashed about wildly, grabbing at his hand, until Jack caught her wrists and held them in a grip of steel. Fury boiled up inside her, and she began to scream. "Monster! I hate you! I *hate* you! You have no right! Let *go* of me!"

"You have the damnedest propensity for making seemingly simple situations incredibly complicated! For God's sake, Kathleen, where did you get the idea that you were responsible for upholding law and order in Columbia?" With an effort, he emptied the last row of type and scattered the pieces across the table.

"*Someone* has to show some concern for justice in this town! No one else seems to give a fig about it . . . except, of course, for our erstwhile champion, the Griffin!" She laughed with false gaiety. "And what a hero *he* turned out to be! In the end, he proved himself a coward like all the rest. After he killed my father, he just slunk away." With one last flurry of resistance, Katie broke free and spun around to face Jack. Almost instantly he had her wrists pinned against her sides. Their bodies were pressed full length, hearts thudding in unison through the layers of clothing that separated them.

"You can't stop me from setting the type again," Katie challenged through clenched teeth.

Jack stared down into her fiery sapphire eyes with a mixture of exasperation and admiration. She made him frustrated, but never bored. In Katie's presence Jack felt keenly, unmistakably *alive*. How ravishing she looked, her cheekbones smudged with rosy color, her exquisite little nose flaring slightly, her full lips parted, her neck arched. Her breasts were like brands against his chest. Instinctively he bent his head, pausing just above her mouth so that their breath mingled.

Katie was so hungry for his kiss that she could barely speak. "Don't you dare kiss me," she gasped.

Jack's green eyes widened, then crinkled at the corners. "I apologize. I don't know what came over me." He drew back. "There, you see? I'm not the brute you accuse me of being. I would never kiss a woman against her will."

Dangerously close to tears, Katie exclaimed, "Just go away and leave me alone!"

"Ah, well, as you might have guessed, I am unable to grant that request. I can't leave you here to typeset that story again." He sighed with mock regret.

"You can't stay here forever!" she cried, enraged.

"I have no intention of doing so." Jack's voice was infuriatingly calm. "As you yourself pointed out, I have better things to do. However, I do have this little problem to take care of first. The obvious solution, as I see it, is to remove *you* from this office."

"What are you talking about? I don't want to leave here. I have work to do!"

"I'm afraid it's for your own good, Miss MacKenzie. You need to rest. If it will make you feel any better, *I'll* write a new story about Tsing Tsing Yee's missing egg. Just the facts. Now then, did you bring a reticule? . . ." The picture of gentlemanly concern, he glanced around the office.

Katie gripped the edge of the table. "I *won't* leave."

Picking up her reticule, Jack walked toward her. His green eyes glowed with the exhilaration of mastering such a challenge. "I'm afraid that you must."

"You can't force me!" Katie's voice rose.

"But, you see, I can," he replied mildly. And with one easy movement, he put his hands around her waist and slung her over his shoulder.

"Heathen!" Katie screamed.

Clasping an arm around her knees to hold her securely, Jack

strode out the door. He took the keys from her reticule, locked the door, then slipped the keys into his pocket. Mrs. Pondhollow tottered forward on her porch to watch their progress down Washington Street. Katie was pummeling Jack's back, to no avail.

"Don't you bother to claim your room, sonny!" the old woman screeched.

He turned his head, laughing. "Let me guess. You won't refund the money."

"Not to your sort!" Mrs. Pondhollow affirmed, patting the five-dollar bill in her pocket. "And don't come begging around here next time you need a place to stay!"

"You have my word, dear lady!"

Katie continued to struggle, ignoring the alarmed stares of passersby, right up until Jack carried her through the saloon and deposited her in the kitchen. Abby was peeling potatoes at the big worktable, chatting with Gideon, who sat on a chair next to the window. Although the MacKenzie Saloon did not serve liquor on Sundays, patrons were always welcome for dinner.

"Gideon!" Katie cried. "This brute has demolished a story I spent hours writing and typesetting, and now he's locked me out of the *Gazette* office! Not to mention the indignity I have suffered at his hands as he carried me like a sack of flour up Main Street!" Her cheeks were aflame with indignation.

Gideon stared at Jack, trying not to smile. "Did you do *that*?"

"It was the only way, I'm afraid." Jack smiled at his friend. "Miss MacKenzie's story about the theft of Yee's jade egg was filled with thinly veiled suggestions that the crime had been committed by Aaron Rush, accompanied by an evaluation of the suspect's character and allusions to his past wrongs. It seemed to me that—"

"You needn't go on," Gideon broke in. "I can guess the rest." He looked at Katie. "How many times do I have to tell you—"

"Don't you scold me! I refuse to be humiliated any further by either of you—you *men*!" Turning her back on them, she glanced through the doorway to the saloon . . . and nearly gasped aloud. Aaron Rush was walking in, accompanied by a stranger who was well dressed to the point of gaudiness. The man wore huge sidewhiskers, a large beaver hat, ruby shirt studs, and a heavy watch chain, and he carried a ruby-topped walking stick. Katie immediately sensed that the proof she sought might well be at hand, if she could only eavesdrop on their conversation.

But first she had to get rid of Jack Adams and keep him from seeing Rush in the process.

"Katie," Gideon was saying, "neither of us means to scold you or treat you like a child. But I can't help being concerned about the fact that you seem determined to place yourself in danger. Not to mention *me*—and our new platen!"

"I'm only trying to do what's *right*," Katie protested. "It seems that I'm the only person left in Columbia who loves justice!"

Jack cocked an eyebrow at Gideon, who rolled his eyes. "I don't know what's come over you," Gideon said to Katie. "I've never seen you with so much . . . fire. It's only been since . . ." His voice trailed off as he met Abby's eyes, then glanced at Jack.

Katie looked out the window, blushing deeply. "I haven't the faintest idea what you're talking about." Lifting her chin, she looked at Jack. "Mr. Adams, if you don't mind, I have work to do. I'd appreciate it if you'd leave—by the back door."

He gave her a reckless grin. "Whatever makes you happy, ma'am."

A smile spread over Katie's face as she watched his departing back. "I feel better already. Abby, could I have a word with you in the storeroom?" They had just begun to walk down the back hallway when she remembered Gideon and turned to shake a playful finger at him. "You must be all worn out from scolding me, but now it's my turn to treat you like a child, and you owe me some indulgence. You stay right where you are and rest. I don't want you to *move*!"

CHAPTER
16

October 15–16, 1864

"Before we go any further, you must give me your word that you won't breathe a word of this to anyone," Katie whispered. "Especially Gideon!"

Abby looked worried. "Is it something dangerous?"

"Don't be silly. Of course not! Would I ask you do anything that would put you at risk? It's just that I find Gideon's overprotective attitude rather annoying."

"I had noticed," Abby said with a weak smile.

"We are grown women after all, and have a right to some independence. We can think for ourselves, can't we?"

"Yes . . ."

"Don't look so nervous!" Katie gave her a big smile and patted her arm. "I'd never admit it to Ja—that is, Mr. Adams, but he was probably right about the article I wrote. It couldn't go to press as it was. I need to have some proof that Aaron Rush stole Mr. Yee's egg, and you can help me get it!"

"I can?" Abby paled.

"You won't be doing anything wrong. Aaron Rush has come into the saloon for supper, and he's with a man I don't recognize. All I want you to do is give them the best service possible, stay near their table almost the entire time they're eating. Offer them more coffee, extra cream, things like that. And when you aren't waiting on them, busy yourself nearby so that you can hear what they're saying. You just might be able to provide the clue I need."

She tugged at a stray golden curl. "Well, I owe you so much, I'd do anything I could to help you, Katie."

"I knew I could count on you! Now, you just go on out there and be your own sweet self. Give them a big smile and don't worry about a thing. I'll take care of the cooking—and Gideon. Then, when Rush and his guest leave, we'll meet back here. All right?"

"I'll do my best."

"That's the spirit!" Katie pointed Abby toward the door and gave her a little nudge. "Good luck!"

For the next hour, Katie cooked, heaped plates with food, and chatted gaily with Gideon. Occasionally she passed by the doorway to the saloon, where she saw Abby hovering over Aaron Rush and his dandified friend. Abby's performance was impeccable. She was always near them, fluffing her burnished curls with a dimpled hand and displaying her bosom before their appreciative eyes. Finally, as the men applied themselves to generous portions of cranberry pudding, Abby glanced toward the doorway and flashed a triumphant smile above their heads. Katie's heart raced with excitement.

As soon as Rush and his guest had departed, Katie gave Gideon a bowl of pudding to keep him occupied and hurried toward the storage room. Abby was waiting for her, her cheeks flushed with excitement.

"That was fun," she whispered, nearly giggling. "I felt like one of those spies!"

Katie could scarcely contain herself. "What did they say?"

"Well, it sounded like the rich-looking gentleman had come all the way from San Francisco. While they were eating dessert, I heard him say, 'I'm eager to see the item. It sounds like just what I've been looking for. One of my clients collects artifacts in that line. When can I see it?' "

Katie clapped her hands with glee. "And what did Rush reply?"

"He dropped his voice real low, and I started talking to another customer at the next table so he wouldn't suspect anything. But I heard him say, 'I'm keeping it away from town, Mr. Armbrewster. We'll have to go by horseback. Can you be ready at six o'clock tomorrow morning?' And the other fellow nodded. Then Mr. Rush says, 'Good. Meet me at the livery stable, all right?' They agreed, then Mr. Rush looked around for me and asked for the bill." Abby's revelations had tumbled out, but now she paused. Then, after a moment, she ventured, "Was that any help? Perhaps you can tell Jack and he'll follow them."

"Yes, of course, that's a wonderful idea," Katie replied distractedly. "But you leave it to me. You don't have to give this matter another thought, Abby. You've done your part splendidly!"

At a quarter to six that next morning, Katie stood in the now vacant icehouse behind the livery stable. During the winter, the ice man took his high-sided freight wagons to the frozen lakes of the Sierras and returned with huge blocks of ice. Properly insulated and stored with several inches of sawdust between them, the past year's ice had lasted through early September. Now the ice man was away visiting his daughter in Sacramento, and Katie was grateful for this hiding place. She stood stroking the velvety nose of her horse, Willoughby, a gray gelding named for the scoundrel in Jane Austen's *Sense and Sensibility*. Her eyes strayed restlessly from one side of the livery stable to the other as she waited for Rush and Armbrewster to appear.

Katie was proud of her disguise. In a pair of old dungarees, battered boots, and a warm gray flannel shirt, she could easily pass as a slight, harmless teenage boy—particularly once she'd pinned up her braided hair and covered it with a large brown felt hat that had belonged to her father.

At last she saw them, entering separately, then emerging onto Fulton Street astride the stable's two best horses. She waited a few minutes before walking Willoughby out onto the street. Rush and Armbrewster were barely in sight, heading east on Yankee Hill Road.

Keeping a safe distance behind them, Katie was grateful for the rain that had fallen during the night. The ground was just damp enough so that the two horses' hooves left a faint impression. If they turned off Yankee Hill Road, she would know it.

The narrow road passed through land now decimated by years of hydraulic mining. What had once been a fragrant pine grove was now a pitted wasteland punctuated by craggy rocks. The mining town of Yankee Hill was nearly dead. Only a few miners' cabins, a tiny store, and a ramshackle saloon attested to its brief, lively past.

The journey seemed to take forever. Twice in two hours, the men stopped to stretch their legs and drink from flasks. Katie assumed that Rush was setting such an easy pace in deference to Mr. Armbrewster, who was obviously no horseman. As the morning sun rose higher, she began to feel tired and warm herself. When she glimpsed Rush and Armbrewster turning off the road onto a path that wound upward through shady pines, she sighed in relief.

Soon, however, her mind turned to more important considerations than the unseasonally balmy weather. Now, she realized, it was imperative that she not be discovered. Anyone could have reason to be on Yankee Hill Road, but what excuse would she offer if they caught her in this much more remote area? Katie had never been on this trail before; she had no idea if anyone even lived nearby. Every time Willoughby stepped on a twig, her heart lurched in utter panic until she was certain Rush hadn't heard. She was afraid to get close enough to see them, afraid that if she could see them, they could see her, too. What if they turned off into the woods again, and the hoofprints were lost in a carpet of pine needles?

For the first time, Katie began to see her situation from Jack and Gideon's point of view. The word *predicament* occurred to her. How was she going to get the proof she sought without being discovered? Even more horrifying to contemplate, what would Rush and Armbrewster do if they caught her? Physically, Katie was no match for two big men, and she had no gun. There was no one around to hear her scream, and no one knew where she had gone. If Rush killed her, it would be as difficult to prove his guilt as in all the other crimes he had committed.

At least another hour had passed, Katie figured. She had dropped farther and farther behind, even stopping once to relieve herself a ways from the trail. Before mounting Willoughby again, she glanced up through the pine trees at the azure sky and said a silent prayer. It occurred to her that she could simply turn back, but stubbornness won out. She decided to keep going for another half hour.

A few minutes later, she spied a narrow path that led through the trees toward the south fork of the Stanislaus River. On a hunch, she tied Willoughby to a branch and walked through the trees, keeping to one side of the path. Soon an abandoned old cabin came into view. Her heart began to pound at the sight of the men's horses tethered outside.

Near the cabin was a clump of lilac bushes, apparently planted by a past owner. Summoning all her courage, Katie scampered across the carpet of pine needles and huddled behind the sheltering bushes. She realized then that her palms were sweaty with fear. She was covered with dust, and her shirt, damp with perspiration, clung to her back. Minutes passed, no one came to flush Katie from her hiding place, and gradually her nerves calmed. She could hear Rush and Armbrewster talking inside the cabin; obviously they were unaware of her presence.

Tentatively, Katie raised her head and peeked through the leaves. There was an open window just a few yards away. Through it she could see Aaron Rush moving about, opening cupboards and drawers, apparently looking for something. Armbrewster stood in the middle of the room, his expression skeptical. Then he turned his back to the window, and Rush walked over to join him.

Were they looking at Tsing Tsing Yee's egg? Frustrated, Katie strained to hear what they were saying.

Finally Armbrewster's voice carried to her on the faint breeze: "I'm prepared to pay handsomely—" But the rest was lost.

Bolder now, Katie convinced herself that the two men were far too preoccupied to notice any activity outside the cabin. She simply had to get close enough to see Aaron Rush in possession of the egg, otherwise she would return with nothing but more charges based solely on speculation. On a rush of adrenaline, she crawled from her hiding place and, head down, approached the cabin. She was nearly there when a rabbit jumped a few feet away, causing her to gasp involuntarily.

"What was that?" said Armbrewster.

Katie scrambled to her feet, trying to decide which way to flee, and for a moment her eyes met those of Aaron Rush.

"You!" he shouted. "Boy! What are you doing out there? Wait!"

She turned to run just as he burst out the cabin door, a revolver in his hand. Certain that death was imminent, Katie ran blindly through the woods. She could hear Rush's heavy footsteps behind her, and his words echoed in her ears.

"Stop or I'll shoot!" A shot rang out each time he uttered the threat.

Every breath Katie took burned. Her legs trembled beneath her as she ran, waiting for the next bullet to hit her in the back, waiting for the fiery pain that would end her life. And as she thought of Jack and all his efforts to keep her from danger, tears scalded her cheeks, caking in the dust that covered her.

"Stop, boy!" The gun cracked again.

Katie felt as if her knees were about to buckle when suddenly she was being hoisted into the air. A horse surged forward beneath her. She leaned against a broad chest, while a strong male arm grasped her securely beneath her breasts. The hand that held the reins was heartbreakingly familiar.

"Jack," she breathed in disbelief.

"Hang on and don't speak," he replied tersely. His arm tightened around Katie's midriff.

They rode recklessly through the woods, narrowly missing trees.

Birds scattered before them, and an occasional pine bough grazed their sides. Finally, after what seemed an eternity to Katie, Jack reined in his horse and turned down toward the river.

"Good work, Byron," he said, leaning forward to pat the stallion's neck.

The south fork of the Stanislaus shimmered invitingly in the sunlight. Jack brought Byron to a stop high on the riverbank, amid a stand of cottonwood trees. Unceremoniously he lifted Katie up and dropped her to the ground, then dismounted. She stood off to one side, too shaken and frightened to speak, watching as Jack led Byron to the river to drink, then tethered him to a tree. Katie wondered what had become of Willoughby.

"My horse . . ." Her voice was a croak.

He was silent for a while before replying coldly, "Worried about him? Perhaps you ought to have given a moment's thought to Willoughby before you tied him to a branch and left to rush blindly toward certain death. As it is, I sent him home. He seemed glad to go."

"I suppose he'll find the way."

Jack walked toward her. "Certainly you couldn't have returned him, and if I hadn't set him free, Rush would have found him by now. Your identity wouldn't have remained a secret very long. Anyone could have told him who owned that horse."

"Jack . . . I—" The words lodged in Katie's throat.

"Yes?" He was standing in front of her, his eyes like chips of green ice, his mouth set dangerously.

"Thank you. For everything. You—you saved my life."

He turned his head. "I'm too angry and tired to talk to you about it now. I'm going to wash up before we head back, and I suggest that you do the same."

"Yes. Of course." At a loss, Katie watched as he walked down to the riverbank and began to strip off his dusty clothing. Did he intend to *bathe*? Jack tossed his boots and shirt onto the grass, then began to peel off his snug-fitting buckskins. Katie turned away, then peeked just in time to catch a glimpse of hard male buttocks and long, muscular legs as he waded into the river and disappeared below the surface.

Jack swam underwater a good distance out, then broke the surface with a shake of his head, sending droplets of water flying in all directions to shimmer in the sunlight. It looked wonderful to Katie, who had never felt more in need of the sort of refreshment he was enjoying.

"Hurry," he called. "We haven't all day."

"But . . ." She flushed.

Jack nearly reminded her that he already had an intimate knowledge of her naked body, but such remarks didn't suit his mood. "Very well, I won't look. Will that suit you?"

Half shielded by a cottonwood tree, Katie shed her boots, trousers, and shirt, but she couldn't bring herself to remove her chemise and drawers. Her hat came off next, and, on a whim, she unbraided her hair and let it fall free. She wanted to feel it floating around her on the surface of the water.

Jack was enjoying himself as Katie gingerly approached the river's edge. He let the current pull him a ways downstream, then swam back against it, apparently oblivious to her presence. Slowly she waded into the cool water, savoring the pleasant shock of the chill as she took herself deeper. Finally she submerged altogether, then popped back out into the sunlight, ebony hair streaming down her back.

"You might as well take those underthings off and hope they'll dry a bit in the sun before you have to dress," Jack called. "Right now they won't help to conceal your body, you know. Wet batiste is provocatively transparent."

His choice of adjectives made her blush. Glancing down, Katie saw that he was right: she could see right through the gauzy cotton, which clung now to her breasts. She stood there a moment, considering. Her underthings were sopping now, and she didn't relish the prospect of wearing her scratchy old clothes without them. . . . Sighing, Katie pulled down her lace-trimmed drawers and draped them over a tree branch that hung low by the water's edge. The sensation of the cool water on her flesh was pure bliss.

The chemise gave her a bit more trouble. The pearl buttons refused to budge from their tiny, wet buttonholes, and Katie soon grew frustrated trying to unfasten them. She'd only managed two when she moved her foot impatiently and came down on something razor sharp.

"Ow!" she screamed, aggravated tears welling in her eyes. Lifting her foot, she saw blood oozing into the water from her big toe. "God's ears!" she cried, borrowing one of Brian's expletives.

Jack watched for a moment as she thrashed about. Then, when she fell backward and disappeared, he swam over.

"Are you all right?"

Katie's face had just emerged from the shallow water. She tried to stand but stepped on her injured foot and let out another yowl of pain. "No! I'm not all right!" When she pushed her hair from her eyes, Jack saw that she was crying. "This has been the worst day of my life!"

"I can assure you," he replied dryly, "that it hasn't been a favorite of mine, either." Reaching out, he put an arm around her waist for support. "Don't cry. Let me take a look at that foot."

"No! I'm not decent!" She pulled the sheer, wet chemise over her breasts and tried not to think about the fact that, under the water, Jack's hand was resting on her bare hip.

"I said I wanted to look at your *foot*," he repeated patiently.

It hurt so badly that Katie complied, still weeping in exhausted frustration. She lifted her foot out of the water and held on to his shoulders with one hand as he bent down to inspect her cut.

"It's not bad," he pronounced, pulling a tiny shard of glass from her toe. "I think you'll live."

Katie's tears subsided as he continued to hold her foot, his hand sliding down to gently massage her instep. To her surprise, his touch sent a current of intense pleasure coursing all the way to her inner thigh. She stared at Jack's wide, brown back and square shoulders, her gaze lingering on the curls at the nape of his neck. Suddenly she found it hard to breathe. "Jack, if you hadn't been there today, he would have killed me." The words spilled out of their own accord. "You were right, right about everything. I should have listened to you. You have every right to be angry with me."

Jack released her foot, straightened, and looked down at Katie for a long moment before gathering her into his arms. "I just couldn't let anything happen to you, Kathleen," he said softly. "I was angry because you'd put yourself in so much danger."

When his hand caressed her back, then pressed her against him until their hips met beneath the water, Katie felt as if a dam had burst inside of her. She melted against Jack's strong body and opened her mouth to receive his kiss.

CHAPTER
17

October 16, 1864

JACK'S MOUTH CAPTURED KATIE'S FULL, RIPE LIPS, AND THEIR tongues met and dueled in a feverish reunion. She couldn't get close enough to him. Her arms wound around his neck as she pressed nearer, and in the chill water, the warmth of her belly nurtured his erection. When she felt him stiffen and rise against her, Katie was utterly lost, consumed with desire. Their hearts pounded in unison as they devoured one another in a frenzy of passion.

The rest of the world slipped away. Katie's reality centered on Jack—the taste of his mouth, the sure touch of his fingers, the warm, strong, living presence of his body—and the currents of energy that flowed between them. It was more than desire or lust: each kiss, each caress, was charged with intense emotion.

Jack's hands disappeared under the water to grip the edges of Katie's chemise, pulling outward to force the recalcitrant buttons from the fabric. Dreamily, she glanced down and watched for a moment as the tiny pearls drifted through the water, zigzagging lazily until they settled on the gravel bed below.

Jack turned so that the current of the river was at his back. As the water lapped against Katie's breasts, they bobbed slightly, the taut, aching nipples turned up as if seeking the sunlight. Occasionally they broke the surface of the water in tantalizing invitation. Jack reached down to cup one breast with both hands, then lowered his head to nip gently at the sensitive pink bud. Katie gasped, astonished by the sudden shock of pleasure. She suffered the sweetest torment as Jack kneaded her swelling breasts and teased each nipple with his tongue and lips. When his mouth moved higher, blazing a fiery trail up to Katie's throat, her head dropped back and her hair floated out on the water behind her.

"Kathleen." He spoke her name with husky warmth. "Kathleen, look at me."

She opened her eyes slowly, unable to speak, and met Jack's passionate gaze.

"You're aware that it's me?" he whispered. "That this is no dream?"

Somehow Katie managed to nod, then twined her arms about his neck in search of his kiss. Jack cupped her buttocks in his hands and lifted her upward. Buoyant in the water, she wrapped her legs around his hips, thrilled to feel the hard pressure of his manhood against the core of her desire. Jack supported her under the water with one hand while the other molded one of her breasts. Shivers of delight transported her as his lips encircled the eager nipple; he swirled his tongue over the swollen peak, sucking gently until she began to pant and move her hips against his in a timeless rhythm. When Jack shifted slightly to position himself between her legs, Katie rocked back and forth against him, her body light in the water. The tip of him teased her bottom as she arched instinctively in response to his thrusts. Aided by the water, she slipped back and forth until, suddenly, there was a burst of delicious, throbbing sensations deep in her loins that undulated in waves over the rest of her body.

Jack's heart tightened with tenderness as he watched her enchanting face contort at the moment of her release. She made a sound of primitive joy, her nails digging into his back and her legs tensing around his hips, and Jack could feel her spasms against the length of his manhood. Again she moaned, this time reaching blindly under the water, begging wordlessly for his entry.

He carried her to a quiet, shallow pool at the river's edge where the thick branch of an oak tree arched out in a curve before them. Still holding her in his arms, he kissed her with sensuous deliberation before setting her on her feet. Katie stood spellbound with anticipation, waiting to discover what would happen next. When he removed her chemise and reached up to drape it over the oak branch, Katie stared boldly at his chiseled body. He was, without a doubt, the most beautiful man in the world.

Jack looked over his shoulder at her, smiling in a way that made her blush with excitement. When he gathered her into his arms, Katie sighed openly and gave herself up to sensation. With feverish abandon, she feasted upon her lover, running her hands down his tapering back, kissing the warm expanse of his chest, then nuzzling his nipples as he had done to hers. When they tautened against her soft lips and she heard Jack's sharp intake of breath, Katie was delighted by her discovery. Her hands strayed lower, exploring and caressing until Jack could stand no more.

Carefully he swept her flowing hair over one shoulder and kissed along the side of her neck, turning her so that her back nestled against his chest. Katie shivered at the twin sensations of Jack's lips on her shoulders and the sweet, sensual play of his fingers down her arms and over the tender insides of her elbows. Finally, he placed her hands on the limb suspended above the water's surface.

Sunlight filtered through the trees, dappling Katie's graceful back and beautifully curved derriere. When Jack moved forward and pressed himself against her, closing his eyes and breathing in the honeyed scent of her hair. Katie felt a fresh surge of arousal and turned to face him, but he held her fast, reaching around to cup her breasts, then trail his hands over her belly to caress her more intimately. Katie gripped the tree branch as Jack gradually entered her from behind. They moaned softly in unison, savoring each sensation, until Katie was completely filled. Jack shut his eyes for a moment, snug inside her warmth. It was as if their bodies had been made to fit together this way.

Then, slowly, he began to move, letting the ecstasy build. Katie held fast to the tree branch and pushed against it to meet Jack's thrusts, while he framed her hips with his hands. The sound of their breathing filled the air, fueling their passion. Each time he pushed into her, a low cry escaped her lips, and when Jack nipped at her neck, then caressed his way down her back with his lips, Katie thought she would explode. The sensations of their coupling were the wildest, keenest, most exquisite she had ever known. Just when she was certain she could bear no more, Jack leaned forward to encircle her with one arm below her breasts, while his other hand reached around in front to brush the soft curls protecting Katie's womanhood. Still moving inside her, he gauged the level of her arousal and lightly pressed his fingers against her. Katie whimpered, in a near frenzy of unbearable pleasure. She wondered how Jack knew exactly how to touch her, how he knew exactly what she needed. As her climax built, his fingers pressed again, paused, then pressed again. Suddenly Katie cried out, shuddering, as Jack thrust deep inside of her, feeling his own spasms begin. It was as if his entire being were centered in his loins, in the shattering contractions that left him pulsing and incredibly sensitized.

A minute passed before Jack could speak, and then his voice was a hoarse whisper. "My God. . . ." He stayed inside Katie, keeping them securely joined, his face buried in the curve of her neck.

Katie let go of the branch and sagged within Jack's embrace. "I feel . . ." Her mouth was parched. "I feel as if I've been turned inside out."

"Well said, my love."

She tensed slightly at the endearment. "I'm so thirsty."

Sensing her uneasiness, Jack gently withdrew and took a step backward. Immediately Katie reached for her chemise and drawers, nearly dry now in the sunlight.

"You must be hungry, too," he said. "I know I am. I have some food and water in my saddlebags."

Katie's cheeks burned, and she kept her eyes averted. What must he think of her? "Yes, I am hungry. I'll dress and join you."

Pulling on his own clothes, Jack pondered the situation. What was Katie feeling? He wasn't even sure what he felt himself, but there was an unsettling ache in the region of his heart.

Katie took her time, waiting until Jack had set out the food and water before she joined him. She could feel his eyes on her, and it worried her to think that he knew her so well. After all, he had awakened parts of her she hadn't even known existed. Could he read her mind as well? Did he understand the confused workings of her heart?

When he handed her a tin cup filled with water, Katie drank deeply, keeping her eyes down to avoid contact. Then she accepted a chunk of bread and an apple and sat down on the ground to eat.

Jack watched her for a long moment. "Kathleen, I think we should talk. . . ."

She shook her head. "No. I don't want to talk about it."

"But we can't pretend it didn't happen—"

"That's exactly what I intend to do," Katie said, hoping he couldn't hear the tremor in her voice. "I intend to pretend that this entire day didn't happen!"

Jack turned away, raking a hand through his tawny hair. He'd let her have her way—for the moment, at least. They both needed time to sort things out. Then he smiled slightly, with a trace of bemusement. Every other woman he'd made love to had clung to him afterward, seeking kisses and declarations of love. With Katie, he'd experienced sensual delights beyond his wildest dreams, and now she treated him like a stranger. Of course, from the first their entire relationship had been unlike any he'd known before. Why should it be any different now?

The afternoon brought a cool breeze that hinted of autumn's late arrival. How appropriate, Katie thought as she and Jack rode down Yankee Hill Road toward Columbia. Clouds gathered over the tree tops, promising rain.

She sat behind him astride Byron, trying not to tighten her hold around Jack's waist or lean against his back. The attraction she felt for this man frightened her. It had been there, simmering, all along, she realized now. The events of the morning made it impossible for her to deny her feelings any longer. She could admit to herself that she craved him helplessly, that she adored everything about his physical presence. His kisses were intoxicating, the scent of his skin made her giddy, just looking at him was a feast for her eyes. She loved to touch him, to feel the warmth of his body and the soft texture of his hair. Worst of all, when he touched *her*, she simply lost her mind. She had no control over her response. He had some sort of magic in his fingers, his mouth, his—

"Are you all right?" Jack asked softly.

Katie flinched. "I'm fine!"

"I thought I heard you sigh."

"I'm a little tired, I suppose."

"Well, we're almost there."

"Good." She was grateful that Jack couldn't see her flaming cheeks. What was this madness that came over her when he was near? She was forced to accept the loss of control of her body; she had no choice. But certainly this did not mean that she was in *love* with Jack Adams. The very thought filled her with panic. No, what she felt was lust, a weakness of the flesh. Now that she understood her malady, she could take steps to effect a cure.

"Here we are," Jack said, reining Byron in in front of Katie's house. This time he played the gentleman and dismounted first, then reached up to assist her.

Steeling herself against the contact, Katie slid from the horse's back into his arms. His touch sent shivers down her spine, but she took a breath and, trying to sound polite and detached, said, "Do you have a few moments to spare? There is something I would like to say to you."

"Certainly." Jack watched as she walked ahead of him up to the house, a model of composure. Would he ever come to know the inner workings of her mind . . . and her heart? He wondered.

"Kathleen—just a moment. I'd like to stable Byron first, and check to make sure Willoughby has returned. Can this wait half an hour?"

She turned back. "All right. But please hurry."

Katie went into the house and made herself a cup of tea. She was too restless to do anything but pace the parlor until she saw Jack striding up the walk. Opening the door, she waved him in.

"Willoughby is fine," he said. "I gave him an extra carrot."

"Thank you. I'd offer you something to drink," Katie said, perching on the edge of the settee, "but I'd like to keep this as brief as possible."

Jack took the rocking chair nearby and leaned forward, forearms resting on his thighs. "Kathleen, why don't you just tell me what is on your mind?"

She found it hard to look at him without feeling that warm, disturbing sensation inside. "All right. I just wanted to say that I am aware of the fact that I seem to be physically attracted to you. I admit it."

He arched an eyebrow slightly. "And?"

"And I see it as a weakness like any other that must be dealt with," she continued primly. "If I were unable to refrain from eating a whole peach pie whenever I baked one, I would not bake them anymore. So, then, must it be where you are concerned."

Jack gave a shout of laughter. "You're comparing me to a *peach pie*?"

"That was just an example."

"Actually, I suppose I should be flattered, considering some of the other things you've compared me to." His eyes twinkled.

Folding her arms across her breasts, Katie persevered. "Abby has realized that she has a weakness for sherry. She does not drink alcohol anymore. The principle is the same. I intend to avoid being alone with you."

He shook his head in disbelief. "Kathleen . . ."

"There's really nothing else to be said."

Jack knew his own share of frustration and confusion where Katie was concerned, but he was also sharply aware of the sweet, welling tenderness that overpowered him when he looked at her. It worried him not a little. "All right. For the time being, we'll leave it at that. Your solution may be the best."

"What other is there?" she replied, blue eyes huge in her delicate, pale face.

A knock at the door interrupted them. Katie answered it and discovered Lim Sung standing on the porch.

"Katie, where have you been? I've looked everywhere!"

"Come in, Lim. What is it?"

He joined them in the tiny parlor, taking in Jack's presence and Katie's disheveled appearance without comment. "There's good news. Tsing Tsing Yee's egg has been returned. He just discovered it on a shelf in the store."

"But certainly you aren't suggesting that it was there all along?" Katie cried. "I'm *positive* that Aaron Rush had it! He was keeping it in a cabin in the woods, and planned to sell it to that Mr. Armbrewster. I followed them there today. They were discussing price—"

"Did you see the egg?" Jack asked.

"Well, no. They seemed to be looking for it—"

"Katie," Lim broke in firmly, "Mr. Yee's egg was returned by the *Griffin*! He left one of his embroidered handkerchiefs under the enamel box."

Katie's mouth dropped open in shock. Jack sat back in the rocking chair and commented, "It sounds as if the Griffin did his work before Rush and Armbrewster reached the cabin this morning."

She sat down weakly, trying to take it all in. "I suppose this makes the Griffin a hero again." She clenched her hands and set her mouth stubbornly. "Well, people can think what they want, but my feelings toward that outlaw will never change. I hate him. I never hated anyone before, but I hate him. He killed my father, and I intend to see justice served. If I ever meet the Griffin face to face, he will die by my hand!"

PART
THREE

CHAPTER
18

October 17, 1864

Iɴ ᴛʜᴇ ᴘᴀʟᴇ ʙʟᴜsʜ ᴏғ ᴇᴀʀʟʏ ᴅᴀᴡɴ, Kᴀᴛɪᴇ ᴀᴡᴏᴋᴇ ʜᴜɢɢɪɴɢ her pillow lengthwise against her body. Her face was buried in it, and she smiled and sighed, dreaming that she was snuggled against Jack's warm, wide, tanned back. This was the ultimate pleasure, to sleep with Jack, to mold herself to the hard curves of his body, to listen to the cadence of his breathing—

Katie's eyes shot open and she sat up, staring in horror at the pillow. What on earth was *wrong* with her? She wished she could shake herself and, in the process, dislodge Jack Adams from her system.

Instead she got up, bathed, and made two large pans of gingerbread, welcoming the flurry of activity as a distraction from disturbing thoughts. When Katie arrived at the saloon, carrying the gingerbread wrapped in towels, she found Gideon sitting at the bar sipping coffee.

"I'm going back to work today, Katie," he announced.

"You are?" She set the pans on the bar and took the stool next to him. "Are you certain you feel well enough?"

He chuckled. "Oh, I think I've been well enough for a while. I've just let Abby convince me otherwise because I enjoyed this life of leisure."

"You've been happy with her, haven't you?" One ebony tendril curled wistfully over Katie's brow, lending her an air of girlish vulnerability. When she reached up absently to push it away, Gideon stopped her.

"Leave it." His smile was warm. "It's pretty. You're pretty, Katie. You look quite . . . uh, womanly lately. Hard to explain. If I weren't in love with Abby, I'd be fully under your spell."

"In love!" she exclaimed triumphantly. "I thought so!"

Gideon pushed up his spectacles and grinned. "I was forced to come to grips with the thing when I realized that I was perfectly well and the time had come to leave here. I think I had the idea that, when my recovery ended, my . . . uh . . . connection with Abby would have to end, too. Then it came to me that we do not necessarily have to deny ourselves those things which give us the most pleasure. So, last night, I spoke to Abby, and she has agreed to marry me."

"Marriage?" Katie repeated, awestruck. "How . . . wonderful! Congratulations!" She leaned forward and kissed his cheek.

"Thank you." Gideon beamed with happiness.

"Will you do it properly in church? With a white for Abby, and flowers, and—"

"A maid of honor?" he supplied, laughing. "Yes, of course. And Abby insists on a church wedding. She feels very close to God these days."

Katie nodded. "Abby has become very wise. When will the wedding take place?"

"In about two weeks, I think. Abby's gone to talk to Mrs. Barnstaple about helping to make her wedding gown. Working here, she simply hasn't the time to do it all herself."

"I'll make the cake," Katie declared. "And we'll have a party here. Who will be the best man?"

Gideon looked at her and swallowed. "I've decided to ask Jack."

"Jack?" she echoed in disbelief.

"Yes." His tone was dry. "You remember Jack Adams, don't you?"

"Of course! You needn't tease me, Gideon. I was just surprised. After all, you barely know the man—"

"He's the best friend I have in this town now. All the men I grew up with here have either gone east to war or off to San Francisco or Nevada to make their fortunes. I've grown to like Jack very much. He has the kind of integrity that's hard to come by these days. I realize that you don't like him, but I certainly can't understand why. He likes *you*, Katie, and he worries about you."

Mixed emotions gave her pause. "In all honesty, I have reason now to like Mr. Adams myself . . . although I have not forgotten that he has serious character defects. For the moment, however, we have called a truce.''

"Won't you tell me why? I'm a terrible snoop, you know." He grinned. "All newspapermen are."

Katie couldn't help laughing. "Well, let's just say that I defied Mr. Adams's warnings about Aaron Rush and nearly got myself killed. It was Jack's concern for me that led him to . . . follow me and, ultimately, rescue me. So, you see, I owe him . . .''

"Your life?"

"Well," she allowed, "at least a debt of gratitude."

"That's good." He watched her with keen gray eyes. "It's a start. You two ought to be friends."

"I think that we are now . . . to a certain extent, at least."

Gideon cleared his throat. "I heard that the Griffin returned Tsing Tsing Yee's egg. I'm sorry you weren't able to get the proof about Aaron Rush that you were looking for. We'd all be better off if you had."

"Oh, don't worry, I'm not finished yet," Katie declared. "That man will be brought to justice—"

"If it's the last thing you do?" a husky, ironic voice interjected from the doorway.

Katie's heart leaped at the sight of Jack striding toward them. His eyes seemed greener, his hair glossier, his tan deeper, and his appeal even more potent than the day before. Katie was stirred by the casual, catlike grace of his movements, the set of his shoulders, the shape of his hands . . .

Stop it! she scolded herself, trying with only momentary success to meet Jack's penetrating gaze. He took the stool next to Gideon and reached forward to pour himself a cup of coffee from the pewter coffeepot on the bar. Then he gave Katie a sidelong glance.

"I think you would be wise to forget about Aaron Rush for the moment. Leave it be."

She smiled sweetly. "I appreciate your advice, Mr. Adams, and I promise to consider it carefully." Turning to Gideon, she inquired, "Aren't you going to announce your good news?"

"Oh—certainly!" He flushed. "I've asked Abby to marry me, and she has agreed."

A sudden, sincere smile lit Jack's face. Putting out his hand, he said, "Congratulations, Gideon! I couldn't be happier for the two of you. Ah, and you're a lucky man, you know. Abby's quite a woman."

Gideon nodded. "I know. And I have you to thank for bringing her into my life."

"It was my pleasure. It's very satisfying to see that two people can successfully navigate the course of true love!"

Katie gave him a quick glance, then looked away as Gideon asked Jack to be his best man.

"Consent? I'd be honored! Except that I'm not certain I'll still be in Columbia. . . ."

"We're hoping to have the wedding as soon as possible. Abby is off right now checking with Mrs. Barnstaple to see how quickly her dress, and Katie's, can be done."

"Katie's?" Jack echoed, his tone casual.

"Katie will be the maid of honor."

"I see." He sipped his coffee. "Well, if this momentous occasion can take place within the next fortnight, you can depend on me to be by your side, my friend. I'll just remain in town a little longer."

Katie felt her cheeks growing warm as the two men shook hands again and was grateful for the distraction when a stranger entered the saloon.

Jack glanced up, too, his mouth going dry at the sight of Samuel Clemens walking toward him. Sam was smiling at the unexpected sight of his friend, and Jack knew a momentary sense of panic. Jumping off the bar stool, he walked forward, hand outstretched.

"Well, if it isn't Samuel Clemens! I hope you remember me. The name is Jack Adams. We met in San Francisco this past summer."

Sam caught the barely perceptible wink that Jack sent his way and managed to conceal his confusion. "Of course I remember you, Jack. I'd hoped that we were friends! I can only assume that you questioned my memory because each time we met you were sober and I was . . . *not*."

"It's good to see you again, Sam, and to discover that your wit remains intact," Jack said, laughing. "Allow me to introduce you to my friends."

As the introductions were made, Katie studied Clemens. His was an interesting face—rather craggy, with deep-set, snapping dark eyes under bushy brows and a mouth that was partially obscured by a thick mustache. His head was crowned by a wild mop of reddish curls. As he smiled at her with frank interest, Katie tried to place his name.

"Aren't you a writer, Mr. Clemens?"

"I like to think so, though there are plenty as would disagree, Miss MacKenzie," he replied with a chuckle.

"I knew it—you're Mark Twain!" she cried. "I've read your work in the Virginia City *Territorial Enterprise*, and more recently in the San Francisco *Morning Star*. The stage drivers are kind enough to bring me newspapers when they think of it. You are very talented, Mr. Clemens!"

"And you are a young lady of rare taste and judgment," Sam replied.

"Miss MacKenzie is not just the owner of this saloon," Jack explained. "She is also a newspaperwoman herself. She is on the staff of the *Columbia Gazette*, which is owned by Mr. Henderson."

"Call me Gideon," the young man protested. "And Katie and I *are* the staff of the *Gazette*. I couldn't do without her."

Unable to suppress her curiosity, Katie inquired, "Will you be in Columbia long, Mr. Clemens? I am eager to learn more about your trade, and would be very grateful for anything you could teach me."

Sam was about to reply that Katie was already acquainted with a great source of knowledge—Jack—but his friend gave him a quelling glance. "Actually, I'm on my way to Jackass Gulch to spend more time with the Gillis brothers, but I'll undoubtedly travel over here from time to time, especially now that I am acquainted with you, Miss MacKenzie—and Mr. Henderson." Sam looked directly at Jack. "Do you know, I thought I was thirstier than anything else, but now I find that I have a powerful longing for a bath and a shave. Mr. Adams, would you mind showing me the way to the best barbershop in town?"

Jack smiled. "I'd be glad to, *Mr.* Clemens. Then you can return here for a hot meal. What are you serving today, Katie?"

"Sausage and beans," she replied, "with fresh gingerbread."

Sam sniffed at the covered pans. "Smells wonderful! Save some for me; I'll be back."

When the two men emerged onto Main Street, Jack closed his eyes and laughed with relief. "My *God*, but the sight of you scared me! That's been my fear all along—that someone from my other life would appear in Columbia and call me 'Wyatt.' "

"Your 'other life'?" Sam peered at him closely. "This is all very interesting. I must say, I wouldn't have taken you for a man with a *secret*." His tone deepened melodramatically. "Out with it now, my friend. Who are you *really*? Jonathan Wyatt—wealthy, fastidious, controlled owner of the San Francisco *Morning Star*? Or

Jack Adams—gold country renegade and . . . and what? Prospector? Barfly?'' Sam's heavy brows rose questioningly.

"If I tell you, you must swear that it will go no further."

"You have my word. I have some dirt of my own that I'll ask you to help me keep under the rug."

Jack nodded. It would be a relief to share the truth with a friend, especially one who was present in Columbia. They walked into a secluded grove of birch trees behind the Wells Fargo building. Jack glanced around to be certain no one could overhear, then said simply, "I'm the Griffin."

Clemens's mouth dropped open. "The foothills' own Robin Hood? Are you serious?"

Jack nodded ruefully. "I'm afraid so. It began simply enough. Rush and Van Hosten had deprived my brother, Conrad, of the gold he discovered near here. I merely came up to Columbia to see that justice was done. . . ."

"Unbeknownst to Conrad?" Sam was fascinated.

"That's right. He still doesn't know. In fact, the only person, outside of yourself now, who does know what I've been doing is my grandfather." He paused to run a hand through his tawny hair. "At any rate, when I discovered how widespread the injustice was, one thing led to another, and I went on with it. I liked balancing the scales for a change—seeing the miners get their due, watching Rush and Van Hosten squirm. Then I returned to my life in San Francisco and thought to put an end to it, but I had to come back. I really hoped to resolve the entire situation without bloodshed."

"Until Van Hosten and that saloon keeper were killed."

"That's right. And the saloon keeper was Brian MacKenzie, Katie's father." It pained Jack to speak the words.

"Oh, Lord." Sam paled.

"It was Van Hosten who shot him, but no one knows that. It shouldn't have happened. Everything began to get complicated when I returned to Columbia last summer and spent enough time here to make real friends. The charade began to seem real. When I went home, just before you and I met, my life as Jonathan Wyatt seemed rather dull and trite. I found that I missed my other identity. Sometimes I'm not certain anymore which man is really me!" Jack bent to pet a calico kitten so that Clemens couldn't read the depth of emotion and conflict in his eyes. Sam watched him sympathetically.

"Now that little talk we had in your office makes more sense than ever. I can certainly see why you were so preoccupied in San Francisco, trying to pick up your ordered existence!" Sam gave a cough of dry laughter. "Believe me, I understand. I've had more than my own share of identities, with occupations of every sort in various locales. I never changed my name—unless my pen name counts, and it probably does!—but I know what it is to feel reborn . . . and to feel a sense of confusion about the direction my life is taking." He shrugged. "I've come to the conclusion that I'm still confused—still searching for the life that's meant for me."

"I suppose I shouldn't have come back here, but I felt compelled. When I heard that Rush's henchmen had wrecked the *Gazette*'s printing press, I brought one up here."

"A noble excuse!" Sam teased knowingly.

Jack smiled, straightening. "Thank you. I thought so at the time. But I didn't consider the complications. I have friends here now, and I don't like lying to them about who I really am." He paused, rubbing his jaw. "It's a mess. I was going to leave in a day or two, but now Gideon Henderson has asked me to stand up with him at his wedding, so I'll have to remain for at least two more weeks."

Sam was contemplating a tree branch as he listened to Jack's story. "Katie MacKenzie doesn't know that you're the Griffin, and she believes that the Griffin is responsible for her father's death."

Jack winced. "That's right."

"What's between the two of you?"

"I'm not entirely certain myself. We're friends, when Kathleen isn't furious with me."

Sam pressed, "But it's more than that, isn't it?"

"What makes you think so?" Jack asked uneasily.

"Well, I'm no expert on this sort of thing, but there seemed to be a kind of energy between the two of you that I've witnessed before. And for what it's worth, I didn't feel it between Jack Wyatt and Genevieve Braithwaite." Clemens sniffed, took out a handkerchief, blew his nose, then added, "But, as I said, I'm no expert."

"I . . . uh, appreciate your opinion, but the fact is that there can't be anything beyond friendship between Kathleen and myself. She doesn't even know my real identity, and of course, beyond that, if she discovered that I was the Griffin, she'd kill me outright." Jack paused, stared back toward the saloon, then shrugged.

Sam nodded slowly. "You're right, my friend. It's a mess."

"Why don't you tell me your own dire story en route to Snyder's Shaving Saloon? Perhaps it will cheer me up!"

Laughing, they set out. The morning was growing warm, and Clemens took off his coarse brown sack coat, a loose-fitting garment with high, short lapels that had become popular for the most informal of occasions. He draped it over his arm, loosened his collar, and began with a question. "Have you ever met my friend, Steve Gillis?"

"No, I don't believe so."

"Well, you will. He left San Francisco with me. Actually, you might say that he *caused* me to leave San Francisco." Sam glanced at Jack, eyes twinkling. "Steve and I are making a history for ourselves of leaving places in a hurry. One day I'll regale you with the full account of our departure from Nevada, which came about at the invitation of the governor himself. Steve had gotten me involved in one of the duels that were fashionable in Nevada then, unaware that there was a new law against it. When the governor pointed it out to us, we decided to go to San Francisco rather than the penitentiary."

Jack felt himself relaxing. Clemens's laconic style both amused and entertained him. "It's coming back to me now. Wasn't Steve Gillis your partner in debauchery when you let rooms from that Frenchwoman?"

"That's right. I'd like to blame him for all our adventures, but I suppose I must play *some* role in them. . . ." Sam grinned. "At any rate, it's been a rather quiet autumn, except for the trouble I've been making for myself as a newspaperman. I've been feeling a bit of heat for my attacks, bravely printed by your paper, on corruption of politicians and police. After you left San Francisco, I wrote a piece damning the mobs who hunt Chinese in the streets, and I received a few threats. Naturally, I'm far too courageous to run away, but Steve took the matter out of my hands." His tone was ironic.

"You know that we'll print anything you write," Jack said seriously. "I gave Edwin Murray orders to that effect before I left."

"I know, and I'm grateful. And I'm sure I'll do more work for you if you'll have me."

"Now that that's settled, tell me what caused you and Steve to make such a speedy exit from San Francisco." The Presbyterian pastor and his wife nodded as they passed the two men, and Jack smiled in response.

"Well, it's a long story, so I'll condense it for your benefit," Sam was replying. "We went out to a saloon one night, bemoaning the sad state of our social lives. But Steve is a man who likes a bit of excitement, especially after consuming whiskey. One thing led to another, and he became involved in a fight which soon took on the proportions of a brawl. The authorities were alerted, Steve was taken into custody, and I was dispatched to raise the money needed to post bond. Once that was accomplished and he was released, it became clear that it might be wise to absent ourselves from San Francisco for a while.''

"I see!" Jack laughed. "Your facility with words serves you well, my friend. What you meant to say was that you are now a fugitive!"

"Why would I *mean* to say a thing like that?" Sam replied innocently, then joined in his friend's laughter.

"I just wanted to be absolutely certain that I understood the situation correctly. You and Gillis ran away from San Francisco, using his run-in with the police and assorted other unsavory types as an *excuse* to escape to Jackass Gulch, which you had been longing to do all the time." Jack's sage-green eyes glinted with amusement.

"I guess grown men need weighty excuses in order to leave the responsibilities of work behind and run off to the foothills," Sam replied calmly.

"Truer words were never spoken."

The two men nodded soberly, in unison. When they reached Snyder's Shaving Saloon, Jack opened the door and smiled as his friend passed by. "I'm glad you're here, Sam."

Their eyes met for an instant in shared understanding. "I'm glad, too, especially now that it's clear I won't be bored!"

CHAPTER
19

October 22, 1864

"Lovely, just lovely!" proclaimed Victoria Barnstaple. She darted forward like a sparrow, hands fluttering to her bosom as she beamed at Katie. "My dear, that color is ideal for you! I could only be more pleased to see you wearing white—as the bride!"

Katie flushed. "Oh, Mrs. Barnstaple, let's not think about that."

"I know that your dear parents would want me to remind you that life's true gifts are only possible when one has a mate to share with," Victoria chirped.

Katie made no reply but waited patiently as the older woman put a few more pins into the yards of lavender-blue silk taffeta that flowed outward from Katie's waist. "This is the stiffest, widest crinoline I've ever worn," she murmured at last, squirming slightly.

"Well, that's good! You should be used to the more disciplined aspects of womanhood by now, my dear. One day, after you're married, you'll be attending all manner of important social occasions, and you must be at ease in your corset and crinoline."

Katie bit her tongue, then tried to change the subject. "I'm anxious to see Abby's gown. She must look very beautiful."

"Oh, yes," Mrs. Barnstaple agreed distractedly. Inserting the last pin, she stood back and examined Katie with a critical eye. "You really do need a new hairstyle, my dear. How will you wear it at the wedding?"

"In a chignon, I thought."

Victoria pursed her lips and narrowed her eyes as if to gauge the overall effect. "Yes . . . Yes, that should look very nice. I wish you'd wear it that way more often. Anything but that braid! You know, Katie darling, you have extraordinary natural beauty. I cannot fathom why you go to such extremes to conceal it."

Her frankness caught Katie off guard. "I'm not entirely certain myself, Mrs. Barnstaple, but I'll think about what you've said."

"Well, good. You may remove that gown now. I suppose you have to be getting back to that saloon." She sniffed as she helped Katie lift the layers of taffeta over her head. "It's not right, you know, a girl your age running a place like that. Some people would call it an open and shameless enticement to evil—"

"But you know our saloon isn't like that!" Katie protested.

"You serve liquor, don't you? I never approved of Brian letting you work there, and I approve even less of you, whose mother was a proper lady, acting as proprietress of such an establishment. It simply isn't right."

Katie stepped out of the crinoline and petticoats, then reached for her own frock of blue-sprigged cotton. "Mrs. Barnstaple, I appreciate your advice, and I know you have my best interests at heart, but the simple truth is that the saloon is the only means of support available to me. I intend to make my own way, without having to depend on others." She cast about for another subject. "Tell me, how is your niece? Is she enjoying her visit to Columbia?"

"Oh, yes, I think so, though she hasn't made the acquaintance of many young women her own age." Victoria began to fasten up the back of Katie's dress. "She spends more time with that Jack Adams than anyone, and I shudder to think what her parents would say. But then, Margaret has always been headstrong. She wouldn't heed my brother and his wife, and she won't heed me. I love the girl, but—"

"I'm sorry. I don't mean to interrupt you, but I do need to get back to the saloon." Katie suddenly felt very warm. "Thank you for making the gown for me, Mrs. Barnstaple. I truly do appreciate it."

"Well, I'm glad to help you and Abigail. She seems to be a nice young lady, and of course, I've always loved Gideon. His mother is one of my best friends."

Katie backed toward the front door and lifted the latch. "I'll see you soon."

"Your gown should be finished by Thursday, which leaves us

time for any last-minute alterations before the wedding on Saturday. Why don't you stay for tea when you come to try it on?''

"I'd love to." She kissed Mrs. Barnstaple's cheek. "Good-bye!"

As she emerged onto Fulton Street, Katie's smile faded. She'd tried not to think about Jack and Maggie Barnstaple; she'd told herself that he couldn't feel anything for the other girl, not when he'd shared such intimacy with *her*. But if the worst were true, it cheapened everything that had passed between them. The fact that she had turned him away was little comfort. Katie continued to feel an intense attraction to Jack, and that shamed her, especially because the memories of their lovemaking were still so vivid.

Fate seemed intent on testing her, for when Katie rounded the corner of Main Street, bound for the saloon, she saw Maggie Barnstaple and Jack standing in front of the dry goods store. He was holding her bolts of lace and striped silk, and the two of them were laughing at the antics of a calico kitten in pursuit of a butterfly.

Before she could think, Katie fled back around the corner. She knew only that she couldn't face them. No sooner had she leaned against the wall of the Douglass Saloon to collect her thoughts than a beefy hand gripped her wrist. She gasped and stared into the face of a man she recognized as one of Aaron Rush's henchmen. He wore a derby that partially covered the scar that slanted across his forehead.

"Excuse me, sir!" She tried to free her wrist from his grasp, fixing him with an angry glare.

"Settle down, missy, and heed my words," the man growled. "You're too pretty to be sticking your nose into affairs that don't concern you. Watch yourself, or something might happen that'd make you wish you'd behaved more like a proper lady!"

In spite of the wave of fear and revulsion that swept over her, Katie's outward composure did not waver. "You may tell Aaron Rush for me that his cowardly threats do not frighten me in the least. Unlike so many of the so-called men in this town, I will not be bullied! Now, unhand me!" She twisted free and walked away, head high.

"You'd better think again, girlie, before you find yourself in the kind of trouble that you can't smart-talk your way out of!" the man hissed after her.

Katie strode onward, sensing that he had turned and gone off down the street. After a minute she realized that she was walking back the way she had come, but she had no desire to return to the saloon. Lim and Abby were both there; they didn't need her. Besides, that hideous man was probably lurking on Main Street, waiting for her to pass him again so that he could mutter more threats in her ear. Without conscious direction, then, she continued up Fulton Street, her mind flashing back and forth between images of the man in the derby and Jack and Maggie laughing together in front of the dry goods store. She ached inside, she felt jumpy, and she longed to escape, if only for a few hours.

Samuel Clemens had stopped in the saloon again only two days ago. Fresh from a bath at the barbershop, and wearing a new shirt, he had regaled Katie with tales of his unsuccessful attempts at pocket mining. And before taking his leave, he had invited her to visit Jackass Gulch any time she wished.

It was the perfect solution, Katie decided, and, feeling a little better, she stopped at last to look around her. To her surprise, she found herself on the very doorstep of the livery stable. When she entered and heard Willoughby's joyful whinny at her appearance, she took it as a sign that she was doing the right thing.

Samuel Clemens stood in the doorway of the Gillis cabin, shading his eyes against the sun as he watched Katie MacKenzie ride up the grassy, golden hillside scattered with scrub oak, pine, and manzanita.

She waved, and Sam waved back, drinking in the sight of her. Katie had hitched up her dress and petticoat to sit astride the horse, and her slim calves gleamed in the sunlight. Her slender shoulders and firm young breasts showed to great advantage in her snug bodice, and her smiling face glowed with good health. The wind had nearly loosened her braid, but it still flew out behind her like a banner, announcing the free spirit of its owner.

When Sam walked forward to help Katie dismount, he found himself mesmerized by her starry-lashed sapphire eyes and her soft, pink lips, and nearly succumbed to an urge to declare her beauty aloud. But he caught himself in time. "Well, this is a surprise," he said instead. "Welcome to Jackass Gulch, Miss MacKenzie."

"Didn't you invite me? I might be mistaken. . . ." Her tone was light, teasing. "And you must call me Katie. Everyone does."

"I seem to remember my friend Jack using a more proper form of address."

"Well"—she turned away to pat Willoughby's damp neck—"I like to keep Mr. Adams at arm's length. We don't always see eye to eye."

Deciding that it might be wise not to pursue the matter further, Sam took the horse's reins and hitched him to the post in front of the cabin. "Tell me, then—to what do I owe the honor of this visit?"

Katie gave him a fresh, honest smile. "I was having one of those days that makes you long more than anything else to *be* anywhere else! This seemed like a good place to escape to, and I knew I'd enjoy your company. I admire you and your work tremendously, Mr. Clemens—"

"Sam," he corrected.

"Sam." Katie beamed. "I've been wanting to have a real conversation with you ever since we met."

"Dear lady, I am at your disposal." His eyes danced above the heavy mustache.

"Are you certain I'm not interrupting? Were you writing when I arrived?"

"No, and no. I've done very little this past week except sleep, eat, exchange yarns with my friends, and make a few halfhearted attempts at pocket mining. I'm afraid I've been shockingly lacking in virtue since I arrived in the foothills."

"Perhaps you needed a respite," Katie suggested.

"I did. We all need one from time to time, for one reason or another, hmm?" He smiled at her and winked almost imperceptibly as they strolled toward a grove of pine trees. "Besides, I'm lazy at heart, and always glad of an excuse not to work. So, you see, your visit is particularly welcome! Why don't you sit down under this tree, I'll get you something cold to drink, and you can tell me what's been frustrating you in Columbia. All right, Katie?"

She nodded and did as he suggested, watching until he disappeared into the spare rectangular cabin with its stone chimney. The rustling pines offered welcome shade from the sun, and Katie leaned against the broad tree trunk behind her and closed her eyes, breathing in the clean, fresh scents of autumn. Sam appeared a few moments later with two battered tin cups.

"I apologize for these," he said with a wry smile. "My host, Jim Gillis, is a mountain bachelor, and lives as such. And all I could find to drink was cold coffee and whiskey, so I brought water instead."

"That sounds wonderful. Thank you." Katie accepted the cup and drank deeply. "I was thirsty!"

Clemens joined her on the ground. "I've heard a little about you already, Katie MacKenzie, but I'd like to know more. Won't you enlighten me?"

"Oh, there's really not much to say." She waved a delicate hand. "I came here to learn about *you*. I'm just a girl who has spent her life in one town. I've never fit in with the other well-behaved, traditional females. I helped Papa in his saloon after my mother died when I was ten, and ever since the Griffin killed Papa I've run the saloon with the help of my friends. I've never yearned to marry and take care of a man. There are too many things I want to do myself! I've read all my life, and dreamed of traveling. I'd like a life like yours, Sam." Katie sighed. "I suppose I ought to have been born a man."

"And deprive the world of your vivacity and beauty?" Sam cried.

"No, my dear, I think not. There isn't the least doubt in my mind that you were born in the right body!" He paused to admire the soft blush that stained Katie's cheeks, charmed by her fresh modesty. "Besides, you don't have to be a man to pursue your dreams. This is the West, Katie. You've flouted convention in Columbia, so why not flout it somewhere else—like San Francisco? What is it you'd like to do?"

"I'd like to write. I want to be a newspaperwoman."

"I thought you already were," he said reasonably.

"Oh—yes, I suppose so, but much of the time it feels as if Gideon and I are children, *playing* at printing a newspaper. How did you get your start, Sam? Did you dream of writing as a child?"

"Lord, no!" He laughed heartily and smoothed his mustache. "I think it is human nature to yearn to be what we were never intended for. I have had just two powerful ambitions in my life thus far. One was to be a riverboat pilot; the other a preacher of the gospel. I accomplished the first, but was interrupted by the war. The second was impossible for me because I hadn't the call, or the gift, if you will. It was the height of presumption on my part to even consider that I might have the qualities necessary to be a minister." Sam leaned back against the tree and paused to drink from his tin cup. "I've become a writer almost by default. It galls me to face facts, but the truth is that this is where my talents lie. I still pretend to myself that I might be able to make a serious contribution to the literary world, but I am slowly coming to terms with my real gift. . . ."

Katie leaned forward, fascinated. "And what is that?"

Clemens smiled crookedly. "My true calling is to literature of a low order—humor. God seems to want me to make others laugh. It strikes me as a rather poor, pitiful business, but I fear it's what I was made for."

Katie was silent for a moment as she digested this. "I think that your gift is great enough that you can put it to any use you choose, but I also believe that the ability to write humor is a rare and special talent. There are very few people who possess real wit, and you are one of them! Wit is what sets your work apart."

"I appreciate your kind words and encouragement, dear Katie."

"I am completely sincere, Sam! And whatever your real gift may be, I must tell you how much I admire the articles you have written speaking out against corruption and the persecution of the Chinese in San Francisco." Her blue eyes were wide and earnest. "You have set an example that I am trying to follow right here in Columbia. You may be aware that we have our share of crime and corruption, too."

"If you mean the Rush mine, yes, I've heard, but I must caution you against using me as a model of any sort, Katie." There was nothing wry or playful about Sam's tone now. "Speaking out against corruption can be a dangerous undertaking, even for a man. Those who mix crime with their business dealings are not above committing other crimes, especially when they're threatened. You might assume that you're safe because you're female, but I wouldn't depend on it."

"But someone has to have the courage to take a stand!" she protested.

"Leave it to the men who can defend themselves, or run away if they smell danger, as I did."

"You?!" she exclaimed in disbelief.

"I hate to disillusion one of my admirers, but that's part of the reason I'm here. I began to hear rumblings, and it seemed wise to remove myself from San Francisco until they died down. And in all honesty, I did have another motive. I'm still young and foolish enough to entertain dreams of easy wealth. Pocket mining could be my ticket to a life of ease! That's what Jim Gillis has been doing while living here in this cabin, so his brother Steve and I thought that we might as well give it a try, too. Let me show you around." Sam got to his feet and held out a hand to her, seizing on the distraction before the conversation could drift onto shakier ground. He didn't know what he'd do if Katie raised the subject of the Griffin.

She was too polite to interrupt him, so she waited, following Clemens over the hillside as he explained pocket mining to her. "You may remember that a dozen years ago, there was a veritable city on this hillside, or at least that's what Jim Gillis tells me." He glanced at Katie and received her nod. "Well, as you know, when the placer gold played out, this town died along with the dreams of its inhabitants. Those who stayed on, however, found an alternative to working for Rush and Van Hosten, an alternative to hydraulic mining.''

Katie found that her interest was piqued. ''I have heard bits and pieces from miners at the saloon, but I've never fully understood what pocket mining meant.''

''Well, it's risky. The men with families who are forced to work for Rush in order to put food on their tables would find this less dependable. Unlike ordinary placer mines, the gold here isn't distributed evenly through the surface dirt. It's collected in little spots, and they are very wide apart and hard to find . . . but when you do discover one, you have yourself a fortune.'' Sam gestured at the gouges in the hillside. ''It can take years. Jim Gillis spent the first eight months of the year digging around this hill, buying his groceries on credit, until he finally discovered a pocket and took out three thousand dollars of gold in a couple of scoops of his shovel. He paid off his debts, then went on a spree until every cent was gone, bought more groceries on credit, and returned here to start digging again.'' Clemens grinned as he told the story.

''Well,'' Katie said doubtfully, ''he sounds like a colorful character. My childhood was crowded with men like Jim Gillis. They settled these hills, and though most either died from hard living or moved on, they've left their stamp. It's just too bad that all their dreams couldn't have come true.''

Sam chuckled. ''I'll echo that sentiment. I confess to having a few dreams of my own in that area, but I haven't much hope that I'll see them realized while I'm here. My luck was abysmal in the mines of Nevada.''

''Well, at least you have some talents and skills to fall back on.'' Katie glanced up at him as she spoke and stepped sideways into a hole that had only been partially filled in. Her ankle turned as she lost her balance and cried out, but Sam reached out and caught her before she could topple over.

''Take care, Katie MacKenzie,'' he said with a fond smile, enjoying the sensation of her soft, female form in his arms. ''Certain people would hold me responsible if you were hurt in my care.''

''What do you mean by that?'' She held on to him and tested her ankle, ignoring the sound of approaching hoofbeats. Sam didn't look, either; he assumed the rider was one of the Gillis brothers, who were due back from Angel's Camp. After a short silence, however, a pair of hands gripped his shirt from behind and yanked him away from Katie.

''What in the hell do you think you're doing, Clemens?'' a hoarse, angry voice demanded.

Before Sam could reply, Katie looked up in shock to see that her friend's attacker was none other than Jack Adams. "Leave him alone!" she cried. "He's been very kind to me!"

"Oh, is that what he calls it? I imagine that there are plenty of women in San Francisco who might use a different word!" Jack released Sam but continued to glare at him. Clemens's own eyes began to twinkle.

"My good friend, I fear that you are giving yourself away. I can assure you that my own motives where Katie is concerned are immaculate. When you rode up, I was merely coming to her aid after she stepped in a hole and lost her balance."

"That's true!" Katie exclaimed. In spite of her outrage, she found that her heart was beating rapidly. Jack looked wildly attractive, his hair windblown, his green eyes blazing, his tanned body taut with anger. She longed to touch him.

"Well, that's not what it looked like," Jack said darkly, slanting a menacing look at Katie. "What are you doing here, anyway? Lim and Abby are out of their minds with worry. For God's sake, we— they thought that you'd been kidnapped by Aaron Rush!"

"Were you looking for me?" She couldn't stop the question. "Were you worried, too?"

Sam cleared his throat. "I think I'll leave you two alone to sort this out. Jim and Steve will be back any minute now, so I guess I'll just head back to the cabin and see what I can scrape together for supper." He gave Katie a smile and a nod of his curly head. "I enjoyed your visit, Katie. Feel free to ride over any time."

"Thanks, Sam. You've been very kind." She favored Clemens with a dazzling grin while Jack continued to glower. When the other man was halfway to the cabin, Katie turned back to Jack.

"Well?" she said sweetly. "Are you going to answer my questions?"

"You're damned right I was looking for you, you little hellion! Just because I feel like wringing your neck most of the time, that doesn't mean I want you dead! What got into you, leaving town like that without telling anyone?"

He'd stepped in front of her, and she could feel the heat and energy emanating from his strong body. "I'm surprised you had time to bother with me," she heard herself snap. "Last I saw you, you were all wrapped up in the simply *darling* presence of Maggie Barnstaple. I wouldn't have believed that you could tear yourself away!"

Suddenly Jack was tired of games. "Jealous?" he taunted softly. "There was no need, my sweet. Maggie is in love with someone back in New York. She's determined to wait out her parents' disapproval and marry him when she goes home. There's never been anything between us except friendship.''

"I distinctly remember you encouraging me to think otherwise!''

"Those were your thoughts, Kathleen. I didn't put them there, nor did I ever verify your suspicions.''

"Well, I didn't put jealous thoughts in *your* mind today, either! I simply rode out here to get away from Columbia for a change. I admire Sam's work, and that's what I came to talk to him about. Nothing happened between us!''

He glanced at Katie's breasts, straining against the thin cotton of her bodice, then his eyes caressed the elegant line of her neck, lingered on her full, parted lips, and finally met her fiery gaze. "Good.''

Suddenly it dawned on her that they were having what amounted to a lover's quarrel, in spite of their agreement and her resolve that nothing loverlike must ever pass between them again. Katie couldn't breathe. She ached for Jack's touch, and when he slipped his hands around her waist and gathered her into his arms, she expelled an almost involuntary sigh of relief.

"You drive me to the brink of madness,'' he whispered. His mouth burned hers in a mutually ravenous kiss, their hearts pounding in unison as Jack thrust his tongue into Katie's mouth. Her fingers kneaded his back, reveling in the feel of his muscular warmth through the fabric of his shirt. Jack's hands slid down to cup Katie's buttocks, fitting their bodies more tightly together and fusing their arousal.

Dimly, Katie realized that she would drop to the ground and give herself to him right there in broad daylight if he wanted her to. "Oh, my God, stop!'' she panted, dragging her mouth away from his. "This is insane!''

Jack released her and took a step backward. Katie lifted her hands to burning cheeks. "I'm sorry,'' he said, his voice rough with shock. "I never meant—''

"It's not your fault.'' She blinked back frustrated tears. "I don't know what possesses us, but it just can't happen again. It just *can't*!''

Jack's body seemed concentrated in the thud of his heart and the wild throb of his desire for Katie. He'd never felt this way before, and that realization sent a stab of fear through him, straight to the hidden depths of his soul. "You're right.'' He nodded. "You are absolutely right. Come on. Let's go home.''

CHAPTER
20

October 22–27, 1864

"WELL, THANK YOU—I GUESS—FOR ESCORTING ME BACK to town," Katie said as she slid from Willoughby's back and handed the reins to Jack. "Are you sure you don't mind returning him to the stable?"

"I have to go there anyway. You go on inside and let your friends know you're all right." Jack's voice was huskier than usual, and he avoided her eyes as he crossed Willoughby's reins with Byron's.

"Yes, I suppose I should." Katie fiddled with the handful of straggly, late-blooming poppies that Jack had picked for her when they'd stopped to stretch their legs on the way back from Jackass Gulch. She wasn't sure why they both were so ill at ease, and further, she didn't want to think about it. "Well, good-bye."

Jack glanced down at her, nodded, and nudged Byron to turn back down Main Street. Katie walked slowly toward the saloon, watching until Jack and the two horses had turned the corner of Fulton Street. Confused, bittersweet emotions assailed her mind and battered her heart, leaving her utterly drained.

Inside the saloon, Lim and Abby rushed to meet her, exclaiming their relief and plying her with questions. When their curiosity had been satisfied, Abby said, "Thank goodness Jack stopped by looking for you. Otherwise, you might still be in Jackass Gulch, and we'd still be worrying about you!"

Katie's eyes widened. "Jack was here? Looking for me? I thought you sent him to find me."

Lim shook his head, watching her all the while. "No, he came here, then he went to look for you at home, then he came back again. He brought you a present."

She was completely confused. "He certainly didn't say anything to me about a present. Where is it?"

"It's a she," laughed Abby, "and she's in the kitchen, lapping milk."

Lim disappeared around the corner and returned holding a tiny bundle of furry patchwork. Katie stared. It was the calico kitten Jack and Maggie had been watching in front of the dry goods store.

"Jack said he was keeping his eye on her most of the day until he was satisfied she was an orphan," Abby explained. "He just had a feeling that you'd be the person who could give her the love she needed."

Tears stung Katie's eyes. "He said that?"

They both nodded. Lim held out the kitten and Katie lifted it, gazing into its bright blue eyes, then held it against her cheek. The warm, velvet-soft body began to purr immediately. "I love her," she whispered. Her eyes fell on the orange poppies that lay on the bar. "I'll call her Poppy."

Turning up the collar of his long tan duster against the evening chill, the Griffin watched Aaron Rush's two assistants leave the mining offices, which were located a short distance south of town. The miners themselves had gone home more than an hour before, and now it seemed that even loyalty to Rush could not keep his closest aides from their supper. The Griffin was concealed behind a cluster of pine trees as the pair walked by. He heard the bigger man say, "Damn it all, I'm starved! The boss has that Chinaman to cook for him when he decides to put the books away and go home, but I don't got servants and I need *food*!" His companion, a thin fellow whose red face bespoke a fondness for whiskey, laughed and nodded his agreement as they reached their horses, mounted, and rode away.

Jack Wyatt narrowed his eyes at the one-story brick building that housed the mine offices. The front windows were lit, and he could see Aaron Rush inside, moving around from time to time. Jack glanced back down the road toward town. He'd been staying away from Columbia, spending most of the past two weeks at the Gillis cabin as he waited for Gideon and Abby's wedding, which would take place tomorrow. There was a war going on inside him over

Katie. He craved her, yet he couldn't let himself go near her. He'd begun to think of her as a fire, warm and inviting, yet dangerous if he got too close. And it seemed that he couldn't stop himself from getting too close. As soon as the wedding was over, he was going back to San Francisco. The Griffin was retiring, but first he had to tend to some unfinished business.

Carrying his hood in one hand and his shotgun in the other, Jack took a circuitous route through the trees that led to the back of the office. Working for Harold Van Hosten had acquainted him well with the floorplan of the building. Pausing outside the rear door, Jack slipped the hood over his head and adjusted the eyeholes. Then, holding the shotgun lightly, he eased open the door and moved silently down the dark hallway. The door to Rush's office was ajar. Jack stood in the narrow bar of light, looking at his nemesis, who sat hunched over a magnificent desk.

Aaron Rush appeared harmless. Sweat soaked his white shirt and unbuttoned brown waistcoat, and his plump, pink face showed signs of obvious fatigue. He took a long drink from the snifter of brandy at his elbow, then rubbed his eyes with meaty fists. Jack wondered how such a man could be capable of so much evil.

Stepping into the room, the Griffin spoke. "Mr. Rush, might I have a few minutes of your time?"

Rush looked up and gasped, paling visibly. "*You!* You devil! How dare you come here and show yourself to me?"

"I simply walked in the door," Jack replied dryly. "It didn't require a surfeit of daring on my part. There are some matters I would like to discuss with you."

Rush fumbled in a drawer, and Jack raised his shotgun and aimed it at the older man. "Looking for your pistol? Take it out and set it on the desk, please."

Now Aaron Rush turned beet red. "Oh, you're smooth, Griffin, but that smart mouth of yours won't save your hide. I'm going to see you dead!"

"Not tonight, however. Just set the gun on the desk," Jack repeated patiently. When Rush had complied, he walked over and picked up the pistol. "Now then, since my more subtle warnings regarding your conduct seem to have had little effect, I thought it might be best to spell things out, so that there would be no room for misunderstanding."

"You're a thief and a murderer!" Rush shouted.

"Then we have something in common," Jack shot back coldly. "I wish I were more inclined toward cold-blooded murder; I could save myself and this town a lot of time and trouble. However, gentleman that I am, I'm going to give you one more chance."

Sweat trickled down Rush's high, flushed forehead. "I'll see you dead, Griffin!"

"You are repeating yourself," Jack replied in bored tones. "Now shut up and listen to me." He placed the cold barrel of the shotgun against Rush's jowl. "Are you listening?"

The older man swallowed, blinking rapidly. "All right. Yes."

"I want you to stop harassing the good people of Columbia. Leave Tsing Tsing Yee in peace. Stop trying to force him, or anyone else, to sell their properties to you. Understand?"

Aaron Rush gave an almost imperceptible nod of assent, his beady eyes straying constantly to the barrel of the shotgun that pressed his hot flesh.

"I want you to start treating the miners fairly. Pay them what they're owed, and stop trying to cheat people out of their claims. You have plenty of gold without taking the small amounts others might find." Jack paused for a moment to let his words sink in. "Finally, leave Gideon Henderson and the *Gazette* alone. Henderson and Kathleen MacKenzie must be allowed to write what they please. If I hear that you have harassed Kathleen any further, or harmed a hair on her head, I'll kill you. That is a promise."

Rush felt a surge of joy as he recognized the tone of the Griffin's voice. A sly smile touched his mouth, and his eyes gleamed triumphantly as he nodded. "Of course. Whatever you say."

There was nothing more that Jack could do. He drew the shotgun back, sick inside with the realization that he'd shown his hand. "I won't take any more of your time, then, Mr. Rush. If you value your life, you'll remember what I've said and behave accordingly."

Aaron Rush waited until the Griffin had gone, then stood to look out his window, watching as the hooded man tossed Rush's pistol into the hydraulic mine pits. When the Griffin swung up onto his horse and rode off into the woods, away from town, Rush allowed a slow, malevolent grin to spread over his face.

"Kathleen MacKenzie, eh?" he whispered. "My dear Griffin, at last I have discovered your Achilles' heel!"

"I can't believe I could have been so *stupid*!" Jack shouted, pacing across the dirt floor of the Gillis cabin.

"Sure you don't want a whiskey?" Sam inquired again. He sat by the fire, thankful that the Gillis brothers had gone off to Tuttletown to take in the show at the fandango hall. In his present mood, Jack didn't seem to care who knew he was the Griffin.

"Even while I was saying those things about Kathleen, warning him to leave her alone, I could hear the—the—"

"Emotion?" Sam suggested helpfully.

Jack stopped in his tracks and threw Clemens a quelling look. "Hmm . . . all right, yes, I could hear the emotion in my own voice. Just that undercurrent of passion, and that was all it took. Suddenly there was this smug twist to Rush's mouth, and this light in his eyes. Instead of sapping his power, I fear I've handed him just the weapon he's been looking for. . . ."

"What are you going to do about it?"

"God, I wish I knew! I only confronted him because I'm leaving for San Francisco tomorrow, after the wedding. Of course, *he* doesn't know that. I thought if I was menacing and mysterious enough—as the Griffin—and if he feared he might die if he defied me, I could leave with some peace of mind. But now I think it may have been a mistake. Rush has the idea that he's omnipotent, that he can do whatever he pleases without consequence. He hates the Griffin, and he may well view Kathleen as a weapon now, to use against me." Jack stopped to stare at Sam, the chiseled planes of his face accentuated in the fire's glow. "It has occurred to me that Rush might try to harm Kathleen in an effort to draw the Griffin out. He won't know that I'm gone."

A long silence fell between them, broken only by the hissing of the damp wood. Finally Clemens puffed at his cigar and shrugged as he exhaled a stream of smoke. "Have you thought of taking Katie with you?"

Jack ran a hand over his tired eyes. "I suppose it might be the only way. If I left here alone and anything happened to her . . ."

"Frankly, my friend, I think it would be the best thing for her, Rush or no Rush." Sam leaned forward, warming to the subject. "That girl needs to spread her wings, and she can't do it here. She's wasted in Columbia, slaving at that saloon and writing newspaper articles that few people ever read. In San Francisco, Katie would thrive, especially with the financial security you could provide."

Suddenly Jack felt drained. He took the chair next to Sam's and stared into the fire. "You're right, of course. The question is, how do I accomplish this?"

"Any ideas?" Sam inquired innocently.

He swallowed, then mustered a bleak smile. "I suppose I could marry her. . . ."

"To tell you the truth, I think you'd be doing both of you a favor!"

Jack pretended not to understand. "Well, under the circumstances, it would hardly be a conventional marriage, but that's not the point right now—''

"I'm not one to interfere," Sam said bluntly, "but if I were you, I'd a damned sight rather be married to Katie MacKenzie than your porcelain-proper Genevieve Braithwaite!"

Jack was numb. He couldn't let himself think past the moment for fear of colliding with emotions that shook him to the core. "I'd rather not debate that issue right now, if you don't mind. Of more immediate concern is how in hell I'm going to talk Kathleen into marrying me at all. It's insane to think that she'll agree to this."

A slow smile spread over Sam's face, widening his mustache. "Never try to second-guess a woman, my friend. I'll wager that if you were to just flat-out *ask* her, adding a sentimental word or two, you might be surprised by her answer."

Jack's eyebrows arched upward as he shook his head doubtfully. "I don't know. . . ." He sighed. "If I tell you something, will you give me your word that it will go no further?"

Clemens nodded. "Of course."

"Nothing's ever scared me more than the idea of proposing marriage to Kathleen MacKenzie."

"Hmm. You don't say." He puffed on his cigar, then added casually, "I wonder why that is?"

"You do?" Jack's tone was acid. "*I* don't, and furthermore, I don't want to discuss it!"

Gideon and Abby's wedding day dawned chilly and overcast. Katie woke at first light after a restless night's sleep. She had bathed the night before, and the curls that tumbled down her back when she got out of bed were still damp and fragrant.

Poppy mewed and stretched at the foot of the bed, watching her mistress pad barefoot out of the bedroom. The kitten considered following, but her little eyes drooped and closed, and soon she was purring through another dream.

Crisp, bright autumn leaves tumbled from the tree in front of the house. Standing at the kitchen window, Katie watched them fall and join the others that covered the neat front yard. Where was Jack? She hadn't seen him, or Sam, since he had left her in front of the saloon days ago, and even Gideon had begun to worry that his best man might have left the foothills. Would he come to the church today? Her heart tightened at the thought of seeing him again. By now she was past wishing she'd never met Jack; he was in her blood—he'd taken her from the achingly sweet fantasies of a young lady to the ardent reality of womanhood, and it was no longer possible to pretend otherwise.

She made a pot of tea and poured a cup. It was halfway to her lips when the sound of hoofbeats startled her, and the hot liquid sloshed over the rim and onto Katie's bare toes. She didn't feel it: her heart seemed to be beating in every part of her body as she peered through the window to see Jack dismount and stroll through the front gate.

There was a knock at the door. Katie managed to return the teacup to its saucer, then crossed to the parlor and opened the door a few inches.

In spite of his preoccupied state, Jack was enchanted by the sight of Katie peeking out, black-lashed sapphire eyes wide in her delicate, pale face. "Kathleen, could I talk to you for a few minutes?"

"I—I'm not dressed." She thought he looked tired, as if he hadn't slept, yet it only intensified his appeal. When he cocked a sardonic brow at the prim flannel nightgown that covered her, neck to toes, Katie saw his point and opened the door. "I suppose it's a bit late to bother with propriety, isn't it."

Jack smiled. "I'm afraid so."

Once he was inside, she kept herself busy fixing another cup of tea while Jack sat at the kitchen table and watched her. Finally there was nothing left to do but join him. "Gideon will be glad to see you. He'd begun to worry that you had gone back to San Francisco."

"What about you? Were you worried?" He watched Katie over the rim of his teacup, green eyes keen. "Did you care?"

She blushed instantly, helplessly. "I thought we agreed that it would be better to omit such personal questions between us."

"I changed my mind. We don't seem to have had much luck trying to undo what's already been done. Perhaps it would be better to go forward instead."

His eyes held hers in a way that made it difficult for Katie to breathe. "I . . . don't understand what you mean."

"Look, Kathleen, I know this is sudden, but only in one respect. There is actually a great deal between us; we already have a relationship of some depth. Only the acknowledgment of it is sudden. I am admitting that I have strong feelings where you are concerned, but before I go any further, perhaps I should ask if you are prepared to be honest about your feelings for me."

Jack's voice was gentle, melting Katie's defenses. Inwardly she groped for a touchstone, some past encounter between them similar to this one, but there was none. This time he wasn't taunting or challenging her, nor was he breaking down her will with the sheer force of his own. At this moment, Katie felt that Jack sincerely wanted to know what was in her heart. She gazed into his eyes, caught by the soft flecks of gold within the green, and just this once allowed herself to trust him. "Yes, I have feelings for you. It's no use pretending otherwise, though I've certainly tried."

"You've already admitted that you're physically attracted to me, and you're certainly aware that it's mutual. Perhaps you've thought that it's simply because you're lovely and available in this rather remote locale. The truth is that I have never felt so powerfully drawn to any other woman." Katie's cheeks grew warm, and she dropped her eyes. Disarmed, Jack smiled and reached across the space between them to take her hand. It was soft and small in his own. "What I would like you to tell me is whether or not you feel something more toward me."

"Are you talking about . . . love?" Katie heard herself speak from far away, over the roaring of blood in her ears.

"Well, not necessarily," he replied carefully. He felt as if he were walking a tightrope: unable or unwilling to fully explore his own feelings where Katie was concerned, yet obliged to bring things out in the open just enough to persuade her to marry him. "Do you think that there is friendship between us? Do you care for me at all?"

She nodded slowly, confused. "Jack, why are you asking me these things?"

He pulled his chair closer to hers and touched her cheek with his fingertips. "Kathleen, I can't ignore the bond that has formed between us any longer. I have to return to San Francisco today, and I don't know when, or if, I'll be back here. I *do* know that I don't want to leave you behind. I'm offering you a new life, in a city that I think you would find very exciting. If you come with me, you'll discover that my existence there is quite different from the one I enjoy here. I know you'll be shocked to hear this, but I actually own a business in San Francisco, and am considered to be—dare I say it?—a respectable citizen. I can offer you a comfortable home and financial security." Jack's tone was wryly detached as he recited the list of his own qualifications. "Actually, I think that we could deal quite well together. I realize that this is sudden . . ."

Katie's head was spinning. Surely this couldn't be happening. Any moment now she would wake up in her bed and find that their entire conversation had been a dream.

"But all I ask," Jack continued, running a fingertip along Katie's jaw that sent delicious shivers racing down her spine, "is that you think about what I've said for the rest of the morning. You can give me your answer when we all meet at the church this afternoon.''

She tried to digest his words. "I'm not sure I understand. Are you asking me to be your . . . mistress?''

Jack stared for a moment, startled, then threw back his head and laughed. "God, no! Did I forget to mention marriage?'' Amused, he dropped to one knee and clasped her hands. "Kathleen, I am asking you to be my wife.''

A knock at the door interrupted them. "Who is it?'' Katie called, her voice cracking.

"It's Mrs. Barnstaple, my dear. I thought I ought to check the hem of your gown one more time, just in case.''

Alarmed and confused, Katie tugged at Jack's hands. "Get up,'' she hissed. "You'll have to go out the back door. I could never explain the two of us, with me in my nightgown, to her! Turning her head, she called again, "Wait just a moment, Mrs. Barnstaple—I'll be right there!''

The absurdity of the situation did not escape Jack as Katie rushed barefoot across the kitchen and opened the door for him.

"Go!'' she urged.

Jack grinned. "Is this any way to treat the man who has just knelt before you and offered you not only his heart, but all his worldly goods as well? Shall I interpret your behavior as a hint to brace myself for rejection later in the day?''

"Will you *go*! I can't even think straight right now—we'll have to discuss it at the church,'' Katie replied, feeling utterly crazed. When he had stepped into the backyard, a thought occurred to her and she stopped in the midst of closing the door. "Wait! I just want to know one thing. Does your sudden desire not to leave me behind in Columbia have anything to do with Aaron Rush?''

Jack met her suspicious gaze unflinchingly. "My dear, if you imagine that I am chivalrous enough to propose marriage to every damsel in distress whom I encounter, you are giving me far too much credit. Believe me, I am no knight in shining armor!''

"Of course. How could I have forgotten?'' she murmured dryly. Still, watching Jack saunter across the yard and vault lightly over the picket fence, his muscular body outlined against dungarees and a faded red flannel shirt, Katie felt the familiar waves of desire wash over her. To say the least, the decision that faced her would necessitate a tug-of-war between her head and her heart. . . .

CHAPTER
21

October 27, 1864

T HE FRAGRANCE OF PINK AND IVORY HOTHOUSE ROSES ENVE-
loped Katie as she held the bride's bouquet together with her own.
Abby stood in front of her, clasping Gideon's hands as they listened
to the minister.

For the most part Katie was far away, her thoughts were a jumble.
But there remained a quiet corner of her mind that attended to the
moment, enjoying the occasion and all its trimmings. She felt quite
beautiful in her gown—a lavender-blue silk taffeta with goffered
flounces around the hem—and she had been surprised and pleased
when she'd first glimpsed herself in the mirror. Wrapped in a sash
of fringed white silk, her waist looked tiny. Her breasts were high,
and her creamy neck and exquisite features were set off perfectly
by the simple, rose-studded chignon at the base of her neck. The
events of the morning left her with pink-smudged cheeks and bright,
thick-lashed blue eyes that were accentuated by the pale violet of
her gown.

Abby, too, looked radiant. Because this was her second marriage, she had opted for a dress of cream-colored muslin in the
same style as Katie's, with a fringed sash of pink silk. Her golden
curls were cunningly adorned with a garland of pink and ivory roses
that matched the bouquet Katie now held for her. Abby's soft doe
eyes were clear as she repeated after Pastor Hitchcock:

"I, Abigail, take thee, Gideon, to be my wedded husband, and I do promise and covenant, before God and these witnesses, to be your loving and faithful wife, in plenty and in want, in joy and in sorrow, in sickness and in health, as long as we both shall live."

Katie heard the words and held them close to her heart. How serious it all was! Gazing past the bride and groom, she saw Jack, his profile burnished by the light that filtered through the stained-glass windows. He was tanned and handsome in his gray suit and blue silk cravat, accented by a white rosebud pinned to a lapel. Katie stared at his roguish features, which were sober yet softened by affection for his two friends. There was a great deal that she didn't know about Jack. For instance, what had become of the woman he had told Abby was "planning a spring wedding"? However, what she did know was important. In spite of their quarrels, he was a good man and a loyal friend. He was intelligent and witty, and he seemed to be honest. He wanted to take her away from Columbia, which both frightened and excited her. Katie was stimulated by his company; she couldn't imagine being bored by Jack, unlike nearly every other man she had met. And last, there was the matter of the intense physical attraction between them and the deeper feelings that she could no longer deny were in her heart.

There had been a certain detachment on Jack's part, even as he proposed marriage, that worried her. There were a great many risks involved if she agreed, but even that thought sent a thrill through her body. The more she considered Jack's proposal, the more she realized that a new life in San Francisco as Jack Adams's wife held the possibility of great happiness and fulfillment.

Pastor Hitchcock was saying, "By the authority vested in me as a minister of the Church of Christ, I now pronounce you man and wife."

As bride and groom kissed, Jack glanced sideways and met Katie's eyes. It was apparent that she had been looking at him; now she blushed tellingly. He suppressed a smile. Caught up in the challenge of convincing her to marry him, Jack had kept his own fears at bay. Now, as they threatened to rise again, he made a conscious effort to suppress them. The thought of committing himself to a lifetime with *any* woman was disquieting, to say the least. But Kathleen MacKenzie was not just any woman. His heart told him that there were good reasons to take her as his wife: she was intelligent, lively, and beautiful. Thoroughly unique. And she excited him physically to an extent that he had not believed possible in the past. But was that a qualification for a wife? Jonathan Wyatt, self-contained, punctilious editor of the *Morning Star*, had his doubts. Katie was nothing like the woman he had long ago decided would make the best sort of wife. When it had become clear that he was reaching the age at which a family was desirable, Wyatt had thought that an *orderly* sort of marriage would be best. Passion, in and out of bed, would be less complicating if sought outside the home.

Well, it was no use having second thoughts now. He'd already proposed. As the organ sounded the recessional and Gideon and Abby walked back down the aisle, Jack went to meet Katie and offer her his arm. She gave him a guileless smile that bespoke her own mixed feelings and softened his heart.

Emerging from the church into the cool, drizzly afternoon, they found a congratulatory crowd already forming around Gideon and Abby. Pastor Hitchcock came over to shake Jack's hand, then he turned to Katie, smiling.

"I have to tell you, my dear, how very beautiful you look today. I confess, as I watched you come down the aisle, I worried for a moment that you might outshine the bride!"

"I appreciate the compliment, Pastor, but I don't think there was any danger of that," Katie replied, laughing. "Abby was the loveliest, most radiant bride I have ever seen."

"Yes, it's a wonderful day, isn't it? Romance is in the air!" The old man breathed deeply and sighed. "This occasion must be the stuff of dreams for you, my dear."

"Actually, it's more the stuff of fear!" She laughed again, nervously. "Marriage is a very serious step, isn't it?" Katie felt Jack's sharp glance but kept her eyes on the minister.

"That's very true, my dear, but that's where the magic of love steps in. Love allows us to take risks and meet challenges that we might otherwise shy away from if . . ."

"We were in our right minds?" Jack supplied helpfully.

Katie shot him a reproving look, while Pastor Hitchcock chuckled uneasily. "Well, I see that the crowd is thinning, so I suppose I should go over and congratulate the happy couple. Thank you for being part of the ceremony, Katie." He clasped both her hands, then turned to Jack and shook his hand again. "You, too, Mr. Adams."

When the minister had walked away, Jack saw his chance and took Katie's arm. "You and I need to talk."

"But we can't just leave!" Panic rose in her.

"This won't take long." He drew her along beside him until they were behind the church, sheltered between two oak trees, their orange leaves spangled against the slate-colored sky. "Have you made up your mind?" Jack asked bluntly.

"I don't know!" she cried, confused by his manner. "This is all so sudden, I haven't had a chance to adjust to the idea—"

"Kathleen, there isn't time for you to adjust. I have to leave today." He stared at her for a moment, then his mouth curved slightly in an ironic smile. "Look at it this way: do you think you'll get a better offer from the men you meet here in Columbia? Setting your feelings for me aside, this is a rare opportunity for you to enrich your life. You have too many gifts to waste them slaving your best years away in that saloon. Columbia is fading; we both know that. San Francisco is in full bloom. Come with me, Kathleen. You can have a home, children, interesting friends, all the books and culture you could possibly desire . . ." Jack paused, gazing into her eyes. "And you can have me. I'm not so bad, am I?"

Katie blushed again, dropping her eyes when he reached out to take her hand. His fingers were warm as he stroked hers, one by one, up to her fingernails. "No . . . of course not. It's just that I'm—afraid, I guess."

"Kathleen," he whispered, "look at me." Tipping up her chin, Jack caressed the delicate line of her jaw with his forefinger. He could feel Katie melting beneath his touch. "There is risk involved for both of us, but I'm a bit tired of playing it safe where my personal life is concerned. I'd rather be married to a warm-blooded woman than a porcelain doll."

Katie gasped when his lips grazed hers. Then Jack was kissing her passionately, holding her chin with one strong hand while his free arm rounded her back to press her body against the length of his own. His mouth was a brand of fire, burning her doubts away, extinguishing all thought. Katie trembled in his embrace, surrendering to his touch with uncontrollable desire.

At length, he lifted his head and commanded roughly, "Say yes."

Katie's senses swam, and she held on to him for fear her knees would give way. Desperately, she sought to retain a measure of dignity and control over the situation. "Just a moment. First you must promise me one thing."

Jack lifted his eyebrows quizzically. "Indeed?"

"You have to promise me that you won't try to rule me. As your wife, I will not be your possession. I have been independent too long to take orders from anyone. Even my husband!"

He grinned, enjoying the light that flashed in her blue eyes. "All right, I promise not to attempt to rule you."

"Then, *yes*, I'll marry you."

If Katie had been expecting Jack to fall to his knees with relief, declaring his love for her, she was doomed to disappointment. "Well, good. That's settled," he said, looking distracted. "There's a stage at three o'clock, and we must be on it. We'll be married in Sacramento tomorrow, and go on to San Francisco by riverboat the next morning."

"Three o'clock!" she exclaimed. "But I have to pack!"

"You won't need much. We'll have new gowns made for you in San Francisco. Just toss the possessions that mean the most to you in a trunk, say good-bye to your friends, and we'll be off. Oh, and don't tell anyone—not even Abby or Lim—where we'll be living. You can write to them later, but for the time being, I'd rather not have it get back to Aaron Rush." Jack's tone was casual.

He was already steering her back around the church, and Katie felt as if she were jumping off a cliff into the vast unknown.

"Are you going to tell Katie that you're the Griffin?" Sam Clemens asked Jack as they walked toward the MacKenzie Saloon.

"Of course not! I haven't even told her yet that I'm Jonathan Wyatt."

"*Really!*" Sam's thick brows jumped at this intriguing bit of information.

"Don't worry, I'll find a way to explain that part. I can *almost* tell her the truth—that I was bored with my respectable existence in San Francisco. She already knows that I have a different sort of life there, with a stable income and a home—"

Clemens laughed. "That's rather an understatement, my friend."

"Do you imagine that Kathleen will be disappointed?" Jack shot back dryly. "As for the Griffin, I'm leaving him behind for good this time. I've done all I can under that guise, and can only hope that Rush will take the Griffin's advice to heart—and the townspeople will stand up to him on their own."

"What will happen to the saloon?"

"Kathleen doesn't want it sold yet. I suppose she half fears she might need to return one day if marriage to me proves too unbearable." His voice was laced with irony. "I spoke to Gideon, Abby, and Lim after the wedding, while Kathleen went home to pack, and they've agreed to run it for her. She has no desire for any share of the profits, only that the place be maintained as in the past, and continue under the MacKenzie name."

The wedding reception, which had been held at the saloon, was ending, and Jack and Sam had to wait for a stream of guests clad in their Sunday best to pass by on their way out before the two men could enter. Inside, the scarred tables were covered with white linen cloths, plates with half-eaten slices of cake, and empty wineglasses. The table in the center of the room held the wreckage of the magnificent tiered wedding cake that Katie had labored over for days. Abby, still clad in her bridal gown, stood near the bar with Gideon, while Katie and Lim were emerging from the kitchen, talking animatedly.

"Hello, Mr. Adams." Maggie Barnstaple approached, resplendent in a gown of sea-green silk, its neckline and hem flounces edged with black guipure lace. Holding out her hands, she clasped his and leaned forward to peck his tanned cheek. "It seems that congratulations are in order for you as well as Mr. and Mrs. Henderson. What a rascal you are, conducting your courtship of Miss MacKenzie in secret!"

"Yes indeed," said Victoria Barnstaple, stepping up beside her niece. Her birdlike features were pinched with suspicious disapproval. "I find it rather curious myself. I would have hoped, since Katie's dear parents are both deceased, that she might have come to me for a few words of advice. But then she tells me that your proposal was rather sudden."

"But no less sincere, I assure you, ma'am," Jack said with all the sobriety he could muster. He introduced Sam to the two women, then continued, "If it will help to allay your concern, Mrs. Barnstaple, I can promise you that Katie will want for nothing as my wife. I'll be good to her."

"She won't even tell me where the two of you will be living!" Victoria protested, her voice rising.

"May I speak to you frankly, trusting that whatever I say will go no further?" Both women nodded, and he continued, "I'm a bit worried about Kathleen's safety. Because of her outspokenness, certain people in Columbia bear her ill will, and I'm anxious to take her away from here. Perhaps I'm merely overreacting like any man in love, but I'd rather wait a while before telling anyone where we're living. It may seem to you that I'm exercising too much caution—"

"Not at all," Mrs. Barnstaple said, her face softening considerably. "Darling Katie's safety must come first, and it pleases me to discover that you share my concern for her welfare. I suppose that there's nothing for me to do but wish you both well, say a prayer, and wait for a letter."

"I appreciate your understanding, ma'am." Jack gave her his most sincere smile and turned to Maggie. "Miss Barnstaple, may

I say that it has been a great pleasure knowing you? You are a delightful young lady, and I wish you all the best."

"Thank you, Mr. Adams. Your friendship has meant a good deal to me, too. I shall miss you."

Looking back over his shoulder at Sam, Jack winked slightly. "Mr. Clemens will be in town from time to time. He's been a great friend to me, and I'm sure he'll be glad to drop by and visit with you."

"It would be my pleasure," Sam affirmed with a grin.

The women bade them farewell then, and Jack turned his attention to Katie. She was behind the bar, dusting the jars of brandied fruit with a wistful expression on her face.

"Look at her," Jack murmured, scarcely aware that he spoke the thought aloud.

"It would be hard not to love such a beautiful creature," Sam observed. "She's glorious to look at, but a good portion of that is radiated from within. In her own way, Katie is untamed, yet also more civilized in her views and values than most people I've known."

Staring at her, Jack felt the familiar rush of desire, admiration, affection, and fear, but he was becoming used to it. He braced himself and waited for it to pass. Then, as if reading his mind and heart from across the room, Abby came over. Jack didn't see her until she put her hand on his shoulder.

"Everything will be fine," she whispered. "Try to relax and put yourself in God's hands."

Jack smiled at her fondly. "Thanks, Abby. You've become quite the sage . . . and you're the most beautiful bride I've ever seen."

"Flatterer." She beamed.

Sam looked at his pocketwatch. "It's half-past two, in case anyone's interested."

"It was good of you to let Katie come alone to make her farewells," Abby told Jack. "It's hard for her to leave Columbia, her friends, and the saloon."

"I think the change will do her good, though, don't you?"

She nodded. "Heavens, yes! She's strong, and she'll adapt—but that doesn't make the parting any easier." Abby met his green eyes earnestly. "You be good to her, Jack. You have a real chance for happiness."

Before Jack had a chance to reply, Katie came out from behind the bar. She wore Brian MacKenzie's favorite dress, the gown of violet-dotted white percale with the lace collar and violet sash. Her hair was still caught back in the smooth chignon that made her eyes look enormous, and she wore her mother's cameo at her neck. Lim and Gideon both hugged her, then walked over with her to say their good-byes to Jack.

"Lim, you mustn't be sad. We'll be together again soon," Katie promised. "You'll all come and visit me—us—and we'll have a fine time." She looked up at Jack. "Isn't that so?"

"Absolutely." He nodded. "You are all welcome at any time in our home."

More farewells were exchanged all around, then they walked as a group down Main Street to the stage depot. Katie found herself thinking back to scenes from her past as she gazed around at the buildings. The doors to the Wells Fargo office were open next door to the stage depot, but William Daegner, the agent, had no customers today. Katie thought back to years gone by, when men had been lined up for over three blocks, waiting to reach the beautiful gold scales where millions of dollars' worth of gold was weighed.

Gideon patted her shoulder, sensing her mood, and Katie looked up into his eyes. "It's sad, isn't it, how Columbia has changed?"

"Well, change is part of life, I think."

"I know." She gave him a brave smile. "I'm ready."

The stagecoach was waiting in front of the depot, ready to depart. There were no passengers from Sonora who were continuing on. Jack had already purchased their tickets, and now he and the driver lifted Katie's hastily packed trunk up on top. Jack's own small bag followed, but Katie insisted on keeping the one she carried with her. Sam, Abby, and Gideon exchanged hugs and good wishes with the departing couple. It wasn't too difficult for Katie to leave them, since she knew that they would all be happy and fulfilled without her. In Lim's case, however, it was different. They had grown up together, sharing their dreams, and Katie found this parting to be the most wrenching of all.

"I'll write to you soon, I promise," she told him through a mist of tears.

Lim held her hands. "Don't worry, I'll be fine. I'll take care of the saloon for you, and we'll look after your house, and Willoughby."

"Only for a little while. Abby and Gideon will look for someone to help at the saloon, and you'll be able to begin a new life in San Francisco. It will be just the way we always dreamed—"

"Yes." He wiped his eyes with the back of his hand. "I hope you find all the happiness and love you deserve, Katie."

"I intend to!" They grinned at each other, and then Jack was gently handing her into the stagecoach.

Moments later Katie was leaning out the window, waving as the stage turned up Washington Street. Jack, meanwhile, admired the curves of her derriere, displayed at eye level for him to appreciate. She continued to look back all the way north on Broadway, until they rumbled onto Parrots Ferry Road and the last building had faded from sight. Then, no sooner had she settled herself next to her betrothed, trying to think of something to say, than a faint "meoww" broke the silence.

Jack looked startled. "What was that?"

Fearlessly she met his gaze. "It's Poppy."

"I beg your pardon?"

"Poppy!" Katie reached into the carpetbag she'd brought on board and lifted out the calico kitten. "You gave her to me, remember? Surely you didn't imagine that I would leave her behind?"

Jack stared, astonished, at the scrappy little kitten, then began to laugh. "To tell you the truth, I'd forgotten all about that kitten, but I can assure you that if I had remembered, I certainly would not have expected you, of all people, to abandon her."

Braced for an argument, Katie felt a trifle deflated. "Well—good!" She sat back against the worn upholstered seat and concentrated on soothing Poppy.

Jack watched, smiling as he thought of Harriet, his grandfather's enormous old gray cat, who took for granted her autocratic position in the Wyatt household. No one, it seemed, would be spared the changes that Katie's arrival would cause, and Jack was beginning to look forward to watching the drama unfold.

CHAPTER
22

Sacramento, California
October 29–31, 1864

F ROM THE MOMENT OF HER DEPARTURE FROM COLUMBIA, KA-
tie had little opportunity to dwell upon the past. She hadn't traveled
to Sacramento since her childhood, and the winding, bumpy journey was fascinating in itself. The weather continued to be chilly,
bleak, and damp, but the landscape was inexpressibly lovely to her
fresh eyes. As they descended toward California's central valley,
the hills softened and the pine trees began to disappear. The
bleached summer grass, not yet returned to green lushness by the
rains of autumn, served as a backdrop for dramatic scrub oak trees.
Their twisted branches were clotted with mistletoe or blanketed in
golden-yellow wild grape. Against the dark background of the oak,
scattered ailanthus trees sprang out in pale lemon, or an occasional
poplar blazed orange fire. Where the dry creekbeds marked canyon
bottoms, there were feathery willows, and the entire underbrush
was a tangle of low-growing wild peach, dense tall manzanita, and
red-berried toyon.

And the views changed constantly. In Calaveras County, the bare
hilltops were littered with chunks of dark porous rock. Ages ago a
volcano had spouted here, and the broken lava mixed with frag-
ments of slate to make it hard going for the stagecoach.

Jack's horse was ridden partway by an extra stage driver. When more passengers joined them, however, Jack gave up his seat and transferred to Byron's back. It left little opportunity for communication between Katie and her future husband, but she found that she didn't mind. His nearness only served to remind her of the chance she was taking, leaving behind a familiar, emotionally safe world and heading toward a future filled with unknowns—as someone's *wife*. Every time Katie glanced out the stagecoach window at Jack, ruggedly graceful astride Byron, countless conflicting emotions rushed over her as she thought of sharing the rest of her life with him. Warm, excited, and panicky, she would turn to one of the other passengers and strike up a diverting conversation or hold the purring Poppy nearer for reassurance.

When they reached Sacramento the next day, Katie was dusty and tired but too excited to think of sleep. With an unsettling mixture of anticipation and fear, she allowed Jack to help her down from the stagecoach. The office for the California Stage Company was located in the Orleans Hotel, where, it developed, they would spend their wedding night.

The Orleans was probably the grandest hotel in Sacramento. Originally it had been shipped, precut, around Cape Horn from New Orleans, then assembled piece by piece on Second Street. After it had burned in the fire of 1852, the Orleans was immediately rebuilt in brick and now boasted a reading room, billiard room, saloon, and the stage office. Upstairs the accommodations ranged from tastefully modest rooms to plush, spacious suites.

Katie moved through the next few hours in a daze. Jack took a suite for them, comprised of a parlor, bathroom, and bedchamber, all decorated in shades of forest green and ivory. Then he went off to make arrangements for their wedding, while Katie took a long, hot bath and washed her hair with French soap that smelled of damask rose. Afterward she put on a soft cotton chemise and dried her hair in the sunlight that streamed through the bedroom windows. Their suite overlooked Sacramento's bustling, muddy streets, while the wide Sacramento River wound behind, barely a quarter-mile in the distance.

Slipping into a wrapper, Katie peeked around the parted draperies and wondered at all the people who walked and rode along the thoroughfare below. Some of them looked like the rough mountain men and miners who frequented her saloon in Columbia, but many more appeared to be prosperous, civilized members of an upper class. Friendly merchants exchanged greetings with passersby, while children walked with their mothers or played together on the wooden sidewalks. There were establishments of every description: general stores, a French importer, provision stores, a daguerrotype gallery, bakeries, liquor stores, a millinery shop, banks, and hotels as far as she could see. A block behind the Orleans was the waterfront, crowded with vessels, while the river was dotted with fishing boats. Sacramento exuded an energy that was irresistible, and Katie found herself looking forward more than ever to discovering the delights of San Francisco.

A knock at the door roused her from her daydreams. Expecting Jack, she was surprised to find a meek-looking maid standing in the hallway.

"Mr. Adams asks that you meet him downstairs at five o'clock."

"What time is it now?" Katie asked.

"It's nearly four," the girl replied. "There's a clock on the table in the parlor."

"Oh. Thank you. Could you come back in half an hour to help me fasten my gown?" Katie asked.

"I'd be happy to, ma'am!"

Katie was glad of the brief respite. It allowed her to lie down for a bit, then dress leisurely. She wondered if Jack intended to be married without a bath and shave, dressed in the flannel shirt and dungarees he had been wearing when they arrived. Would he then come to their marriage bed with the dust of the road on him? Katie decided not to think about it. Instead, she thought of the vices Jack did *not* have. Unlike nearly every man she knew, he did not drink liquor, smoke cigars, or chew tobacco. During the years spent in the saloon, Katie had developed a powerful aversion to the smelly brown liquid filling the spittoons. A little dust on Jack's body would be a blessing compared to tobacco juice in his mouth!

At ten minutes before five o'clock, the maid had departed again, and Katie stood surveying herself before the full-length cheval mirror in the bedroom. She wore the gown from Abby and Gideon's wedding because it was the best one she owned. Perhaps it was too fancy for the wedding Jack had in mind, but stubbornly, Katie didn't care. Even though they wouldn't be married in a church, with all their friends present, she still wanted to look as much like a bride as possible.

It took her a few minutes to pin her ebony hair into a smooth, loose chignon at the base of her neck. Her sapphire eyes were brilliant with excitement, her cheeks were slightly flushed, and she had applied some rose-tinted salve to her full lips. The gown fit beautifully, showing off her white shoulders and nipping in at her waist. As her only adornment, Katie pinned her mother's cameo between her breasts. She wished she had flowers and suddenly found herself remembering her birthday, and the bouquet of lilies and larkspur that her father had given her. She had met Jack that day. How long ago it seemed! For a moment, she closed her eyes and pictured both her parents in her mind, together, watching over her and smiling. This was her wedding day, and she knew they were with her in spirit, praying for her happiness.

Poppy was curled in the corner of a green velvet settee in the parlor, purring contentedly after her lunch of fresh salmon. Katie paused to stroke the kitten, then rustled into the hall and closed the door. The walk downstairs seemed endless. Her palms were damp, and she felt slightly nauseous. Would Jack laugh when he saw that she had dressed so elaborately? What if he made her go back upstairs and change into a dress that better matched his own attire?

Then she stepped into the ornate lobby and saw Jack stand and come forward to meet her. Clad in a perfectly tailored midnight-blue morning coat over a crisp white shirt, simple wrapped cravat, double-breasted waistcoat, and black trousers, he was indescribably handsome. His tawny hair had been trimmed, he was freshly shaven, and his clean, tanned face looked appealingly healthy against the white of his collar.

Although overwhelmed at the sight of him, Katie was determined not to show more emotion than he did. Taking her cue from his friendly but polite smile, she held out her hand and said, "How did you manage this miraculous transformation?"

"Surely you didn't expect me to attend my own wedding in the guise of a grimy frontiersman?" He laughed softly. "Actually I have friends here in Sacramento, and in the past I have kept some clothes at their house against the occasional concert or play. Today, I visited Stephen and Amanda to ask them to act as witnesses for our wedding—and while I was there, I bathed, shaved, and put on more suitable clothing. I thought you might appreciate the time alone."

During this speech, Katie sensed a preoccupation in Jack as he steered her through the lobby of the Orleans Hotel and out onto Second Street. Now she could feel the tension emanating from his strong body, which fueled her own anxiety. "Jack, is something bothering you? Have you changed your mind? If so, you may certainly tell me, and I can assure you that I will understand. I mean—"

Looking down, he gently placed a silencing finger over her mouth. "Hush. No, I haven't changed my mind, but yes, I admit that something is bothering me. I thought we would walk to the church so that I could talk to you about it."

"All right."

They walked in silence for a few minutes, turning west onto K Street and heading away from the river. Jack guided her through the muddy thoroughfare and up onto the wooden sidewalk as Katie gingerly held up her skirts. Finally he said, "Jack Adams is not my real name."

"I beg your pardon?"

"Your name, when we marry, will be Wyatt. My true name is Jonathan Wyatt. Adams is my mother's maiden name."

"I don't understand!"

"I became Jack Adams when I went to the foothills because the life I led there was so different from the one I have in San Francisco. I felt like a different man, and I suppose it was an escape. When I was there, I gradually *became* another man, and in time that identity seemed more real to me than the one I had as Jonathan Wyatt, in San Francisco."

Katie was shaking her head. "It's so confusing . . . but perhaps I do understand. Perhaps I'm just stunned. It simply never occurred to me . . ." She twisted her hands together, thinking. "It makes sense, in a way—your trips back to San Francisco and the vagueness of your answers whenever I asked about your life in the city. Looking back, you did seem torn between the two existences. What concerns me most right now, however, is—" Katie broke off, wondering how to phrase her thoughts.

"Yes?"

"Who *is* Jonathan Wyatt? Do I know the man I am about to marry?"

Jack turned and looked down at her, his sage-green eyes sober. "I can't imagine that the man I am when I am with you will change very much, but on the other hand, I hesitate to make any promises. I honestly don't know. You'll understand better when we arrive in San Francisco and you are able to see for yourself what your life will be like." He started to walk again, steering Katie around the traffic outside a dry goods store. "Perhaps it would be best for you to approach this marriage from a practical standpoint, rather than dwelling on my personal qualities as a husband."

Katie's head was spinning. "What do you mean?"

"You haven't forgotten what we talked about when I first suggested marriage to you?"

"Don't you mean *proposed* marriage?" Somewhere at the back of her mind an alarm was sounding, setting her nerves on edge and alerting all her senses. Jack's tone of voice was too studied, too casual. He'd been holding her at arm's length ever since the scene between them at the Gillis cabin, and at the time that had suited her own need to keep a safe distance from her feelings. Now, however, on the brink of their wedding, he was withdrawing even further, and it frightened her.

Jack ignored her correction. "We agreed that there were plenty of sound reasons for you to marry me, aside from the relationship between us. It might be wiser for you to focus on those for the time being, rather than on me. I feel confident that you and I will have a perfectly respectable marriage if we allow enough time to get our bearings." He gave her what was meant to be a reassuring smile. "There's the church."

Startled, Katie found that they'd turned the corner of Sixth Street and were approaching a handsome brick church. A well-dressed young man and woman were standing on the steps, waving.

"Hello, Jack," the woman called. "I'm so excited! Do hurry and introduce us to your beautiful bride!"

The next few hours passed in a blur of unreality for Katie. Reverend Benton, a dynamic Congregational minister who had already made his mark in Sacramento, performed the wedding ceremony in a church that was empty except for the bride, groom, and Stephen and Amanda Knauer, who acted as witnesses. Reverend Benton had agreed to marry them as a favor to Jack, who apparently was a long-standing friend. The Knauers seemed overjoyed that Jack was finally taking a wife, and it soon became clear to Katie that they believed he had been overcome by true love. Amanda found the sheer romance of it all positively thrilling.

During the ceremony, Jack was irresistibly charming. He had even arranged for a small bouquet of white roses to be delivered for the bride. Everyone exuded pleasure, so Katie tried her best to act her part, too. She smiled into Jack's eyes as she recited her vows, promising to love, honor, and cherish Jonathan Wyatt, although the name meant nothing to her and the man himself was little more than a stranger. As if sensing her numbness, Jack elicited a shock of passion from her by kissing her intimately after they were pronounced man and wife.

The Knauers took the Wyatts in their carriage to their large brick home on Third and N streets, and there the newlyweds were treated to a delicious candlelight supper of pea soup, pheasant, apples and rice, carrot pudding, and Damson plum tart. Katie ate and chatted dutifully, though she couldn't taste the food and the champagne went to her head. She wished that she had followed Jack's example and declined it. When Amanda Knauer remarked worriedly that

Katie appeared to be a bit pale, Jack replied that she was merely tired from the long journey and the excitement of the day. Fondly he patted her hand, and Katie nodded and smiled agreement. She felt as if she had been dropped into a play set on an unfamiliar stage with actors who were all playing their roles to perfection—and demanded the same of her. Even Jack seemed transformed; sophisticated and at ease among Sacramento's most elite citizens, he bore little resemblance to the man she had known in Columbia. His voice seemed more cultured, his laughter softer, his conversation more careful and intelligent. His movements were more controlled, less infused with masculine energy. In short, Jonathan Wyatt was a gentleman.

It was past nine o'clock when the Knauers' carriage deposited them at the Orleans Hotel. Katie had never felt more drained, and desired only to climb into bed, pull the covers over her head, and sleep endlessly. She moved up the stairs in a fog, barely aware of Jack walking next to her until he unlocked the door to their suite and lightly touched the small of her back to signal her to enter. Even through her gown and corset, the brush of his fingers sent fire streaking over her nerves. Involuntarily her eyes were drawn to the wide gold band on her left hand as she remembered that the wedding night still loomed before them. Her heart began to pound so loudly, she was certain he must hear it.

Inside, Jack went immediately into the bedroom and lit the lamp next to the magnificently carved Gothic revival bed. Katie hovered in the doorway, watching as he stripped off his coat and sat down on the forest-green velvet bedspread. She liked to watch Jack move: he was graceful and masculine all at once, the muscles in his arms and shoulders flexing against the fine linen of his shirt as he bent to remove his shoes. Soft lamplight burnished his hair, and when he looked up at her, Katie was enthralled by the sober male beauty of his face.

"How are you feeling, Mrs. Wyatt?" he asked softly.

"Fine, I think." She tried to smile. "A little tired." She prayed that he would suggest she get a good night's sleep.

He stood up and held out his hands to her. "Why don't you let me help you relax?"

Katie went to him with trepidation. Her cheeks were warm, but her hands were cold as she put them in Jack's. "It's hard to believe that we're really married."

"But it's true. You are my wife now, Kathleen."

The tone of his voice told her that he fully intended to exercise his rights as her husband. She had come to believe that the physical attraction between them was too vital to extinguish, but now she felt as shy as if Jack were touching her for the first time. In the past, she had given herself over to the loss of control, to the flame that caught and spread in spite of its forbidden nature. It had seemed to Katie that they were both powerless . . . then. Was that passion lost now? Everything seemed different, including Jack himself. It was as if they were strangers who had met on their wedding day. ·

Slowly Jack turned her around and began to unfasten the back of her gown. She felt freezing cold; it was all she could do to keep from shivering. After sliding the sleeves down her arms to free the top half of her body, Jack put his hands on her shoulders and kneaded gently, soothingly. Something seemed to break inside of Katie. She nearly sagged against him and whimpered with pleasure. His fingers found every source of hidden tension, probing expertly until she sighed with gratitude. When the touching ceased she held her breath, eyes closed. Time seemed suspended . . . and then warm, firm lips pressed the nape of her neck, burning, sending shivers down her spine. Suddenly Katie was anticipating the next step, when he would pull her into his arms and kiss her in earnest.

"Relax, Kathleen," he whispered, his breath tickling her ear. "And wait."

His tone was seductive, and she was startled to feel a hot twinge between her legs. Jack removed her gown and unwieldy crinoline, leaving Katie standing in stockings, lace-trimmed drawers, chemise, and corset. He surveyed her, and the patient, predatory gleam in his eyes made her blush. Her heart beat not with fear, but with expectation. From beneath her lashes, Katie watched as he removed his waistcoat and unbuttoned his snow-white shirt to give her a glimpse of the tanned, lean-muscled chest behind it. The memory of his scent and warmth heightened her desire.

With excruciating slowness, Jack unlaced Katie's corset, tossed it aside, then slid down her gauzy drawers so that she could step out of them. Then he stood back and gazed at her for a moment. Her legs were slim and sleek in the creamy stockings, and the simple cotton-and-lace chemise nipped in at her waist and clung to the curves of her full breasts. Jack's blood pounded with pure lust. Reaching around, he removed the pins from her hair so that it spilled in soft, fragrant waves to her hips.

"My God, but you are beautiful," he murmured. Try as he might to distance himself from her emotionally, the physical passion Katie elicited from him always caught him off guard. There was something about her—that mixture of intelligence, naiveté, gloriously innocent beauty, and lush, untutored sexuality—that aroused him in a way that no other woman ever had.

Katie could feel Jack's heat as he stood before her and ran his fingers lightly up her arms, caressing her throat and shoulders, then down over the sides of her chemise. His eyes held hers as he paused for a moment before grazing her breasts with his fingertips. Instantly Katie's breathing changed. The tingling ache in her breasts was almost unbearable. Her nipples tautened against the thin cotton of the chemise, and she felt an ache begin to build deep inside her, a throbbing that left her moist with desire. Still gazing into Katie's eyes, Jack reached for her trembling hand and placed it over the ridge outlined against his trousers. Her blush deepened even as she curved her fingers around him.

"I want you, my beautiful wife," he said huskily.

Katie nodded. "I want you, too," she managed to whisper.

He flicked open the tiny buttons of her chemise, his green eyes devouring her body as it slipped to the ground. Proud and shy, she stood before him, naked except for the pale stockings. Jack moved closer and traced the curve of her waist and hips with wondering hands, then cupped her buttocks and drew her against him. Involuntarily, she arched against the hardness of his manhood. Her nipples, pink and soft as rosebuds, pressed the crisp hair on his chest. His shirt had disappeared, and now Katie fumbled boldly with the buttons on his trousers. When he was naked she longed to touch him, but the sight of his erection and the male strength of his body made her shy. Smiling, Jack drew back the bedclothes, scooped Katie up, and deposited her on the soft sheets.

Katie stretched like a cat, luxuriating in her own sensuousness. As the lamplight spread its amber glow over the tantalizing curves of her body, she looked up to see Jack poised above her like a bronzed god. There was nothing similar about their bodies except for a common beauty.

Jack knelt between her legs and slowly lifted one so that the ankle rested on his broad shoulder. With exquisite deliberation, he rolled the stocking down Katie's leg, his fingers trailing fire. When her foot was bare, he kissed her instep, the slim curve of her ankle, and then each toe until she nearly cried out from the rush of intense sensations.

Through the mist of her arousal, Katie marveled dreamily at the sight of Jack's torso as he knelt before her: the muscled definition of his chest, the ridges of his flat belly and narrowness of his hips, the line of dark hair that led downward to the proud essence of his masculinity. She loved the strong, leonine curve of his head and neck as he bent toward her. The painstaking care he took to bring her to new heights of pleasure made her feel precious and more feminine than she had ever imagined possible.

By the time Jack had removed Katie's other stocking and paid homage to her left foot, she thought she would go mad with longing. Every nerve ached for him, and now, as he came to her, she held up her arms in welcome. The sensation of his hard, warm body pressing against the length of her own made her gasp. She drank in the feel of his back, she sought his mouth, she rubbed against his chest, and she yearned for release from the feverish pressure in her loins.

Jack was hungry, too. Katie's mouth was ambrosia, and he drank his fill before tasting her neck, shoulders, and, finally, her breasts. They were swollen with desire, the rosy nipples eager for his lips. Katie strained against him as he suckled, molding a breast with one hand while his other strayed lower, caressing the satiny surface of her belly until he found the moist, hot place between her legs. His fingers surprised her. His evocative probing, combined with the sensation of his mouth at her breast, made her pant. She writhed helplessly as Jack's skilled touch brought her higher and higher until, at last, she seemed to burst under a tidal wave of acute ecstasy. For a moment she felt paralyzed, as if she'd been cast up on a beach after a storm. Blissful sensations continued to radiate from her loins, but she ached for something more.

Jack moved upward to kiss her again, his tongue working its magic with ease. Then Katie's hands sought and found his pulsing shaft, which suddenly seemed to grow even larger as he groaned with pleasure. When he moved inside her hands, her hips joined in the rhythm, and then, when the ache had reached the point of pain, Katie guided him home. His first thrust gave them both a jolt, and Jack paused for a moment, reveling in the sensation. They mated then in earnest, their damp bodies straining together, the world and all its cares forgotten. Through it all, they kissed and touched, as if they couldn't get close enough. Katie spiraled higher and higher, crying out when she climaxed again, arching against him with all her might. Jack's own release came soon after in a burning series of contractions that left him spent and dazed. Slowly he lowered himself next to Katie and, gazing deeply into her eyes, reached out to caress her cheek with reverent fingers. He'd almost forgotten what it was like with Katie. . . .

"Meoww!"

Poppy sprang blindly into the air, hooked her claws into the velvet bedspread, and hoisted herself to safety near their feet. Katie managed a soft giggle as she lay cradled in against Jack's chest, trying to get her breath back. The kitten scrambled toward them. Her mistress reached out to pet her, and Poppy purred and writhed with pleasure.

"Are you all right?" Jack inquired.

"Yes. . . ." Was it simply weariness that she detected in his tone? "How do you feel?"

Jack stroked the damp curls back from Katie's brow and sighed. "Well, I don't think there's any doubt that this marriage has been consummated," he said dryly. "There's no turning back now. . . ."

CHAPTER
23

November 1–2, 1864

"SACRAMENTO IS SAID TO BE ANOTHER WONDER OF THE world," Amanda Knauer announced proudly, "for it has risen as rapidly, and been burned down as many times, as San Francisco. We have floods to contend with, too. And yet Sacramento thrives, even though the prosperity brought by gold is past. Other towns have died in the last few years, but we will continue to grow because we were wise enough not to rely on the gold for our security."

Katie looked around the bustling waterfront. Jack and Stephen were off making certain that Katie's trunk was loaded properly on the steamer they were about to board for San Francisco. She wasn't particularly interested in discussing the economy of Sacramento, but Amanda seemed so earnest, and it was, after all, a way to pass the time. Katie certainly didn't want to answer questions about her relationship with Jack, several of which Amanda had already attempted to pose. "It clearly is evident that Sacramento has become quite the shipping center." She gestured below them at the river, which was crowded with barks, brigs, schooners, sloops, steamers, and barges.

Amanda nodded, dark eyes wide in her pale, thin face. "That's only part of it. This valley is going to provide a bounty of food. Already we have many flour mills, and thousands of acres are planted with fruit orchards and other crops. We have dozens of brickyards, several lumber mills—''

"Kathleen, it's time to board!" Jack approached, winding his way through the bales, crates, and boxes that were being unloaded along the levee.

Katie glanced back at the unfinished-looking city, shrouded in the pinkish-gray fog that marked most sunrises in the Central Valley at this time of year. The distant mountains where she had spent nearly all her life were hidden from view. In the midst of her excitement, Katie felt a bittersweet pang for the life she was leaving behind. "I want to thank you and Mr. Knauer for your many kindnesses," she said, taking Amanda's hand. "I'll always remember Sacramento as the place where I began my marriage."

"It was our pleasure." Amanda beamed. "I hope you realize how lucky you are to have caught Jack Wyatt. Wait until the female population of San Francisco hears! I wish I could be there to witness the reaction as the word spreads. . . .''

Jack took his wife's arm, giving Amanda a sharp look as he did so. "Don't talk nonsense, Mandy. I'm certain that the only response to the news of our marriage will be warm congratulations."

"What about Gen—" Amanda caught herself, realizing that Katie might not even know about Genevieve Braithwaite. "Of course, you're right. You know how we women are, we just love the thought of gossip! Now you two have a wonderful trip, and give our love to—"

"I'll be sure to pass along your regards to all your friends," Jack cut in. He gave Amanda a kiss, shook hands with Stephen, and waited while Katie made her good-byes. At last the newlyweds boarded the magnificent steamer.

Jack told Katie that the steamships that plied the Sacramento River were known as water palaces, and she mentioned that Samuel Clemens had called the riverboats he had piloted "wedding cakes on water." Jack laughed at that, and Katie delighted briefly in the conversational spark. It was reassuring to recall that they had once engaged in heated verbal exchanges, matching wits with gusto.

Soon after they boarded the *Senator*, however, Jack slipped back into his role of detached husband. He stood on deck chatting with some businessmen he knew who were traveling to San Francisco, while Katie strolled around and admired the steamer. The *Senator* was indeed a water palace. From the dock it had looked like a splendid white house, a first impression unsullied by the view close up, for inside it boasted fine, large doors, spacious windows, and galleries with fittings and furniture to match. In the ornate saloon,

Katie observed the rather curious mixture of passengers. The women were nearly all well dressed and appeared to be refined, but such was not the case with the men. Although some, like Jack, wore tailored suits, most looked as if they had come from the foothills in their worn jackets and work boots.

Every male on the steamer seemed to be chewing tobacco, even the boys. Katie found this disheartening, for she'd hoped the habit would not be so widespread in the larger cities. At least they didn't spit as often as the miners of Columbia, although many of the men used their fingers for handkerchiefs. Katie reminded herself that she was still in the West, where men rejoiced in defying rules of etiquette.

South of Sacramento, the river was beautiful. Sloughs and hidden coves branched off in every direction, thick with water hyacinths. Katie smiled with pleasure at the sight of the blue flowers standing up in contrast with the green leaves that lapped at the surface of the water. Fish jumped as they fed, and flocks of geese and ducks flew overhead, their cries filling the morning air. It was a new world for Katie, and she loved it all.

At length, Jack found Katie and took her to the dining salon for lunch. In spite of the room's elegant appointments, the passengers' manners made the meal a crowded, rushed affair. While they ate, Jack remarked that the steamer was making excellent time. It was always much quicker to travel downstream to San Francisco rather than the reverse, and the tide was out, which further hastened their journey. With luck, they would dock before sunset.

"I hope that you'll have your first look at San Francisco in daylight," Jack said, spearing a last bit of potato. "It's nothing like Columbia. . . ."

He gave her a wry smile, and Katie returned it mechanically. The future was rushing toward her now, and there was nothing she could do to slow its approach. In a way, she was glad. Soon she would see her new city, her new home, and have some idea what life would be like from now on. She told herself that in just a few hours, the uncertainty would be over. She should have been happy, but in truth she was terrified.

"It's a great pleasure to meet you, Mrs. Wyatt," Elijah said, receiving the news of his employer's marriage with his usual unruffled composure. If he was shocked, he didn't show it. "Welcome to San Francisco."

The black manservant's warmth came as a great relief to Katie. As Jack handed her up into the beautiful carriage awaiting them near the Pacific Street wharf, she returned Elijah's smile. "Thank you very much! I'm glad to meet you, too, Elijah."

For his part, Jack ignored the other man's keen, amused glance. "I appreciate your meeting us, and hope you didn't have to wait long. How is everything at home?"

"Just fine, sir. Your grandfather and brother were happy to receive your telegram and are looking forward to your arrival, but they failed to mention Mrs. Wyatt to me. . . ."

"That's because they don't know," Jack replied laconically. "You may take a more scenic route to Rincon Hill, so that my wife can have a look at San Francisco before the light goes completely."

As the carriage set off toward the hills of downtown, now plum-tinted in the twilight, Katie turned to Jack and murmured politely, "I didn't know that you had a grandfather and brother at home."

"Yes, you did. I told you last July, when I first suggested that you come to San Francisco with me." His tone was matter-of-fact.

Katie's voice rose. "Are you referring to a conversation that took place between us on the night that my father died? How could you possibly expect me to remember information imparted to me at such a time?"

"Kathleen," he warned, inclining his head toward Elijah, "I would prefer to have this discussion later, when we are alone."

Tears stung her eyes. "Fine." Why, she wanted to ask, had he not prepared her more fully for the circumstances of this new life? Why had he not told her all about his house, his business, and the family members who shared his home? Katie felt powerless, and it frustrated her. She wanted to be happy and excited about the future that stretched before her, but Jack's attitude thwarted that.

It was hard not to be stirred by her first sights of San Francisco, however. The busy streets were crowded with people, wagons, and carriages of every description. Store owners were bringing in their merchandise off the sidewalks as Elijah drove the carriage up Clay Street, and men were crowding into the doors of saloons. When Katie remarked on the number of buildings under construction, Jack explained:

"San Francisco is being rebuilt with Nevada silver. This is a boom that rivals the gold rush. The silver mines have yielded more than fifteen million dollars so far this year, and I'd estimate that more than a thousand new buildings have gone up here as a result of the fortunes made in Nevada. We're beginning to have a city of quality."

"I have always heard that it is quite fabulous."

Jack arched an eyebrow. "Fabulous, perhaps, but not always in the best of taste."

Katie opened her mouth to reply, then closed it, dumbfounded. Was this the down-to-earth, unpretentious man she had known in Columbia?

Sandy hills rose up around Stockton Street, imposing a western barricade. Elijah turned south, and before long they emerged into virtual countryside. Katie stared out the window with interest, while Poppy scrambled onto Jack's lap. When he began to stroke her, gently rubbing her neck with his strong fingers, the noise of the kitten's purring filled the carriage.

Rincon Hill curved around the foot of the bay, much of which had been filled in in recent years to create a straighter waterfront for the city. Rincon Hill rose above the fog, majestic and imposing with its elegant brick homes—particularly those of South Park, which was built along the western slope. South Park consisted of mews patterned after those in London; residential blocks were centered on a floral park, and the whole area was enclosed by a locked iron fence. Katie stared in astonishment when Elijah pulled up at the gate and got out to unlock it.

"You don't live *here*, do you?" she exclaimed.

"Any complaints?" Jack countered mildly, his large hand stroking Poppy's tiny body.

"Why didn't you tell me? All you said was that you had 'a house.' I expected something considerably more modest!" She fell silent when Elijah climbed back up onto his seat.

"Kathleen, are you familiar with the expression 'pleasant surprise'? Usually it evokes elation, smiles . . . that sort of thing."

He looked so calm, even amused, as he reclined against the upholstered seat, watching her with hooded green eyes and petting the besotted Poppy. Her husband made her furious. And how could *her* kitten turn traitor this way? Poppy appeared to be enamored of Jack to the point of forgetting her mistress completely.

The carriage drew up before a handsome brick house embellished with Palladian windows, pillars, and porches. The house was flanked by cypress trees and surrounded by a graceful iron fence. Elijah got down to open the door for them, and Katie turned to Jack, intent on speaking her mind.

"I assume that your reference to the 'pleasant surprise' was meant to infer that I am reacting inappropriately. I do not appreciate your attempt to turn this around so that I appear to be at fault." Her blue eyes blazed at him. "When I accepted your proposal of marriage, I asked you to promise not to try to rule me, and you agreed. May

I suggest, sir, that your purposeful withholding of information is nothing more than a means to exercise power over me. Keeping me ignorant for as long as possible ensures control for *you*! I do not even know what your occupation is. You hold all the cards and make all the rules, but I am raising an objection. Perhaps you imagine that you have married the sort of woman who will meekly acquiesce, settling for a pat on the head and a crumb of information. If so, pray allow me to correct that misconception. If you are unable to accord me the respect I deserve as your wife and partner, then perhaps you ought to send me back to Columbia right now!''

Jack returned her glare coolly. "That's a tempting suggestion. I'll think about it. In the meantime, why don't we go inside and have supper.''

Elijah, waiting outside the carriage for the storm to pass, now opened the door and helped Katie down. As Jack passed him, he carefully avoided his employer's eyes, but the merest suggestion of a smile tugged at his mouth. Until now, working for Jonathan Wyatt had been an ordered affair, so much so that it threatened to become tedious at times. It was also financially secure, which Elijah appreciated, but he had always hoped to see the day when someone or something would shake up the Wyatt household. Obviously that day had come, courtesy of Kathleen MacKenzie Wyatt, and Elijah could not have been more delighted.

Ambrose Summers sat on a maroon wing chair in the parlor. The cavernous, mahogany-paneled room was dark except for the small lamp at his elbow and the fire blazing in the marble fireplace. A worn copy of *David Copperfield* lay open on the curve of his belly, below which curled the fat, furry body of Harriet the cat.

Half dozing, the old man raised his head and pushed back his spectacles when the sound of voices reached him from the entry hall. So, his grandson had come home at last. Summers smiled, pleased. Perhaps now Jonathan would settle in and stay put. Ambrose wasn't particularly fond of Genevieve Braithwaite, but one couldn't be choosy in the West, and Genevieve *was* the most beautiful woman in San Francisco. She'd be a proper, elegant wife, and she'd give Jack beautiful babies. That's what the boy needed: a family. Then he'd abandon these mad jaunts to the gold country and stay home where he belonged. He'd have to be a fool to leave if Genevieve was in his bed.

Ambrose turned dreamy at the thought of becoming a great-grandfather. It would be wonderful to dandle an infant on his knee for a few minutes, then turn it back over to its parents. All the benefits of parenthood with none of the responsibilities. . . .

"Grandfather?"

Squinting at the shadowy figure in the doorway, Ambrose struggled to sit up, but Harriet's weight proved too great a burden. "Jack? Welcome home! Come in here and give your grandfather a proper greeting. Was that Genevieve's voice I heard?"

"No, Grandfather." Wyatt reached back and drew into the doorway a figure wearing what appeared to be a dark, shapeless dress, but the light was too dim to make out the woman's identity. "There is someone I'd like to introduce to you."

As they crossed the shadowy room, Harriet began to dig her claws into Summers's legs and emit a low growl. "Harriet, behave yourself! What's gotten into you, you cantankerous old woman? Don't you remember Jack?"

Jack himself had forgotten all about Poppy, who was curled into the crook of Katie's arm, half-hidden in the folds of her blue-gray traveling cloak. Just as he was about to reach for her, the calico kitten sprang forward and landed on Harriet, who was several times larger. Horrified and furious, the old cat hissed menacingly, but Poppy batted at her bewhiskered face before springing down to the Persian carpet and running for shelter.

"God's eyebrows!" Ambrose exclaimed, hoisting himself to a full sitting position. "How did that thing get into the house? Jack, find that little beast and get rid of it before it attacks Harriet again!"

"I'm afraid I can't do that, Grandfather," Wyatt replied with a weary sigh.

"What the devil are you talking about?" he blustered. Leaning forward, Ambrose finally got a good look at the woman standing beside his grandson. "Jonathan, who—"

"The kitten belongs to my wife, I'm afraid. Grandfather, I'd like you to meet Kathleen MacKenzie Wyatt, your new granddaughter-in-law. Kathleen, this is my grandfather, Ambrose Summers."

The old man peered over his spectacles at Katie. Through the shadows, he saw that the young woman's body was swathed in a dark cloak that belled out over her gown and crinoline. She had glossy black hair smoothed back into a chignon and a delicate, pale face. What immediately struck him, however, were her eyes. Large, sapphire blue, and thickly fringed with long dark lashes, Kathleen's eyes sparkled with a mixture of defiance, intelligence, and uncertainty. Ambrose was intrigued. Apparently his new granddaughter-in-law had character.

"So, you're the girl from Columbia," he muttered, thinking aloud.

Katie was startled. Could Jack have told his grandfather about her before returning to the foothills last month? "Yes, I'm from Columbia, Mr. Summers, and I'm glad to meet you."

"Call me Ambrose—or even Grandfather. Whatever suits you." His sweeping mustache curved upward as he chuckled absently. "I think I'm going to like you, Kathleen, even if you have brought another cat in to invade poor Harriet's territory. Just between us, I suspect that it will be good for *all* of us to have our routines upset a bit. I'm glad you decided to leave Columbia after all, and I'm glad you did Jack the favor of becoming his wife!"

Katie's heart felt immeasurably lighter. "I can't tell you how relieved I am to hear you say that, Mr.—Ambrose. Your kindness is deeply appreciated at this moment." She shook the hand he held up to her. "Everyone calls me Katie except for Jack, so you also may choose the name you prefer."

Summers turned to his grandson, who was observing this exchange with mixed emotions. "I'm pleased to see that you did the right thing, my boy!"

Jack didn't particularly care to have this conversation in front of Katie. "Well, I'm pleased that you're pleased." He turned to his bride. "Mrs. Gosling is waiting to take you upstairs to freshen up, darling, and Elijah has already brought up your trunk. Wouldn't you like a bath before dinner?"

"That would be nice," she said politely. "Will you excuse me, Ambrose?"

The old man's round cheeks turned pink as he beamed at Katie. "Of course, my dear. Enjoy your bath. I hope you'll pardon me for not standing. It's not for lack of manners, I assure you. My legs simply aren't what they used to be."

She grinned. "To tell you the truth, sir, neither are mine!"

Katie left the two men then and returned to the entry hall to join the waiting Mrs. Gosling. The housekeeper was more than a little unnerved at this unexpected turn of events. What would her life be like now that she was no longer the only woman of influence in the Wyatt house? When Katie appeared before her, however, Mrs. Gosling's heart softened. The girl was young, and she looked rather lost. The older woman smiled at her warmly and was encouraged by the sweetness of the new Mrs. Wyatt's answering smile. They had just started up the stairs when Ambrose Summers's voice carried out from the parlor:

"Tell me now, Jack, what the devil do you intend to do with

Genevieve Braithwaite? She dropped by the other day and was prattling on about the new draperies she has in mind for the parlor and dining room! You're going to have a mess on your hands when she and her mama hear that you've gone and married someone else!''

Katie stood in the middle of the stunning Turkey carpet, cleverly woven in shades of blue, cream, and blood red, that dominated Jack's spacious bedroom. Never in her wildest dreams had she imagined that he might live like this. She felt out of place, not only because of the grandeur of her surroundings, but also because the room was unequivocally masculine, from its color scheme to its handsome Hepplewhite furnishings. It was impossible not to wonder if she might always feel like a guest in her husband's bed.

Elijah had started a fire in the walnut-framed fireplace, which added an element of cheery warmth. The bathroom echoed with the sound of running water, and a moment later Mrs. Gosling emerged.

"I've started your bath, Mrs. Wyatt, and you'll find towels on Mr. Wyatt's dressing table. I've brought in some more feminine soap from the guest bathroom."

Katie smiled wanly. "Thank you, Mrs. Gosling. I truly appreciate your help." Her knuckles were white as she clutched her folded cloak in front of her, looking for all the world as if she were interviewing for the position of housemaid.

"How remiss of me not to take your wrap when you came in!" the older woman exclaimed. "I suppose my only excuse is that I was too surprised by Mr. Wyatt's news." She took matters in hand then, draping the cloak over her own arm, unfastening Katie's dress and unlacing her corset, and finally leading her into the bathroom. "Now you just get undressed and have a good long soak. It'll do you a world of good. I'm going to go next door and prepare your own rooms for you."

Alone again, Katie obeyed mechanically. She was sitting in the beautiful porcelain bathtub, steaming water gushing out of the brass faucet in front of her, when Mrs. Gosling's words sank in. Her *own* rooms? Did that mean that she would not sleep with Jack? Before she could assimilate this latest turn of events, Jack's voice drifted to her from the other side of the wall, where, apparently, her own bedroom was located. Quickly she turned off the taps and strained to hear what he was saying. Most of it was muffled, but she did manage to make out a few phrases:

". . . because I'd like these rooms ready before we retire tonight. Mrs Wyatt will doubtless be exhausted from her travels, and I would hate to wake her in the morning.''

Waves of confusion washed over Katie, but she managed to compose herself when she heard Jack enter the bedroom through the connecting door.

''How are you doing?'' he called, peeking around the entrance to the tiled bathroom. ''Is the water hot enough?''

Katie crossed her arms in front of her breasts. ''It's fine,'' she answered politely. ''May I ask you a question?''

''Of course.'' Jack had removed his coat and cravat and looked engagingly relaxed as he leaned against the door frame.

''What sort of wife do you intend that I shall be? Will we lead separate lives and only meet for distant conversation over the dinner table? Will you come and go as you please from *your* rooms, carrying on your life as you did before I came here, deigning to share my bed only when the spirit moves you?'' She was shivering in the hot water, her face strained and pale.

''Kathleen—'' Straightening, Jack sighed and raked a hand through his tawny hair. ''I think that you are overreacting. You're tired. Why don't you relax and enjoy your bath, and we'll talk about this when you have dressed.''

''No!'' she cried, on the verge of tears. ''I want to know *now*!''

They were interrupted by a series of loud knocks on the door to Jack's bedroom. He excused himself and left the bathroom. Crossing the carpet, he opened the door to discover an incredulous-looking Conrad, skin white against his flaming red hair and wild blue eyes.

''Jack!'' cried the younger man. ''Is it true? I can't believe it! Has Grandfather finally gone soft in the head during his waning years, or have you actually gotten married to a stranger?''

''Frankly, I tend to think you have all gone a little soft in the head around here,'' Jack replied sarcastically. ''But to answer your question more directly—yes, I have gotten married, and yes, she is a stranger to *you*, though obviously not to me.'' He took his brother's elbow. ''Why don't we go downstairs and continue this conversation?''

Conrad froze in the doorway as Jack tried to steer him into the hall. ''But what about *Genevieve*?'' he burst out in near hysteria. ''All hell is going to break loose when she hears about this!''

''Will you *move*!?'' Wyatt barked, at the end of his patience. ''And keep your voice down, you dolt!''

Katie heard the door close behind them. Blindly, she reached for the bar of lilac-scented soap and began to rub it into a furious lather.

The water was cooling rapidly, she was cold, and she felt utterly naked in every sense of the word. As she washed, tears slipped down her cheeks, tears she was determined that Jack would never see.

CHAPTER
24

November 3, 1864

IT WAS GOOD TO BE HOME. WALKING LIGHTLY DOWN THE STAIRS, Jack stopped for a moment in the entry hall, which was awash with hazy morning sunlight. He took his watch out of his vest pocket and checked the time: seven-thirty, exactly. The chaos of last night was behind him, he mused, smiling. Somehow, they'd all gotten through dinner, during which Katie appeared to win the hearts of both Conrad and their grandfather, and she'd been too tired at bedtime to resume the argument begun during her bath. He'd made an effort to be pleasant, tucking her into bed in her lovely room decorated in rosewood and carnation-pink silk. Katie had been exhausted and accepted his explanation that he had work to catch up on in his study before he could go to bed himself. They'd shared an affectionate kiss, and then she'd gone to sleep.

Now life was assuming its former structure, and Jack was relieved to be able to let his guard down. This morning he had risen at the usual time, had his bath and dressed in peaceful solitude, and now, after the usual ritual of tea and fruit over the newspaper, he could leave for work just as he always had. He and Katie would chat when he returned in the evening, and perhaps he'd even visit her bed. However, there would not be a repeat performance of their wedding night, at least not for a while. Jack felt uneasy whenever he recalled the force of his own passion—a passion unknown to him before Katie, and one that was entwined with emotions that threatened to consume him. The next time they made love, he was determined to keep it uncomplicated.

Feeling that he had regained a measure of control over his own life, Jack smiled to himself as he opened the paneled door to his study. As usual, on the Chippendale desk across the room, tea and a plate of sliced fruit awaited him next to the folded newspaper. The house was agreeably quiet, and Jack welcomed this interlude to organize his thoughts and prepare for the day ahead. He had just started across the carpet when a voice startled him.

"Good morning, Jack! Did you sleep well?"

Stunned, he stood frozen for a moment, then turned slowly. There, perched high on the ladder that could be pushed on rollers around the walls of books that lined the study, was Katie. Stock-inged feet peeped out of a flurry of soft petticoats covered by a simple periwinkle-blue gown that buttoned most of the way up her throat. She had resumed wearing her hair in a single braid again, but soft black tendrils curled about her exquisite face. Jack thought that his wife was looking especially appealing this morning, her cheeks stained pink and her eyes sparkling; but he resisted his attraction to her.

"Hello, Kathleen," he said in what he hoped was a calm, friendly voice. "I'm surprised to find you here—I thought you were still sleeping."

"Heavens, no!" She laughed. "Had you forgotten that I am an incurably early riser? Why, when you were staying with Papa and me, I used to leave the house most mornings before you were even awake!"

"You're right, I had forgotten." Jack smiled and nodded, struggling to suppress his growing irritation. Why did she always have to do something other than what he wanted her to do? Just once, why couldn't she have stayed in bed, out of his way and out of trouble? No one ever entered this sacred study without an invitation from him, *especially* during this sacred half hour before he left the house. He was beginning to think that Katie was somehow able to divine precisely what would bother him the most, and then set out to do it. Still, he kept his tone even as he inquired, "What made you decide to come in here?"

Katie laughed, nearly losing her balance. "Must you speak to me as if I were a particularly annoying little child? Is this not my house now as well as yours, or are there rules concerning where I may and may not go?" She sounded amused, but there was a spark of defiance in her blue eyes. "I came to the study to see your books, you silly man! When I peeked in earlier, the first glimpse I had of this wonderful library made me happier than I've felt in a very long time.''

Jack was trying to decide how to react as Katie turned around and climbed down the ladder. She was so damned stubborn and independent! Trying to gain a measure of control in this relationship was like wrestling with a ghost; each time he thought he had a grip on the situation, Katie slipped through his fingers. Even more frustrating was the pang of admiration and attraction he felt as he watched her descend the ladder. Her waist looked tiny enough to encircle with his hands, and the curves of her hips stirred up memories of the sheer perfection and responsiveness of her body. He fought the urge to take her in his arms and kiss her. One inner voice argued that there must be *some* redeeming feature to the marriage, while another warned him not to yield to temptation or he'd end up falling in love with her. And falling in love with Katie seemed tantamount to falling into an abyss. . . .

''Good morning, Mr. Wyatt!'' Mrs. Gosling exclaimed as she entered the study carrying a tray of apple muffins. Her eyes touched on Jack, then warmed at the sight of Katie. ''Mrs. Wyatt, these turned out beautifully. You have a magic touch! Did you tell Mr. Wyatt that you have already been at work in the kitchen? He'd doubtless scold me for letting you toil at dawn on your honeymoon, but when he tastes the results, he'll sing a different tune.'' Setting the tray on the desk, she turned to beam at Jack. ''I was telling your bride about the day you came home last summer and asked for muffins. Why, I never thought you *liked* muffins! I didn't understand then, but now I do, and I think that it's terribly romantic. You were missing her, weren't you, sir?''

Jack thought he must be losing his mind. ''Isn't it possible that I simply had a craving for muffins?''

Katie wrapped her arms around him from behind and smiled when she felt him flinch. ''My husband is shy about expressing his feelings,'' she told Mrs. Gosling as if Jack were not present, ''but I don't mind because we know the truth, don't we, darling?''

''Ah, young love!'' said Mrs. Gosling, sighing. ''It does my old heart good to see it, and to see you looking so happy, Mr. Wyatt. I thought the day would never come.''

''So did I,'' muttered Jack. He was burningly aware of Katie's breasts pressed against his wide back.

''Well, I'll leave you two lovebirds alone before Mr. Wyatt has to leave for the office. Do let me know if there is anything else I can get you.''

When the elderly housekeeper had closed the door on her way out, Jack reached down to pry Katie's hands loose. "You are a little devil, do you know that?"

She held on stubbornly. "Don't you want to take advantage of our time alone?" she teased.

Jack turned in her arms and stared down at her, their faces only a few inches apart. Katie smelled faintly of apples and cinnamon, and her lips looked delicious. "Damn you," he said hoarsely before covering her mouth with his own. It was a scorching kiss, and his arms seemed to have a will of their own as they encircled her slim back and pressed her firmly against his body. Katie warmed and softened in his embrace, molding herself to him. It occurred to Jack that he could lock the door and take her right there on the rug, but a moment before he lost all sense of reason, he pulled himself back from the precipice.

"What are you up to?" he inquired, his voice husky with desire and a telltale trace of affection.

Katie was all innocence. "I don't know what you mean. Is it wrong for a wife to flirt with her husband?"

"Well, I suppose not," Jack muttered, clearing his throat, "but this is hardly the time." He walked around the desk and poured himself a cup of tea. "You have to understand, Kathleen, that I have a fairly rigid schedule here. My life is very different from the one I led in Columbia. I have a business to run, and I never allow myself more than a half hour to bathe and dress, then another half hour for tea here in my study. This is a very important interlude for me. It gives me a chance to organize my thoughts for the day ahead, to relax in solitude before I begin what amounts to a day-long marathon."

Katie liked to look at Jack. When she was able to remain objective, she felt a little surge of pride at the realization that he was her husband. His tawny hair gleamed in the morning sunlight that poured through the window behind the desk, his face was golden brown against the white of his shirt, and he wore his expensive, tasteful clothes with the grace of a lion that *seemed* to be tamed. "I think that the routine you have described is fairly typical of bachelors," Katie said. "When one operates independently, it's quite easy to make an art out of organizing one's life. However, when one marries, the art becomes that of learning to compromise."

He glanced up from the newspaper, his green eyes sharp. "I think that if *one* is earning the family living, one can have the last word."

Katie narrowed her eyes and smiled at the same time. "That doesn't sound very fair to me," she said sweetly.

Jack merely shrugged, sat down, and tried to concentrate on the morning's headlines. He hoped that Katie would take the rather heavy hint and leave. Instead, she pulled a chair up to the desk and inquired:

"What exactly do you do to earn the family living?"

"I am the publisher and editor-in-chief of the *Morning Star*," Jack replied casually.

Katie sank back against the tufted velvet upholstery, unable to conceal her shock. It was almost impossible to reconcile this disclosure with what she'd believed about the man she had known in Columbia. Memories crowded her mind: Jack's interference with her work at the *Gazette*, the platen he had acquired from some "anonymous donor" and then insisted on testing, and his insufferable penchant for giving her advice about newspaper writing. A flush spread over her cheeks as she recalled her superior attitude toward him when they were in the *Gazette* office, and suddenly she heard his angry voice again, shouting, "You have no idea what I do and do not know!"

"The *Morning Star* is one of the finest newspapers in the West," Katie murmured at length. "Why didn't you tell us?"

Jack looked up, one eyebrow arched. "I wasn't there as Jonathan Wyatt, I was there as Jack Adams."

"But, I don't understand. *Why* were you—"

"Kathleen, I can't go into all that now. In fact, it's a subject that I consider closed. My reasons for needing to get away from San Francisco and live more simply were personal, and a part of the past. I think that we have enough to deal with in the present, many adjustments to make, and I just don't see the point in wasting valuable time talking about something that is no longer relevant." With that, he consulted his watch, snapped the newspaper closed, and stood up. "Now, if you'll excuse me—"

"Wait!" Katie stood up, too, prepared to block the doorway if necessary. She wanted to protest that Jack didn't want to talk about *anything* personal, including the marriage that they had just embarked upon, but she sensed that one more outburst from her would only cause him to retreat further. "What am I supposed to do all day?"

"What do wives usually do?" he replied absently.

"I have always worked, and I want to continue to work. You know that I have skills as a newspaper reporter. Why can't I come to work at the *Star*?"

Jack stared, then gave a short laugh. "Ridiculous! Absolutely not."

"That's not an answer! You have to give me a reason." Her sapphire eyes flashed, and spots of color stained her cheeks.

"You are the wife of a wealthy man, Kathleen, and you do not have to work," he said coolly, gathering up his business papers. "There is a great deal to occupy you in this house. Have Mrs. Gosling hire a maid for you. Go out and purchase some new gowns. God knows you need a proper wardrobe! Have you no feminine instincts? Act like a wife! You'll have to learn that you aren't in the foothills anymore."

"Don't you dare speak to me that way!" Katie followed him across the study, longing to jump onto his back, wrestle him to the carpet, and sit on him until he heard her out. "You knew what I was like when you married me. If you wanted a San Francisco society belle, you should have married *Genevieve*, the way everyone expected you to!"

Her risk paid off, if only for an instant. Jack paled, then turned back to grip her arm. "You're going to make me wish I had, you little vixen," he said in a dangerously low voice. His eyes were like green ice, and a vein throbbed in his forehead. "I'm going to work now, and I trust that when I return tonight you will have settled on a more pleasing topic of conversation!"

Katie had no choice but to watch him walk away. When she heard the heavy front door slam with a thud, she nearly vented her frustrations in a long, loud scream, but then she remembered that the house was full of people. All of them were still virtual strangers, and she didn't want them to think that Jack had married a madwoman. . . .

"Well, if it isn't my new granddaughter!" Ambrose looked up from his place at the end of the empty dining room table and gave Katie a welcoming smile. "What do you have there, sweetheart?"

She stood in the doorway holding the plate of muffins. "I thought you might like one of these. I baked them earlier for Jack's breakfast, but . . . he wasn't very hungry."

"Come on in and sit down. I won't bite, and neither will Harriet. Where's that little tiger of yours, by the way?"

"Up on my bed, I think. She's getting used to the house one room at a time, I guess." Katie walked the length of the long table and took the chair at Ambrose's left. It warmed her heart to see the old man snatch a muffin immediately and eat it in three large bites.

"Jack doesn't care for muffins," he confided, swallowing the last of it and reaching for another.

"I don't think Jack cares for much of anything," she said.

"You know, my dear, I was about to tell you how pretty you look this morning, but I can't do that until you give me a smile!" He chuckled at her attempt to oblige. "Well, that's a little better. Now, tell your old grandfather what's bothering you."

Tears welled in her eyes. "I am used to having a great deal of freedom. I grew up in a town where I didn't have to follow all the usual rules for feminine etiquette. I worked alongside my father in our saloon, and I ran it myself after he died a few months ago. And, I wrote articles for the *Columbia Gazette*. Jack knew me quite well there. He's certainly aware that I am not some simpering female who delights in taking tea and embroidering all day long. And yet—" Her voice caught.

"Yes?" Summers prodded gently.

"And yet he seems to expect me to become that sort of woman, that sort of *wife*, now. He doesn't want me in his way, he doesn't want to hear my opinions, and he certainly doesn't want me to *work*!" Katie laughed shakily.

Ambrose patted her hand. "I'd urge you not to let him bully you, sweetheart, but I'm sure there's no danger of that! Now then, without betraying Jack's confidence, I will tell you that there are reasons for his need for discipline. There was a time when he didn't live by any rules or impose any restraints on himself, and he nearly lost everything. He had the good sense, however, to stop before it was too late. While rebuilding his life, Jack may have overcompensated in the area of discipline. There's more to it than that, and I don't doubt that the day will come when he will discuss this with you in depth, but for now I can only urge you to be patient with him." Ambrose took another bite of muffin. "Mm! Delicious! . . . Anyway, as I was saying, I happen to believe that Jack has slowly been outgrowing the rigid rules he made for himself. He tested his wings during the weeks he spent as Jack Adams—"

"Do you know all about that? He's so secretive that I wasn't certain how much the family knew."

"I'm the only one Jack confided in. Conrad knows very little, so it's best for you to restrict your conversation to the here and now when we're all together. I'm not even sure it's a good idea for me to be discussing this with you, except that you deserve at least a semblance of an explanation for Jack's behavior."

"But you think that he is changing?" Katie's eyes were wide with hope.

"You, my dear, are the surest sign of that. The fact that he married at all is a tremendous leap, and the type of woman he chose seems a clear indication of the new direction in his life. I think that, whether he realizes it or not, Jack hopes to incorporate the freedom of choice and zest for life he rediscovered in the gold country within the structure of his existence here. Step by step he'll discover that he can bend without breaking, that he can feel passion again without losing control of his life. . . ."

Katie considered this, her brow furrowed and her chin propped on her palm. "I hope you are right, Ambrose," she murmured at length.

"Trust me, my dear." His eyes twinkled behind the spectacles he wore. "Are you in love with my grandson?"

She blushed. "Well, I . . ."

"You owe me a secret!"

"Yes. Yes, I suppose that I am, but he must not know it. Not yet."

"Don't worry, I won't say a word. It would spoil all the fun! I plan to enjoy watching this drama unfold."

"But what shall I do in the meantime? Just be patient with him?"

Ambrose laughed heartily. "On the contrary! Don't give him an inch—continue to challenge and confront him at every turn. Make him *feel* again!"

"But how?" Katie asked plaintively. "I don't think he wants me to *do* anything. When I asked how I should spend my days if he won't let me work, he barked that I should be a *wife*, whatever that means." She made a face.

"You are enchanting, Katie!" Leaning forward, Ambrose patted her cheek. "If I were a few decades younger, I'd give my grandson a run for his money. As it is, I'll have my fun helping you torment him."

Katie felt a little thrill of excitement at his words. "Just tell me how and I'll do it," she exclaimed.

"Take him at his word. Be a wife until he cries for mercy. First of all, you must go shopping for a new wardrobe. I have a friend who will be delighted to take you, and I'll send for her immediately. Leave no stone unturned. Jack is quite wealthy, and he can afford whatever you buy."

"He suggested some new gowns himself, but somehow the project sounds much more appealing the way you describe it!" Katie laughed.

"Next, turn your attention to this house."

"But it's beautiful," she protested.

Ambrose gave a derisive snort. "For a family of men, it's fine, but there's a woman here now. *Change* things—it will drive Jack insane! Add a feminine touch."

"I'm not certain I know how. . . ."

"Believe me, my dear, once you begin touring the finest shops and stores San Francisco has to offer, you'll have ideas galore. And then, once your wardrobe and the house are complete, you must announce to Jack that you want to have a huge party so that you can meet his friends. Christmas is coming soon, and that sounds like the perfect time, don't you think?"

Katie sat back, her mind spinning, and giggled like a little girl. "You're a naughty man, Grandfather."

"All for a good cause, darling Katie!"

CHAPTER
25

November 3, 1864

"**I** HOPE THAT I AM NOT TAKING YOU AWAY FROM SOME OTHER obligation, Mrs. Menloe," Katie said to the charming older woman who perched on the Empire side chair in the corner of the dressing room. Nelle Braust's fancy dress shop on Kearny Street was all the rage among San Francisco's elite, having sprung up in the past year to provide a fresh outlet for the money that was burning holes in the pockets of the silver barons.

"Nonsense, my dear," Hope Menloe replied, waving her slender hand. As she spoke, she kept a close eye on the work of the dressmaker's assistant who was pinning a gown on Katie. "I couldn't be happier to help you in this matter. I must tell you that Ambrose is very dear to me. He was a great friend of my husband's, and since Theodore died last spring, Ambrose has been extraordinarily kind to me. This morning, when he sent word of Jonathan's marriage and explained your predicament, I was overjoyed to be of service. I know how it feels to come to a new city, knowing no one except your husband. Theodore and I sailed here from Boston thirteen years ago, and for months I was positively bereft. I hated San Francisco, and was certain I would never be happy here. Everything seemed so *different*!" She rose and came over to feel the pale Russian gray silk of the visiting dress in progress. "I couldn't have been more mistaken. This is a very exciting place in which to live, and I have scores of intimate friends. I simply had to learn to see things and meet people with an open mind.''

"Well, Jack was right: San Francisco is nothing like Columbia, but I am determined to like it, and I appreciate your encouragement, Mrs. Menloe. So far, everyone has been extremely kind to me.''

"And there is nothing like a new wardrobe to cheer one up!'' Mrs. Menloe proclaimed. "This color is divine with your eyes and hair, my dear, and the gown is in perfect taste, as are all that you chose today. Jonathan will be prouder than ever to introduce you as his wife.''

"I've never been very interested in clothes,'' Katie admitted, "so I am counting on you to be painfully honest. I welcome your advice, and hope that you will speak up if I err.'' Her eyes swept enviously over the older woman. Hope Menloe appeared to be in her fifties, and she was still a beauty. Tall and elegant, she had wavy titian hair laced with silver that was cunningly styled in a coil at the base of her neck. Her keen blue-gray eyes were set off by arching brows, and high cheekbones lent her a timeless dignity. Every detail of her appearance was perfect. Small deep purple bows of *moiré d'antique* marched down the bodice of her silk gown, which was black because she was still in mourning for her husband, and there were graceful gathers at her hem. Tasteful pearl-and-diamond earrings added the perfect finishing touch. When they had arrived at Madame Braust's shop, Katie had honestly admitted her ignorance, and Hope had tactfully helped to choose styles and fabrics that showed Katie's figure and coloring to exquisite advantage.

"You are a rare beauty,'' Mrs. Menloe said now, "and it is exciting to witness this transformation.''

"I have to admit that I am quite excited myself!''

"Next we will go to the milliner's, and tomorrow I will take you to be fitted for shoes. You must have Jonathan show you his mother's jewelry collection, so that you will know what you lack. I know the very best place to go. . . .''

They were finished for the morning, and Katie put on one of the gowns Madame Braust had in stock that fit her already: a lovely confection of sea-green silk with cream lace at the neck and sleeves, and a wide skirt that belled out over a hooped petticoat. The color was perfect with her ebony hair and somehow made her eyes look even more blue than usual. When Hope turned Katie to face the mirror and described the ideal bonnet and jewelry for the gown, the younger woman nodded happily.

"I have always been too busy working and using my mind to

bother with such things, but now I am determined to enjoy my femininity!'' Katie laughed. The thought of Jack's reaction to her enhanced beauty intensified her self-satisfaction.

"Your husband will fall in love with you all over again," Mrs. Menloe assured her, as if reading Katie's mind. "And that reminds me, we must purchase a large assortment of lacy undergarments for you. I know of some that are imported from France. They are very expensive, but they are made of pure silk."

They walked together into the shop's main salon, where Hope looked for Madame Braust so that she could confirm the details of Katie's order. As they talked, Katie stood off to one side and observed the other women who had entered the shop. All seemed to have achieved a level of sophistication that she feared she could never match. But perhaps she didn't have to. Katie felt an instinctive twinge of resentment at the notion that she might be pressured to change in order to fit in with San Francisco society. She decided then that she wouldn't try. Either she would win the acceptance of Jack's friends on her own merits or not at all. Katie couldn't change to win Jack's love, either. The gowns, bonnets, and jewelry were only useful to enhance her physical beauty; she must not allow them to alter her character.

A stunning, slim young woman with pale blond hair had come into the shop and now stood near Katie talking to a companion who appeared to be her mother. Even from a few feet away, Katie could smell her light, lavender-scented perfume. The young woman wore a unique gown of soft pink cambric, stamped with a design that resembled black braiding, and her face shone as she whispered excitedly:

"Oh, Mother, wasn't it fortunate that we encountered Marabelle on the street just now? If we had arrived here a few minutes later, she would have already been gone and I still would not know that Jonathan is home!"

Katie froze, wondering if it were possible that this could be the woman whose name she had heard so frequently since arriving in San Francisco.

"Marabelle said that she saw him in his carriage, Genevieve," replied Elizabeth Braithwaite. "She may have been mistaken."

"Mother, she saw Elijah, too, and the carriage was in front of the newspaper offices. I hardly think it could have been a mistake." Genevieve's voice rose impatiently. "Oh, how I have missed him! We must hurry with our errands so that I will be at home if he should send word, or even come himself. What shall I wear tonight?"

"Perhaps Madame Braust will tell us that the pearl silk gown is ready," Mrs. Braithwaite suggested. "I must admit, I hope you are right, and I hope that Mr. Wyatt will stay put and declare himself at last."

"I'm certain that he shall!" Genevieve fairly sang. "A Christmas wedding—isn't that a sumptuous prospect?" Sensing that someone was staring at her, she turned and met the wide blue eyes of a complete stranger. The young woman looked somewhat uneasy in what was obviously a new gown. Although pretty enough, she seemed out of place, and Genevieve guessed that she had probably just arrived from some tawdry provincial outpost like Sacramento or San Jose. And of course she stared because she hadn't the manners to know any better. Deciding that she was to be pitied, Genevieve gave her a condescending smile and turned back to her mother. "I do wish that Mrs. Menloe wouldn't monopolize Madame Braust. Doesn't she realize that there are other patrons in the shop?"

Moments later, Hope Menloe bade the dressmaker good day. Turning, she saw Mrs. Braithwaite and her daughter, smiled and nodded at them, and then took Katie's arm as they exited the shop.

Genevieve was curious now, for Hope was a pillar of San Francisco society. "Madame Braust," she said sweetly, approaching the statuesque German woman. "who was that young woman with Hope Menloe? I don't think I know her. Is she some relation from the foothills that Hope has taken under her wing?"

A slow, vaguely malicious smile spread over Madame Braust's powdered face. She had never cared for Miss Braithwaite's incorrigibly superior airs, and now she relished the opportunity to deflate them. "My dear Miss Braithwaite, hadn't you heard? That was Jonathan Wyatt's new bride. They just arrived in San Francisco last night, and Mrs. Menloe was arranging for an exquisite new wardrobe for Mrs. Wyatt—at Mr. Wyatt's request, of course. He insists that no expense be spared."

The blood drained from Genevieve's face as she managed a hollow reply: "How . . . lovely."

Outside on Kearny Street, Hope Menloe was all business as she steered Katie through the crowds toward a charming millinery shop on the corner.

"That young woman we just saw," Katie began tentatively. "I heard her talking about Jack, and I heard her mother call her 'Genevieve.' People have been mentioning that name to Jack ever since we arrived last night, and I am not a fool. Mrs. Menloe, won't you tell me what existed between them?"

Hope put an arm around her and squeezed reassuringly. "My dear, I think that is a question for your husband." Then, seeing Katie's crestfallen expression, she relented. "Well, I know very little. Yes, it is true that their names have been linked for some months, but marriage was never proposed, at least as far as anyone knows. I saw them together on many occasions, and I did not perceive that Jonathan was in love with Miss Braithwaite. If he were, would he have married you?"

Katie tried to smile. "No, I don't suppose that he would have," she murmured, wishing that she could believe it herself.

Jack's office at the *Star* was in a state of comfortable disarray. Papers were scattered over his desk, his coat was draped over the back of his chair, and he'd left the remains of his lunch on a plate that he had deposited atop a stack of books. Jack himself leaned back in his leather chair, sleeves rolled up and collar loosened, proofreading an editorial that he had just completed about the possible outcome and ramifications of General Sherman's march in progress through Georgia.

He was just reaching for his pen to make a correction when the door to his office flew open and his secretary appeared.

"Excuse me, sir!" cried an agitated Bradley Hughes. "I told Miss Braithwaite that you asked not to be disturbed, but she insisted—"

Genevieve pushed past the young man. "This is *crucially* important, Jonathan! Surely you won't deny me a few minutes of your precious time?" Her beautiful face was pale with rage. "I think that you owe me that much, at least."

"You may leave us, Bradley." Jack got to his feet. "And close the door behind you."

Genevieve was momentarily at a loss as she faced Jack across the office. She hadn't expected this to be so simple.

"Won't you sit down?" Jack asked calmly.

She marched over to the chair he indicated, then paced back and forth in front of it. "I don't know if I'm able to sit still! I can't recall ever feeling more agitated than I do at this very moment!"

"Genevieve—"

"Have you any idea how I feel? How humiliated and insulted and foolish I feel?"

"I was going to tell you about the marriage myself," he said, reaching up to massage the sudden tightness in his neck. "I realize that you are probably shocked, and that's understandable—"

"*Shocked?!*" Her voice rose to a near shriek. "I had to hear it from Madame *Braust*! I had to come face to face with that little *peahen* who calls herself your *wife*—"

"Leave Kathleen out of this," he said coldly. "She is completely innocent."

"Oh, *certainly* she is. Where did you find her, in those Nevada silver mines you haven't been able to stay away from? It's horrible enough that you led me on, allowing me to believe that I would one day become your wife. But did you have to marry someone so utterly lacking in style and social graces? Why, I'll wager that she can't even read or write. Is that why you married her, because she hasn't a thought of her own?"

He almost laughed at that. "No, Kathleen has plenty of thoughts, and they're all her own. Don't underestimate her, Genevieve. She's a match for any woman in San Francisco when it comes to intelligence and character. In fact, she's more than a match . . . and perhaps that's why I married her. I may have believed that I wanted a proper, obedient wife, but when it came down to it, I chose Kathleen."

"Oh, spare me a speech about the limitless virtues of that little trollop." Her voice shook with anger. "That's what she really is, isn't it? Have you gotten her with child? Was that the reason for this sudden marriage?"

"No." There was a warning glint in his eyes, but Genevieve was too upset to notice it.

"Do you know why I really think you did this? Can you bear to hear the truth?"

"I assure you, anything you can bear to say, I can bear to hear," he replied caustically, losing patience.

"I think you were afraid. Afraid to love me, afraid to marry a real woman who would make you a real wife. So instead you went out and picked a drab little miner's daughter and put a ring on her before you came home, because you knew that if you saw me first, you'd lose your nerve!"

"Genevieve, there is no point in this conversation. You don't want to hear the truth, and I have better things to do than waste my time listening to your fairy stories." He came around the desk to face her. "I am sorry if you've been hurt, but the fact is, I never asked you to marry me. If you'll think back to the months I was here before leaving town in October, you'll remember that I was far from an amorous suitor. You simply chose to ignore the truth." Jack's voice softened. "I didn't plan it this way, Genevieve. If I'd known all along that I was going to marry Kathleen, I would have had a talk with you before I left San Francisco the last time. But fate sped things along. I know it doesn't seem possible now, but someday you'll realize that this is for the best. We weren't right for each other. Before long, you'll meet the right man and thank God you didn't marry me!''

Stepping up to him, Genevieve rested her face against Jack's shoulder, dropping her eyes so that he couldn't see the fury that still burned in their depths. ''I suppose you're right, and I should accept the inevitable with good grace. I wish you all the best, Jonathan, and I'm sorry I behaved so rudely.''

''I'm relieved to hear you say that, and of course, I feel the same way. I have only fond memories of the times we shared.'' He put an arm around her shoulders and escorted her to the door. ''Take care of yourself, and give my regards to your family. I trust they'll understand.''

''I'll see to it that Papa doesn't come looking for you with a gun,'' she replied archly.

Jack suppressed a sigh of relief as he watched her go. Genevieve turned at the end of the hallway and gave him a brave smile, but inside she was still seething. When she rejoined her mother in their carriage on California Street, her face was contorted with rage.

''If he thinks I am going to give up so easily, he has gravely underestimated me. It isn't too late to get rid of that mousy little slut! Jonathan Wyatt belongs to *me*, and I intend to have him!''

Clad in a new, lace-edged nightdress, Katie sat at her rosewood dressing table, brushing her hair by firelight. It was pleasant to sit alone and reflect on the day. Ambrose had reminded her not to expect miracles instantly, to be content with progress rather than perfection in her marriage, and it was reassuring advice. Katie was doing what she could to effect change without demanding it from Jack, and that felt good.

There had been no opportunity to ask Ambrose or Conrad about Genevieve, and Katie wasn't entirely certain that she wanted to. If they answered her questions honestly, it would only make Genevieve—and her relationship with Jack—more real, and therefore more threatening. For the moment she could only trust that it was over—a part of Jack's past. Besides, she had enough to contend with without manufacturing problems that might not even exist.

The evening had been quite enjoyable, all in all. They had all eaten dinner together, while Jack explained to Conrad that he had spent some time in Columbia during his travels to and from Nevada. That, he said, was where he'd met Katie. She added little, letting him take the lead. Then, when Samuel Clemens was mentioned, both Jack's brother and his grandfather reacted with surprised delight. Katie was happy to join Jack in relating stories of Sam's attempts at pocket mining in Jackass Gulch.

After dinner, Katie had played a spirited game of piquet with Conrad, while Ambrose read and dozed and Jack finished proofreading his editorial. When she paused to reflect on the sense of contentment she felt, Katie realized that she already felt part of the family. She was the first to say good night, coming upstairs to indulge in a luxurious bath. Now, as she brushed her damp, silky hair, Katie was proud that she hadn't lingered downstairs waiting for Jack. If he wanted to be alone with her, it was better that he make the choice of his own free will.

"Can I do that for you?"

Startled, Katie looked around, remembering that the connecting door between their rooms was open. Jack stood in a pool of lamplight that spilled over from his bedroom. He wore a dressing gown of slate-gray silk that exposed a portion of his strong chest, and his hair was appealingly tousled.

Silently, Katie held out the silver-backed brush. Crossing the room, Jack took it from her and slowly ran it down the length of her hair. From time to time his fingers brushed Katie's neck as he lifted her hair, and shivers raced down her spine.

For long minutes they said nothing, Jack stroking her hair and Katie reveling in the sensuousness of his touch. Finally the silence became too fraught with intimacy for Jack to bear. His purpose in visiting his wife's bedroom had been to establish a sense of normalcy in their marriage. He wanted Katie to know that she had a husband, but that did not mean he was willing to open his heart and make a gift of it to her. Jack understood little enough of its workings himself.

What he had in mind for tonight was something much more conventional . . . and controlled.

"Did you enjoy yourself today? The shopping excursion, I mean?" Jack asked, his tone pleasantly conversational.

His voice startled Katie, breaking the spell. For a moment she was unable to respond. "Yes. Yes, I did."

"I meant to tell you how lovely you looked tonight in your new gown, Kathleen. You must feel free to buy as many as you wish, to purchase anything that you like that will make you happy."

Katie squirmed a little. "That's very kind of you." She suppressed the urge to tell him that it would take more than material possessions to make her happy. Instead she said, "I was also grateful today for the opportunity to see more of San Francisco, and I enjoyed Mrs. Menloe's company. She's a very impressive woman.''

''I am not surprised that you would think so,'' he replied wryly. ''Hope is certainly strong, intelligent, and independent, which are qualities that not everyone admires in a woman. . . .''

She dropped her head back to look at him, brow furrowed. ''That's an odd remark. Are you trying to lure me into an argument?''

''No! At least, that was not my intention when I came in here.'' Jack laughed softly, shaking his head. ''Perhaps it would be better if we didn't talk for a while. Are you ready to get in bed?''

Suddenly shy, Katie nodded and stood up. Jack took her hand, led her over to the Empire-style bed, and drew back the covers. In spite of her rebelliousness at his attempts to control her behavior outside the bedroom, Katie thrilled as a woman when Jack took charge during these amorous adventures. Now, she could hardly wait to unleash her passion, to have an excuse to open the floodgates of her love.

The fire was nearly out, and it was hard for her to see Jack. When he slipped off his dressing gown, she felt cheated because she could make out only dimly the chiseled lines of his body. She hadn't realized how important the element of sight had become in their lovemaking. True, the first time they had been together it had been dark, but that darkness, combined with her sleep state, had dissolved her inhibitions. Now, being deprived of the sight of each other seemed to detract from the intimacy between them.

Jack eased Katie onto the bed and lay down facing her. Without removing her nightdress, he slipped his arms around her and kissed her gently. His hands moved over her body, and his lips were skilled, but there was a deliberation about his lovemaking that made Katie feel awkward. Occasionally, as he nibbled at her neck and cupped her breast through the thin lawn fabric of her nightdress, a spark would flare, but it never ignited into the exquisite rapture she had come to expect.

Pushing up the hem of her nightdress, Jack caressed Katie's thighs and the curves of her derriere. When he softly probed between her legs, Katie was encouraged to feel herself moisten with a tentative surge of desire. She sighed, expecting him to remove the garment that separated them, but instead Jack pressed her back into the pillows and shifted so that he was above her. Katie was shocked to feel him enter her. Was this all? She wondered. Tears stung her eyes as she tried to meet Jack's thrusts, unable to get the rhythm just right. She put her arms around him, but his body felt like that of a stranger. After what seemed an eternity, Jack groaned, pushing into her to the hilt, then let his arms bend so that he was lying fully on top of her.

She felt the thud of his heartbeat and tried not to weep. Then, turning her face against his neck, Katie caught the scent of lavender on his skin. Genevieve! It was as if a knife had been plunged into her heart, and she held her breath, waiting for the pain to subside.

Jack raised his head and kissed her lightly. "Mmm, that was nice." He rolled off her then and patted her bare thigh. "At this rate, it shouldn't take long to enlarge our family. I must admit, I'm looking forward to becoming a father. . . ." He sat up and offered her a benevolent smile. "Well, my dear, I'll leave you to freshen up," he said. "We're both tired, and will undoubtedly sleep better in our own beds."

"Good night, Jack," Katie managed to whisper. When he was gone, she lay still, letting the waves of indignation wash over her, her hands balled into fists at her sides. Did he think that she was some sort of brood mare who would docilely live by his rules while he cavorted as he pleased away from home? If so, Jack Wyatt was sadly mistaken! Until he was prepared to make this a real marriage, bound together with love, laughter, honesty, and loyalty, Katie vowed not to submit to his will. This was one filly he would find impossible to tame unless he was willing to domesticate himself *first*.

PART
FOUR

CHAPTER
26

November 10–28, 1864

"ARE YOU CERTAIN THAT JACK WON'T OBJECT TO THIS?" Conrad asked worriedly as he helped Katie rearrange the parlor. They had just finished grouping new overstuffed chairs and a sofa, upholstered in moss-green velvet, around the fireplace.

"Frankly, I don't mind if he does object! It would do Jack good to be shaken up a bit." Laughing, Katie stood back, hands on hips, to survey their work. "Well, I like it! What do you think, Conrad?"

"It's a big change," he said slowly, gazing around the parlor.

In truth, it didn't even look like the same room. Jack was due back momentarily from a three-day trip to Sacramento. He had gone to try to lure one of the *Union*'s best reporters over to the *Star*. No sooner had he bade them good-bye than a wagon had arrived to cart away all the old parlor furniture, and that had been just the beginning. The walls had been painted eggshell white, and new draperies of cream silk had been hung to replace the dark blue velvet curtains Jack had purchased. A magnificent Aubusson rug of green, ivory, and deep rose covered the floor, and now all the furniture was coordinated in those colors. The room seemed much brighter. A cozy carved tête-à-tête, where two people could sit facing each other on opposite sides, was bathed in sunlight from the front windows. Nearby reposed an étagère with marble shelves which Katie intended to line with china figurines and knickknacks belonging to Jack and Conrad's mother. Already she had set bowls of bright chrysanthemums around the parlor.

"Is that all you can say?" Katie asked, disappointed.

"No, I can truthfully say that I love it," he replied, turning to grin at her. "It's light and warm and in the best of taste. I don't see how Jack can object."

"Neither can I. After all, he told me to be a *wife*, insisting that I occupy myself with the house. *And*, he told me to purchase anything that would make me happy. In a way, this was his idea!"

Conrad thought that Katie sounded almost rebellious, as if she had redecorated the parlor to irritate rather than please her husband. He never knew what to expect from his sister-in-law, and now he watched fondly as she moved a candy dish and fussed with an arrangement of miniature mauve-and-white chrysanthemums. She had undergone quite a transformation herself in the past few days. Clad in a stylish morning dress of white French muslin with a bright blue vest, Katie looked fetching and elegant at the same time. Her glossy black hair was caught up in back in a *cache-peigne* of net and ribbons, while soft curls escaped to frame her face. Although she was more beautiful than ever, and certainly more self-assured, Conrad thought that he detected an undercurrent of sadness in Katie's sapphire eyes. It wouldn't have been noticeable if there weren't moments when it lifted, moments when Jack was near and looked at or touched his wife with unguarded affection. Then Katie's face would radiate joy until Jack remembered himself and drew away from her.

Conrad was more than a little puzzled by his brother's marriage. He had expected Jack to make a marriage of convenience, most predictably with Genevieve Braithwaite. She was beautiful and poised, would make an efficient wife, mother, and hostess, and she was already established in San Francisco society. Physically, Genevieve was desirable, and Conrad suspected that Jack also liked the fact that she was not warm and loving and thus would make few demands on him in that area.

Then, out of the blue, Katie had appeared, with her winsome looks, warm, carefree charm, and expressive, intelligent eyes. It had been logical to conclude that Jack had slipped and fallen helplessly in love. Yet the outward signs of that love, if it existed, were few and far between. Jack was friendly toward his bride, but little more. Conrad knew that they slept in separate beds, and Katie had taken to reading next to Ambrose in the parlor after Jack went to bed at night. It was all very curious.

"Katie, can I ask you a question?" he said suddenly.

"Of course, Con! Let's rest for a moment, shall we?" Smiling, she sat down on the new sofa and patted the spot next to her. "What would you like to know?"

"More about you, actually. I've never really heard about your life before you married Jack. I think you mentioned the foothills once, but then Jack changed the subject."

Poppy, who was venturing out of the bedroom now if Katie was close by for protection, jumped onto the sofa and snuggled between them, purring. Katie began to stroke the kitten. "Well, my parents came west when I was four years old, and I was raised in the town of Columbia, up in Tuolumne County—"

"I've been to Columbia!" Conrad cried in surprise.

"Have you?" Her eyes twinkled. "Did you go there thinking to strike it rich?"

"Well, yes, and I *did*, in a manner of speaking," he said with a frown. "But that's another story. You tell me yours first."

"My mother was a lady of culture, and I loved her very much, but she died when I was ten. After that, my father raised me, which meant that I was pretty much able to do as I pleased. What few girls there were in Columbia had mothers who taught them the rules of proper feminine etiquette, but Papa hadn't the vaguest notion about such things. I guess he thought I would just *become* ladylike through instinct." Katie paused, smiling as she thought of her father. "Of course it didn't work that way. I wore breeches for the most part until I was sixteen, and although I went to school, I often stole away to my favorite spot above the Stanislaus River and read the classics instead. My mother had a beautiful library of books."

"It sounds idyllic," Conrad murmured.

"I suppose it was, in a way . . . but not exactly the proper training for the wife of the wealthy, influential owner and editor of the San Francisco *Morning Star*, do you think?" She laughed. "I grew up working alongside my father in the saloon he owned—"

"A saloon? A *real* saloon?" Conrad echoed in amazement.

"Yes, except that we didn't have dance hall girls. And I began writing articles for the *Columbia Gazette* a year or two ago. So, you see, although there weren't many rules in my life, I did have to work very hard. Much harder than most boys at the same age." She rubbed behind Poppy's ears. "I also kept house for my father, and I set high standards for myself there. I was always looking up to Mama's example. . . ."

"How did you meet Jack?"

Katie chose her words carefully, aware that Conrad didn't know about Jack's other life in the foothills but thought that his brother had been in Nevada during his absences from San Francisco. "Jack used to pass through Columbia on his travels, and he got to know my father. I met him in the saloon on my eighteenth birthday."

"When was that?"

"On the twenty-first of June."

Conrad smoothed back his red hair, pondering this information. "So, Jack knew you when he came home in July. . . ." He grinned. "That's very interesting!"

"Why do you say that?"

"Because he seemed *different*, somehow. More restless and moody. And—" He broke off, blushing.

"And?" Katie pressed.

"Well, there was a woman Jack had been seeing . . ."

"Genevieve Braithwaite," she supplied.

Conrad was shocked. "You know about her?"

"Not from Jack, but from everyone else. In fact, I overheard you carrying on about her the night I arrived, when I was in the bathtub and you knocked on Jack's door. Since then, I saw her in the dress shop the morning after we arrived here, and Hope Menloe confirmed her identity." Katie smiled wryly. "I had the impression that Miss Braithwaite thought her relationship with Jack was still in full flower, so I don't imagine that she was very happy when she learned of my existence."

"No, she's not," Conrad replied hesitantly. "I work in her father's bank, and she's had words with me about it. She's not the sort of woman who gives up easily. But what I was going to say before was that Jack changed toward Genevieve after he came home in July. He was definitely cooler."

Katie sat back against the green velvet upholstery and stroked Poppy's back thoughtfully. "Life is interesting, isn't it? I've come to believe in fate, and to resign myself to it, at least to an extent. There is a reason I met Jack and a reason for our marriage. I have to believe that God had a hand in it. So many twists of fate came into play . . . for instance, if my father hadn't died, it probably would have taken a great deal more to convince me to leave Columbia."

"How did your father die?" Conrad asked softly.

Before Katie could reply, the front door opened and Jack's step sounded in the entry hall.

They both jumped up, suddenly remembering that the parlor had changed completely in his absence. Katie was surprised to discover that she could scarcely wait to see him. For three days she had kept busy with her projects, trying to pretend that she didn't miss Jack, but now the promise of his physical presence filled her with elation.

At last Jack appeared, framed in the arched entrance to the parlor. His tawny hair seemed dusted with sunlight after two long days on the *Senator*, and his face was more deeply tanned than ever. He wore an impeccably tailored morning coat and trousers of lightweight, charcoal-gray wool, a double-breasted waistcoat, a starched white shirt, and a simple wrapped cravat.

He froze in the act of drawing off his dove-gray gloves and stared. "Am I in the right house?"

Katie went to him and stood on tiptoe to kiss his cheek. "Welcome home, Jack. Do you like it?"

Conrad watched them both with a rather anxious expression on his face. "In my opinion, Katie's done a wonderful job," he offered helpfully.

"Leave us alone, would you, Con?" Jack's tone made it an order rather than a request. When his brother had gone, he turned to Katie, his cat's eyes dazzling with anger. "How dare you do"—he gestured at the parlor—"*this* without consulting me?"

"Don't you like it?"

"That's not the point! I chose the things that were in this room after I purchased the house. They belonged to *me*, and you had no right to dispose of them and put something else in their place!"

"That's not fair!" Katie retaliated. "First of all, you are *married* now, so it's absolutely *wrong* for you to keep saying 'I' and 'me' that way. There are two of us now. Secondly, you *told* me to busy myself with the house, that there was more than enough for me to do here, and when I asked you what those things might be, you had no answer. So I had to look around and see what I could do to make this male house into a home. Thirdly—"

"For God's sake, Katie, how long is this tirade going to last?"

"Don't you *dare* act bored and cut me off," she told him in menacing tones. "*Thirdly*, you insisted that I buy anything that would make me happy. I happen to find that a pitifully condescending thing to say to anyone, and the sort of sentiment that is peculiar to your sex, but I decided to take you at your word. Fourthly—"

"I'm not sure that's a word." Jack was beginning to enjoy her performance. There was something especially stimulating about Katie when she was furious.

"I beg your pardon?" She paused impatiently for breath.

"I don't think that 'fourthly' is a word," he explained, leaning against the wall.

"Kindly refrain from patronizing me! *Fourthly*, I objected to the former style of this room. I'm not criticizing your taste, I'm talking about the taste of this entire period. I find most of the supposedly fashionable homes I have seen in San Francisco too dark, too cluttered, and the furniture too overbearing. I think that *our* parlor, now, is much more aesthetically pleasing, and if you will look at it with an unbiased eye, I don't see how you can disagree.''

Jack gave Katie a smile that made her heart skip a beat. "You're right.''

She paused in midbreath and frowned. "What?''

"I can't disagree. You are absolutely right.''

"Do you mean—''

"I mean that I like the parlor. It will take some getting used to—''

"That was going to be 'fifthly.' I think that you simply resist change, even change for the better—''

"Kathleen, be quiet.'' His eyes crinkled gently at the corners.

"How dare you talk—''

"No more.'' Jack drew her firmly into his arms. "Kiss your husband; welcome me home properly.''

"But Jack—'' Katie felt that somehow he had taken control of the argument, defusing it before she was finished.

He reached up with one hand to hold her face still, then covered her mouth with his own. He kissed her hungrily, drinking in the lithe, female warmth of her body pressed full length against his. Katie was intoxicated by the taste of him, the smell of his clothes and his skin, the forcefulness of his embrace. As long as Jack seemed to have lost control, perhaps it would be all right for her to lose control, too. Just this once. . . .

"Grandfather, you really don't have to do this. We have gardeners, you know.'' Jack crossed the lawn through the cool morning mist to join Ambrose, who was cutting back the rosebushes that grew along the tall iron fence.

The old man scowled at him. "Why do you say that to me, Jack? You know that I *want* to do this, so leave me alone!''

"My apologies.'' Jack smiled, fiddling with a cuff link. "Perhaps I said it so I would have an excuse to come over here and talk to you.''

"Then just say what's on your mind, boy!''

"It's Kathleen.''

"Katie? What about her?'' Ambrose clipped the last ivory rosebud of the season and tucked it in his grandson's lapel.

"I—I guess I feel that she isn't putting enough effort into our marriage. She's been so busy with the house, her new wardrobe . . ."

"Hmm." The old man continued to prune, not looking up. "Go on, I'm listening."

"I didn't mind when she ordered the first batch of new gowns, or even when she redecorated the parlor, but then came elaborate preparations for Thanksgiving, and now she's changing the dining room, and she's being fitted for a riding habit this morning, and—"

"Seems to me that you *told* her to occupy herself with this sort of thing," Ambrose remarked reasonably. "Or am I wrong?"

"Well, I didn't expect it to occupy her every waking hour!" Jack loosened his cravat and hunkered down next to his grandfather. "Night before last, when I went to bed, she and Hope Menloe were looking at sketches for her new cloak and riding habit. Then, last night, I went to Kathleen's room and discovered that she had installed a new *desk* for herself! She was working at it busily—"

"Oh, yes, I heard about that desk." Ambrose smiled, scratching his bald head. "I think Katie's planning to turn the morning room into a little study for herself, with her new desk, and a chaise, and bookshelves for *her* books. She wants to send to Columbia for the books that belonged to her mother, but was worried about the expense. I told her to go ahead. The study is a spectacular idea, and just what she deserves."

"Are you two in league to drive me insane?" Jack felt a pang of jealousy that Katie was sharing dreams with his grandfather that were unknown to him.

The old man chuckled. "Don't mind me. Go on with your story."

"Well, when I went to her room, I thought that we might spend a little time *alone*, if you take my meaning." He flushed, slightly embarrassed to be confiding such things to his grandfather. "I've barely kissed her since the night I returned from Sacramento over a fortnight ago! But she announced that she couldn't join me until she finished her lists, and that might take another hour." Jack's voice dropped to a deadly whisper. "*Lists*. Have you heard about those?"

"No, I don't think so."

"What a surprise! You seem to know everything else!" He drew a long breath to calm himself. "Kathleen is planning a huge Christmas party. An 'affair of significance,' she called it. If I hadn't seen the lists with my own eyes, I'd think she was in jest! There are moments when I can't believe this is the same girl I knew in Columbia. . . ."

"Isn't this what you wanted in a wife? Didn't you encourage her to be a lady?" Ambrose asked simply. "And perhaps she's just trying to redirect her life now that she's accepted reality. Perhaps she's trying to fill the space that she hoped you would occupy."

Jack stared, jaw tensed, mouth grim. Then he looked away. "What do you mean by *that*? I went to her room to be with her, didn't I?"

"Jack, you must know Katie better than to think that she could be content with the mere trappings of a marriage. I suspect that going through the motions hurts her more than not being with you at all. And the decision rests with you: either simply share space with your wife or make a real marriage. My guess is, with Katie, there can be no in between."

Jack's knuckles were white as he gripped the iron fence for support. "Oh, God."

"Would you like to hear what I think?" Summers asked gently.

"I imagine so. . . ."

"I believe that you hold Katie away from yourself because of your guilt about her father. Perhaps one day you can tell her, and she'll understand, but in the meantime the best thing you can do for Brian MacKenzie's daughter is to be a flesh-and-blood husband to her. Let yourself love her."

"That isn't as easy as it sounds," Jack said, his voice husky.

"Perhaps it's too easy. You think too much, my boy. You've gotten so used to thinking rather than feeling these past few years that your heart is out of practice. Listen to it for a change." He pulled away a thorny branch and cast it to the side.

Sighing deeply, Jack uncoiled his strong body and stood up. "I'll think about it."

"There you go again." Ambrose chuckled. "Will you listen to a piece of advice from an old man who's learned a few things the hard way? Miracles don't happen overnight, even to you, Jack. Real change comes slowly, and you'll have to learn patience. Trust yourself. You're an extraordinary man . . . and Katie knows that."

CHAPTER
27

December 10–18, 1864

DECEMBER BROUGHT A STATE OF CHAOS TO THE WYATT household. New servants were hired, including a ladies' maid for Katie named Judith, but most of the preparations for Christmas and the party that was planned were made by Katie herself. She was in the kitchen at dawn with a ruffled white apron over her dress, working alongside the cook and her staff to make fruitcakes and plum puddings. Some were for the family, but most would be given as gifts and distributed to the poor. Fragrant, fresh green garlands trimmed with red velvet bows were strung over every wall downstairs and also festooned the mantels, doorways, banisters, and chandeliers. Katie made the wreath for the front door herself. It was huge, consisting of pine boughs, sprigs of red-berried holly, tiny pine cones, and a big bow of red-and-green plaid silk. A single candle burned in every window, and the house was redolent with the scents of spices and evergreen.

Midway through the second week of the month, Hope Menloe came over to help Katie plan the food for the party. Invitations had gone out for the eighteenth, and already more than two dozen acceptances had been received. The two women were seated in the breakfast room, heads bent over cookery books and lists, when Jack and Conrad stopped in to say good-bye.

"I'm going to take Con to the bank on my way to the office," Jack said.

Katie looked up distractedly. "That's nice. I hope your day goes well, Jack." She smiled at her brother-in-law. "And yours, Conrad."

Jack started to go over and give her a kiss, but when Katie turned back to Hope to point out another recipe, he thought better of it. Sighing, he drew on his gloves as they went out the door.

"Is something wrong?" Conrad asked, summoning up his courage.

Jack arched an eyebrow and shrugged. "No, not really. We always long for the thing that eludes us, don't we? I'm no different."

"What is it you long for?"

Jack almost rebuked him for being too inquisitive, but a sudden impulse made him reply instead, "The company of my wife."

"Do you really! That's the first time I've heard you admit that you care for Katie."

"Well, I wouldn't attach too much importance to it, Con." His tone was light now as they climbed into the carriage. "All I meant was that a house full of Christmas cheer isn't much use if there's no one to share it with."

"Well, perhaps it's not an issue of crucial importance to you, but I know that if I were married to Katie, I'd hoard her like a miser. I think she's nothing short of magic. Not only is she simply enchanting to behold, but the air around her is filled with a kind of vibrant goodness—"

"Conrad," Jack interrupted in mock consternation, "your enthusiasm borders on delirium. Are you harboring a secret passion for my wife?"

"I wish I'd met her first, I'll say that much!" The young man blushed a little. "No, I'm not in love with her, any more than I was in love with Genevieve, even though I lusted after her mightily."

"*Lusted?*" Jack blinked, amused. "Good God!"

"I'm a man, too, and I'm only human," Conrad countered, lifting his chin. "As for Katie, it would mean living in fantasy if I were to let myself fall in love her. The reality is that she's in love with you, and she's your wife." He gathered his hat and papers as the carriage approached the First Western Bank, which was owned by Gerald Braithwaite. "My own reality is less exciting, but comforting nonetheless. I think I'll propose to Emma on Christmas Eve. It's time, I suppose, for the plunge into manhood."

With that, Conrad stepped down from the carriage, waved to his brother, and dodged other vehicles and pedestrians as he hurried toward the bank. Jack leaned back against the upholstery and smiled to himself. How typical of a young pup like his brother to lust after an empty shell of a glamorous woman like Genevieve while worshiping Katie as if she were a goddess. The truth was that Katie, with her warmth and goodness, was far more desirable than Genevieve, because of her *own* capacity for desire, which was as great as it was for all other human emotions. Arousal fueled arousal, and love fueled love. These past weeks, during which Katie had steadily blocked him from enjoying her spiritual and physical passions, Jack had slowly begun to understand and then to accept the meaning behind her actions. Now, he had to show his wife that he was willing to change—not just his own life, but the life he shared with her.

Conrad's office was a small, dimly lit, airless room dominated by a scarred desk. As a clerk, he worked hard, poring methodically over columns of figures in search of errors, not because he enjoyed it, but because Mr. Braithwaite held out the promise of a promotion "one of these days." The accounts manager was getting older and was frequently ill. It was this job, which involved interaction with real human beings, that Conrad craved.

"I hope I'm not disturbing you, Conrad."

Startled, he pivoted on his chair and saw Genevieve Braithwaite peeking around the door to his office. "My gosh! I mean—no, of course not! Can I do something for you?"

She closed the door and stood there for a moment, smiling, so he could fully appreciate the beautiful picture she made. Her dress was powder-blue silk with a daringly low neckline that left little to the imagination. The bodice fit tightly, hugging every curve and accentuating her perfect eighteen-inch waist, then the skirt flared out over her crinoline. Genevieve had removed her bonnet to show off her silky blond curls, which were caught up in a profusion of ringlets next to one ear. Her provocative mouth was rosy and moist as she said, "I was just visiting Daddy, and I thought about you, Conrad. I've *missed* you." She glided the few steps to his desk and stopped in front of him. "Have you missed me?"

Mesmerized, he stared at her breasts, which were level with his eyes, noticing the way they swelled with each breath she took. "Missed you? . . . Well, yes, of course."

She perched on the edge of his desk, slightly higher than Conrad and just inches away. "How have you been? And how is dear Mr. Summers?"

"I've been—about the same, I guess. Nothing new. Grandfather is . . . fine, too. The same."

"But things are *not* the same at your house, are they? You've avoided talking to me about this before, Conrad, but is it really fair of you? Can you not understand how I feel? Not knowing what is happening or who this woman is who took my place only makes me feel more confused!" Looking as if she might weep, Genevieve leaned forward until one breast lightly grazed the side of his face. "Won't you help me?"

Conrad thanked God that he was sitting down. "Well, wh-what can I do to help you?" he heard himself say hoarsely. She was so close that he could smell her perfume, and her skin looked incredibly soft. Dizzily, he imagined what her breasts would look like if she were to open her gown.

"Tell me about her. Maybe if I understand, if I can think of her as a *person*, I can wish them well. . . ." Her voice was low, hypnotic.

Conrad cleared his throat and tried to respond rationally. His loins ached so that he could scarcely think, let alone speak. "Well, Katie's actually a very nice person. She's friendly, and—"

"Are they happy?" Genevieve broke in.

He squirmed. "I—I imagine so. They have a few problems, but I believe they'll work them out."

Stroking his red hair and side-whiskers, she purred, "Do you know, you're a good-looking man, Conrad. Your features are more classical than Jonathan's. Tell me some more about Katie. Where is she from? How did she meet your brother?"

"She's from Columbia." He heard his own voice from a distance. "They met at her saloon. . . ."

"Indeed? How quaint." Genevieve tried not to betray her glee. Standing, she reached over to pat Conrad's cheek and said, "Well I must be going, Conrad. I have a luncheon engagement. But it's been lovely seeing you again. Do give my regards to your family."

Conrad panicked, not only because of what he had said about Katie, but also because he didn't want Genevieve to leave. "No wait I ought to explain about the saloon. It wasn't the way i sounds—"

"It probably wasn't like other saloons simply because your sister in-law was in it, hmm?" she replied sweetly. "I understand. Now you take good care of yourself, and tell Papa I said he mustn't work you too hard!"

With a rustle of crinoline and an intoxicating swirl of lavende scent, Genevieve sailed out of the office. Alone again, Conrad sa at his desk in a daze. It seemed that he could almost feel the blood slowly leaving his groin and returning to his brain. How could he have been so stupid? Not only had he completely forgotten his commitment to Emma, but he had also discussed Katie with Genevieve in spite of his resolve not to. Still, what harm could she do? Jack and Katie were married, and Genevieve had no choice but to accept the fact that she had lost . . . didn't she?

"Judith, could you come in here for a moment?" Jack called from his bedroom.

The young, sweet-faced ladies' maid, whom Katie had hired for her disposition rather than her experience, hurried in from her mistress's dressing room. At the doorway she stopped, paralyzed by the sight of Jonathan Wyatt.

He wore a dashingly cut black tailcoat, black trousers, and a white silk waistcoat, all of which fit to perfection on his tall, strong body. Jack's white tie and shirt, with its starched turnover collar, contrasted strikingly with his tanned, roguishly handsome face. His ruffled hair was the color of melted caramel, and his sage-green eyes sparkled with flecks of gold.

"Anything wrong, Judith?" he asked, trying not to betray his amusement.

"Yes—I mean, no, sir! It's just that . . . well, I hope you won't think I'm speaking out of turn, but I've never seen a finer-looking man than you, Mr. Wyatt."

"That's very loyal of you, Judith," Jack said, the corners of his eyes crinkling, "and I appreciate it. In fact, I appreciate it so much that I'm sending you downstairs for a hot buttered rum."

"Yes, sir. I'll bring it right back to you!"

He held out his hand, laughing. "No, no, I want *you* to drink it! If you don't care for spirits, have a cup of tea. Just sit down, put your feet up, and sip it slowly. I'll help Mrs. Wyatt finish dressing."

Judith's dark eyes were like saucers. "Oh, no, sir, I couldn't possibly—"

"I insist."

Looking confused, the little maid did as she was told, while Jack walked through the connecting door and turned into Katie's dressing room. She was standing before a bureau, examining a collection of jewelry, the back of her silk ball gown open to the waist.

"What did Mr. Wyatt want, Judith?" she asked without looking up.

Jack came up behind her and slipped his hand into her open

gown, curving it around her midriff to draw her against him. "He
wanted to be alone with Mrs. Wyatt."

Katie gasped at his touch, then leaned back and laughed nervously. "It's very bad of you to startle me that way, Jack, and very
bad of you to spoil my surprise. I didn't want you to see me until I
was completely dressed."

"I like you better this way." He lowered his mouth to the place
where her neck curved into her shoulder. "God, but you smell good
. . . and your skin is like satin."

"My, aren't we frisky tonight," Katie teased, trying to ignore
her own response.

"I'm more than frisky," Jack said in a husky voice. He wanted
to tell her that he'd missed her, that he hoped they could make a
fresh start tonight, but Katie was drawing away from him.

"Well, you'll have to hold yourself in check for a bit, because
it's getting late and the guests will be arriving soon. Fasten my
gown, won't you, please?" She stood motionless while he complied, the touch of his fingers sending little shivers down her spine.
Then she turned slowly to face him. "I confess that I'm a little
nervous about this dress. What do you think?"

"I think . . . that I can hardly believe you are the same girl I
knew in Columbia." It was the same sentiment he had expressed
to his grandfather, but this time his tone was warm with approval
and admiration.

Katie wore a stunning gown fashioned of Chinese-red silk. The
deeply scooped bodice revealed her creamy shoulders, then
wrapped over her breasts. Her tiny waist was accentuated by a red
sash that tied in a bow in back. A cluster of soft little ermine tails
swayed from the ends of the sash and marched around the gown's
wide hem.

"It's so different from anything I've seen," Katie said, surveying
herself a trifle nervously. "The color, the ermine—"

"It's inspired," Jack assured her, "and you look spectacular.
That red is beautiful with your hair and eyes. You ought to wear it
more often."

"Oh, I don't think so!" She laughed, unused to such lavish and
sincere compliments. "My only hope is that people will indulge
me because it is Christmas. I had it designed for the holiday." She
pointed to the cluster of holly she wore in her hair, which was
caught up on one side in a mass of long curls. "You see? I'm
striving for a festive effect."

"You don't need an excuse to stand out in a crowd, Kathleen.

You're an extraordinarily beautiful woman; you deserve to be stared at.''

She colored slightly, her sparkling blue eyes smiling at him. "You look quite extraordinary yourself, Mr. Wyatt." His gaze held hers so intimately that she turned back to her jewelry. "I thought I might wear the ruby-and-pearl necklace and earrings that belonged to your mother."

"Perfect." Jack fastened the necklace for her, then kissed the feather-soft curls that brushed the nape of her neck. Slowly, then, he turned her in his arms and they embraced. Currents of emotion passed between their bodies, warming each of them with hope, until a knock sounded at the door to Jack's bedroom.

"Mrs. Gosling wants to know if Katie's going to check the table," Conrad called. "All the food has been set out."

Jack released Katie, and she quickly fastened her earrings, each of which consisted of one simple, square-cut ruby crowned by a lustrous pearl. Then she picked up a little spray of holly. "Stand still," she told Jack, and pinned the holly to his lapel.

Walking down the hall, she took Jack's arm, and he smiled to himself.

"Did I tell you that I sought out Lim Sung's parents in the Chinese quarter the other day?" she asked.

"You *know* that you didn't tell me, Kathleen!" he replied instantly exasperated. "I never would have allowed you to go there without me."

"Elijah took me, so I was perfectly safe. And fortunately I found them quite easily. It was wonderful to see Yong and Choy Sung again, and they agreed, after much persuasion, to come to our party tonight. Lim will be so pleased when he hears."

Jack looked bemused. "I'm glad you invited them, Kathleen, but don't be surprised if some of the other guests have a different reaction."

"Then they needn't stay," she said briskly.

As they descended the wide staircase, he remarked, "I learned today that Grant Phillips will also be attending tonight—the reporter who has just arrived from Sacramento to work for me. Perhaps he'll make a new friend or two."

"That's nice. You must make a point of introducing us." With studied nonchalance, Katie added, "Oh, by the way, Mr. and Mrs. Braithwaite sent their regrets."

Jack glanced down at her. They were approaching the dining room as he said, "That's just as well, for the time being. Kathleen,

I've been meaning to talk to you about them . . . well, about their daughter, to be more specific. . . ."

The embers of hope burned brighter in Katie's heart. Could Jack actually intend to begin revealing more of himself to her? Mrs. Gosling, clad in a black taffeta gown and crisp white apron, was hurrying toward them as she replied, "Unfortunately, it will have to wait. I seem to have other obligations. . . ."

Everything looked magnificent. The carved sliding doors between the drawing and dining rooms had been opened to form one huge room that seemed to exude Christmas cheer. A long buffet table stretched across one wall, covered with a snowy white cloth and studded with artful centerpieces of evergreen, candles, and fruit. Around them was arranged food of every description. There were dishes with various pâtés, scalloped oysters, lobster patties, sausage rolls, salads, iced prawns, and galantines of duck and tongue. A huge roast goose with chestnut stuffing had been artfully arranged beside a garnished, glazed pink ham, and both were surrounded by raised chicken pies, woodcocks, plovers, and cracked crabs. There were plates of fresh biscuits, bowls of pumpkins squash and green beans with almonds, compotes of fruit, tartlets of jam, bonbons, sweetmeats, tiny cheesecakes, plum puddings, dates, and nuts. The pièce de résistance had been baked by Katie—a magnificent Christmas cake covered with snowy white frosting and decorated with sprigs of holly.

There were several small Christmas trees on tabletops throughout the house, glowing with the light of miniature candles. Each was gaily decorated with strings of glass beads and cranberries and hung with tiny brightly wrapped packages, colorful blown-glass balls, crystal snowflakes, and little birds with real feathers.

The magical effect was made complete by the hundreds of candles that illumined the entire downstairs of the house. A fire danced in every fireplace, and on the parlor mantel Katie had arranged an exquisite hand-carved crèche she'd discovered in a box in the attic.

Now she paused in front of it, remembering what her mother had told her each Christmas. As Jack came up to give her a cup of hot mulled cider, Katie murmured, "This is the essence of Christmas for me. Mama used to say that the celebration of the Christ child's birth should be a time of rebirth for all of us, that winter could bring more new growth than spring . . . new growth in our hearts. That's the gift I want most for Christmas. I want to be cleansed, to replace my fears and pain with courage and serenity as I enter the new year." Her eyes glistened. "I believe it's possible, with God's grace."

Jack felt a tightening in his chest and a surge of tenderness toward his wife. He wanted to tell her that his dream for 1865 was the same as hers, but before he could speak, there was a resounding knock at the front door and guests began to arrive.

A stringed quartet began to play in a corner of the drawing room while the house slowly filled with the richly garbed cream of San Francisco society, as well as many of Jack's less wealthy but more colorful friends. Ambrose Summers and Conrad, both clad in white tie and tailcoats, were there to help assume some of the hosting duties, but everyone wanted to meet the new Mrs. Wyatt. All were gracious when presented to her, though Katie was well aware of the curious stares and whispers from across the room and the occasional eyebrow that arched at her red gown. But she didn't care. Tonight she could feel headstrong Katie MacKenzie from Columbia merging with the more womanly Kathleen Wyatt, and she knew a sense of peace that she had never experienced before.

Polished servants, under the watchful eye of Mrs. Gosling, moved discreetly through the crowd with bottles of French champagne, while others served hot buttered rum, mulled cider, eggnog, and wassail from huge silver bowls. Guests milled around the buffet table, filling their plates, and a few couples began to dance in the drawing room.

Bret Harte and Edwin Murray, the *Morning Star*'s city editor, approached Jack. Between sips of champagne, the dandified Harte clapped Wyatt on the back and remarked, "We were just saying how very beautiful your bride is, old boy. I cannot remember ever being in the company of a more fresh and radiant woman."

"I'll second that." Edwin nodded, hiccuping. "If you don't mind my saying so, sir, you made the right choice. Mrs. Wyatt is a stunner."

"Thank you," Jack said, grinning. "For once I agree with both of you at the same time." He indulged himself in a long look across the room at Katie, who was hugging the newly arrived Hope Menloe. She was surrounded by several admirers, many of whom were neighbors or members of their church whom Katie hadn't met until now. Even from a distance, Jack could see and feel the radiance Bret Harte had spoken of. It shone from inside Katie and was reflected in her eyes, her glowing skin, her smile, even the bounce of her glossy black curls.

"Well, well, look who's just arrived." Harte cocked an eyebrow as he stared toward the entry hall. "It's the overrated star reporter from the *Sacramento Union*. Oh, sorry, I've put my foot in it again. Phillips works for you now, doesn't he?"

Jack was glad of an excuse to leave Harte and Murray, both of whom had obviously sampled a bit too much champagne. Weaving through the crowd, he kept Grant Phillips's blond head in sight. Katie was moving toward him, too, and Jack was just a few steps behind when she reached the new guest.

"I'm so pleased that you could come," Katie said, reaching for his hand with both of hers. "I'm Kathleen Wyatt, Jack's wife."

"I'm Grant Phillips." Hazel eyes smiled at her from behind steel spectacles. "It's a pleasure to meet you, Mrs. Wyatt. As you may have heard, I am newly arrived in San Francisco, so I'm grateful to you and your husband for inviting me to your home."

"Of course!" Katie's face brightened with recognition. "You're from Sacramento, aren't you? I've only been here a few weeks myself, so we have something in common."

Jack came up behind his wife and shook Grant's hand. "I'm glad you could make it. Did you take my advice and search out a young lady to escort?"

Grant smiled. "I did indeed—the prettiest girl I've seen in San Francisco, present company excepted, of course. She is just handing over her cloak to your maid. . . ." He turned toward the entry hall, and his smile widened. "Here she is! Mr. and Mrs. Wyatt, are you acquainted with Miss Genevieve Braithwaite?"

Katie paled, and she felt Jack's arm tense around her back. "I don't believe we've been formally introduced," she murmured.

Taking her place at Grant's side, Genevieve smiled coolly and said in a loud voice, "Jack and I are old and intimate friends, aren't we, Jack? And this must be your bride. I would have known you anywhere, Mrs. Wyatt, by your scarlet dress. Isn't that the color de rigueur for saloon girls?"

CHAPTER
28

December 18–19, 1864

A HUSH FELL OVER THE CROWD OF GUESTS, WHILE OTHERS across the long room whispered, "What did she say?"

Jack gave Genevieve a murderous look. "Miss Braithwaite, I think you owe my wife an apology."

"Do I?" Her shrill voice carried easily. "Oh, my, I didn't realize it was a secret that she was working in a saloon when you met. If I've spoken out of turn, I *do* apologize. I don't suppose I can blame you for being embarrassed by your past, Miss—I mean, Mrs. Wyatt."

"My wife *owned* the MacKenzie Saloon," Jack said, his voice carrying. "She was *not* a 'saloon girl'."

Katie felt faint. She was trying to find her voice when she glimpsed Yong and Choy Sung peeking into the dining room. Yong wore an ill-fitting brown suit, and his hair was slicked back into a long queue, while Choy was clad in the traditional Chinese costume of a long, embroidered tunic with a high collar fastened to one side, over loose silk pants. Their faces shone with loving smiles when they saw Katie.

The assembled guests, already staring attentively at the scene between the Wyatts and Genevieve Braithwaite, now wore expressions of undisguised shock. It seemed that everyone began to whisper at once. When Katie moved forward to embrace the new arrivals, a few of the women gasped aloud. San Francisco's upper class was noticeably more tolerant of the Chinese than other Californians, and appreciative of their contribution to the city, but socializing with them was unthinkable. Although Katie could feel the tension in the air around her, she proceeded to introduce the Sungs to other guests, who had no choice but to smile, nod, and mouth polite amenities.

Jack was torn between two crises. He felt bound to give Katie support with the Sungs and so helped her make introductions all the way over to the buffet table. She was explaining the various dishes to Yong and Choy when Conrad came up behind Jack.

"You'd better do something about Genevieve," he murmured. "She's telling everyone who'll listen about Katie's life as a saloon girl, and adding spiteful comments about her choice of friends"— he nodded at the Sungs—"for good measure."

Conrad's face was even whiter than usual in contrast with his bright red hair and side-whiskers. He was in an agony of guilt over his own part in the havoc Genevieve was wreaking on Katie's lovingly planned party, and he was also more than a little worried that she might decide to tell Emma Pierce about the cozy scene between them in his office.

Leaning toward Katie, Jack whispered, "I'll be right back." Her only response was a nod; she didn't look up.

As he strode across the room, he could clearly hear Genevieve saying to Charles Henry Webb, founder of the literary weekly, the *Californian*, "I hardly think that it can come as a surprise, that woman bringing Chinese into Jonathan's house as guests! How could she possible know better? I mean, just look at that gaudy dress she's wearing. The poor thing was raised in the mountains, and she worked in a saloon until Jonathan took pity and married her. I shudder to think whom she'll invite next to this beautiful home. Can you *imagine* the sorts of friends she must have?" She widened her beautiful green eyes to suggest various unmentionable possibilities.

People around Genevieve pretended to sip their drinks and chat, while listening with one ear to everything that she was saying. Jack was rigid with fury. Coming up behind her, he gripped her elbow and said softly, "Come with me."

"Of course, Jonathan darling." She looked around until she spotted Grant Phillips and then called, "Now, don't you worry about me, Grant—I'm just going to have a moment alone with Jonathan. Old times, you know!"

Jack could hear the buzzing that began as soon as they reached the entry hall, but he didn't care, nor did he care if he bruised Genevieve's arm as he dragged her into his study and slammed the door.

"You *bitch*! I could kill you for this!"

Genevieve reclined gracefully against the overstuffed armchair Jack all but tossed her onto and smiled up at him, one eyebrow arched. "I can't imagine what you mean, darling. All I did was tell the truth. If the truth is unpalatable, perhaps you had better seek another." The challenge in her eyes was unmistakable. "It's not too late to admit that you've made a mistake, you know."

Jack stared, incredulous. "You must be out of your mind!"

"On the contrary, I am saner than you. My mother always told me that an inability to admit mistakes was a flaw inherent in men, but somehow I hoped that you were better than that, Jonathan."

"I don't know what the devil you're babbling about, and furthermore, I don't care—"

"I'm talking about that woman you're trying to pass off as your wife. You must see by now that she can never do justice to your fine family name. Jonathan, you can tell me how you really feel; I of all people will understand. And I'll wait for you while you disentangle yourself from this disastrous marriage."

Jack longed to smash something, but instead he clenched his jaw and drew up a straight-backed chair next to Genevieve. Slowly he said, "Obviously this is not an argument worthy of my time. You are a spoiled, self-centered girl who is so used to having her own way that you distort other people's lives until they suit your purposes. I thank God for bringing Kathleen to me, thereby delivering me from doing something insane in a weak moment—like marrying you!"

Genevieve's lustrous green eyes widened. "But Jonathan—"

"Be quiet and listen for a change! Kathleen is nothing like the person you imagine her to be. She is educated, tasteful, loving, and good, and she is the finest thing that ever happened to me." He paused. "Now listen carefully, Genevieve: I love Kathleen with all my heart, and I believe that she loves me. Nothing is more important to me than the success of our marriage, and I intend to do everything in my power to make her happy." Jack took a deep breath. "If you say one more word against my wife, or do anything to harm her or her reputation, I won't be responsible for my actions. Is that clear?"

"Mm." Sulking, she twisted her hands together in her lap, staring down at them.

Jack stood up. "Look at me! Is that clear?"

Genevieve returned his stare defiantly. "Yes! Yes, it's *clear*. But don't come to me later, when you've seen that I'm right, and beg for another chance!"

Walking toward the door, he said over his shoulder in icy tones, "I'll have Elijah drive you home. Do not rejoin the party."

When the last guest had departed, Ambrose discovered his grandson in the parlor, gazing pensively into the dying fire.

"I'd say that the party was a success, in spite of everything," the old man murmured. "After you sent Miss Braithwaite home, I thought you and Katie did an excellent job of repairing the damage she tried to do."

Jack smiled bleakly. "People seemed to understand that Genevieve was acting out of jealousy, and Kathleen is so obviously genuine that our guests couldn't help being charmed by her. She went right on with the party as if Genevieve didn't matter. Kathleen won them over simply by being herself."

"Your support counted for a great deal, my boy," Ambrose assured him. "And now that they've all gone home, Katie might welcome some personal attention. She's organizing the cleanup with Mrs. Gosling. Why don't you lend her a hand?"

Jack's white tie was already loosened, and now he unfastened his starched collar and sighed. "I already tried. Kathleen doesn't seem to want anything to do with me. To be honest, Grandfather, I'm afraid I waited too long to tell her how I feel, to show her how much I love her. She's been drawing away from me for a long time, and that scene with Genevieve tonight may have killed whatever feelings she had left for me. . . ."

Ambrose frowned. "Nonsense."

"You wouldn't say that if you'd seen the way she looked at me." He stripped off his tailcoat, slung it over the back of one of the new moss-green velvet chairs, and walked to the sideboard. Pulling the stopper from a decanter of brandy, he sloshed some of the liquor into a glass.

"What are you doing?"

"Having a drink." He returned to the fire and stared into the glass.

"Don't be a fool, boy. That brandy's not going to help you! Only you can fix this problem, and you need to start this very moment. Go to her and *tell* her how you feel! Do you expect her to be able to read your mind? Hasn't it occurred to you that she might be as confused as you are? For God's sake—"

Jack threw the glass into the fireplace, splashing brandy and shattering the crystal over the flames. Bracing himself against the mantel, he let his eyes rest upon the crèche, and Katie's words came back to him. Fears replaced by courage, she had said. . . . "All right," he whispered. "I'll talk to her."

"Come over here for a moment," Ambrose ordered gruffly. He embraced Jack with all his might and muttered, "I'm proud of you, and I love you."

"I love you, too, Grandfather. Wish me luck."

Crossing the hall, Jack found that there were only two kitchen maids removing the last of the food. They told him that Mrs. Wyatt had just retired for the night. He ran lightly up the stairs, then turned the corners of the hallway until he saw Katie passing the door to his bedroom. Carrying her shoes in one hand and holding her skirts with the other, she looked so small and vulnerable.

"Kathleen."

She stopped but did not look back.

Jack came up behind her. "I'd like to talk to you."

"I'm very tired." Katie lifted eyes clouded with pain to meet his.

"Please, just give me a few minutes. It's important." He opened the door to his room and gestured for her to precede him. She bit her lip doubtfully but entered. Elijah had lighted a fire and turned back the covers on the bed to reveal two plump, inviting pillows. Turning her back on the bed, Katie stood stiffly in the middle of the magnificent Turkey carpet, waiting. Jack approached but stopped a few feet away, and when she looked at his face, she found it different somehow. His eyes and mouth looked more boyish, unguarded, and hopeful than Katie had ever seen them before.

"I'm sorry about the way the party turned out," Jack said.

She blinked back tears. "So am I."

"I know how much it meant to you—"

"Well, I think that the guests certainly had a good time, and that was most important." Her chin trembled. "I'm so very tired. Was that what you wanted to say to me?"

"No. Please . . . won't you sit down with me?" Jack led Katie over to the bed and perched next to her on the edge, holding her cold hands. "I have to tell you that . . . I love you, Kathleen. I love you and I need you. It's taken me a long time to realize just how strong my feelings are, but that's my fault, not yours. If you'll give me a chance, I'll try to be a husband to you in every sense of the word, in every way that you long for." Bending his head, he kissed her fingers. "Tell me that I haven't waited too long."

Katie began to weep. "Oh, Jack, I just think that Genevieve

Braithwaite may be right after all. I don't think I can ever be the wife that you deserve, and I can't change the person that I am. It would have been better if you'd married someone who was born to this life. I'll always be doing things like inviting the wrong people and speaking my mind at the wrong time and—''

"But that's what I *want*!" he said hoarsely. "I want *you*, just the way you are—''

"You wanted to get away from me tonight, after *she* told everyone about my past, and then Yong and Choy came. Weren't you embarrassed? Isn't that why you left? Everyone was whispering during the time you and Miss Braithwaite were off alone together, whispering that you and she—''

Jack took a snowy linen handkerchief from his breast pocket and gently dried her tears. "Kathleen, my love, nothing could be more ludicrous, and I think you know that. I feel nothing but contempt for Genevieve, and I made that clear to her tonight. The only reason I took her to the study was to make certain she understood that her little scheme wouldn't work. I told her that I love you and would not tolerate another word spoken against you. Then I sent her home." Tenderly he kissed Katie's brow and stroked her hair. "I could never be embarrassed by anything you say or do. On the other hand, I was embarrassed tonight to think that my name had ever been linked with Genevieve Braithwaite's.''

"But you must have loved her once," she said brokenly.

Jack smiled. "No. I didn't know the meaning of the word until I met you, and after that, I realized just how shallow my relationship with her was." He felt Katie soften against him, and his heart swelled with hope. "Can we forget about Genevieve now and talk about you . . . and me?''

"Yes." Her eyes were huge as she looked at Jack, searching his face. "Are you certain we're awake, that this isn't a dream?''

"If it is, we're having the same one. Kathleen, do you believe that I love you, that the future can be different for us?''

Katie saw the truth in his eyes, heard it in his tone more than his words, and felt it in the warmth of his body and the beat of his heart. She nodded. "I love you, Jack." Another tear spilled onto her cheek. "I'm so afraid to hope for fear I'll be disappointed. More than anything, I yearn to have a real marriage with you. . . .''

"Sweetheart, I give you my word that from now on I intend to share myself with you, and I hope that you'll want to do the same. I'll be your best friend, if you'll let me, and I'll keep all your secrets. You can tell me your dreams and your frustrations, and I'll never tire of listening. I want to make love to you, and then hold you in my arms and keep you warm all night long—''

Katie stared in amazement. "What happened to the man who said that we'd sleep better apart?"

"That's right, make me cringe by reminding me of every stupid thing I've said since our wedding day!" He laughed. "Only a very frightened man could have spoken words as ridiculous as those, especially considering the fact that his wife was incredibly desirable." Jack paused. "Do you want to know a secret of mine?"

A tingling warmth was spreading over Katie's body. "I want to know everything about you. You can trust me with all your secrets."

"Our wedding night scared the life out of me. Somehow, when we made love before, in Columbia, the loss of control seemed excusable because there was no commitment, and it was—"

"Unplanned," she finished excitedly. "I know, I felt the same way! Jack, I was as afraid to let myself love you as you were to love me! I couldn't face it, either!"

"And that night in Sacramento, I felt—exposed. I knew that if we kept on that way, I wouldn't be able to stop the momentum, and so I tried to go backward."

Katie stroked his cheek with loving tenderness. "Why did you stop being afraid?"

"I think I finally found the holding back more painful than letting go. And . . . Grandfather's been urging me on. I didn't want to lose you, Kathleen. I want to spend the rest of my life discovering you." Jack lowered his head and kissed the tears from her cheeks before covering her mouth with his own. They kissed wonderingly for long minutes before drawing back to stare into each other's eyes.

Without speaking they stood, and Jack undressed Katie before stripping off his own clothes. Then, in one fluid movement, they embraced. Their bodies were warm and clean, and it felt as if they were touching for the first time. Katie stood on tiptoe, her arms around Jack's shoulders, pressing herself against him, while he embraced her with his entire being, his face buried in the fragrant tumble of her hair. Time seemed suspended as they remained thus, hearts beating in unison.

Sometime later Jack slipped an arm under Katie's knees, lifted her up, and carried her to the bed. He ached with love as he kissed her mouth, her eyes, her temples, the hollows of her throat. Both felt keenly sensitized; every touch and kiss was almost unbearably acute. Katie lay back, smiling dreamily, as Jack explored her body with his mouth and fingertips. The sensations he evoked were exquisite and mingled with the joy that surged through her veins to bring her nearer to paradise than she had ever imagined possible.

When Jack's face appeared again above her, Katie lovingly drew him down to meet her hungry mouth. Their lips brushed, tasting . . . Then, in a surge of passion, Jack deepened his kiss. Katie's hips arched involuntarily as she welcomed the slow, sensuous dance of his tongue, engaging in a duel of intense erotic pleasure that left her weak and breathless.

Jack stared down at her, his heart revealed in his warm green eyes. "Dear God, how I love you," he murmured.

A tear trickled down Katie's cheek. "And I you."

He entered her with excruciating slowness until their bodies were one; then, together, they began to move—still slowly, reveling in each sweet sensation. When Jack took Katie's arms and turned her so that she lay on top of him, she beamed. It was a joy to behold him lying there in the firelight, so appealingly strong and handsome against the white pillows. Still joined to him, she caressed his glossy hair and proud face. She ran her fingertips over his corded neck, broad shoulders, and powerful arms, while Jack reached up to fondle her breasts. Katie arched forward slightly so that he could take a nipple into his mouth. Little currents of sharp pleasure radiated out from her breast, intensifying the arousal between her legs.

Katie tightened around Jack's hardness and bent to rub her brow over his chest; she loved the feel of his crisp hair, loved the smell of him. Jack's hips moved slowly, and tentatively Katie found an answering rhythm, dropping her head back as the sensations built. Her hands braced against his chest, she rode harder, her ebony hair swirling about her shoulders. Jack was enthralled by his wife's wild beauty. He held himself back, waiting, waiting, until at last Katie drew in a shallow, gasping breath, then let it out in a series of shuddering, whimpering cries. Her back arched, and as Jack felt her spasm, he found his own hot, convulsive release.

Afterward Katie lay full length on top of him, Jack pulsing inside her. Neither spoke for many minutes, yet their silence was more moving than words. Jack stroked her gleaming hair, and he could feel her smiling against his shoulder.

"Ohhh . . ." Katie moaned at last.

He chuckled. "We're going to have a lot of fun, my love."

She flopped over onto her back next to him, took his hand, and pressed the palm between her breasts so that he could feel her heart pounding. "I didn't know it could be done . . . like that," she said in a small, delighted voice. "I liked it."

"I liked it, too." He traced the fullness of her breasts with a fingertip. "I'm very happy, Kathleen."

She giggled. "So am I!"

"And, I'm very *hungry*. Let's go downstairs and have a private feast. I don't think I ate a bite all evening."

Jack went into his dressing room and came back wearing his gray silk dressing gown. He carried one of Prussian-blue silk for Katie and helped her into it, tying the sash around her slender waist. Like high-spirited children, they crept barefoot down the corridors to the staircase. The house below them was dark except for the faint orange glow cast by the fireplace embers in each room. Jack held Katie's hand as they made their way into the kitchen, where he turned on a gaslight.

The iceboxes and sideboards were filled with covered dishes. They loaded their plates with sliced ham, oysters, biscuits and honey, cold chicken pie, jam tarts, plum pudding, and sweetmeats. Jack hooked one finger around a jug of cider, and they returned to his room. There they lit candles and made a picnic on the bed.

Katie sat cross-legged in Jack's voluminous dressing gown, exposing her bare limbs unselfconsciously. As she devoured a tart, she gazed around and her smile broadened. "When I was a little girl, Mrs. Barnstaple ordered a testered bed like this from New York, and I'd never seen anything like it. Sometimes she let me play on it when we visited. It was pine, and not as magnificent as this one, but it had a wonderful muslin canopy and curtains. I used to pretend that the bed was a ship, the hangings were sails, and the blue braided rug underneath was the ocean. . . ."

"You must have been an enchanting child," Jack said fondly. He leaned back against the pillows and poured cider into cups. As he handed Katie hers, he looked into her eyes. "Do you have any idea why I don't drink spirits?"

She shook her head. "I just assumed that you liked to keep your wits about you."

"It's a little more involved than that." Jack took a deep breath. "I was raised in Philadelphia, and my father died when I was a boy. Mother took us to live with Grandfather, then I came west at eighteen. Up until I was twenty-five or so, I drank brandy—or whiskey, or champagne. Lots of it. I was what you would probably call a libertine. I made a lot of easy money during the gold rush, and this was an exciting place to be young."

"I imagine so," Katie agreed.

"I broke a few hearts and I broke my word in some business dealings and I lost money gambling, but the brandy took the edge off my conscience. It wasn't until my mother died and Grandfather brought Conrad here from Philadelphia to live with me that I began to take a look at my life. Conrad was thirteen, and extremely impressionable. Since he'd lost his father when he was a baby, he decided that I would be his role model.'' Jack smiled bitterly. ''One morning, after I hadn't come home for two days, Con came looking for me. He found me passed out in the bed of a less-than-reputable lady above my favorite saloon. I thank God that at least *she* was not there by then. Anyway, I didn't drink after that.''

Katie squeezed Jack's hand. ''It couldn't have been easy,'' she murmured.

''Giving up the brandy was the least of it. When my brain cleared and I took a good look at the wreckage of my life, I set about repairing it with a vengeance. I worked hard, and I was determined that, from then on, I would keep my life in order. I never broke my word, I was never late, and I adhered to a schedule at home, too.'' Jack felt a pervasive sense of peace stealing over him as he shared this part of his past with Katie. ''When I stopped drinking, I began to feel things again, and those feelings made me uncomfortable. The sterile routine I made for myself helped, because it kept me out of volatile situations. Of course, it was only a matter of time before the human being in me wanted to live again. I found an excuse to go to the foothills, and you know the rest. I've been torn between the two worlds, and my two selves, ever since.''

''But now you've resolved the conflict?''

Jack smiled at her over the rim of his cup. ''With your help, Kathleen. I've finally come to realize that the key to making it all work is balance. Sam Clemens used to talk to me about his need for *passion* in his life, and it scared the hell out of me because I realized that I needed it, too. I've finally discovered that opening up and letting myself feel again doesn't mean my life is going to career off a cliff. I can lose control in some areas . . . like right here in this bed with you''—his eyes twinkled at the sight of her blush—''and still retain discipline in other areas, like my business dealings. Over all, however, I've decided to loosen the reins on my life. If I don't eat the same thing for breakfast every day, or take the afternoon off to go riding with my wife, the world won't come to an end, and I'll doubtless be happier for it. . . .''

Katie grinned. ''Balance. I like that.''

''Good. Why don't you snuggle up to me and balance your plate next to mine?''

CHAPTER
29

January 24–25, 1864

"**C**AN'T YOU DO SOMETHING ABOUT THAT KITTEN?" Ambrose Summers demanded, looming in the doorway to the morning room. "Poor Harriet was just attacked! She was lying on my lap, licking the last of the egg yolk, when that young marauder leaped onto the dining room table and pounced on her from above. Then, adding insult to injury, she put her face up to my plate and began nosing around. Harriet was so outraged that she has taken refuge under the sideboard!"

"Where's Poppy now?" asked Katie, who sat curled on an over-stuffed chair, a notebook in her lap.

"Mrs. Gosling came running in response to my cry, and her idea of saving the situation was to take your kitten to the kitchen and *feed* her! Now she'll think that there's a reward in store if she abuses Harriet!"

Jack looked at Katie from across his desk and bit his lip to keep from laughing. "What do you suggest we do, Grandfather? Turn Poppy out of the house?"

"Well, no, I don't suppose that's the solution . . . though the idea has merit." His eyes twinkled slightly as he glanced at Katie. She gave him a look of mock horror in reply. "I just wanted you to be aware of this . . . misbehavior. Take it under advisement." Ambrose cleared his throat. "Say there, young lady, why aren't you working at your own desk in the morning room? What's the point of having an office if you're going to fritter away the daylight hours in here with this character?''

"Grandfather, it's only eight o'clock!" she protested, laughing. "Besides, I'm looking over my notes for an article I'm going to start today."

"Well . . . good." He brushed a crumb from his drooping mustache. "I'll leave you two to your own devices, then. I think I may take a stroll. Hope wants me to have a look at the calla lilies she's started in her new greenhouse."

When the sound of his footsteps had grown faint, Katie exclaimed softly, "Isn't it exciting? I think Grandfather is forming an attachment to Hope."

"Kathleen, you've become a hopeless romantic. They were dear friends long before you came here."

"But this is different. I just *know* it. Women can sense these things."

Jack arched a brow suggestively. "If I weren't already late, I'd tell you to come over here and sense something else."

"And I would have to refuse you, sir." She lifted her dainty nose. "I have *work* to do."

"I notice that, as usual, you are going ahead with this article without clearing it first with your editor—"

"Edwin knows about it," Katie declared.

"Yes, and Edwin is a notoriously soft touch where you are concerned. What are you writing about?" He came around the desk to glance down at her notebook, but Katie's scribblings were illegible to all but their author.

"Chinese prostitution," she replied casually.

"*What?*" Jack looked heavenward as if for guidance. "Kathleen, I don't really think that—"

"This is a very serious problem, Jack. If you won't print a story about it, I'm sure I can find a newspaper that will." She met his gaze with calm defiance.

"I won't be blackmailed with that threat forever, you know! You and I are both aware that other papers would love to print a sensational article under the byline of the *wife* of the *Star*'s editor, but those are not fair tactics on your part. You cannot coerce—"

"Jack, I believe that this is a story that needs to be in print, and when you read it, you'll agree. Listen to me a moment." She waited. "Are you listening?"

He perched on the edge of the desk and replied with exaggerated patience, "Yes."

"It's really hideous, Jack. Most of the girls who come over from China have no choice about doing this, and when they arrive here they're assigned to tongs, those secret Chinese societies that make them sign seven-year indenture contracts. Can you imagine? Their living standards are deplorable, and they routinely contract venereal diseases and receive no medical treatment. Is it any wonder that they turn to opium to—"

"Have you been spending time in the Chinese quarter again, Kathleen?" he interrupted in ominous tones.

Before she could reply, Mrs. Gosling appeared in the doorway. "Sir, there is a Mr. Clemens here to see you. I thought that perhaps you had already left—"

Katie and Jack both stood up immediately. "Show him in, Mrs. Gosling," said Jack.

Sam entered to an enthusiastic chorus of greetings and hugs.

"This is an unexpected surprise," Jack said as they settled down around the fire. "You look as if you just stepped off the steamboat!"

Clemens smiled sheepishly. He was, if possible, even more disheveled than usual. His tousled hair and mustache were in need of a trim, he hadn't shaved, and his clothes were rumpled, as if he'd slept in them. "That was tactfully put, my friend. I apologize for not preparing myself properly for this event, but I fear that an eagerness to reunite with the two of you overcame me." Sam's eyes danced. "I just arrived last night, went straight to the Occidental Hotel and slept for fourteen hours, and now I am here. Do you mind?"

"We are simply delighted!" Katie exclaimed as Mrs. Gosling placed a tray of coffee and cakes on the marble-topped table before them. "Do you want a proper breakfast? The cook would be glad to prepare one for you."

"Maybe later." Smiling, Sam gazed upon them with affectionate eyes. "Katie, you look spectacular, and it's not just the dress and the hair. Stand up and let me feast my eyes on you for a moment."

She complied, pirouetting in her laurel blossom–pink gown with its fashionable Zouave jacket. Her black curls were caught in a thick cluster at the nape of her neck, and her lovely face shone with happiness and fulfillment.

"Good God, the headstrong little sprite I knew just three months ago has been transformed into a radiant woman!" Clemens exclaimed, then added warmly, "I'm glad to see that the two of you are so happy. It renews my faith in the dream of romantic love and the institution of marriage.''

''Kathleen may be a radiant woman, but the headstrong sprite hasn't departed,'' Jack told him as they ate cranberry cakes that tasted suspiciously like Katie's muffins. ''She's led me on a merry chase all this past month.''

''I wanted to work,'' she protested. ''Once everyone found out about my lurid past in the saloon, and branded me a wild woman, I decided that it was no use keeping up pretenses any longer. When I told Jack of my intention to write for a newspaper, he refused to give me a job at the *Morning Star*. So, I went to the *Morning Call*—''

''Oh, no!'' Sam laughed. ''If you had written me for advice, I could have told you to avoid that paper at all costs!''

''Well, it was all a ruse, anyway,'' Jack interjected. ''Katie didn't *really* mean to write for the *Call*, she just wanted to scare me into giving her a place at the *Star*.''

''And it worked,'' she confirmed, grinning. ''I am now a reporter for the *Star*—and a good one. Isn't that so, Jack?''

''You may be competent, but you're incorrigible. If you continue to write such controversial articles, you're going to make enemies, and you're going to get into trouble.'' He turned to his friend. ''She won't listen to me, Sam. Every time I threaten not to publish what she writes, she starts talking about looking for work elsewhere.'' He narrowed his eyes at Katie, but there was an undeniable note of affectionate respect in his voice.

''Sounds to me like you two have a rollicking good marriage, and I'm not fool enough to take sides,'' Sam declared. ''Besides, if Katie gets into trouble here, she can always run away like I did. She has a ready-made refuge in Columbia!''

''Oh, God,'' Jack said, giving him a dark look. ''You're a great help.''

''Enough about us,'' Katie declared, offering Sam another cranberry cake. ''What's been happening in Columbia? Did you ever find your pocket of gold in Jackass Gulch? How are Lim, and Gideon and Abby? Has the Griffin returned?''

''Whoa!'' Clemens held up his hands. ''One thing at a time. I know you will both be shocked to hear it, but I never did strike it rich pocket mining. Matter of fact, I didn't strike much of anything at all.'' His eyes twinkled under bushy brows as he took a sip of his coffee. ''Finally, I decided that I'd rather be poor and ragged in San Francisco than in Jackass Gulch, especially during the winter. Oh—I almost forgot. I do have one accomplishment to report.

I have an idea for a story that I started writing last week. It sounds crazy—it's about a jumping frog contest in Angel's Camp—but I think it will work. As for Columbia, little has changed. Gideon and Abby are very happy. I saw them at Christmastime; they invited me to the saloon for roast turkey, and it was the best meal I'd had in weeks. Lim Sung, as I recall, is planning to come to San Francisco. In fact, he may have left already.''

''His mother told me that she had found a lovely girl for him,'' Katie said, nodding. ''I think he's too young to marry, but it's none of my business, and of course, I'd be delighted if he were in San Francisco. Yong Sung has *two* laundries and a herb shop here now, so Lim is needed.'' She paused. ''Is there any news regarding Aaron Rush—or the Griffin?''

Sam glanced at Jack. ''Well, Rush continues to be a rather ominous presence in Columbia, although he hasn't done anything too dastardly of late. His main weapon is fear.''

''And the Griffin?'' Katie persisted. ''Has he returned?''

Jack almost spilled his coffee when he heard Sam reply, ''As a matter of fact, he has. It would appear that this has been a lean winter for the Griffin, because he can no longer afford to play Robin Hood. Word has it that he's held up two stages this past month and robbed *everyone* on board, and none of the passengers had any connection to Aaron Rush. In fact, both stages were carrying shipments from the only two independent gold strikes made in the Columbia area this winter.'' Stroking his mustache, Clemens observed, ''If I didn't know better, I'd think that the Griffin was in league with Aaron Rush.''

As Jack stared in consternation, Katie leaped to her feet and cried, ''I *knew* it! That highwayman is as low a villain as Aaron Rush himself!''

''What the devil possessed you to spin that preposterous tale about the Griffin?'' Jack demanded. ''Have you lost your mind?''

Jack had brought Sam to the Bank Exchange Saloon on Montgomery Street because it was one of the few places he could be certain that Katie wouldn't suddenly appear to interrupt or overhear their conversation. Jack drank water, while Clemens sipped Pisco punch, a Peruvian brandy concoction invented by Duncan Nichols, the colorful man who presided over the saloon.

''As a matter of fact, I thought that it was quite ingenious of me to tell Katie that the Griffin had returned. Don't you see? Now there is absolutely no possibility that she will ever suspect *you*. You need worry no longer on that score.'' Sam gazed around the marble-floored saloon as he spoke, drinking in the sight of valuable oil paintings hanging on the walls and fabulous crystal chandeliers dangling from the high ceilings. "Good Lord, it's good to be back in civilization again! The foothills hold many charms, but I've missed this bawdy city."

"Would you mind returning to the subject of the Griffin for a moment?" Jack asked through clenched teeth.

"Of course not. As a matter of fact, that's the main reason I came back. You see, I wasn't actually spinning tales when I said that the Griffin had reappeared in the Columbia area and was robbing stages. Someone is impersonating you, Jack."

Wyatt's face darkened. "Aaron Rush?"

"Or one of his henchmen," Sam agreed. "That does seem to be the likely answer, doesn't it? He's doing what he and Van Hosten liked to do best—take gold from the few men who are still lucky enough to find it on their own, only this time pinning the blame on the Griffin. You must have really made him angry when you went to see him that night. He couldn't take revenge through Katie, and the Griffin disappeared as well, so he's found more devious means."

"Christ!" Jack raked a hand through his tawny hair and glared at his glass of water. "It begins to seem that there's only one way to put an end to this madness once and for all."

"I'm sorry to have brought you this news. It would appear that you and Katie have found happiness together; that you have filled the emptiness in your life . . ."

"And now I'll have to go back to Columbia."

"Well, perhaps it would be best to put an end to this business once and for all. I certainly wish you luck." Pensively, he drained his Pisco punch. "I wish there were something I could do. . . ."

Jack grinned at him, one brow arched. "Oh, but there is. You're going with me, Sam."

Clemens responded with a sickly smile. "I was afraid of that." He sighed, "No, strike that. Actually, I was resigned to it before I left Jackass Gulch. I had hoped to indulge in a bit of female company first, however. How soon do you want to leave?"

"Tomorrow."

Sam groaned. "You're a cruel man. I doubt that even *my* considerable charms will win me the . . . affections of a desirable woman in one night!" Jack's only response was unsympathetic laughter, so he sighed in resignation. "All right. Tomorrow, then. What about Katie? What will you tell her?"

"I sure as hell can't let her know where I'm going, because she'd want to come, too. The truth will have to wait again, but it will be told. Even before you arrived today, I had made up my mind to tell Kathleen the truth about her father's death. I hate having secrets of any kind from her; it goes against all the principles upon which our marriage is based. But first I had to win her trust. When I return from Columbia, and this mess is cleared up once and for all, I'll tell her that I was the Griffin." A tiny muscle pulsed in his jaw. "I'll tell her the truth and take my chances. . . ."

"But not now," Sam clarified.

"No." Jack sighed harshly. "Not now."

Hazy moonlight, filtered by fog, drifted softly over the large testered bed. Katie liked to awaken to light in the morning, so Jack no longer slept with the curtains closed. It was one of the many compromises and alterations he had made in his life-style over the past weeks, and he found that they were surprisingly painless. Jack had learned, as Ambrose had predicted, that he could bend without breaking, and that the process itself was oddly satisfying.

Now, in the timeless hours between midnight and dawn, Jack and Katie lay next to one another, her slim body snuggled into the curve of his. Jack's arm was around her, his hand cupping her breast. He had swept her long hair up over the top of the pillow so that he could smell the sweetness of her neck, kissing her there from time to time. Katie imagined that she had never in her life felt as secure, serene, and protected as she did during these exquisite nights in Jack's arms.

On this particular night, however, her sleep was troubled. Finally, turning onto her back, she awoke with a start to find Jack staring down at her.

"Are you all right?"

His face, strong and tender, was poignantly dear to her. She hadn't grown complacent about waking up next to Jack. It was as if each morning were both Christmas and her birthday. "Oh, Jack," she whispered brokenly, "must you go away?"

He cradled her against his chest. "I've told you that I must, sweetheart, and that I'll be back as soon as I can." He took a deep breath, grateful for the darkness as he lied, "Sam is certain that this newspaper in Carson City is the perfect one for me to buy, and you know how much I've been longing to make that sort of investment. We'll ride straight through, spend as little time as possible doing business, and come back. I'll be home before you have time to miss me."

Katie tried to swallow her tears. "But I miss you already."

Taking her chin between his thumb and forefinger, Jack turned her face up so that he could gaze into her glistening eyes. "I love you with all my heart, Kathleen. Do you believe me?"

She nodded. "Yes."

"I swear before God that it's the truth, and I want you to hold my love close to you while we're apart." He kissed her gently. "Promise?"

Katie tasted him on her lips and smiled. "Yes." She snuggled nearer, closing her eyes. "I promise."

"What am I going to do all day today with Emma ill?" Conrad mourned, staring out the window at the unseasonably sunny Saturday morning.

Katie, who was pacing restlessly across the parlor, whirled on him. "I would appreciate it if you would keep your petty troubles to yourself! You are looking at a woman who is in the first hour of a separation from her beloved husband, a separation that is bound to last at least a *fortnight*! Although I didn't say as much to Jack, I am well aware of the risks and inevitable delays that one faces when crossing the Sierras during the winter. And business meetings always take longer than anyone thinks they will. St. Valentine's Day will probably be here by the time he returns. . . ."

Conrad put an arm around her shoulder sympathetically. "Well, at least Sam went with him. You don't have to worry about him getting into trouble alone."

"Sometimes I think that Sam takes trouble with him," Katie said. "Like a carpetbag."

"Let's talk about something else, shall we?" He steered her over to a sofa.

"Conrad, I hardly think that you can distract me for two weeks!" Reluctantly, Katie sat down beside him and accepted a cookie from the plate he picked up from the side table.

Conrad smiled. "What news did Sam bring from the foothills?"

Briefly, she told him about the Griffin's latest attacks on stagecoaches. When Aaron Rush's name came up, her brother-in-law colored angrily.

"I hate that man!"

Katie stared. "How do you know Aaron Rush?"

"Do you remember my telling you that I once spent some time in Columbia? Actually, I was nearer Murphy's, but I did go to Columbia from time to time. We may even have seen each other. It was two years ago, at a time when I was feeling a need to make my own mark on the world rather than trade on my brother's reputation. I decided that I would go to the foothills to make my fortune, unaware that most of the surface gold was already gone. To make a long story short, I did happen to find three reasonably large nuggets. Fool that I was, I went to the saloon in Murphy's and was showing them off. Harold Van Hosten was there. He told me that he could get me a better price than they were paying in Columbia, and he seemed so respectable that I believed him.''

Katie cringed. "Oh, no, Conrad!" It was almost painful for her to imagine her brother-in-law as a prospector in the clutches of Rush and Van Hosten.

"Oh, yes, it's true. I was an idiot!" His voice rose. "I gave him the gold . . . and that was the last I ever saw of it. When I tried to stake a claim, Van Hosten had beaten me to it, and when I confronted him and his partner at their office, he denied ever seeing me before." Conrad became increasingly agitated as he told his story and got up to pace across the parlor. "No one would listen to me or do anything about it. I thought I'd go mad! In the end, I came back home with nothing. To be perfectly honest, I was overjoyed last summer when I heard that Van Hosten had been killed by the Griffin. Sometimes, when I heard and read the tales about that highwayman, it seemed that he was avenging *me*. It's disillusioning to learn that he's no different from the rest of them. . . .'' He sank down on the sofa and stared into the cold fireplace.

"Conrad, that's a terrible story! Why didn't you tell me before?" Katie exclaimed, putting a hand on his arm.

"Well, I meant to, but to tell the truth, I try not to think about it very much.''

"I know how you feel about the Griffin. I used to revere him, too, until he killed my father." Her pretty mouth hardened.

"What?!"

She leaned back beside him. "It's true. My father was on the same stagecoach as Harold Van Hosten, the one the Griffin attacked in June. There's some confusion about exactly what happened, but as I understand it, the Griffin had them both get out of the coach and took them behind it to search Van Hosten." Katie's voice was choked with tears. "A struggle ensued, and at the end of it, Papa and Harold Van Hosten were dead . . . and the Griffin escaped with his life.''

"But perhaps Van Hosten had a gun. Do you know for certain that it was the Griffin who shot your father?''

"No, but I do know that if he hadn't attacked that stage, Papa would be alive. No explanation can change that.''

"Well, I can certainly understand how you feel," Conrad said hastily, taken aback by her icy demeanor. They sat in silence for several minutes, each lost in thought. Conrad ate two cookies before Katie spoke again.

"Con, I was just thinking . . . there is something very productive that we both could do during Jack's absence."

There was a strange gleam in Katie's eyes. Unnerved, Conrad replied carefully, "What's that?"

"Wouldn't you like to feel that you had taken some action to right the wrong perpetrated against you by Rush and Van Hosten? Wouldn't you feel better if you knew that you had pursued justice?"

"Well, yes, certainly . . ." He straightened his shoulders.

"I feel the same way about the Griffin—and I also have a few grudges of my own against Aaron Rush. I could help you confront Rush if you would help me trap the Griffin—"

"Katie," he exclaimed, "that's insane! Are you suggesting that we run off to Columbia and do this while Jack is away?"

"Yes, that's exactly what I'm suggesting."

"But what would Jack say?"

"Stop worrying about Jack! We're adults, aren't we?" Her face was animated. "We have just as much right to leave San Francisco as Jack does. More, maybe, because we have just causes. And you certainly don't need your brother's permission. Besides, I miss my friends in Columbia, and this would be a perfect opportunity for me to see them again. Please, Conrad! When was the last time that you had a real *adventure*?"

He looked uncertain. "Well, it's been a while. . . ."

"Say you'll go with me, please? We can go to Columbia via Stockton—we'll be there in no time! And we'll make a pact to stay no longer than four days. If we've accomplished nothing by that time, at least we'll know we tried, and we can return home with that knowledge. What do you say?"

Conrad sat up straight and expanded his chest. "I say—*yes*! I'm older now. This time I'm going to confront Aaron Rush like a man and demand justice. I want to be paid for that gold, and any more that they took from what should have been my claim!"

"And I'll help you!" Katie cried, filled with the spirit of adventure and justice. "We'll show Aaron Rush and the Griffin that they can't toy with Kathleen and Conrad Wyatt and get away with it!"

Jumping awkwardly to his feet, Conrad thrust his fist into the air and shouted, "Hear, hear!"

CHAPTER
30

January 28–30, 1864

A FULL MOON WAS THE WHITE AND LUMINOUS CENTERPIECE in the star-strewn midnight sky. Jack stood for a moment outside the Rush Mine office, staring down at the lot below, which had been raped by hydraulic mining. Bathed in a hazy silver glow, the huge, oblong boulders of granite, limestone, and marble looked eerie, as if part of some other, uninhabitable world.

Jack shrugged off the chill that crept over him and walked soundlessly around to the back of the mine offices. Without rushing, he picked the lock on the back door and stepped inside, thankful for the moonlight that streamed in to aid his progress. The doors off the narrow hallways were unlocked. He started in Rush's office, searching through the cabinets, then crossed to what had been Van Hosten's room. Stripped now of its paintings and handsome cherry desk, it was filled with several tables and chairs and apparently served as an office for Rush's assistants.

Jack had no luck there, either, and was losing hope as he stepped back into the central corridor. Then, spying the outline of a narrow door off to one side, he remembered the small storage room and flashed a grin in the darkness. The latch was difficult, but Van Hosten had taught him the trick. Inside, his eyes wandered over the shadowy shapes of trunks and crates containing books and papers until he spied the cupboards built into the far wall. Sensing somehow that success was at hand, he crossed the room and opened them. The deep shelves inside were stacked with a wide variety of miscellaneous office items—books, folded curtains, objects from Van Hosten's office, rolled scatter rugs, bottles of brandy, and odd pieces of crockery. Jack yearned for a candle. Carefully he withdrew the curtains from the lowest shelf, bent down, and reached behind them. His hand made contact with a long object wrapped in cloth.

Heart pounding, he drew it out into the dim light. He carefully unfolded the garment on the floor and saw what he'd known he would find: a handsome double-barreled shotgun identical to the one he himself had wielded as the Griffin. It had been wrapped in a long, tan linen duster. A hood, with holes cut out for eyes, lay next to the shotgun.

"Ah, Mr. Rush," he said softly, "I have you now."

"And you just put it all back?" Sam exclaimed. Rubbing his eyes, he staggered from his bed and poked at the fire. Across the cabin, Jim and Steve Gillis snored blissfully.

Jack dropped onto his own cot and pulled off his boots. "He'll never know. Everything is just as I found it. Not even a lock was disturbed." He yawned. "God, I'm tired."

"Well, it's your own fault for going over there the same night we arrived." Sam was wide awake now. Pouring himself a finger of whiskey, he returned to bed, ready to hear every detail of Jack's midnight adventure. "These have been the most exhausting three days of my life."

"Well, get a good night's sleep, because you go on stage tomorrow, and I don't want you to forget your part."

"How can you be certain Aaron Rush will be there?"

"Obviously we can't be *certain*, but you yourself told me that his wife had grown bored with life in the foothills and had returned to New York. Didn't Lim say that ever since she left, Rush has been plaguing the saloon with his company at lunchtime? Didn't you tell me those things?"

Sam scowled. "Aren't you even going with me? You wouldn't have to come into the saloon."

"You know I can't, Sam! I can't take even a small risk that I'll be seen by Aaron Rush. If there's any chance at all that he suspects I might be the Griffin, he mustn't know I'm in the area." Stretching out in his dusty buckskins and gray woolen shirt, Jack closed his eyes. "Everything has to go perfectly; there is no room for error . . . and no time. I want to go home to Kathleen."

* * *

Columbia was indeed having a lean winter, Samuel Clemens thought to himself as he tied his horse to the hitching post in front of the MacKenzie Saloon. A cold wind blew through the leafless trees of heaven, and Main Street was nearly deserted except for a weary old prospector asleep on a bench in front of the bank. The old man's dog, a mangy mutt with protruding ribs, lifted his head with an effort and gave Sam a sorrowful look.

Clemens rubbed a hand over his reddish curls, took a deep breath, and pushed open the door to the saloon. The immediate sight of familiar faces calmed him somewhat. Lim Sung was behind the bar, polishing the jars of brandied fruit that marched under the mirror. He looked preoccupied, as did Abby, who was sweeping the floor. At the sound of Sam's step, however, she looked up and broke into a wide smile.

"Why, Samuel Clemens! I thought you left for San Francisco a week ago!"

"Well, no." Sam blushed. "I wasn't in the mood after all."

"Have you been working on that story about the jumping frog all this time?"

"Yes. Yes, that's it." He took a stool at the bar and greeted Lim, bursting to tell them about Katie. How happy they would be to learn that she had found her niche in San Francisco, that she looked more beautiful than ever, and that she and Jack were in love. Instead he said, "What's for lunch, Abby?"

"Chicken pie." She rolled her eyes. "Aaron Rush gave me his wife's recipe and asked that I make it today. Can you imagine? He even brought me the chickens."

Breathing a sigh of relief, Sam chatted idly with Lim about the young man's plans to leave Columbia. When his chicken pie arrived, he picked at it.

"Is something wrong?" Abby asked. "Is it too salty?"

Clemens grinned. "No, it's fine. I'm just taking my time. Lunch with the two of you is the high point of my week!" He was fascinated by Abby, for in just a few short months she had changed dramatically. Her coquettish appearance and behavior had ripened into the rounder, contented look of a wife. When Sam inquired after Gideon, Abby's doe eyes softened.

"He couldn't be better. He's working hard at the *Gazette*, putting it out all by himself with a little help from Dusty Shaw, even though there's hardly anyone to buy it. Have you seen him since Christmas? I'd wager that he's put on another five pounds." Her smile widened, and she patted her own belly. "And so have I. We're going to have a baby late this summer."

"Abby, that's wonderful news! Please convey my congratulations to the proud father." Sam took a bite of potato. "Won't Katie and Jack be pleased!"

"Oh, Sam, just the sound of their names brings tears to my eyes. . . . I pray every day that Katie will find happiness with Jack. The last letter we received, around Christmas, was full of news, but it didn't really say one way or the other how she felt. That's not like Katie, and I just had a notion that something might be wrong underneath all her talk about new gowns and parties and how grand San Francisco is."

"Jack had better be good to her," Lim put in. "If Katie isn't happy when I get there, he'll have me to deal with!"

"Well, of course, I don't know any more than you do," Sam said, "but I just have a feeling that it's all right. All the ingredients were there for a very loving marriage."

Abby looked reassured. "Yes, you're right, of course. That makes me feel a little better. Lim, pour Samuel a beer. On the house!"

"Ah!" boomed a voice from the doorway. "Is that chicken pie I smell?"

Sam looked around to see Aaron Rush lumbering across the saloon. His cheeks were pinker than usual from the cold, and he wore a topcoat with a fur collar over his brown suit and waistcoat.

As Abby scurried off to fill a plate and Lim poured the drinks, Rush heaved himself onto the stool next to Sam's. Suddenly Sam's palms felt damp.

"Hello, Mr. Rush," he said.

The older man appeared to be in a jovial mood. "Hello, Clemens! Ah, I've been looking forward to this chicken pie all morning. As you can see, I've been wasting away since my dear wife journeyed to New York. I need to put on a bit of fat to keep my bones warm!" Rush opened his coat to reveal a considerably thinner body and shook his head ruefully. As Abby set the plate before him, he looked at her. "Not too much salt, I hope? You know I don't care for salty food."

Abby's eyes widened apprehensively. "No, sir. I don't think so, sir."

Rush took up a healthy forkful and tasted it. "Well, it's not quite up to Ellen's standard, but it will suffice," he pronounced a moment later. "Next time, Abby, you must cut the carrots and potatoes into bigger pieces, and add a bit more pepper. All right?"

"Yes, Mr. Rush." Nodding to Sam, she disappeared into the kitchen.

Sam could think of nothing that appealed to him less than a conversation with Aaron Rush, but he had his orders, and Jack had been very specific. First, he mentioned casually that he had seen one of the drivers of the stage to Stockton during a layover in Angel's Camp a few days earlier. Rush's ears pricked up.

"Charlie gave me a few newspapers," Sam said, beginning to warm to his role, "and from the looks of things, the war will be over before long. General Sherman's on his way to connect with Grant, and instead of going by sea, he's raiding his way through the Carolinas. The Confederacy's barely breathing, it seems to me."

"You're forgetting General Lee's army," Rush said between bites of chicken pie and swigs of whiskey-laced tea. "That's one very important arm of the Confederacy that's still alive. The war can't be won until Lee is beaten. But let me ask you—"

Knowing that Rush was eager to learn more about his supposed conversation with the stage driver, Sam interrupted with another argument about the war. He had to admire Jack's thinking. There was no possibility that Aaron Rush would suspect he was being set up for a trap. Finally, as they started on pieces of pumpkin pie, Sam let the older man get a word in.

Rush was the essence of nonchalance as he remarked, "Sounds as if you and Charlie had quite a lengthy conversation. Did he have anything else worthwhile to say?"

Sam shrugged. "Well, he did mention that he was going to pick up two wealthy businessmen when he returned to Stockton. They're coming up here with a fortune in gold, thinking to take over the mi—" He looked shocked at his own slip. "I mean, the *bank*, as I recall."

Rush's face reddened with concern. "Are you sure that was what you were going to say?"

"I just stumbled over my own tongue, Mr. Rush," Sam assured him unconvincingly. "Too much beer, I reckon. Well . . ." He got to his feet. "I'd better be on my way. I have to get back to the cabin and wash out my socks. Nice seeing you, Mr. Rush. Good luck!" With that, Clemens bade Lim and Abby farewell, put three times more than he owed on the bar, and sauntered out into the afternoon sunshine.

As the stagecoach climbed the oak-and-pine-studded hills east of Angel's Camp, Katie perused her new copy of *Godey's Lady's*

Book. Her mind, however, was not on the embroidery pattern detailed on the page before her.

Conrad squirmed restlessly on the seat opposite her. The other passengers had disembarked at Angel's Camp, except for one fat young man whose head kept bouncing backward as he snorted and moaned in his sleep. The closer they got to Columbia, the more nervous Conrad felt.

"I wish you'd let me have that . . . that *thing*," he hissed at his sister-in-law.

Katie smiled. "Are you referring to—*this*?" she inquired sweetly, patting the neat little derringer hidden inside her cloak. "No, thank you, Conrad. I'll keep it with me for the time being."

"I'm beginning to understand why Jack loses patience with you upon occasion!" he whispered hoarsely. "You are—"

"Stubborn? Headstrong?" She grinned. "Incorrigible, perhaps?"

"Yes!"

"You sound just like your brother." Katie was enjoying herself immensely. As they drew nearer and nearer to real adventure, her pain over the separation from Jack lessened. She only wished that Conrad were a bit more like his sibling, because it was clear to her that he would never be dashing or courageous enough to carry off the kind of confrontation she anticipated. Sitting across from her now, in a loud rust-and-brown-checked waistcoat that he insisted was the very height of fashion, Conrad looked like a frightened boy. If she were to turn over their weapon to him, he would probably shoot himself by accident. "Don't be so fretful, Con," Katie soothed. "Nothing is going to happen yet."

"Then why won't you give that thing to me?"

"Because if anything *does* happen . . . and you know what I mean"—she glanced at their snoring companion—"I must be the one to act. That person who shall remain nameless is my enemy, not yours."

"Oh, God, I wish we'd never come! I must have been mad to ever consider this escapade!" He raked a hand through his hair, and it stood up in red spikes. "Jack would murder me if he knew what we were doing! I should have insisted that we remain in San Francisco—"

"In that instance I should probably have come alone, so you can absolve yourself of blame."

He sighed in exasperation and looked out the window. They were ascending a particularly steep hill overlooking the Stanislaus River, and he began to feel queasy. The stagecoach was traveling perilously close to the edge of a cliff that plummeted hundreds of feet to the water below. If a wheel were to come loose . . .

"Oh, my, isn't it beautiful?" Katie exclaimed, leaning out the window for a better view. "I hadn't realized how much I missed this country."

"I think a more appropriate adjective would be 'terrifying,' " Conrad replied in a tight voice.

Katie glanced at him. "You know, Con, I think you're getting old before your time. Where is your spirit of adventure?"

They were slowing down for a blind curve, and as they rounded it, a man's voice rang out.

"Halt, sir!"

Katie and Conrad scrambled to look out the other window. There, standing in front of a grove of scrub oak trees, was a man wearing a long linen duster and a hood with holes cut out for his eyes . . . and carrying a double-barreled shotgun. "Kindly throw down your box!" the man cried. "And I'll have a look at those passengers, too. I hear there is a pair on board from Stockton."

Katie knew a pang of disappointment. The Griffin was neither as tall nor as well built as she had imagined, and his voice was not as thrilling as people had said. Obviously he had been romanticized like so many other folk heroes. She reached inside her cloak for her derringer, while Conrad looked on in horror.

Suddenly another figure jumped down from a clump of bushes on a ledge above. The Griffin started to turn, but it was too late. A shotgun barrel was shoved into his back.

"I don't appreciate being impersonated by such a pale imitation," the other man said in a low, husky voice. "Remove your hood, sir."

Katie and Conrad watched, their mouths open. The man who claimed to be the real Griffin was dressed in an identical duster and hood, and he was tall and strong-looking, like the Griffin of legend.

Aaron Rush knew that if he unmasked, his life would be over. Seeing no choice, he whirled around and grabbed for the other man's shotgun, but his reflexes were far too slow. The gun went off in the ensuing struggle, and he sagged to the ground with a hole in his belly.

The stage driver was fumbling for his own rifle, but the other man was quicker. He leveled his shotgun at the driver and said, "There's no need, sir. I mean you no harm, any more than I intended for this man to die. You see, I am the real Griffin, and I had a score to settle. This impersonator has been sullying my reputation by robbing virtuous townsfolk, and I had to put a stop to that."

Katie's heart was pounding madly. This was her chance to avenge her father's death! Here was his killer, standing before her. Without stopping to think further, she drew out her derringer and threw open the stage door. "And I have a score to settle with you, sir! Throw down your gun!"

The Griffin froze at the sound of her voice, then turned to look at her through the holes cut in his hood. He sighed audibly. "Don't shoot, Mrs. Wyatt." His hoarse voice sent chills down Katie's back. Dropping the rifle on the ground next to Rush's body, he slowly drew the hood from his head. "I am your husband."

CHAPTER
31

January 31, 1864

"**B**UT IT CAN'T BE TRUE!" ABBY GASPED. "IF JACK IS THE Griffin, that means that he . . . he killed—"

"Papa," Katie supplied tonelessly.

The two women were gathered with Lim, Gideon, and Conrad in the tiny, makeshift kitchen of the saloon. Katie, who was trembling with shock, sipped tea as she sat on a stool near the cast-iron stove. Her friends were gathered around her, but Conrad paced restlessly. Outside the window, clouds were gathering in the waning light of late afternoon.

"There has to be another explanation," he cried. "It just doesn't make sense!"

"It certainly doesn't," Abby agreed. "Jack was very fond of Mr. MacKenzie. They were *friends*!"

"Now let's calm down and look at the facts," Gideon said. "Right from the beginning, on the very day that Brian was shot, there was confusion about the circumstances. No one actually saw the Griffin shoot Brian. Van Hosten may have had a gun, or a struggle may have ensued. Whatever the case, I have always believed that Brian's death was pure accident. It went against everything that the Griffin had stood for up to that moment. He had always striven for justice, and he'd achieved a large measure of that without firing a shot. I'm sure it was no coincidence that the first blood was shed when Harold Van Hosten was present. It's always been my belief that Van Hosten was the cause not only of Brian's death, but of his own.''

"But if Jack hadn't attacked the stage . . .'' Katie heard her own voice from a distance. So much had happened in such a short space of time, she was barely able to take it all in. Her husband, whom she loved deeply, was in jail. And not only was he responsible for the death of her adored father, but he had lied to her. He had married her knowing that he was also the man she despised more than anyone else in the world. "He should have told me,'' Katie whispered now. "He married me with blood on his hands.''

Conrad spoke up as if he hadn't heard her. "Everything makes sense now! Jack became the Griffin to avenge *me*! He wasn't going to Nevada at all. He was coming up here in search of justice—''

"And he found a new life,'' Gideon said.

Lim pulled a chair up next to Katie and patted her hand. "How did you feel about Jack before today?''

Something broke inside of her. "I—I loved him. We had become so happy together—not just husband and wife, but also the best of friends. This past month has been so very wonderful, it was almost like a dream. But perhaps that is just what it was. An illusion, with lies at its core. . . .''

"Perhaps he was afraid to tell you the truth,'' Lim suggested gently. "If, as you say, he had fallen in love with you, he had much to lose.''

"I feel as if I've been tricked. Tricked into marrying Jack, and then tricked into loving him.'' Katie began to weep, silently. "I'm so confused! It's as if I don't know him anymore.''

"I feel certain that his conscience must have been bothering him, Katie,'' Gideon said, frowning. "He probably has longed to tell you, and I'm sure Lim is right. He must have been afraid to, knowing how you feel about the Griffin—that even if he didn't directly cause Brian's death, he was still responsible.''

"Jack's a very honest person,'' Conrad exclaimed. "He would never have misled you without good reason.''

A voice spoke from the doorway. "Perhaps I can help to clear up some of this mystery.''

Katie looked up to see Sam Clemens, his hair in wild disarray above his pale face. "Sam! You're here!'' Her elation drained away as she remembered. "But of course you'd have come with him. I shouldn't be surprised. You and Jack have been in league to deceive me for some time, haven't you? You lied to me very glibly in San Francisco. There is no newspaper for sale in Carson City, is there?

And your tale about the Griffin robbing stages again was for my benefit, wasn't it? How could I ever imagine that my own husband was the Griffin, if he was in San Francisco and the Griffin had been sighted again in the foothills? After all, Jack couldn't possibly be in two places at once, could he?''

''My dear Katie, your hostility is sadly misplaced. Do you love Jack so little that you are able to condemn him without hearing his story?'' Sam's eyes were filled with sadness as he crossed to perch on the worktable in front of her. ''Have you never made a mistake, that you are so inflexible when it comes to the humanity of your husband?''

Suddenly Katie felt guiltily disloyal. ''All I can sort out right now is what I know to be the truth,'' she said. ''I hurt too much to go beyond that.''

''Do you want some help?'' he asked in a kinder tone.

Katie nodded, fresh tears welling in her eyes.

''Perhaps we should leave the two of you alone,'' Gideon said.

Conrad opened his mouth to protest, but Sam saved him the trouble by replying, ''No, I think you all should hear what I have to say. You're Jack's friends, and he very well may need your help.''

''Oh, God,'' moaned Conrad. ''I knew we shouldn't have left San Francisco! If not for us, Jack would have had his confrontation with that imposter and gotten clean away. Katie, he might hang because of our interference!''

By now Katie was beginning to feel that perhaps she, not Jack, was to blame for the mess spread out around her. ''Conrad,'' she countered stubbornly, ''I don't think that's fair! If Jack—''

''Let's not waste precious time pointing fingers,'' Sam interrupted. ''I've just seen Jack, and I think we'd all be better served by some explanations, don't you? I'll try to be brief.''

Katie and Conrad closed their mouths and waited. Abby brought Sam a beer and then went to stand in the shelter of Gideon's protective arm. Lim still sat close to Katie, a comforting source of silent support.

''I'm going to go back a bit, back to a time before I came to Jackass Gulch. Jack told me everything, and I think that I'm the only person who knows the whole story besides Mr. Summers, his grandfather.''

Katie gasped. ''Ambrose—knew?''

Clemens continued as if she hadn't spoken. ''Conrad, you were quite right; Jack started this masquerade because of what Rush and Van Hosten did to you. It took on a life of its own after he became aware that other human beings were suffering as a result of the unfair practices at the mine. He continued to play the Griffin long after Conrad's injustice had been corrected because of all those other miners . . . and because, I believe, Jack's new life here was a blessed relief from his structured existence in San Francisco.''

"Yes!" cried Conrad. "It makes perfect sense!"

"Then the situation became more complicated after he became friends with Katie and her father. He grew very fond of Mr. MacKenzie." Sam focused on Katie. "Katie, Jack told me how your father died. The truth is that Van Hosten had a gun. He tried to shoot Jack, and your father grabbed for the gun. Jack told him that he should let go and leave Van Hosten to him, but then the gun went off, and Brian MacKenzie fell.''

"Oh, Papa," Katie breathed, closing her eyes.

"Van Hosten then fired at Jack, and he fired back, killing him. Jack went to your father and held him in his arms, but he had already died. He was in agony, Katie, that's why he returned to Columbia to be with you when you heard the news, and that's why he wanted to take you with him to San Francisco. He felt that he owed it to your father to do everything in his power to make certain you had a safe and secure future." Sam smiled slightly. "Also, I suspect Jack was already falling in love with you, and in light of what had happened, and your animosity toward the Griffin, it seemed an impossible situation.''

"Poor Jack," Abby said softly.

"Well, at that point, he thought that he was finished with the whole business of the Griffin. Van Hosten was dead, and Rush, who had seldom been in town, seemed harmless enough. Then, back in San Francisco, I innocently told him about the attack on Gideon and the *Gazette*'s printing press. I think you all know the rest. After Jack came back up here, he did what he could to subdue Aaron Rush, including stealing back Tsing Tsing Yee's valuable egg.''

Katie's eyes were wide. "That's why he was in the woods near that cabin when I needed rescuing!"

"Yes. The bad blood between you and Rush was a constant worry for him. Finally, when he felt he couldn't stay here any longer, he went to confront Rush in the Griffin's guise and, among other things, warned him to leave you alone. Rush looked delighted, as if he'd found the Griffin's weakness, and so Jack felt that he couldn't leave Columbia unless you came with him.''

"So he married me because he felt obligated?" she asked in a small voice.

"Well," Sam replied dryly, "I think that was the excuse, but you know better than anyone that both of you were a long ways from acknowledging your feelings when you got married. The fact is that, by the time I returned to San Francisco the other day, you and Jack had a real marriage. He loves you with all his heart, Katie, and the last thing he wanted to do was come back here and become the Griffin again.''

"Then why did he?" Lim asked.

"Yes, what about all those recent stage robberies? The Griffin had gone from hero to villain," Gideon said. "Even I had to admit that Katie had been right all along. I wrote editorials condemning him. . . ."

"*That's* why Jack returned—just two days ago. When I told him what had been happening up here, we realized that it must be Aaron Rush impersonating the Griffin, serving his own needs while blackening the Griffin's name. Jack decided to deal with him once and for all, by exposing him.''

"So that's what that scene on the road today was all about!" Conrad exclaimed.

"I was so confused," Katie said. "When the stage driver climbed down to take Jack prisoner, and then pulled the hood off Aaron Rush, I felt that it was all some sort of bizarre nightmare."

"Of course Jack never meant for Rush to *die*," Sam said. "He just wanted him unmasked and brought to trial. If you hadn't been on that stage, brandishing your derringer, he would have made a clean escape and the two of us would be on our way back to San Francisco right now.''

"And I never would have known the truth," Katie murmured, a note of bitterness in her voice.

Sam drained his beer. "No, my dear, that's where you're wrong. Jack intended to tell you everything when this situation was settled here. He told me that he couldn't lie to you anymore, that it went against all the principles of your marriage, and that he meant to tell you the truth and take his chances.''

It was hard for Katie to breathe. "What's going to happen now?" She paused, her heart aching. "How is Jack?"

"He's in jail in Angel's Camp, and more than anything else, he's concerned about you. He knows the pain you must be in, and he blames himself for it." Clemens sighed. "The judge is in town, and one of Rush's henchmen, a big fellow named Potter, is pushing for an immediate trial. So the jury is being assembled, and I'd imagine that the trial will be tomorrow or the next day. Potter is telling everyone in town that he intends to see Jack hang for the

murders of Aaron Rush, Harold Van Hosten, and Brian Mac-
Kenzie.''

"But that's not fair," cried Conrad. "It was Rush's own fault
that he was shot. It was an accident! And Jack didn't even shoot
Mr. MacKenzie!''

Sam shrugged. "This is the West, Con, where life isn't always
fair. People have little tolerance for highwaymen; they want to see
them punished as a warning to others with similar ambitions. It
would be one thing if we could prove that Jack was innocent in
those deaths, but I don't see how that's possible. . . .''

The little white frame house on the corner of Jackson Street
looked forlorn to Katie as she came through the gate. The morning
glory vines atop the porch roof were brown and withered, and the
grass needed cutting. As she opened the front door, Katie felt as if
she were stepping into the past. Only three months had passed since
she had last been here, yet it seemed an eternity. The air smelled
faintly musty, and a thin layer of dust covered the tables. Abby and
Lim had been taking care of the house and yard, but what was the
point of regular cleaning when no one lived here?

As she gazed around the parlor and the kitchen, memories
crowded her mind and an odd, bittersweet feeling crept over her.
The winter of Katie's eighth year had been unusually rainy and
snowy, and each afternoon Mary MacKenzie had curled up with
her daughter on the settee to read from *Tales of the Arabian Nights*.
What magical hours those had been! That winter their parlor had
been steeped in the wonder of genies, talking birds, cities of brass,
pirates, turbans, and silks, colossal jewels, and unforgettable characters like Ali Baba, Sinbad, and Aladdin. And, for Katie, that
enchantment would always be laced with the warm sound of her
mother's voice. Looking now at the settee, she could almost see
Mary MacKenzie sitting there, the big book open on her lap and
her blue eyes brimming with pleasure.

Katie walked slowly into the kitchen, almost expecting Brian to
be pulling a chair up to the table, his suspenders dangling and his
woolen shirt open at the neck. They'd been so happy in each other's
company, taking care of one another, sitting down together for the
evening meal and sharing stories of the day. Katie always knew that
Brian had never stopped grieving for his wife, but he hadn't let that
cloud his life with Katie. It had been awkward for him at times,
trying to be a mother as well as a father to a growing girl, yet Katie
had never doubted his devotion to her. Tears stung her eyes now as
she felt his big-hearted hug and heard the love in his voice as he

murmured "Katie darlin'." It still seemed impossible that she would never see her father again.

Her own bedroom was untouched, the narrow bed neatly made. *Wuthering Heights* lay on the dresser, apparently overlooked by Lim when he'd packed her books and shipped them to San Francisco. Katie picked it up, thinking that her birthday seemed part of a distant past. That June morning when Brian had given her this book, she had been a girl, innocently living in a fantasy world. And then Jack had come into the saloon, and her life hadn't been the same since. She was a woman now, and there was no going back. . . .

Katie stepped out the back door and looked at the little yard with its lovingly tended flower and vegetable gardens. They had been a source of great pride and pleasure, particularly in the spring when the new seedlings sprouted and then thrived under her careful ministrations. She had always loved to sink her hands into the soil, loved the challenge of coaxing plants to grow. Lim had kept up the gardens, planting winter vegetables and pruning back the rosebushes. Katie paused at the gate for a last look, then wandered out of the yard.

Her thoughts were far away as she strolled west on Jackson Street toward St. Andrew's Church. Memories of her childhood flooded back, and Katie could almost see herself running along as a little girl, chasing Lim. Her eyes misted again, and she wondered at the emotions that seemed so near the surface these days. Ever since she and Jack had opened their hearts to each other, Katie had found that she felt both joy and pain more keenly.

Passing the Barnstaple house, she saw Victoria peeking out the window, staring as if she'd seen a ghost. When Katie waved, the older woman threw open the window and leaned out.

"Katie!" she cried. "You're here! Is it true what I've heard about your husband?"

"Mrs. Barnstaple, there is something I have to do now, but I would like to come by in a little while and talk to you. Would that be all right?"

"Of course, darling!"

Katie waved then and continued on her way. The sun was setting slowly, a blazing sphere of apricot and plum behind the blue spruce trees that ringed the church. Although she wore a plaid wool cloak, the chill wind nipped at her cheeks and nose, and she rubbed her gloved hands together to warm them. After a bit she quickened her pace, lifting her petticoats as she strode up the hill to the church.

Stopping inside, she knelt and said a silent prayer, and felt better immediately. As she rose, a sense of peace stole over her.

Back outside, Katie walked behind the church to the small fenced cemetery. Her parents' graves were marked with wooden crosses engraved with their names. Tears slipped down her cheeks as she sensed their nearness.

"Mama and Papa, I want to tell you thank you for all the love you gave to me. I miss you both. . . ." Pausing, she swallowed, then whispered, "I miss you, but I'm going to be all right. I promise."

CHAPTER
32

February 2, 1864

"I T WOULD SEEM THAT MY HUSBAND'S DEFENSE HAS HAD LIT-tle opportunity to prepare a case," Katie remarked to the sheriff as she waited to see Jack. Since San Andreas was the Calaveras County seat, Jack had been brought there to await his trial, which was scheduled to begin at ten o'clock, less than an hour away. Outside, in front of the courthouse, a crowd was forming in spite of the snow that had begun to fall.

"Well, ma'am, what's there to prepare? Wyatt himself has ad-mitted that he was the Griffin. The Griffin killed Aaron Rush, Har-old Van Hosten, and your own father. Seems pretty simple to me." Sheriff Jones leaned back in his chair, one cheek bulging with to-bacco, and appraised the lady who stood near his desk.

Katie looked elegant, wealthy, and gloriously beautiful; the vi-olet of her ruched silk gown set off the deep blue of her eyes, while the indigo shimmer of her matching silk jacket instantly drew the eye to her glossy black tresses, which had been caught back in a full chignon. An amethyst-and-pearl brooch was pinned at her col-lar, and more amethysts gleamed in her ears. At the moment, it was hard to tell whether the color in her cheeks and the sparkle in her eyes was a result of the weather or her own emotions.

"You sure you're from these parts?" Sheriff Jones asked with a trace of sarcasm.

"I may look a bit different now that I live in San Francisco, but I can assure you that my roots and my loyalties will always lie in the foothills, sir," Katie replied coolly. "It may be that my husband is a rich man, but that has only affected my outward appearance."

"Of course the Griffin's rich!" Jones guffawed. "He's been robbing stages of all the gold from the Rush Mine!"

"He owns a newspaper, Sheriff. He was wealthy long before he became the Griffin."

"And you'll be a rich widow, I reckon, hmm?" He eyed her shrewdly, then aimed a stream of tobacco juice in the direction of a tarnished brass spittoon. "Well, that's justice, isn't it. After all, Wyatt did kill your father."

"That's crudely put, Sheriff, but I suppose that the truth speaks for itself. . . ."

The deputy came out then to say that the prisoner was now washed and dressed, and his wife might see him.

"Five minutes," Sheriff Jones warned. "And my deputy will have to watch. We can't afford to take chances with *this* prisoner."

Katie's face betrayed no emotion as she nodded, then followed the young deputy down a short stone corridor to the two tiny cells in back. One was empty, and the other held Jack, who stood next to a low iron bunk. A tiny slit in the wall provided the only light, but in spite of the dingy surroundings, Katie was rendered breathless by the sight of her husband. If not for the deputy lurking in the background, she might have wept.

Jack was tanned a warm shade of dark gold, and his tawny hair was appealingly in need of a trim. He wore neat charcoal-gray trousers and a starched white shirt, and when Katie appeared in the doorway of his cell, he looked at her with his heart in his eyes.

"Kathleen," he said softly.

Disarmed by his engaging smile, she forced herself to remember that they were being watched. "I thought I ought to see you, Jack. Under the circumstances, I don't think I could stand to attend the trial."

He had started toward her, but now he froze. "Oh, God. My darling, will you ever be able to forgive me? I wanted to tell you—"

"Never mind." Katie's tone was cold, but her eyes brimmed with tears. "Your friend Sam has already pleaded your case to me, but that won't bring Papa back, will it?" Seeing the pain on his face, she rushed on. "I might be able to forgive you for Papa if our marriage had turned out differently, if I could believe that you were a good man with a heart capable of love. As it is, I don't see how

I can forgive you for Papa when I haven't forgiven you for . . . that night."

"What night?" Jack demanded, frowning.

"The night of our Christmas party."

He hesitated, his eyes intent now on hers. "I don't know what you're talking about."

"You and Miss Braithwaite . . . in your study . . . for what seemed like an eternity."

Slowly he nodded, then backed away a step. "Well, I guess you're right. I'm a cad, and I deserve whatever I get today, hmm?"

Katie sighed. "I couldn't agree more." She put out her hand, and when he came forward and took it, the warm familiar strength of his touch sent a shiver of longing over her. "Well, I suppose everything has turned out the way it was meant to. I'll say a prayer for a fair outcome of your trial, Jack."

"Kathleen." Once again his sage-green eyes held hers. "I'm not sorry I married you. We had our moments. . . ."

"A few." Katie forced herself to step back and disengage her hand. Glancing over at the waistcoat and jacket on the bunk, she added, "I see that you have some suitable clothing to wear in court."

"Sam brought those. He's been a faithful friend." When Jack saw that she was about to step out of the cell, he couldn't resist the urge to look upon her face one more time. "Wait . . . How is Conrad?"

She glanced back over her shoulder. "He's distraught, as you might imagine, but he won't let anyone speak ill of you. He's very loyal."

"Give him my love."

"You will probably see him before I do. I'm quite certain he means to be at the trial." Katie nodded to the deputy. "I have to go now. The sheriff said just five minutes."

"Good-bye, Kathleen," Jack said huskily.

"Good-bye, Jack." She glanced at him once more, then followed the deputy down the dank corridor, her throat aching with tears.

Back in the sheriff's office, Katie recognized the man sitting with Sheriff Jones as the ruffian who had threatened her in Columbia. She took a chance. "Good morning, Mr. Potter."

He gave her a curt nod. When Katie had left the office, Potter listened as the deputy related the details of the meeting between the Wyatts. When the young man had finished, Jones and Potter exchanged satisfied smiles.

"Don't sound to me like you have anything to worry about," the sheriff remarked. "If Wyatt's own wife won't do anything to help him, it'll be a short trial."

Potter lit a fat cigar. "Wouldn't matter much if she did care. We made sure that there was barely time for Wyatt to find a lawyer, let alone anyone to testify for him. It'd take a miracle to save him now."

Across the street from the courthouse and jail, Katie seated herself in the lobby of the hotel and waited.

Jack's lawyer, Abraham Humphrey, was a grizzled old man whom Sam had persuaded to travel down from Jackson to take the case for a sizable fee. Now, sitting next to him in court, Jack prayed that his attorney would at least be able to argue effectively before the jury, because he certainly seemed to have no other strategies for exonerating his client. The prosecution—aided by such witnesses as Benjamin Potter, who testified that his employer, Aaron Rush, had been threatened by the Griffin just a few weeks ago—had presented a strong case. Most of the testimony consisted of hearsay, but people had come forward all the same, all seemingly intent on seeing the Griffin hang. Jack felt certain they'd been paid off. The morticians who had prepared Brian MacKenzie, Harold Van Hosten, and Aaron Rush for burial spoke in gruesome detail of their mortal wounds. And the driver of the stagecoach on which Katie and Conrad had been passengers had been questioned so skillfully that he'd said little more than, "It was the Griffin who fired the shot that killed Aaron Rush. And when he removed his hood, he turned out to be that man—" pointing theatrically toward Jack. When cross-examining, Humphrey did little to erase that image from the jury's mind. Potter had done his work well over the past two days, raising a hue and cry against highwaymen. Jack could tell from looking at the jury that they had forgotten how beloved the Griffin had been just a few months earlier. Aaron Rush's recent exploits had blackened the Griffin's name beyond repair.

Jack wouldn't let himself think ahead to the probable outcome of his trial. The possibility that he would hang, that his life with Katie was over, was very real, but it would do no good to dwell on that now. He felt slightly ill whenever he thought of his meeting with Katie earlier that morning. More than anything else he had wanted to hold her in his arms, to kiss her lips, to reaffirm the precious bond between them. But obviously she had had other ideas. That might have been their last chance to speak privately and touch each other! He had managed to translate the cryptic things Katie had said—he understood that she forgave him for his part in Brian's death and that Sam had told her all about the tragic accident—but still he longed to talk with her openly. He simply couldn't imagine what she thought to accomplish by pretending to hate him and staying away from the trial.

Now, as he walked forward to take the witness stand on his own behalf, a murmur swept over the courtroom. Jack swore on a Bible to tell the truth, then sat down and looked out over the sea of unfriendly faces. The only person there to give him support was Conrad, looking more frightened than Jack had ever seen him.

"Now, then, Mr. Wyatt," Abraham Humphrey began soberly, "I am going to ask you tell us your story in your own words. Who are you in reality, and why did you become the Griffin?"

Jack was glad of the opportunity to explain. As sincerely and concisely as he was able, he told the jury about Conrad's misfortune with his gold and how he, as the older brother, had decided to correct the injustice. Then he explained that the corruption he found at the Rush Mine went much deeper than he had expected, and that he had become concerned for all the miners. Insisting that he had never intended to hurt anyone, Jack further swore that he had not kept any of the confiscated gold for himself but had made anonymous gifts to the poverty-stricken miners and their families.

Humphrey then brought up the day MacKenzie and Van Hosten had been shot. When Jack told his side of that story, the whispers of disbelief in the courtroom grew louder. The general sentiment seemed to be that Jack was a rich man from San Francisco playing games with the lives of people in the foothills. After Jack had finished telling the story of Rush's death and his own capture, Charles Milton, the lawyer for the prosecution, stood up to cross-examine.

"My, my, Mr. Wyatt—or should I call you Mr. *Griffin*? You certainly do have a knack for *accidentally* killing your enemies!" Milton paused, smiling as a wave of taunting laughter rippled through the courtroom. After a moment he continued, picking apart Jack's story point by point, and with much caustic cynicism, to end with, "Well, sir, I must say that it does seem odd that there is no one here to support *your* claims, while there are plenty of witnesses for the prosecution. If I were on the jury—"

"Objection, Your Honor!" Humphrey cried, heaving himself to his feet.

"Sustained," muttered Judge Kincaid.

"Well, I think I've made my points," Milton said with a snide smile. "I have no more ques—"

"Wait!" cried a female voice from the back of the courtroom.

Jack gazed out over the crowd to see Katie entering through the double doors. Next to her were Sam, Victoria Barnstaple, and a heavy-set young man whom Jack vaguely recognized. Could it be . . . ?

"What is the meaning of this outburst?" the judge demanded.

"I am Mrs. Jonathan Wyatt, and my friend, Samuel Clemens, has brought two very important witnesses to testify on my husband's behalf. They were delayed by the snowstorm, and have only just arrived in San Andreas. Please, Your Honor, give them a chance to speak!"

The judge was silent a moment, then nodded. "Well, as there have been no witnesses for the defense except the defendant himself, I suppose it would be only fair to hear these two out."

Seated in the courtroom, Potter glared at Sheriff Jones and hissed, "I thought you said Mrs. Wyatt was no threat! I'd've seen to it that she was out of the way today if I'd known she'd try to interfere!"

Katie hurried toward the defense table and whispered to Humphrey. Places were made for her, Sam, and the unidentified man to sit on the bench behind the table, and Victoria was sworn in. When Jack returned to his chair, Katie leaned forward to clasp his hand. Beaming, she whispered, "I love you." Jack's heart swelled with relief and hope.

"So, Mrs. Barnstaple, I understand that you were a passenger on the stagecoach the day Harold Van Hosten and Brian MacKenzie were shot," Humphrey began. "Why didn't you come forward sooner if you saw what happened?"

"Well, the Griffin wasn't caught, and I suppose I was afraid to get involved. It was a very shocking experience. I didn't want to think about it afterward." She trembled like a frightened sparrow at the memory. "Also, I was a close friend of Brian MacKenzie's, and I was very upset by his death. I was angry at the Griffin for attacking the stagecoach! But if he might be hanged for this, it's only right that I come forward and tell the truth."

"And what is that?" prompted Humphrey.

"I saw it all. Harold Van Hosten had a gun, and Brian tried to get it away from him. The Griffin told Brian not to interfere, but he was too good and brave. . . ." Victoria began to weep. "Such a good man! Mr. Van Hosten's gun went off, and that was how Brian died. Then, Mr. Van Hosten tried to shoot the Griffin, who fired in self-defense."

Charles Milton gruffly declined to cross-examine.

Next, the fat young man took the stand, identifying himself as Lawrence Learoyd of Sonora. He testified that he had been on the stagecoach with Katie and Conrad when it was stopped by the Griffin. "I had been sleeping, and at first I thought I was having a hideous nightmare!" he cried dramatically. "The man demanded our money, and then another man, also dressed in a long duster and hood, jumped down from a ledge on the cliff above. He told the first man to throw down his shotgun, but he—the first man, that is—tried to fight instead, and the gun went off. Soon after that, he—the first man, that is, the one who was killed—was unmasked, and I recognized him as Aaron Rush, the mine owner. He was an acquaintance of my uncle's. What I want to say is that the killing was accidental. I believe in doing what's right, and that's why when Mrs. Wyatt and Mr. Clemens sought me out yesterday, I agreed to come here and testify. I don't know any of these people. I just want to do what's right." Learoyd extracted a handkerchief from his pocket and wiped his moist, moon-shaped face.

"Will you cross-examine, Mr. Milton?" the judge asked.

"No," he muttered sourly.

"Thank you, Mr. Learoyd," said Humphrey, smiling. "You may step down. Your Honor, lastly I would like to call Mrs. Jonathan Wyatt to the stand."

Katie strode regally to the front of the courtroom, her violet silk dress rustling softly. When she began to testify, her voice was clear and calm.

"I would like first of all to verify what Mr. Learoyd has said. I was also a passenger on that stage, but since I am Jack's wife, I knew that my testimony would not be sufficient to convince the jury. I didn't know then that my husband was the Griffin. The truth is, I hated the Griffin because I believed that he was responsible for my father's death. I understand now that it was an accident, and I know that Jonathan Wyatt would have died himself before knowingly allowing any harm to come to my father. They were very fond of each other. Papa would not have wanted Jack to be blamed in any way for his death. The truth is that Harold Van Hosten caused not only Papa's death, but his own, just as Aaron Rush chose his own fate rather than be exposed for the truly evil man he was." Katie paused to take a deep breath, then continued, "I didn't know Jonathan Wyatt very well when I married him—at least, not in the way I had expected I would know my husband. I learned to trust him with time as I discovered what a truly fine man he is. I love him, but I also respect him, and I know that there isn't a mean or violent bone in his body. As the Griffin, he only tried to see that justice was done. Aaron Rush impersonated him and sullied his reputation, but I can testify that it absolutely could not have been

Jack acting as the Griffin during the past three months, because he was in San Francisco with me." One crystal tear spilled onto her cheek. "I realize that the jury may think I am biased, but I am also honest. Jonathan Wyatt is the best man I know, and he deserves to be free."

At four o'clock, barely an hour after the jury had retired to deliberate the case, they sent word that they had reached a verdict. Jack was returned from his jail cell, and Sam and Katie both stood up as he approached the defense table. Sam gave his friend a hug, and Katie wrapped her arms around his neck and kissed him.

"I love you, sweetheart," Jack said hoarsely. "And, no man could ask for a better friend, Sam. . . . Thank you."

He was told to stand as the jury filed in and the foreman stood to read the verdict. Jack said a silent prayer, while Katie began to tremble as she clutched Sam's hand. Her heart threatened to burst, it was beating so hard.

"Gentlemen of the jury, have you reached a verdict?" Judge Kincaíd intoned.

"We have, Your Honor," replied the foreman. "We the jury find Jonathan Wyatt innocent in the deaths of Harold Van Hosten, Brian MacKenzie, and Aaron Rush."

The judge looked at Jack. "You're a lucky man, Mr. Wyatt. I suggest that you take your wife home to San Francisco and forget about this Griffin business once and for all."

Jack flashed him a grin. "With pleasure, Your Honor."

EPILOGUE

"**H**APPY BIRTHDAY, KATIE!" THE GUESTS CHORUSED AS
Mrs. Gosling set the beautifully decorated cake on the marble table
in the parlor.

"Do you have a birthday wish?" asked Hope Menloe.

Katie turned to Jack, who smiled at her with sleepy green eyes,
thinking that his wife had never looked more beautiful. Clad in a
gown of pale yellow muslin that flowed gracefully over her swollen
belly, she was a vision of summer radiance, her black curls swept
back in a simple yellow ribbon.

"I couldn't wish for anything more than I have right now, unless
it might be an extra prayer for a healthy baby."

"The baby is coming in August, isn't it?" asked Hope. Smiling
at Ambrose she added, "Goodness! You'll be a great-grandfather!"

Katie nodded. "We can hardly wait. You'll help me decorate the
nursery and pick out baby clothes, won't you?"

"I've already begun embroidering little dresses!" Hope laughed.

"I still can't believe that you were . . . with child when we
traveled to Columbia in January, Katie," Conrad complained for
the dozenth time in four months. "Why, all sorts of things could
have gone amiss—"

"But they didn't did they?" she replied sweetly. "Don't fret so,
Conrad. You're getting those little wrinkles between your eye-

brows. Besides, I believe that God meant us to make that journey. Everything turned out just as it should have—even Jack's trial.'' She laughed. ''Thank goodness for that, otherwise Sam and I would have been forced to put our alternate plan into action.''

''Do I want to know about this?'' Jack asked, pretending to cringe.

''I don't know why not. We were simply going to break you out of jail if they'd sentenced you to hang,'' she replied offhandedly.

''Of course,'' he murmured. ''I should have guessed.''

Katie began to cut the cake, all the while surveying her guests. ''I am so very happy!'' she announced. ''It's staggering to think how much my life has changed since my last birthday. Then, I never would have imagined that I would find a man to love, let alone get married . . . or leave Columbia. I miss Papa at times like this, yet I have to remember that other people have entered my life who love me. I have a tremendous amount to be grateful for.''

''Well, we're grateful, too, sweetheart,'' said Ambrose. ''You've been a ray of sunshine in this house.''

Katie grinned at him. ''I love you, too, Grandfather!'' Then, handing a cake-laden plate to Lim Sung, she inquired, ''Lim, how have you been? I don't think you've come to see me all this month.''

''I'm happy, Katie. I like San Francisco, and I'm glad to be with my family again.'' He lowered his voice, blushing slightly. ''You haven't seen me very much because I've been courting Li Wong, the girl my parents introduced me to. I like her very much. . . .''

''Well, you are seventeen now,'' Katie said doubtfully. ''You'll have to bring Li to dinner soon. We'd like to meet her.'' She glanced over at Conrad and Emma. Sunlight glinted off the new diamond ring Emma wore on her left hand. ''Love certainly seems to be in the air.''

Ambrose cleared his throat suddenly, and Hope turned pink. Katie, in the process of passing out the last pieces of cake, gave Jack a mischievous look.

Then they all took seats and chatted amiably over coffee and birthday cake. Katie shared the news from Abby's latest letter. The Hendersons had purchased the saloon but kept the name unchanged in honor of Brian, and they had moved into Katie's house in March ''It was silly for them to live with Gideon's mother while my house stood empty,'' Katie explained. ''I wanted it to be lived in, and with a baby coming, they can certainly use the extra space. They both sound very happy, and apparently the town is, too. Finally after I don't know how many years of doing without, Columbia has found a sheriff. Jack's old friend Missouri Dan has taken the job!''

"Just the man to breathe some new life into that town," Jack said, chuckling.

Hope spoke up. "I have a bit of news, too. I saw Elizabeth Braithwaite at Madame Braust's yesterday, and she said that Genevieve is engaged to marry a wealthy banker from New York. They'll make their home there, and apparently will be sailing next week."

"How lovely," Katie remarked. "I can't think of a better place for Miss Braithwaite than New York." While her guests laughed, she gazed pensively out the window.

"What's wrong, darling?" Jack smoothed back one of the loose curls that had fallen over her brow.

Katie sighed and turned to him with a wistful smile.

"I miss Sam. How I wish he could be here today! It seems like an eternity since he left for the Sandwich Islands. I keep thinking about the fate that befell Captain Cook, and I can't help worrying about Sam."

Jack laughed. "Allow me to set your mind at ease, my sweet." He reached into the inner pocket of his coat and withdrew a letter. "This arrived two days ago, but Sam asked that I save it for your birthday."

"He remembered?" Katie exclaimed, delighted.

"Kathleen, *no* one forgets about you!" Eyes twinkling, he opened the letter and read aloud: " 'Birthday Greetings, dear Katie! I should be back soon, and we'll celebrate again, but in the meantime, I am sending a hug in this letter. I haven't much time, because the schooner is leaving within the hour, but I wanted to assure you and Jack that I am well. I have been hard at work on my articles for the *Union* about the sugar interest, and recently managed to carry off an exclusive story that you may have heard about. While in Honolulu, I met with the survivors of the clipper *Hornet*, which had burned on the line. They were mere skin-and-bone relics, having spent forty-three days in an open boat on ten days' provisions. After working all day and all night, I produced an account of the matter and flung it aboard a schooner that was going to California. It should be the only full account in print. Aren't you sorry now that you didn't pay my way to the Sandwich Islands, Jack? Perhaps when I return to San Francisco, I'll break into the lecture field. . . . In the meantime, Katie, you have my permission to steal any or all of what I wrote in the *Union* for an article of your own. I'm glad to hear that your 'condition' hasn't put a stop to your journalistic pursuits, and I eagerly await your next letter.

" 'I miss you both, and often reminisce mistily of our adventures in the foothills. I hope to be on hand when your baby is born, trusting that he will be named Samuel—or, Mark, perhaps? Either one will do. Until then, I remain, your faithful comrade, Sam.' ''

''Oh, how good to hear from him,'' Katie said happily.

''You know,'' mused Jack, ''I predict that Sam won't linger long in San Francisco once he returns from the Sandwich Islands. His reputation is growing even in his absence, and intuition tells me that he'll soon travel east in pursuit of real fame and fortune.''

''Yes, you're probably right,'' Katie agreed, ''but in the meantime, we can enjoy him for as long as he does remain with us.''

Before long, the guests began to depart, and Katie thanked each of them for their gifts and their friendship. Conrad and Ambrose left to escort their ladies home, and then Lim, who was the last to leave, said good-bye as well. As Katie closed the front door behind him, Jack gathered her into his strong embrace, and she pressed her face against his chest contentedly.

''I love the way you smell,'' she murmured.

''I'm glad.'' Jack laughed, caressing the curve of her belly. ''How are you feeling?''

''Wonderful. Happier than I've ever been in my entire life.'' Katie turned her face up to him, and it shone with love and serenity. ''I can't wait to have our baby.''

''Are you ready to open your gift from me?''

''You shouldn't buy me things! All I ever want or need is your love.''

''Indulge me, Kathleen.''

''Well, all right,'' she teased. ''Just this once.''

They went up the wide stairway to their sun-washed bedroom, and Katie obediently sat down on the edge of the bed and closed her eyes. Jack disappeared into his dressing room, then returned with a small velvet box which he placed in her hands. When he pushed a tiny button, the lid sprang open.

''You can look now.''

Slowly, Katie opened her eyes and beheld an exquisite locket on a thin golden chain. The locket was oval, also made of gold, and edged with tiny diamonds. In the middle were the linked initials KMW.

''Oh, Jack,'' Katie whispered.

''Turn it over, darling.''

She did so and found the inscription: ''I love you—Jack. June 21, 1865.''

''It's so beautiful. I adore it.'' Her eyes glistened with tears.

''There's room inside for two pictures. I thought you might want to save a place for the baby.''

Katie reached out to touch his face and shining hair, and then she kissed his mouth. The feel and taste of him were as familiar to her as her own body, yet she never tired of him. Each embrace seemed sweeter than the last. Gazing down, Katie gently ran her thumb over the surface of the locket, glimpsing a reflection of herself.

"It's a perfect present, because it's a symbol," she declared as Jack fastened the chain around her neck. "Gold may be more precious to some people than anything else in life, but we have something that's much brighter than gold." She held the locket against her heart. "It's in here."

Jack pressed the middle of his own chest. "And here. I love you, Kathleen."

"I love you, Jack."

He kissed her, tasting the salt of her tears, and felt the baby move against him. "Happy birthday."

About the Author

Cynthia Wright now lives with her dashing husband, Jim Hunt, and her sixteen-year-old daughter, Jenna, in the small town of Elk Point, South Dakota. They share their large, cozy home with cats Whitney and Baxter, and a new black labrador retriever named Holly. Cindy and Jim enjoy fishing, gardening, sneaking away for weekends, laughing, and what friend Catherine Coulter calls "oozing."

Cynthia is currently finishing the wonderful tale of Natalya Beauvisage, daughter of Caro and Alec from *Caroline*. It's been a joy for Cindy to return to Philadelphia and revisit characters from earlier books, who she has discovered have grown even livelier during the intervening years.

Cynthia sends fond greetings to all her readers and invites letters to her at P.O. Box 862, Elk Point, SD, 57025.

One of the most beloved historical romance writers...
CYNTHIA WRIGHT
...casts her magic spell.